GW00360789

THIS
UNQUIET
LAND

Stories from India's Fault Lines

BARKHA DUTT

ALEPH

ALEPH

ALEPH BOOK COMPANY
An independent publishing firm
promoted by *Rupa Publications India*

Published in India in 2016 by
Aleph Book Company
7/16 Ansari Road, Daryaganj
New Delhi 110 002

ISBN: 978-93-82277-16-3

1 3 5 7 9 10 8 6 4 2

For my mother and father—Prabha Dutt and S. P. Dutt,
For your love, your courage, your integrity,
and for your belief in me.

CONTENTS

INTRODUCTION

ROOP LAL WAS a seemingly ordinary man. With extraordinary problems. He had been imprisoned in Pakistan for twenty-six years for 'straying' across the border. He had narrowly escaped the gallows. His wife had left him for another man. He was a stranger to his twenty-six-year-old daughter, who had grown up without ever seeing her father. But now it appeared his luck was turning. Roop Lal was coming home, a free man at last.

A group of journalists had gathered at Delhi's Indira Gandhi International Airport to record Roop Lal's homecoming in April 2000. This was because he was no ordinary victim of bad luck. Roop Lal was an Indian spy. Naturally, his country would not admit to this, given the fractious relationship between the two countries. As soon as the Pakistan International Airlines plane carrying him touched down, Roop Lal, a scruffy looking man with a luxuriant moustache, was whisked away by officials of the Research and Analysis Wing (RAW)—India's primary external intelligence agency.

At the time, private media had not yet exploded into hundreds of news channels. But there was a media scrum at the airport anyway as print reporters, cameras and sundry police officers elbowed each other for space. Suddenly, we realized we had been duped. Roop Lal, who was partially paralysed as a result of torture, and wheelchair bound, was being wheeled out of a different exit from the one we were waiting at. Now there was chaos with microphones flying and people tripping over cables to try and get to him. I dashed to the Ambassador car he was to be driven away in and knocked on the windows, but the officials wouldn't let me talk to the spy. As we argued back and forth, I spontaneously jumped onto the bonnet, and then pulled myself up to the roof of the car and stubbornly sat there surveying the crowd below; I assumed that our spooks wouldn't drive off with me perched on their car's carrier. At first it appeared I was wrong; the car continued to inch along to the exit.

But when the officials inside the vehicle realized I had no intention of getting off, they slowed to a halt and allowed me to ask Roop Lal a few quick questions.

As I was writing this introduction, I happened to see a photograph of me sitting cross-legged on that car fifteen years ago and it made me laugh. Nothing, no matter how crazy, would stop me in my efforts to get a good story.

The inordinate hard work and risk-taking aside, there were some funny moments as well. I remember an incident in a district court in Delhi when I had gone to cover the trial of Congress leader Kalpnath Rai, who had been accused of harbouring terrorists. I sneaked under the security cordon thrown around Rai by seventy police officers and, before they could stop me, climbed onto a ledge three feet from the ground, one leg dangling in mid-air, just so that I could put a microphone to him before he was jailed. As he spouted his own version of Shakespeare on justice and the quality of mercy, I burst into tears. Not because Rai—he of the 'Rajiv Gandhi is just like a diamond' fame—had stirred my soul, but because at the exact same moment, the court's resident rhesus monkey had sunk his teeth deep into my dangling ankle, apparently panicked by my sprint across the courtroom complex. Writing about the incident in 1997, *India Today* magazine said: 'This is truly journalism's new breed'. It went on to describe me and my contemporaries as 'brash-brat TV kids' who were now a 'permanent part of the journalistic stratosphere, willing to do anything for a story'. I'd like to think that I still remain as determined as ever to pursue a promising lead or interview. The passion has not dimmed.

■

I began working in 1994 for a news show originally broadcast on Doordarshan; my entry into journalism coincided with the birth of private TV news. As a first generation child of the industry I would often tell people who, at first, dismissed us as facile 'soundbite soldiers' that if the printed word was a symphony of ideas, television was opera—filled with a furious energy, often in your face, and wasting no time in getting to the heart of the matter. Television journalists like us approached every assignment, big or small, with the same mixture of wonderment and passion. We didn't do it for the money, journalists were not at all well paid at the time, or the importance—no one gave us any, anyway. We did it because television news excited us like nothing else did. We loved the sheer adventure of it, the opportunity to be chroniclers of history as it unfolded.

I would get so consumed by an assignment I was on (I still do) that almost nothing else would matter. I spent days and days on the road, often in some of the most violent and perilous parts of the world. I was hopelessly addicted to the nomadic life that journalism mandated and at one point got so toxically hooked to the adrenalin rush of dangerous conflict and war zones that I became maladjusted to a 'normal' city life. So viscerally drawn have I remained to the adventure and experience that the world of news reporting offers that I thought nothing of crossing over illegally from Egypt into conflict-torn Libya, accompanied only by my much-younger producer, Ruby, and cameraman, Manoj, without bulletproof vests, any knowledge of Arabic or even one local contact to guide us—we didn't even have the satellite phone that all the other international crews were armed with. The stranger with the cold, vacant stare whom we finally requested to take us around Benghazi carried a knife and a gun. Anything could have happened. And yet, when a Michael Jackson song filtered out of his car stereo and he wordlessly handed us a bar of Snickers each, the nervousness ebbed away to be replaced by that familiar sensation of excitement welling up inside. The anticipation of adventure is one of journalism's many blessings in my life.

■

My tryst with the news began early. At the age of five, my parents would make me identify little-known world leaders on the covers of *Time* magazine. Around the dining table, politics was a staple diet, right up there with the obligatory portions of yucky daily greens.

Growing up as a journalist's daughter—at a time when women in the media were expected to write about flower shows and fashion—I watched my mother, Prabha Dutt, wrestle every single day of her working life with gender-driven preconceptions. Even getting hired had been difficult. She rose to become the first woman chief reporter of the *Hindustan Times*, but the badge came with an initial rejection—she was told that the paper did not hire women in mainstream reporting roles. She went on to become a tough-as-nails investigative journalist scooping such stories as the use of beef tallow in shudh vanaspati and a major scam at the All India Institute of Medical Sciences, undeterred by threats and warnings from those she was going after. My sister and I worried as children when she received ominous phone calls in the dead of night or shadowy men showed up at the door. But she was relentless in her pursuit of a good story and taught us never to take no for an answer.

When she sought to interview the notorious murderers Billa and Ranga, who had made national headlines after kidnapping and killing two schoolchildren, Geeta and Sanjay Chopra, in 1978, the jail authorities declined her request. She went to court against the decision and secured her interview just before the two men were executed, finding a place with her petition in the annals of case law.

Despite the demands of the profession she would find the time to call us at periodic intervals to check on homework and meals. Sometimes, when there was no help available at home or when we had to be dropped off for dance or swimming lessons, we would accompany her to work and play on the noisy newsroom floor as she furiously typed away to meet the day's deadline. In an unconventional personal decision, when my father, an Air India official, was transferred to New York for several years, my mother opted to stay back in India for at least half of that posting so as to not lose the momentum of her professional life; she only shifted to the US when she got a job with the United Nations. It was never assumed that one career took precedence over the other; both my parents had to make adjustments to accommodate their individual and collective dreams. As I grew older and started working, I often wondered whether I would have my mother's gumption.

In 1965, when war broke out between India and Pakistan, my mother, still single and in her twenties, asked to be sent to the front line. Her proposal was rejected outright; there was no question of sending a woman to a war zone. It was still tough for women to get the so-called hard-news assignments of reporting on politics or crime, conflict reporting was beyond the pale. So Prabha Dutt requested a few days of leave to visit her parents in Punjab. No sooner was her leave granted than she made her way to the front line in Khem Karan—all alone and without any infrastructural support or backup. From there she began sending war dispatches to the paper, which were too good not to be published prominently. And so was born India's first woman war correspondent. Thirty-three years later, when I attempted to convince the army that I be allowed to report from the combat zone of the Kargil War, that my being a woman would not cause them any inconvenience, I remembered the battle that my mother and women of her generation had fought, opening the way for us to follow.

My defining memory of my mother would remain a photograph of her balanced precariously on the edge of an army tank, surrounded by soldiers, her head, protected by an olive green helmet, thrown back in a full-toothed smile, happy and utterly free.

Though she died from a sudden brain haemorrhage when I was just thirteen, my mother's appetite for adventure, her dogged pursuit of a story, her rejection of anything that sought to constrict her, and her determination to be her own person even when it made her unpopular, would remain the deepest influences on my own life.

Much before her journalism would nudge me towards the world of news, her interventions as a parent had introduced me to the lifelong battle that being a woman entailed. When I was still in middle school, I remember her storming into school to know why I had been denied my choice of woodcraft as an extracurricular activity and been pushed into home science instead. The woodcraft class involved the use of saws and sandpaper and heavy machinery that the school thought was unsuitable for girls. It took some vociferous arguing by my mother before the school authorities wilted and allowed me entry into the woodworking class. Prabha Dutt was a staunch defender of the right of women to be treated on a par with men long before this notion became an idea that society was forced to take seriously.

■

I learnt early enough that a successful woman, especially one with a public profile, would be scrutinized in the most unsparing and, quite often, unfair way. As an unabashed feminist who has spent her life shrugging off 'woman' as a prefix to her identity as a journalist, I have always been loath to play the gender card when things go wrong. I am level-headed enough to recognize that neither praise nor criticism need to be taken too seriously. But the extraordinary malice that I have had to contend with from time to time has made me pause and wonder—was I having to deal with such nonsense because I was a woman or was it because I didn't conform to conventional notions of what a woman ought to be, or was it something else altogether? I can't say I have been able to find any clinching evidence for any of the foregoing, but whatever the reason, there has certainly been some strange fiction that was peddled about me. When I was younger it would hurt me just a little bit (despite my mother's steely voice in my head encouraging me to not give a toss). In 1999, when I came back to Delhi after a long, difficult stint on the front lines of the Kargil War, I was astounded by the avalanche of praise and positive feedback I received. But there were a few venomous whispers as well. It was said that my use of an iridium phone had given away a troop location. Soon after I returned to Delhi, I was invited by General V. P. Malik, the then army chief, for a cup of tea where he complimented me for television coverage that he believed had been a force multiplier in the conflict. I thanked him, but also asked him if there was any truth to what was being said about my use of an iridium phone. He laughed and said the army used the same phones and added that the Pakistani military did not have the ability to monitor such devices. He said that all journalists at the front had used the same phones since there was no other way to communicate. The general would go on to record this conversation in his Kargil memoirs. But the internet, with its army of anonymous hatemongers, still tried to keep the absurd story alive. As I grew older, and more experienced in my profession, I recognized that every achievement would provoke a round of antipathy; it just came with the turf.

What I have never quite been able to comprehend is why I have often been singled out and made a symbol of everything that has been wrong about the media coverage of a major incident or event, even if hundreds of other journalists have also been present—as they were in Mumbai when the terror strikes took place on 26/11—or even for stories I had not reported on personally, such as the night police officer Hemant Karkare was killed. In particular, I was taken aback by the vitriol of an Amsterdam-based blogger, whose vituperative rant was filled with all sorts of defamatory inaccuracies, including the old Kargil slander. His post was being emailed and shared on social media sites like Facebook. I decided to stand up to the lies that were masquerading as a media critique and sent him a legal notice. He hastily took his post down; a development that would generate fresh controversy. The blogger would justify his article later by saying that he had drawn his information from user-edited Wikipedia. Wiki's many gems about me included gifting me two Kashmiri husbands I never had. Apparently, it still has a spouse entry for me, though I have never been married.

A few years later, I was—to my astonishment—charged with helping a Dravida Munnetra Kazhagam (DMK) politician, A. Raja—a man I have never met—secure a Cabinet berth in the United Progressive Alliance (UPA) government. This was despite the fact that I had reported extensively on how the then Prime Minister Manmohan Singh was firmly opposed to his presence in the Cabinet. The controversy, fuelled by some fellow journalists, broke after 100-odd phone conversations between Nira Radia and hundreds of people, including me, was leaked. Apart from the ludicrousness of the assumption that I had the clout to influence Cabinet formation—or any interest in it—what struck me as odd was that only a fraction of the 5,800 recorded conversations was leaked and nobody quite knows who picked what to keep secret and what to make public. I knew Radia (though not particularly well), like hundreds of other senior journalists, because she was the public relations strategist for two of the biggest names in business—Mukesh Ambani and Ratan Tata. At one point in 2009, when the DMK and the Congress were at loggerheads because of Manmohan Singh's reluctance to take Raja and T. R. Baalu into the Cabinet, I was keen to hear the DMK side of the story. I knew absolutely no one in the DMK, perhaps because of my north-Indian focus. Somebody told me that Radia was close to the DMK's Kanimozhi, so I spoke to her as one among multiple sources to get a fix on what was going on behind the scenes. A journalist's relationship with a source—any source—is always part-acting; you flatter to deceive and act friendlier than you feel in order to elicit the maximum information. My conversation with her was no different—a gossipy exchange of notes on who was in and who was out, what the DMK might settle for and how much the Congress might be willing to compromise. On air, I kept underlining how opposed Manmohan Singh was to the entry of Raja, something he failed to prevent because of—what his former media adviser Sanjaya Baru would later confirm in his memoirs—pressure from the party.

Why don't you just say sorry and be done with it? This was the advice given to me by some well-meaning colleagues as a way to end the controversy. I remember one of them even saying people derived psychological satisfaction from an apology: that was the way to deal with the situation, rather than to aggressively defend oneself, which was my way. I refused point blank—there was absolutely no way I was going to apologize for something I hadn't done. But to make the point that just like I asked questions of other people, they must also have the same right to put questions to me, I opened myself to being grilled by a panel of four editors on an unedited programme that was aired on prime time. If I have one regret about those hurtful few weeks, it's only that I spent too much energy explaining myself; I should have let my work speak for me instead. But stuff like this remained, at best, an episodic blip on what has been an extraordinary opportunity for me to understand India.

Being a television journalist at a time that has recorded some of the most seismic shifts in Indian society has allowed me rare insights into the way my country works. It was my desire to explore what to me are the most interesting aspects of the ongoing churning within Indian society that made me first want to write this book.

■

It is true in many ways that India has changed more dramatically over the last twenty-five years than at any other period since

Independence. That massive and rapid change is also reflected in the transformation of my own industry.

As a journalist—and a generalist—who is more suited to working from deadline to deadline, you may wonder what made me actually go through with the writing of *This Unquiet Land*. First, I felt that it would be interesting for me to explore the underlying causes and effects (some obvious, some less apparent) of the cataclysmic change that I had been reporting on for decades. Second, I wanted to write about the impact my profession—the world of television news—has had on every major Indian event from the 1990s onwards. Riots, the challenge of left-wing extremism, our staggering economic and social inequities, the centre-staging of corruption, the evolution of politics as a performance made for TV and the birth of middle-class activism (and thus, middle-class politics) have all been framed by television discourse.

Like the country, my own industry today stands at the edge of major transformation. Anchors have become more glamorous, some networks even have in-house stylists. Talking heads have ousted on-the-ground reportage during prime time. Hashtags occupy the space once meant for pictures in a perfect illustration of a reductionist national debate. Judgement is served as instantly as 2-minute Maggi noodles and the more strident and hyperbolic you are, the better. Television news has begun to feel the pressure of social media, and Twitter trends tend to determine the 'content hierarchy' of a news bulletin. Because the online commentary is so politically polarized there is increasing pressure on journalists to affiliate themselves to stated ideologies and take sides. Most worryingly, journalists—especially younger ones who are less used to being constantly judged by viewers—have begun to worry far too much about being 'liked' on Twitter or Facebook, often modulating what they say based on the sort of abuse they think they may have to face online.

The flux within media, the clash between old (mainstream) media and social media mirrors the multiple battles being waged between Old and New India every day. It is these strands of change that bind my narrative together. I am neither a pundit, nor an academic; I have only written about areas that I have reported on. Many of the conversations and encounters in this book took place over the course of my career. I have identified those I was talking to, barring a few cases where I have not in order to protect the confidentiality of the source. I should also say that this is not the definitive 'India' book—not that there has ever been, or can ever be, such a thing. Rather, this is a book about some of the major fault lines that I have followed for nearly four decades.

The place of women, terrorism, sectarianism, Kashmir, the games politicians play, the rapidly changing class and caste equations within our society—all these are aspects of India that I have obsessed about throughout my career, and it is these that I have explored as deeply as possible in the book, although each of these subjects could do with a book to themselves. I have not gone too deep into the law and order situation, the judiciary, the crying lack of infrastructure, corruption, our defective education and healthcare sectors, pollution, environmental degradation, our foreign policy and corporate scams, among others, because these aren't necessarily stories I have reported on at any great length. However, many of these fault lines make their appearance in various chapters, because nothing that is good or bad about society exists on its own (to state the obvious—everything is linked in one way or the other).

As I have said earlier, the great advantage of exploring ideas and events, at some length, and after the passage of time, is that one is able to have a better sense of them. Working on the book gave me the opportunity to get a proper handle on the rumblings beneath the surface of this unquiet land and enabled me to measure visible and unmeasurable tremors that will change it for the better or worse in the near future. And when I finished writing it I realized it had helped me understand my country better.

One

THE PLACE OF WOMEN

I

ON MY EIGHTEENTH birthday, my father asked me to choose any two books I wanted as a gift. I picked *Daughter of the East* by Benazir Bhutto and a collection of essays by Germaine Greer entitled *The Madwoman's Underclothes*. At the time, my often impetuous formulations on the gender debate had little nuance, and my understanding of poverty, privilege, caste and other elements of my country was limited; consequently my feminism was simplistic, and without context.

Regardless, I was proud of my feminist sensibility. As I have said, it was largely shaped by a real person—my gutsy, unconventional mother—but also by the much more abstract world of books by writers like Greer, Gloria Steinem, Virginia Woolf and, much later, Naomi Wolf and Susan Faludi. That I did not read the great Urdu writer Ismat Chughtai's iconoclastic *Terhi Lakeer* (The Crooked Line) or Sarojini Naidu's poems until long afterwards was evidence of just how culturally unidimensional I was during my student days.

Back then—on the cusp of the nineties—we debated gender with a certitude that left no room for the slightest self-doubt. Why was the woman expected to take her husband's name after marriage? Did the institution of marriage even make sense? Why did we bring up our daughters on a Barbie diet and our sons on a staple of mindlessly violent video games? Was waxing our legs and painting our toenails an example of pandering to the male gaze?

This is not to say that these do not remain valid questions in the eternal, and I would argue, universal, debate around what makes us women who we are. I have never understood the scorn with which these issues were, and are, sometimes dismissed as 'westernized'.

Today, more than two decades later, I still get worked up over these intractable questions. But, in the years of our youthful feminism, we certainly didn't understand just how different things were outside our circle of comfort for millions of Indian women who were battling brutality of a kind that made some of our concerns seem luxuriously self-indulgent.

As young student activists and feminists, our battles were sincere. We vowed never to accept a 'Ladies' seat in the overcrowded university bus. We petitioned the well-heeled St Stephen's establishment to open its doors to women in the BA Pass programme—no one had thought of questioning why they weren't allowed, to begin with. We fought with our male friends to get St Stephen's to open its Residence (hostel accommodation) to female students. Only students-in-residence could run for college president; with no such option for women, the top union post was closed to them. The boys, only half jokingly, argued that women-in-residence would take away their freedom to walk about the corridors half-naked. Dr John Hala, a former principal, had quipped, without the slightest trace of embarrassment, that he'd have to open a maternity ward on campus if he accepted the demand for half the residence blocks to be reserved for women. He'd shown the same brazen chauvinism during one of the institution's most infamous controversies in 1985 when three male students had smuggled skirts, shorts and panties out of the ladies' common room and strung them across the cross in the main balcony of the college. As protests erupted, Hala told newspapers it was a 'domestic issue'.

There was a seeming paradox about this. On the one hand, our beloved college was steeped in the best liberal traditions—it encouraged dissent, argument and rebellion. At the same time, it would keep throwing up instances of sexism within its precincts, some subterranean, some overt. Authors and bureaucrats, ministers and artists—some of India's biggest names had graduated from St Stephen's. Yet, all these years, the tradition of the 'Chick Chart'—a public roster listing the 'sexiest' women in college—had survived in the name of ritual and custom. Were we going to be 'cool' and laugh along, replace it with a list of our own that similarly objectified the men, or protest its very existence?

We remained preoccupied with these battles—big and small. In our little world, we saw ourselves as crusaders for equality, unmindful of an entire universe of gross prejudices that lay outside the boundaries of our socio-economic cocoon. It would be many years before we understood how class and culture complicated the gender discourse.

There was only one issue that did cross the economic and social barrier—sexual violence and abuse. Even though every single girl I knew had her own sordid experience to share, oddly, it was not at the forefront of our heated college conversations. For all our ostensible empowerment, like so many Indian women, we had probably come to accept, albeit subconsciously, that some form of sexual violation was an inevitable consequence of our coming of age. So, day after day, crushed into a corner of a packed public bus, we would alternate between anger and resignation when leery men pawed our breasts or pinched our bottoms.

Some days, we would slap our assaulters, on other days we would push them away or shrug them off. In both situations a voice inside us would suggest that we were lucky—this was not rape or abuse, it was what was (and continues to be) hideously described as 'eve-teasing'. This was the level to which we had internalized society's denial of sexual dignity to us. We mentally calculated how bad the abuse could have been and were 'relieved' when it didn't plummet to the absolute depths of depravity.

In the middle-class neighbourhood of South Delhi where I lived, boys who were not yet eighteen would stalk me on their two wheelers, swerving towards me as they whizzed past, an arm outstretched to grab my breasts or pull my hair, laughing and whistling with glee at my visible rage. When I wasn't feeling combative, I learnt, like many women of my generation, to walk alongside the rows of residential houses instead of on the road, so that I could quickly slip inside an open gate and pretend it was my own home if I needed to duck an especially unpleasant set of goons. Yet, there was no conscious sense of victimhood to our lives. Instead, I suspect, in a peculiar Indian version of boot camp we saw ourselves as hardy women made stronger by the wars we fought against the frequent infiltrations into our private spaces. We came to treat such instances of harassment and abuse as the rites of passage of growing up female in India.

II

In 1990, around the time I was proudly proclaiming my feminism in college, the Nobel prize-winning economist Amartya Sen wrote a discomfiting essay in the *New York Review of Books* that revealed that 100 million women were 'missing' from Asia and parts of Africa, most of them in China and India. A few years later, in 1995, a UNICEF report revealed that there were between 40 and 50 million girls and women 'missing' from India's population. Missing was a polite euphemism for gender-driven genocide.

In 2006, the UN published another staggering statistic: every day 7,000 baby girls were aborted or killed right after being born. In other words, a girl was aborted or murdered every twelve seconds in India. If she wasn't murdered in the womb, sand or tobacco juice was forced down her nostrils when she opened her mouth to cry so that she would choke and die. Renuka Chowdhury, the then Minister for Women and Child Development in the UPA government at the centre, admitted that in the previous two decades alone, 10 million girl children in India had been killed by their parents. She called it a 'national crisis'.

But, on the sun-soaked lawns of St Stephen's College, in our well-intentioned if elitist bubble none of this was what we were anxious or outraged about. Our privileged existence channelled our aggressive fight for identity and equality in other directions. Indeed, most of us thought of ourselves as glass-ceiling busters, supremely independent and free of the shackles that women in other countries were ensnared by. I remember the sense of superiority I felt years later when I found a copy of the *The Rules* by Ellen Fein and Sherrie Schneider tucked away in the underwear drawer of my American roommate at Columbia University. It was self-help pap that ostensibly helped you land Mr Right. The book urged women to be 'easy to be with, but hard to get'. I would watch in astonishment as my super-bright roommate, a post-doctoral history candidate, fought back her urge to phone the attractive man she'd just been out on a date with, because *The Rules* forbade the woman from making the first move. She had all the usual questions about arranged marriages in India and whether my father was going to bundle me off with some man I'd never met. I didn't fit a single one of her stereotypes about India, I thought rather smugly to myself. Instead, I sneered at the institutionalized dating rituals that trapped otherwise accomplished women, even in New York, the world's grittiest city. I would proudly list the many women who had become prime ministers and presidents in South Asia, astonished that Americans had been unable to crack the political glass ceiling in their country.

At Columbia—while filming a documentary about the premium placed on motherhood and the lengths couples were ready to go to for a biological child—I remember standing on the editing room's radiator in frustrated anger when a classmate from the Midwest demanded that the clips of Betty Friedan and Gloria Steinem leading an abortion-rights rally be deleted from the finished version of our student project. An otherwise laid-back and quiet sort of guy, he was an adamant pro-lifer who did not believe in a woman's fundamental right to abortion.

Once again, I retaliated with the Indian example of how we had closed the debate on abortion and women's reproductive rights long ago, while the so-called developed world still grappled with these issues. My self-righteous outbursts made no space for gender-driven illegal abortions—mass murders really—that were my country's abiding shame; quite truthfully, in the sliver of India that had been my little universe, I did not even stop to think about them. In effect, I had confused the many paradoxes of India for progressiveness. It would be several years before I would confront the fact that, for a woman, India was one of the most hostile and unequal countries in the world.

This wasn't to say that the generalizations made about India and the place of women, especially in the West, weren't infuriatingly distorted or, worse still, lacking in any self-awareness. I sometimes wrestled with competing impulses—rage at the relentless horrors women battled every day and simultaneous impatience at the Western world's many caricatural notions about us. But this was not before I had undertaken my own journey of 'unlearning' and introspection.

The first challenge to my simplistic certitudes came from reporting on the gang rape of a grassroots activist in a dusty Rajasthan village in 1992. I had just become a journalist and this was one of my earliest assignments.

Her saffron dupatta draped around her head, red bindi gleaming in the sun, her demeanour stoic, her body hunched over a potter's wheel, Bhanwari Devi betrayed little emotion as she spoke about how she had been sexually assaulted by a group of so-called upper caste men. Her husband, Mohan, was forced to watch mutely as the men took turns at thrusting themselves on her. They assaulted her with impunity because they were protected by custom and village tradition. Bhanwari Devi was a Dalit, an 'untouchable' who was expected to keep a respectful social distance, draw water from a different village well and accept and obey all that she was commanded to do. She was theirs to do with as they pleased.

In the eyes of the accused, there were many reasons for Bhanwari Devi to be a ready target—her caste, her gender and the fact that she had dared to campaign against child marriages in the village. In this instance, she had tried to stop her rapists from marrying off a nine-month-old baby to a one-year-old child. Ironically, as a saathin or volunteer with a government-sponsored campaign, she had only been doing her job; one for which she was then paid all of Rs 200 a month. For this, and for daring to take the perpetrators to court after she was raped, Bhanwari Devi had been pushed to the outskirts of Bhateri village, where she lived ostracized by the rest of the community.

When I arrived in the village with a television crew to report on her battle, the men were aggressive and hostile to our questions. The leader of the gang that had raped Bhanwari—Ram Karan Gujjar, also the father of the infant who was being married off—scoffed at the charge against him and said Bhanwari had fabricated the entire story. The panchayat—meant to function as a self-governing, locally elected body—led the tirade against her. Thirty-nine village heads came together from across the district to demand that Bhanwari withdraw the case. If she failed to do so, every saathin attached to women's groups in the area would be boycotted.

'Hum tumhare saath nahin rahenge aur na hi sahyog denge (You cannot live as our neighbour and we will not support you in any way),' bellowed the sarpanch of Bhateri to Bhanwari Devi, happy to go on the record and on camera to issue his threat. But unfazed and determined, Bhanwari Devi was adamant about punishing the men who had violated her 'izzat'. Most rape survivors choose to hide behind a veil of anonymity, daunted by the stigma that still attaches itself to rape, but not Bhanwari Devi. She refused to pull her pallu over her face. She wanted the world to see the rage in her eyes. With virtually no one to support her but her husband—even her brothers cut off ties with her for refusing to accept the monetary compensation later offered by the accused—she stood alone, and strong.

In the immediate aftermath of the rape, Mohan told his wife he wanted to drown himself in the village stream. She urged him to be stronger. The nearest police chowki was ten kilometres away but was manned by an officer who was a Gujjar, the same caste as that of the accused. Bhanwari Devi knew she would have no luck there; she'd have to travel further, closer to the state capital Jaipur. The next morning, they took a bus for the city, in what would be the beginning of an interminably long journey.

At the police station, she was called a whore, even by women constables. The magistrate's office ordered that a test be done to check her age, the suggestion being that she was too old to be raped (she was thirty-five). There was no female doctor available to conduct a medical test; it would be fifty-two hours before she could get one. Back at the police station, she was asked to strip and leave her ghagra behind as evidence. It was past midnight when she made her way home draped in the thin cloth of her husband's turban.

A few months after I met Bhanwari, the local trial court acquitted all five accused and ordered their release. Among the observations made by the judge was one that held that an upper-caste man would not rape someone of a caste he considered 'untouchable'. Other absurdities used to buttress his argument were that a husband would never passively watch his wife being raped and that a rapist would not assault a woman in the presence of his nephew. The case had to travel to a higher court, journeying through the minefields of intimidation, insinuations and insensitivity.

At Bhateri village, Bhanwari continued to live an isolated existence, shunned by the village community. No one was willing to buy the clay pots that Mohan made. There were even days when they refused to sell essential commodities like milk to her. She was surviving on the trifling amount she earned from the government-run community programme.

For me, reporting as a twenty-something on her fight for justice had meant unpacking a vast quantity of ignorance. How could I afford to dismiss the exacerbated impact of caste on gender discrimination, for instance, when I had never known what it was to experience that sort of oppression? The certainty of my college years and my assertions that caste was an irrelevance began to seem naive and— looking at what was happening to Bhanwari—even nonsensical. My feminist preoccupations began to feel more text-bookish than fully thought through. I became acutely aware of how much the class I belonged to had protected me. I was filled with ideological self-doubt as I listened to Bhanwari Devi say, 'There may be no justice in the courts, but in God's house, one day, I will get justice'. Though her resolve never weakened, there was a good reason for her cynicism. Her appeal against the court acquittal of her rapists had been slotted by the High Court to be heard 'in due course'. More than a thousand appeals, pending from the 1980s, had to first be processed by the slow-moving judicial system before it would be her turn. Years would pass before her petition was even heard.

Ironically, India's women have her to thank for the fact that we finally have legal cover against sexual harassment. Because Bhanwari Devi had been raped while she was doing her job— anti-child-marriage advocacy—her case gave birth to what came to be known as the 'Vishaka Guidelines': court administered norms on how an employer must respond to complaints of sexual violation at the workplace. A dispossessed, poor, 'lower-caste' woman's brave battle had given birth to the first authoritative set of rules in the country to protect working women against sexual intimidation. But while she has waited for decades to see her fight translate into justice, a slew of urban professional women have been able to use the Vishaka code for redress. In recent times, a Nobel Laureate (R. K. Pachauri) and a celebrated editor (Tarun Tejpal) have had to contend with criminal charges, one for harassment, another for rape, because the Vishaka Guidelines exist.

The Supreme Court framed the Vishaka Guidelines after a collective petition was filed by women's groups who took the Rajasthan government to court after the Bhanwari Devi gang rape. In August 1997, nearly six years later, India got its first official framework that laid out the process that government offices and private companies alike should follow if a female worker complained of sexual harassment. The onus of providing a working environment that 'prevents or deters' abuse was placed on the employer. The court defined sexual harassment to include not only unwelcome physical contact or demand for sexual favours but any unwanted 'verbal or non-verbal conduct of a sexual nature'. It also asked managers to put a complaint mechanism in place—with at least one external representative—that would provide for time-bound decisions.

Despite all this, in December 2012, when the country witnessed widespread street protests over the gang rape of a young medical student in the capital—a moment widely seen to be an inflection point for the fight against gender injustice in India—the men who raped Bhanwari Devi had still not been convicted. It had been twenty-two years since she was raped. 'Time bound resolution', as mandated in the Vishaka Guidelines and made possible by Bhanwari Devi's courage, was a cruel joke when it came to her own specific case. Two of the five men charged with the rape were dead; in all this time, her appeal had not even been heard in the High Court. She had been all but forgotten even as an enraged country finally put violence against women at the centre of public attention.

III

That sunless winter in December 2012, when the cold bit hard and the skies turned grey with smog, citizens literally took control of the capital's King's Way (as the British used to call it); 'Rajpath', as it is now known, had become 'Janpath' in the metaphorical geography mapped by popular anger.

This is the grandest part of Delhi. Edwin Lutyens had designed the boulevard for an unobstructed, panoramic view of the city from the British viceroy's residence, which became Rashtrapati Bhavan when India got independence. Rajpath runs all the way from Rashtrapati Bhavan on Raisina Hill through Vijay Chowk to India Gate and then beyond to the city's National Stadium. It is on this ceremonial avenue that the Indian republic shows off its might every January during the annual parade. It is here that, every year on Republic Day, camel mounted troops and military bands signal a ceremonial 'retreat' from battle as the sun sets and the surrounding buildings are illuminated.

But that December, what was a historic symbol of India's nationhood was pressed into service as a stage on which to highlight a moment of national shame. Along the entire stretch of the avenue, right up to the president's house, where barricades prevented them from going further, was a sea of protesters. In their thousands, young men and women marched along, their fists punching the cold winter air in anger and determination, their placards held high like badges of honour. 'We are angry', 'It's a dress, not a yes', 'Stop telling us what to wear, ask your sons not to rape', 'Where I am, at what time, is no excuse for rape', 'You raped her, because her clothes provoked you, I should break your face because your stupidity provokes me'.

School-going teenagers, men and women from Delhi University, middle-aged professionals, homemakers—the protests drew all ages, all classes, all faiths and all types. It was the largest popular mobilization India had seen against sexual violence. The unspeakable horror of what had happened to a young woman in her early twenties, who could just as easily have been you or me or any college-going student in any Indian city, had made it impossible to look away. She had been beaten so badly by her rapists that 95 per cent of her intestines had to be removed. The iron rod used to bludgeon her into submission had also been repeatedly rammed into her abdominal cavity. As the men took turns to violate her, they had wrenched out some of her vital organs with their bare hands.

The young woman and her male friend had clambered onto a

chartered bus as they made their way home from watching *Life of Pi* at a popular city-mall. They paid the Rs 20 the conductor demanded at the door and settled into the red seats, staring out of the darkened tinted windows with yellow curtains. At first they thought the men in the bus were passengers as well. Later, in her dying declaration, the woman who came to be known by many names—Nirbhaya (the one without fear), Damini (lightning), Braveheart—would ask for her rapists to be 'burnt alive'. She would recount how one man would take the wheel, while the others would gather at the back of the bus, taking turns to brutalize her body. The bus was driven past several police check posts without a trace of fear. Forty-five minutes later the men pushed her and her companion out onto a deserted street, naked and bleeding. The doctors would find bite marks on the girl's body and at least eighteen injuries to her internal organs. A portion of her intestines had been pulled out by her rapists and doctors had to surgically remove the rest because it had become infected and gangrenous. Even then, the twenty-three-year-old fought to live. Unable to speak, she scribbled down brief notes to her parents, enquiring about the health of her friend, and imploring them to help her. 'Save me, I want to live', she would tell her brother. Airlifted to a super-specialty hospital in Singapore a few days later, as the New Year approached, she died.

Public rage over the rape and murder spilled onto the streets. The government and the police got nervous and made a terrible situation even worse. Cold jets of water slammed into the heads of young students as the cops trained water cannons on them. Lathis were used to clobber the demonstrators as they pushed past security barricades. But they kept moving forward, inching closer to the president's house and the North and South Block buildings from where India is governed. A smart, empathetic politician—or even president—would have come out to meet them or, at the very least, would have invited a smaller delegation inside for discussions. But instead of an official or unofficial acknowledgement of their agitation, clouds of tear gas began to darken the winter sky over Raisina Hill. Some protesters fell to the ground, others tried to shield their friends from a battering by police lathis. And all the while, thousands more pressed forward through the stinging smoke and water. The protests lasted several days and were misjudged and mishandled from the beginning. Finally, a hapless police force began shutting down metro lines to stop the crowds from reaching the centre of the city.

Why had this rape—in a country where a woman is raped every twenty-two minutes—moved so many thousands out of their apathy and onto the roads? The monstrous nature of the crime was only one explanation for the mass outpouring of support. There were two other important reasons that marked this moment. The rape of Nirbhaya may have generated headlines globally about how unsafe India was for women but the demonstrations it had sparked were in fact a gigantic moment of hope. The media activism, the sloganeering, the public marches and the candlelight vigils had all captured a freeze frame of change in the country's gender discourse. India's younger generation—and it was heartening to see how many men were among the crowds—were no longer willing to treat sexual violence as routine. And the other reason, of course, was that the victim's own story was, once again, so much about the aspirations and ambitions of an India that was altering. She was the daughter of a baggage handler at the Delhi airport. At a time when infanticide and female foeticide remain blots on the country's claims of modernity, here was a father who described his daughter as the 'engine of the family'. He had sold the only piece of land he owned so that he could educate her and finance her dreams to become a physiotherapist.

In so many ways Nirbhaya's story had come to be the story of Everywoman in an India that was lost in transition, caught in the flux created by globalization, the creation of a neo-middle class and the competing forces of conservatism and change. In her death, Nirbhaya gave birth to a robust new law to punish sexual crimes. Under acute pressure, the government announced the setting up of a special panel headed by a retired judge of the Supreme Court to re-examine existing legislation on sexual violence. In an ironic coincidence, the judge was Justice J. S. Verma, the same judge who had first delivered the verdict on the Vishaka sexual harassment guidelines after the rape of Bhanwari Devi. In so many ways, though she never got the same public attention (perhaps because she was poor and lived in a village or perhaps because it was much before India had transformed enough to rise up in solidarity), the gang rape of Bhanwari Devi gave rise to the Nirbhaya moment.

Verma, a soft-spoken jurist respected for his unflinching probity and simplicity—he typed parts of his report himself with one finger as he couldn't afford to hire staff on his meagre pension—received more than 80,000 suggestions from the general public and from lawyers and activists. In twenty-nine days, his team (which included the trailblazing female jurist Leila Seth) and he drew up a path-breaking blueprint for change. His recommendations included making voyeurism and stalking a criminal offence, a separate set of laws for acid attacks, tougher punishment for gang rapes, the barring of politicians charged with rape from contesting elections, a review of legislative immunity to security forces in conflict zones and the recognition of marital rape as a criminal offence. The Verma panel, however, opposed the death penalty for rapists.

When the government legislated on the new law it accepted some of the suggestions by the Verma panel and rejected others. Rape was now redefined as the forced penetration of any orifice of the female body not just the vagina, using not just the penis but also fingers, hands, bottles or any other object. (This would be the basis of the rape charge against Tarun Tejpal.) It also allowed for the death penalty to be applied in especially brutal gang rapes. India's Parliament rejected the proposal to criminalize marital rape and remained silent on the recommendation that politicians facing charges of sexual assault be prohibited from becoming candidates.

∎

While the mass protests had forced the political establishment into action it soon became clear that not enough would be done. It also became apparent that although there were a fair number of women in positions of political power, that was not necessarily going to translate into a more empathetic response. While everyone made the right noises, for the most part, women politicians displayed no extra sensitivity or visible identification with the young people out on the streets.

Women may not have been in a dominant position in the political establishment in December 2012, but enough key positions were occupied by female politicians. Yet, this did not mean much. Sheila Dikshit, the grandmotherly chief minister of Delhi, had already been criticized for her use of the word 'adventurous' to describe journalist Soumya Viswanathan who was murdered in 2008 as she drove home late from work. By the time Dikshit made belated attempts to join the protesters, she was heckled and kept out.

It could be argued that the most powerful woman politician at the time—Congress President Sonia Gandhi—also failed to understand the import of the moment. Ironically, just a year ago, she had shown intuitive political sagacity by joining delirious fans celebrating India's cricket World Cup victory on the streets of the capital. She had waded into the crowd, waving the national flag, happy to shake hands and pose for photographs. But now, she showed no such spontaneity or willingness to dispense with security protocols. She did emerge from inside her fortified residence to meet with a tiny group of demonstrators, but by the time this happened the moment seemed emotionally aloof and more formal than felt. The defining image on national television was of men and women in their twenties being contained by the police force with tear gas and water cannons. The dissonance—between the seething, genuine sense of outrage in the crowd of protesters and the stiff, formal way in which the country's leadership, especially its women leaders, responded—was enormous.

The muted response of women politicians to the outcry was ironical as for two decades now, there has been a battle in Parliament to reserve one-third of the seats in the legislature for women. This has often provoked violent resistance—disruptions, scuffles and documents thrown about. The Lok Sabha is yet to pass the legislation and, given the resistance within, it's unlikely that this will happen any time soon. I remember after one such scuffle inside Parliament, I waylaid Sharad Yadav, a veteran politician from Bihar and vocal opponent of the proposed law, as he was getting into his car; I jumped in from the other side to take a seat beside him as his car drove out of Parliament. He was stumped to see me there and even more taken aback at my many questions on his opposition to the bill.

Later, Yadav dismissed me (and those like me) as an elite 'par kati mahila' (woman with short hair) who was out of sync with issues that really mattered to the masses.

In the aftermath of the Delhi gang rape, the question resurfaced: Would the presence of more women in the political space automatically make governments more gender-sensitive? Or were women as conditioned as the men by the patriarchal society that India was? And, once in politics, did their compulsions and compromises become identical to those of their male counterparts? Perhaps, just like in other professions dominated by men, women politicians in India spent too much time proving that they too could be tough and ruthless.

To some degree, India mirrored a universal phenomenon of the push-back women face when they have the guts to jump into politics and public life. In May 2012, when Hillary Clinton was visiting India as the US Secretary of State, and was considered among the most powerful women in the world, she told me, in all seriousness, that the fastest way to get a story about herself on the front page was to change her hairstyle. We were together in West Bengal, a state governed by a feisty and unpredictable woman politician—Mamata Banerjee. Hillary had recently met the ex-defence minister of Finland, Elisabeth Rehn, and they had talked about how when they read about themselves in the media the coverage usually went something like this, 'It'll be my name, comma, wearing a spring suit of pastel hues, comma, spoke of—'. Speaking of her own run for president of the United States she freely admitted that it was 'a pretty hard glass ceiling' that had not yet been broken. 'I think we just have to keep persevering and not be deterred from supporting women who have the gumption to get out into the political arena.'

But in India, the sexism went well beyond prefacing every analysis of female politicians with a fashion critique. This was because in a gender contradiction typical of this country, unlike in the West, many of the women were socially unconventional by the standards of a deeply orthodox country. Several of them were, for instance, single women who had lived openly with mentors or partners or, in some cases, were divorced. In the United States, which has not voted for an unmarried president since 1885, it's impossible that Hillary could have run for office as a divorced or single woman. In India, Mayawati, Uma Bharti, Vasundhara Raje, Mehbooba Mufti, Mamata Banerjee and Jayalalithaa were among the more prominent politicians who had never bothered to present the picture postcard image of domesticity, marital bliss or motherhood that is expected of women in public life in even the most modern of democracies. Yet, they have won elections in a deeply orthodox country. At the same time, these women have also been mercilessly picked on. In drawing rooms that considered themselves intellectually sophisticated, I had heard the most crass jokes about these 'frustrated' women who 'weren't getting any', a gross sexual subtext to their single status. In more than twenty years of reporting on politics I have never heard unmarried male political leaders spoken of in the same terms.

It is true, of course, that many of these women have their eccentricities and quirks, just like everyone else, but because they are women their idiosyncrasies are scrutinized to a degree that male politicians do not have to deal with. The word 'hysterical' was the most commonly heard adjective if a woman flared up in public. I had never heard it used for a man in public life. The humorous, politically incorrect asides of Lalu Prasad Yadav who often gave interviews dressed only in a 'banian' and pyjamas while milking one of his cows were treated indulgently as eccentricities (both the job and the rustic garb). If a man showed tears in public—the present prime minister, for instance, has choked up twice—he was rightfully applauded for being modern enough to wear his emotions on his sleeve. But for fear of being considered too female, a woman politician would not be able to cry in public. In short, despite their ability to win elections, women in Indian politics are most definitely victims of misogyny. But in a perplexing paradox, as their response to the Nirbhaya protests showed, they are also guilty of behaving in ways that are worthy of criticism.

Several female politicians are autocratic one-woman armies; men in their parties are terrified of them. They have imbibed the more unsavoury characteristics of male-dominated politics, the display of punitive authority and a hierarchical embrace of power, among them. For instance, it may have been her way of asserting her hold over the party, but when Jayalalithaa—the 'Amma' (mother) of Tamil Nadu politics—encouraged the practice of party members prostrating themselves before her or carrying pictures of her in the front pocket of white shirts so transparent that her face would shine right through, it was also anti-democratic and the antithesis of the transformative politics that feminists had hoped would accompany the entry of more women into politics.

Worse, administrations headed by women have shown no special sensitivity when it comes to handling incidents of sexual abuse and violence. The chief minister of West Bengal, Mamata Banerjee, for example, walked into a minefield for suggesting that a woman raped at gunpoint on Kolkata's Park Street in February 2012, had 'cooked up' the entire incident at the behest of Opposition parties. She even transferred the police officer who had successfully investigated the case. Later, she argued that her statements had been distorted by the media, but her actions were evidence of the fact that increasing the representation of women in politics would not by itself herald dramatic change.

Political responses after the Delhi gang rape could at best be called lacklustre and at worst, ignorant. The Delhi chief minister, who had won three consecutive elections, possibly lost the fourth time she ran because of her seeming indifference to the protests that followed.

Even women who wielded great power were bound by the political ecosystem they operated within. After the rape of Nirbhaya, I reached out to Sonia Gandhi's office and asked whether she might want to give an interview. Sonia was infamously camera-shy but I thought she might want to speak out on this particular issue. I was given an appointment to meet her at her residence. She explained to me why she was unwilling to speak on the record. She said she did not want to contradict any statements that might have been made by the Manmohan Singh government in public and be accused of undermining its authority—an allegation that had often been made about her.

She believed Delhi's police commissioner, Neeraj Kumar, should have been replaced or removed after the police used force against protesting students. The home minister—the constable turned politician Sushil Kumar Shinde—differed with his party president and backed the commissioner's continuing in office. Sonia didn't push the matter. I didn't know what to make of this. The awkward duality of power-sharing between the Manmohan Singh-led UPA government and Sonia Gandhi, the Congress party president, made it impossible to locate direct accountability as the party and the government would often lapse into blaming each other in times of trouble. But this wouldn't have been the first time that the Congress president disagreed with the government. It was unfathomable to me that as the most prominent woman politician in the country when the rape, and the subsequent agitation, took place, she was unwilling to take a more public and direct position on the events that had unfolded.

She asked me what I thought. I said that I thought it was imperative that she speak out. I also said that young politicians, men and women, including her son Rahul, should be out there, meeting students in universities and on college campuses, openly discussing issues of women's safety and equality. None of it ever happened.

Women politicians, from any party, also refused to directly address the issue of the grave charges of sexual violence against fellow parliamentarians and legislators. Days after the gang rape, the Association for Democratic Reforms, a not-for-profit advocacy group, released statistics that underpinned this hypocrisy. In the past five years, it said, 260 candidates facing varied charges of crimes against women, including rape, assault and what Indian law old-fashionedly calls 'outraging the modesty' of a woman (an ambiguous phrase in the penal code that covers everything from stalking to molestation) had contested assembly elections. Prominent among the parties who gave these candidates election tickets, were the Congress and the Bahujan Samaj Party (BSP), both helmed by women presidents. Even with the opportunity to change this on the law books, Parliament ignored the specific recommendation of the Justice Verma Committee. Men were still free to pursue electoral power even if charged with rape. The irony was that the same political establishment which debated the new rape laws had two sitting MPs and six MLAs facing rape charges.

Forgotten in the frenzy of rage against the Delhi gang rape were women for whom no one had ever marched. Bhanwari Devi had faded from the headlines, others who lived in the dusty districts of the hinterland struggled even to have their stories told. In the media we were certainly guilty of class bias. Not that the Delhi rape was not a turning point; it certainly was. But it was true that sexual assaults just as horrific, away from the cities or centres of power, never got similar air time in the media or the attention of the wider public.

■

Banda, in Uttar Pradesh, is among the 250 most backward districts in India, and was one of those first targeted by the government's massive rural employment programme. Located in the arid, underdeveloped area of Bundelkhand in Uttar Pradesh, it has been a cesspool of feudalism, caste bias, bigotry and oppression of women. With an estimated 20 per cent of its 1.6 million people belonging to the so-called lower castes, it is women who bear the brunt of institutionalized and caste-driven discrimination. The district is home to the 'Gulabi Gang', a glamorous, pink-sari-draped group of women vigilantes who beat up men who are violent, abusive or alcoholic. Led by the full-blooded Sampat Pal Devi, a mother of five who gave birth to her first child when she was just thirteen, the 'gang' has even inspired the movie star Madhuri Dixit to enact their exploits on film.

In the winter of 2012, I met Sheelu Nishad, a young girl from this very district who had come to Delhi. There were no movie stars or sari-clad avengers rallying around her; she sat by herself in a frayed beige jacket buttoned to the neck to ward off the cold. In hesitant, soft-spoken words, she told me the story of her battle to get justice. She was still a minor when she was kidnapped and raped by the local legislator Purushottam Naresh Dwivedi, a representative of the BSP. Once again her story could only be understood at the intersection of caste, class and gender prejudices. Dwivedi, a Brahmin, had kept Sheelu, who was from the backward caste of boatmen, captive in his house for four days. He repeatedly raped her until she somehow managed to escape. She was rescued from under a small bridge in the village, where she had been lying semi-conscious for two days. The legislator then accused her of theft and trespassing, and put pressure on her family to withdraw the rape charge. 'We have to find the strength to fight our own battles so that other women gain confidence from us. A number of women get scared and withdraw their complaint for some money or simply from fear. This is completely wrong. It is our failure,' she said on the TV show I had invited her to participate in. Her words were met with a roar of applause from the audience of young men and women. 'If I do not get justice, I will turn into a bandit and seek revenge.' These words from Sheelu may have sounded hyperbolic at first but there was a historic precedent for them. Phoolan Devi, who came to be known as India's 'Bandit Queen', was born into the same 'Nishad' caste as Sheelu; like her, Phoolan was gang-raped and humiliated repeatedly over several days by upper-caste men—the land-owning Thakurs. She was then paraded naked around the village. After escaping, Phoolan's life was fuelled by revenge and retribution, for the indignities heaped on her, and for the murder of her lover Vikram Mallah. In India's collective memory her definitive image came to be that of a woman in khaki trousers with her hair pulled back in a bandanna, a Sten gun slung across her shoulder, a flaming red shawl adding authority and awe to her otherwise diminutive five-foot-tall frame. She rose from poverty, abuse and sexual violence to infamy and near-mythical status on Valentine's Day in 1981 when she rounded up twenty-two upper-caste men and shot them all dead. Two years later she negotiated her own surrender, spent eleven years in Gwalior jail without trial, until all the criminal charges against her were dropped in 1994 by Mulayam Singh Yadav, the then chief minister of Uttar Pradesh. In 1996, the former outlaw was elected to the Lok Sabha; I remember being naively captivated by her personal history and voting for her party that year when she made her debut as a politician.

I asked Sheelu whether she had ever considered telling her story from behind the protective cover of anonymity. 'Why should I hide my face or name?' she snapped back. 'If they play with our honour, should we be ashamed or should they?' But women like Sheelu were still the exception not the rule. It called for extraordinary mettle and gumption and the readiness to have your integrity relentlessly questioned but it was heartening to see that the outrage over Nirbhaya's rape and murder had bolstered the resolve of a few women to fight their oppressors and the society that had victimized them.

After Sheelu left, my thoughts drifted to Bhanwari Devi from all those years ago, hunched over her husband's potter's wheel, determined to keep making clay pots that no one in the village was ready to buy. Not once had she opted for namelessness or facelessness, not even when the men who raped her walked free from jail, with an I-told-you-so dare in their eyes. Almost seventeen years after I reported on her rape as a rookie journalist, I met another woman from whom the same exceptional courage emanated.

With her cropped hair, no-fuss jacket-and-jeans ensemble and pocket-sized frame, Sunitha Krishnan's pluck was inversely proportional to her four-foot-six-inch frame. Raped by eight men when she was just fifteen, Sunitha had evolved from survivor to saviour—she had committed her entire life to rescuing women and children from the multi-billion dollar industry of sexual trafficking (valued at an approximate $9 billion; according to a UN report, trafficking in persons is estimated to be the fastest growing enterprise of the twenty-first century). According to the Ministry of Home Affairs, there were nearly 5,000 reported victims of sexual trafficking in India in 2013 alone.

'I refused to believe that I was spoilt or that I had been destroyed or that my soul could be broken by the eight men who gang-raped me,' she told me, explaining why she didn't need dimmed lights or the cover of a scarf while going on camera to talk about how she had been violated as a teenager. It had been more than two decades since the rape, but she still woke up every single morning gripped by a rage that hadn't diminished with the passage of time. 'The anger of exclusion, the anger at being questioned for your pain, for being blamed for something you have never done and society conspiring to make you feel cheap and ashamed...' she said, as she tried to explain how being angry had helped her shrug off victimhood. 'It bothered many people that I didn't cry,' she laughed, throwing her head back, 'they called me arrogant for not weeping. Look at her, they taunted, so much has happened to her and she is walking freely and lightly. They blamed my parents for giving me too much freedom. The worst was the attempt by society to make me feel ashamed of myself.' Sunitha had become something of a heroic figure, inspiring other women to be stronger, rescuing little girls sold into the sex trade by their own relatives, providing shelter for children infected with HIV as a result of rape and sexual violence. She had freed 8,000 girls from sexual slavery; she personified strength. Yet the valour never took away her essential vulnerability.

'What people never understand is that I am brave in the daytime, but at night I have to deal with myself,' she said, her eyes welling up behind the glasses that covered most of her tiny face. 'You have to deal with your nightmares, you have to deal with the memory of the sixteen hands that groped you, you have to deal with the pain and shame and loneliness that you are going through, because you can't talk to anyone. If you tell anyone they will always say you asked for it. I don't feel my face needs to be blurred: I think the men who did this to me should hide their faces. But what bothers me is from the time this happened to me twenty-four years ago till this moment, the attitude of our society has not changed.' Ironically, for all her pluck, her rapists never got punished; she said there was just too much pressure on her from her family to not pursue the case. And she wasn't confident of identifying them. 'I definitely felt guilt and shame for dropping the case. But what I want to ask today is whether we will ever act (together) as a people?'

Sunitha was prescient in her understanding that the appearance of fundamental change in the aftermath of the Delhi gang rape was illusory. 'Today this is a lovely story,' she said mocking the media's notorious fickleness, 'tomorrow this will go away and everything will be forgotten. Then a bigger gang rape has to happen, maybe a few more rods have to be thrust into a woman for us to feel outraged. We get outraged about Delhi; we don't get outraged about Kozhikode or Palakkad or Uttar Pradesh, do we?'

The country had a new rape law, but one that failed to recognize that for many women in India, the enemy was firmly inside the circle of trust. Neighbours, uncles, cousins, old family friends, even husbands were often the perpetrators; the familial connections pushed the women deeper and deeper into awkward silence. One survey said that one in every five Indian men admitted that they had forced their wives into having sex with them. Yet, Parliament ignored the Justice Verma Committee's recommendation to legally acknowledge marital rape as a criminal offence. First, the government justified leaving it out of the law, describing it as a 'difficult issue that needed more consultations'. Then, an all-party parliamentary forum, which had several women as its members, backed the government on this decision. 'The committee agrees with the government that we should not disrupt the family system,' said Venkaiah Naidu, the chairman of the panel; he would later become a senior minister in the Narendra Modi-led Bharatiya Janata Party (BJP) government. The panel admitted that 'consent in marriage cannot be consent forever', but went on to argue that bringing marital rape within the purview of the law could 'destroy the institution of marriage' and family life. The refusal to acknowledge the reality of marital rape went against the international trend; the United States began criminalizing rape within marriage in the 1970s; most European countries had amended their laws by the 1990s. More recently even countries such as Turkey and Malaysia, both regarded as more socially conservative than India, changed their laws, in 2005 and 2007 respectively.

The remarks of India's parliamentarians betrayed an archaic, conservative notion that women are the 'property' of their husbands and that sex is a guaranteed male entitlement of marriage, irrespective of whether the woman wants it or not. In law, the marital rape exemption can be traced back to Matthew Hale, the Chief Justice of England, who wrote in the mid-seventeenth century that the 'husband cannot be guilty of a rape committed by himself upon his lawful wife, for by their mutual consent and contract, the wife hath given up herself in this kind unto her husband which she cannot retract.' The United Kingdom finally changed its law in 1991, but in India the only protection against marital rape is for child-brides who are under the age of fifteen.

When Naidu announced the decision to keep marital rape off

the law books he was supported by parties across the spectrum, including those, like the Congress, which were headed by women. The resistance to change reflected the enormous premium placed on the continuation of marriage at all costs—the harsh truth of a society that saw women primarily as wives (or mothers) and denied them the sexual agency to make their own choices. Over the next few months I would meet scores of women who had been sexually abused, or beaten by their husbands.

In Mumbai, there was Anjum, her head swathed in a black veil, who looked down at her feet and spoke quietly about how her husband wanted her to replicate the pornographic positions he downloaded on his mobile phone. Every time she refused, he would thrash her into submission till she fell to the floor, bleeding from the mouth and nose. When she turned to her parents for help they told her that what happened within her marriage was her problem; she would have to find a way of dealing with it. Illiterate and disempowered, she was not permitted to step out of the house alone. She had often contemplated going to the police, but told me she had no idea how to even begin the process. Her movement outside the house was restricted to visiting her parents and returning home. When she fought with her in-laws to let her leave, they forcibly held her down. Finally, distraught, exhausted and helpless, she tried to kill herself by swallowing poison. 'I thought it was better to die than to live like this. My own parents dismissed my pain and told me I could not turn against my husband. I had no one to talk to,' she told me in tears.

And then there were others who were brutalized by those they knew. From Uttar Pradesh's Bulandshahr district, there was Archana, her face covered by giant black shades in the middle of the day to hide the ridged and scored skin corroded by acid. She had been stalked for five years by a man obsessed with her, the acid was the man's answer to her lack of romantic interest in him. In a country where it is not uncommon for Hindi cinema to indulgently show a persistent suitor who never takes no for an answer, courting and cajoling, even breaking into song whilst pulling at the heroine's dupatta, the idea that a woman had the right to set her own boundaries of space and privacy was still an alien one. Archana's stalker started harassing her when she was still a student at school and finally insisted that she marry him. When she declined he entered her house and flung acid on her face and simply walked away. 'I felt as if the sky had opened up and collapsed on me; my life changed in an instant,' Archana said, showing me a photograph of herself before the attack. Flawless skin, deep black eyes set apart by a distinctive, aquiline nose, a bright smile that travelled right up to the corner of her eyes—it was the look of a confident young woman who was dreaming of a life bigger and better than anything the village of Dulhara had to offer her. Today, despite twenty-three surgeries—operations for which the family had sold the little land they owned and every piece of jewellery they possessed—craters and cracks indent the surface of her face. 'The acid slashed the skin off my face; my appearance was so frightening that adults would look at me strangely and little children were too scared to talk to me,' Archana said, her voice more matter of fact than anguished. Her father was now undergoing psychiatric treatment and her mother had to take pills just to sleep at night. Sitting by her side, fighting back tears, her mother told me she had had big dreams for Archana, but the man who had done this to her daughter had destroyed them all. 'At least I still have the confidence to speak to you and the world at large,' Archana said, consoling her mother. 'I keep thinking how many other women like me must be suffering in silence. Who do they unburden their hearts to? Let me tell you, for all your kind words and sympathy, no one else can ever feel my pain or what my parents have gone through.'

IV

I was not even ten when I was first sexually abused. The perpetrator was a distant older relative who had come to stay with us for a short period of time. Like many Punjabi households, ours was an open house, always welcoming to cousins and their friends, and their friends in turn. Today, decades later, I cannot even recall the precise connection of this man to my family. But, to a child's eye, he was avuncular and affectionate and, in any case, I just assumed I was safe in my own home.

Little did I imagine that this much-older, family figure—someone who would take the kids for piggy-back rides and twirl us around in the air—could be such a monster. Worse still, as a child unable to process the magnitude of what had happened—I was the one who felt grotesque and dirty. The concept of teaching your child to distinguish between 'good touch' and 'bad touch' had not yet become the enlightened norm. But after the first few times I had innocently followed him to 'play' with him in his room, I was overcome by panic and disgust.

Ridden with guilt, unable to shake off the feeling of being dirty and trapped in a sink of fear, I finally told my mother that something terrible had happened. My assaulter was immediately thrown out of the house and I buried the awfulness of the memory in a deep, dark place that I hoped I would never have to revisit. As I grew older, what stayed with me, strangely enough, was the rancid smell of hair-oil; even years later, anything that smelt faintly similar made me nauseous. In my growing years, I blocked out the man's face, his name, in fact the very incident was banished to the recesses of my consciousness; but from that moment onwards, sexual abuse had an odour.

It was the loneliest and most frightened I had felt as a child and the fear lurked in the shadows, following me into adulthood. I discovered that I was often wary, even scared, of sexual relations—a familiar consequence for those who had experienced abuse as children.

I didn't know it then but my experience, horrible as it was, was hardly uncommon. In 2007, the first ever government survey of child sexual abuse uncovered that more than half the children spoken to (53 per cent) said they had experienced some form of sexual abuse. Twenty per cent of those interviewed said they had been subjected to severe abuse, which the report defined as 'sexual assault, making the child fondle private parts, making the child exhibit private body parts and being photographed in the nude'. Yet, the silence of young victims and the misplaced shame they felt shielded the perpetrators. These were men deeply embedded in the family structure, it made it that much more difficult to call them out. The report found that

31 per cent of the sexual assaults were by an uncle or neighbour. So it wasn't surprising that over 70 per cent of children had never spoken to anyone of what was done to them.

The toughest discovery for me was to find that feminism offered no shield against the vulnerability, confusion, guilt and rage you felt when you were abused.

As a young adult who experienced violence in a personal relationship for the very first time as a postgraduate student at Delhi's Jamia Millia Islamia University, my response was less confused but no easier to act on. By now I was a self-aware young woman with strong opinions. I thought I was difficult to intimidate. I believed I would know exactly what to do if a man I was dating ever hit me. Of course I would take him to the cops, I would say with confidence when we sat around discussing how unfriendly the legal system was towards women. I thought I was never going to stand for anything like domestic abuse. It went against every book I had read, every principle I held as sacred and every bit of my self-image. Until it happened.

I was briefly in a relationship with a fellow student at the university's mass communication centre. It was a very different environment from the people-like-us safety of St Stephen's. Budding filmmakers exemplified every depressing cliché you could think of. Everyone smoked; you even lit up in class because the zany graphic design teacher did; everyone was filled with angst and cynicism and everyone thought 'intense' and 'dysfunctional' were interchangeable adjectives.

I was a bit of a misfit. I did not smoke, I hadn't yet had my first drink and I was considered puritanical and uptight in an environment where it was assumed that creative people were sexually promiscuous. I don't quite remember how I ended up straying into an unlikely involvement with a fellow student who was studying to be a cinematographer. Quite soon I knew that the relationship was wrong for me. Warning bells began sounding the day the man suddenly grabbed a razor blade and opened up his wrists when we had an argument and I told him I no longer wanted to be with him. In absolute horror I watched him wrap his scratched wrists

in strips of white Band-Aid and calmly smoke a cigarette, his eyes
fixed on me in a cold, hard stare. It could have been a bad movie,
except this was my life, it was happening to me. I knew I was being
manipulated and blackmailed, yet I was terrified. I didn't end the
relationship that day.

The next time we met I was categorical that I was not going to
allow myself to be emotionally and mentally bullied. When I told
him that it was over between us he sprang up from the floor where
he had been lounging, pinned me to the ground and lay on top of
me, trying to sexually force himself on me. I slapped him. He hit
me hard, grabbed me by my arm, shoved me around, slapped me
and pushed me against the wall. My face was burning up with pain
and anger. I pushed him away, walked out and took a rickshaw back
home. My right cheek was now a purplish blue mass. Initially, I told
my family that I had walked into a door.

But I had resolved that I was never going to be a woman who
would hide abuse because of a misplaced sense of embarrassment. I
was determined to complain officially to the campus authorities and
contemplated going to the police. But this was still the early nineties.
There were no sexual harassment guidelines, there was no rape law,
there was no environment of support that is available to women
in these situations today. Still, I took the faculty into confidence.
Some of my teachers were progressive feminists themselves. They
were empathetic but also practical. They explained that I still had
two years of my programme left before I would get my degree. The
university was unlikely to act on a 'he said, she said' complaint.

To reiterate, at the time, there were no mandated sexual
harassment committees in existence. The Vishaka Guidelines would
only be passed in 1997 and the Domestic Violence Act even later,
in 2005. To review the options I had, I went to meet lawyers who
worked in a women's collective. Could I take this to court, I asked?
They told me, as kindly as they could, that I would spend the next
two decades in court and the fact that the violence had taken place
within a relationship would only be held against me.

I spoke to other students and discovered that other women too
had been hit and abused by the same man who had done this to me.

But they weren't willing to put their names down on any kind of official petition asking for his expulsion. For all the fight I thought I had in me, I was effectively helpless. The most I managed was to get myself placed in a separate working group where I would never have to interact with him again. As I went about my work on campus as bravely as I could, I could hear the sniggers and the gossip behind my back. It was I who was considered the troublemaker, not the actual perpetrator.

In 1994 when I applied for my first job at New Delhi Television Limited (NDTV) I had only one request. If 'that man' from Jamia was going to be hired as a cameraman (remember, private television had not yet taken off in India and the pool of trained people available was very small), I could not accept the job. They agreed. And I never saw him again. It was perhaps the most isolating experience of my adult life.

Much later in life, I would discover that I was not alone; almost every young woman I knew had experienced something essentially similar—not just out on the streets, but within the so-called safe zone. This was not startling for a country in which government data itself shows that even today, 90 per cent of Indian women who have been sexually abused know their assaulter. What broke us internally and what we could not fight publicly was the abuse we experienced within the circle of trust. We could slap the molester on the local train but were almost never able to say out loud that among our uncles, cousins and family friends were sexual predators who had manipulated us into feeling a shame that should have been theirs. We buried it deep within us, unable, even years later, to excavate the pain, the anger and the confusion.

In Bangalore, Suja Jones uncovered a truth that was probably worse than being violated yourself—that the man she was married to was sexually abusing her children. She believes it all started when she was expecting their third child. Her infant daughter would use broken baby words to indicate that all was not well. The first time her baby girl said 'Papa hurt me down there,' Suja's husband explained it away by saying he'd bathed her with soap which may have caused discomfort. 'I am a woman who comes from an educated, privileged background. But I loved my husband, I was dependent on him. At first, I thought I am sitting at home with two children, maybe I am the one going crazy,' she said explaining how she kept living in denial. 'I didn't want the pretty picture of my family to collapse. It tears me up today that my daughter was trying to tell me something in her faltering baby language and I chose not to understand it.' It was another year before her daughter was able to construct a full sentence and tell her mother why it suddenly hurt to urinate. The internal struggle was as fierce as external pressure; Suja didn't tell her parents until the news of her filing a criminal case against her husband was out in the papers. 'I kept rationalizing things to myself, denying even what the doctors were telling me in their initial evaluation. When the hospital test confirmed presence of sperm, it was a slap on my face. After that there was no looking back possible,' she said, consumed by the guilt of her initial inaction.

In 2013, just a few months after the Delhi gang rape, the same sort of anger that had galvanized public opinion after 16 December erupted again—this time, after the sexual assault of a five-year-old. 'Gudiya', as she was christened by the media, was found tied up in a basement where she had been locked up for over forty hours. She had suffered chronic internal injuries; a bottle of hair oil and candles had been forced into her private parts. Her rapists, who lived in the same building, had lured her into the basement with the promise of potato chips. Her father, a daily-wage labourer, had migrated to the capital from Sitamarhi in Bihar, one of the poorest districts in India, so underdeveloped that according to the 2001 census, 92 per cent of its villagers lived without any medical facilities. Now, as he stood in the ICU of the All India Institute of Medical Sciences, watching his infant daughter going through her fifth reconstructive surgery, he recounted how he had been offered Rs 2,000 to withdraw his criminal complaint. It was heartbreaking to observe the little girl, dressed in a purple frock, frail and so very tiny, enveloped by the sheets of the hospital bed she lay on. Her internal organs had been damaged and she was awaiting a colostomy; a bag had to be created to divert her stool while her doctors tried to repair the damaged organs. Four surgeries later the hospital discharged her but her family discovered that they would need to keep changing neighbourhoods. As murmurs began to spread about what had happened to their daughter, people began to blame them for not 'controlling' Gudiya. They had shifted four homes already; the victim—even when she was a child—had been made the accused.

V

Unlike India, much of the western world took its time to grant women the right to vote or run for office. Women were not allowed to vote in ancient Greece and Rome and it wasn't until the nineteenth century that women's suffrage even became a rallying point. It would take until after World War I for the electoral empowerment of women to gather momentum. The suffragette movement that swept through countries like Great Britain and the United States seemed odd to us here in India as women had had voting rights from the time independent India held its first election in 1952. A few years later, in 1955, the Hindu Marriage Act gave women the right to own and inherit property and the right to divorce. As a new nation, India was far more forward-thinking than many much older democracies.

All the more reason then, for the patriarchal nature of Indian society to be such a contradiction in terms. The country's culture of patriarchy has its origins, not in its Constitution, but in age-old religious scriptures, tenets and traditions. What is one to make of a country that worships women but blesses new mothers with the exhortation to give birth to a 'hundred sons'? How does one reconcile that places of worship, the famous Sabarimala Temple among them, often forbid menstruating women from entering their compounds, even as 'infertile' women are scorned and rejected by society? When I put this question to Rahul Easwar, a trustee of the Sabarimala temple board, he called me a 'fundamentalist feminist'.

I met with women of the Bharatiya Muslim Mahila Andolan who have been fighting for years to abolish the 'triple talaq' diktat which allows a Muslim man to divorce his wife simply by uttering the word talaq thrice. Even though the seventh-century law has been reformed or abolished across much of the Muslim world, it continues to thrive in India. And the Muslim Personal Law Board has openly scorned women of the community who are fighting for reform.

There has been a highly-charged and politicized debate around a uniform civil code for India, a directive principle in the Constitution. Because of the politics, consensus has been elusive and the orthodoxy of personal laws—across religions—continues to militate against gender equality.

The confusion and contradictions of India's feminist movement can be traced back to the paradoxes of the country's ancient cultural and religious traditions. In her critique of Indian feminism, *Why Kali Won't Rage*, Rita Banerji has explored why women's movements in the West have been much angrier than in India. Banerji locates what she calls the relative 'passivity in the face of extreme tyranny' to the cultural constructs built by ancient religious texts like the *Manusmriti* that offers, among other things, this set of instructions:

> A girl, a young woman, or even an old woman should not do anything independently, even in her own house. In childhood a woman should be under her father's control, in youth under her husband's, and when her husband is dead, under her sons.

On the other hand, Banerji points out, the Shakta cults that arose in the first millennium AD, believed in worshipping women:

> The *Shakta* goddesses were immodest, and assertive in their needs and demands, in all arenas, including sex. As in the myths of Radha and Sati, the goddess broke social conventions of marriage, caste and clan in her choice of sexual partners. And when confronted with men who wanted to sexually exploit her, the goddess would, as Durga or Kali, respond to the affront with fearsome rage and spectacular battle skills—destroying the men in a bloody battle and then wearing their decapitated heads in a victory garland around her neck.

The anti-women diktats of Manu and the ferocious feminism of Durga reflect what Banerji believes may have been a violent confrontation between matriarchal and patriarchal communities. It is these cultural incongruities that Indian society has inherited and been subconsciously shaped by.

So, well beyond the daily battles against sexual violence stretches an even larger war-zone—the gladiatorial ring where women must first fight the contradictions of this historic conditioning and learn that insidious gender bias can often be subliminal and not overt.

■

The company I worked for would periodically run media campaigns for women's equality. I had imagined that as a female mentor to an editorial and production team dominated by young women, we were all strengthened by each other to live lives unfettered by stereotypical sexism. Many of the women in my team had accompanied me into conflict, war, floods and the fury of angry crowds. They were extraordinarily talented and spunky, often outperforming men in the same roles. Yet, over the years, I watched in dismay as that familiar work–life balance bogey aborted some brilliant careers. Marriage, or even children, did not drag down the professional graph of a single male colleague. Yet, the ambition of more than a few women I knew declined once they had to juggle managing a home along with a career. Many asked for less strenuous shifts, some opted out entirely. I cajoled, sulked, lost my temper, offered friendly counsel to try and change their minds. I even argued that we were betraying the battle fought by the generation of women who had gone before us, professionals who had struggled to get past a glass ceiling that their best efforts could only crack, not break. Perhaps I was not empathetic enough; perhaps as a beneficiary of exceptional personal freedom I was not sensitive to the pressures and demands made of women by their families. But I worried—how could we break down barriers at work when it was not at all certain that women themselves would grab opportunities that were presented to them with the same fervour and staying power as men?

My experience was anecdotal but statistics about the female labour force in India told their own dire story. Data from the National Sample Survey Organization (NSSO) showed that the proportion of working women had actually plummeted from 40 per cent in 1990 to less than 23 per cent by 2012. According to the International Labour Organization (ILO), India ranked eleventh from the bottom

on a list of 131 countries when it came to female participation in
the workforce. So had India's years of economic liberalization simply
bypassed women? Or was there some other explanation?

Ironically, the percentage of women who worked in the villages
was much higher than in the cities, where globalization had brought
malls and McDonald's and ostensibly a slew of new opportunities
for employment. In a definitive study, economists Surjit Bhalla and
Ravinder Kaur analysed the numbers to show that in urban India,
the percentage of women in the labour force was 'much lower and
with a labour force pattern not very dissimilar from that prevailing
in most Islamic countries'. Their study also showed how as incomes
and education levels of men increased the women they were married
to showed a greater inclination to stop working. At poor and low
levels of family incomes the very need to survive ensured that women
worked as well as managed the home and children. They plotted a
U-curve for the number of working women in India—the numbers
were high among the poor but declined steeply as income levels of
the family began climbing before registering an increase again at
much higher levels of income.

Another study by Vinoj Abraham conclusively showed that greater
education was no guarantee of greater economic independence or
self-reliance for India's women. In urban India, for instance, the
proportion of working women graduates had plunged from over 60
per cent in the 1980s to 26 per cent in 2010. Abraham argued that
institutionalized patriarchy and the peculiar socio-cultural norms of
Indian society associated upward mobility with the 'labour market
participation of men, marginalization of women in the labour force
and the domestication of women'. In other words, status-seeking
households continued to idealize domesticity when it came to
women. Social scientist M. N. Srinivas had described this process
as 'sanskritization' in which women's seclusion was traditionally
a marker of high status among upper castes and was now being
emulated by castes and communities seeking to rise to the same
level in the social pecking order.

The peculiar social norms, the engrained societal hierarchies,
the absence of shared responsibility in household chores and no

guaranteed infrastructural support for child care meant that women who chose to be as professionally driven as men were expected to either be magicians or surrender at least one dream to privilege another. Even India-born Indra Nooyi, the global CEO of PepsiCo—who was No. 15 on the *Forbes* list of the most powerful women in the world in 2015—declared that women could not 'have it all'. Biological determinism remained an unalterable impediment to free will and Nooyi was absolutely on target when she said that the biological clock was in 'total and complete conflict' with the career clock.

I have often been quizzed about parenthood and whether I had never wanted it for myself. The truth is that as an adrenalin junkie, whose job comes with unpredictable hours and travels to dangerous hotspots, I was too obsessed with work to think about much else in my twenties and thirties. When the passage of time began to shrink the space left to make a free choice, I began to feel conflicted. I wrestled with questions millions of women have had to deal with. Could I go off to report on the fall of Gaddafi in Libya (as I had for days on end, illegally crossing over into Benghazi, from the Egypt border in the darkness of night, with gun-toting strangers for company) with a baby at home? Would I have taken the same risks at the front line of the Kargil War if I was also responsible for a young life? Would my drifter instincts and love for being on the road for long stretches interfere with my capability as a mother? I don't know if a man in my role would have struggled with the same dilemmas; logically, any parent—man or woman—would have had to agonize over these questions, but I suspect this hand-wringing and second guessing is particular to women. It wasn't until I was in my forties, just about the time that biological fatalism had in any case sealed my choices, that I could answer the question—do you want to be a mother?—without getting annoyed or defensive.

Nooyi's philosophical acceptance that women, as distinct from men, would have to junk some desires to fulfil others remains true for the majority of Indian women. But a telling anecdote she recounted about her own mother also offered a glimpse as to why. Seemingly without rancour or anger, she remembered how she had come home excitedly one night to share the news of a promotion at work. But she found her mother disapproving and barely interested in the news from the office. Instead, she wanted to know why Nooyi had forgotten to buy milk for the household. When the PepsiCo CEO asked why the errand could not have been run by her husband who happened to be at home, she was reprimanded by her mother: 'When you are at home, you are first a daughter and a wife.'

Nooyi did not tell us whether, today, one generation later, she would say the same to her daughter. But the argument echoed the conversations that many of my own female colleagues were negotiating in their newly married lives. Whenever a colleague would confide in me about irritable in-laws or a demanding husband and concede that domestic pressures were beginning to impinge upon her performance at work, I would urge her to ask for more parity at home. But, in India, the combination of socialization and cultural pressures has led to women just accepting that they can't have it all or resigning themselves to the fact that they would still have to 'do' it all. In an interview with me, actress turned politician Kirron Kher freely admitted that she had opted not to work till her son was fourteen; her husband Anupam Kher had a demanding work schedule and she believed the obligations of marriage and parenting could not accommodate two equal ambitions. Firuza Parikh, one of India's pre-eminent IVF doctors, told me how every landmark achievement in her career came with a subliminal sense of loss. 'I would cringe with pain when they called me a superdoctor every time we had an innovation or breakthrough, because I felt if I am a superdoctor, I can't be a supermom. At that point I made a choice; I can't differentiate between my family and my patients, I can't draw a neat line. My family got used to my missing birthdays because I had to cut a cake with a baby I'd just helped deliver.'

The 'superwoman' and 'supermom' story has become a staple of glossies and advertisements (usually for pressure cookers or washing machines); this has created a fundamentally unfair and unrealistic standard for women to live up to. By internalizing the notion that both the boardroom and the household would belong to our domain of responsibility, by unquestioningly embracing the dual role of boss and homemaker, we have made things even tougher for ourselves. Whenever we women pay ourselves compliments rooted in gender generalizations—for example, the favourite theory that women are better than men at multi-tasking—we are complicating things even further for ourselves. These ways of thinking only reinforce the argument that some talents in the workplace are gender-specific, opening us to discriminatory evaluations based on our sex that we have spent years shrugging off. The new cliché is the image of the perfectly put-together female corporate executive, a string of grey pearls framing her elegant neck as she works the phones to instruct the domestic help on what to cook for that evening's dinner while simultaneously hammering out the last stages of a million-dollar deal. It is an obvious glorification of subtle, but age-old cultural prejudices that deify domesticity when it comes to women. The superwoman tag is effectively a self-inflicted wound masquerading as a compliment. Indian men are not grappling with any of this; they are not agonizing over whether being a super-banker means they can never be a superdad.

And, as before, women who were educated and well off and should have thus felt more empowered were the ones who were more inclined to surrender to societal expectations. Among the poor, the very debate was redundant; there was no choice but for women to do everything. Bhagwani Devi, who mopped floors and washed utensils in tony colonies of Delhi, also ran the kitchen in her own home, brought up her children and looked after her husband who worked as a daily-wage labourer. Though he had long spells of free time at home, 'He wouldn't even get up to get a glass of water for himself,' she said, resigned to the many jobs that were left to her.

VI

In today's India, the millennial generation has thrown up what I call the 'new rebels'. Young women are embracing things that were once taboo, or words that are typically used as pejoratives against them, and converting them into provocative statements of power. So whether these are 'slut walks' or slogans of equality scribbled on sanitary napkins that are plastered across campus walls, the new urban feminist is looking for a fresh idiom to express herself in.

That clash between the old feminism and the new was reflected in the cultural debate triggered by the Nirbhaya rape. On one of my shows soon after the Delhi rape, veteran actress Shabana Azmi and the much younger star Priyanka Chopra got into a raging argument over what Hindi films call the 'item number'.

While Indian society remains puritanical and closed when it comes to talking openly about sex, the portrayal of women in popular culture is hyper-sexualized like never before. Is the formal advent of the 'item girl' in Indian films—a flamboyant serenade extraneous to the plot and inserted just for its in-your-face sexuality—a sign of emancipation or another manifestation of the male gaze?

Shabana believed it was the latter and called for women in the industry to make informed decisions about songs that were sexualizing even little girls who would then repeat the pouty gyrations at weddings. And then there were the lyrics. Did women really want to be referred to as 'tandoori murgi' or 'chikni chameli'? Priyanka argued that it was about choice and that free choice was the cornerstone of all feminism.

Had someone asked me to take a side I would have found it difficult. I remember feeling entirely conflicted when, during the course of a television debate on censorship, I met Mumaith Khan, a sultry beauty best known for her gyrating and pouting to the camera. At one point, springing to her feet, she pointed to the short skirt riding up her toned thighs and proclaimed aggressively that this was the freedom women wanted. The age of draping women only in salwar kameezes was over, she yelled, to thunderous applause. As a young Muslim woman from a conservative Lucknow family, she had defied several norms and cultural assumptions. But in the process had she just adopted an alternative stereotype where her freedom was to be defined by a camera travelling up to her navel?

Unlike the naive years of my youth I had finally come to understand that the gender debate was impossible to dislocate from parallel arguments about social heterogeneity, economic equality, globalization and, of course, caste in India and race in the West. Nothing exemplified the dilemma for liberal feminists more than the

THE PLACE OF WOMEN

debate around the veil. My feminist impulse opposed it completely; my support for multiculturalism in an increasingly homogenized world and for the rights of women to choose for themselves weakened that certitude.

I found myself similarly conflicted following the global row over *India's Daughter*, a BBC documentary on the Nirbhaya rape. The filmmaker, Leslee Udwin, a survivor of rape herself, had got rare access inside a Delhi prison to interview Mukesh Singh, one of the men convicted for the crime. The film was to air on NDTV when the government, in a knee-jerk and indefensible response, decided to ban it. The self-goal shifted the debate from the merits of the film and the wisdom of giving a rapist a platform to amplify his views to one of censorship. There could be no basis to rationalize the ban (which was later upheld in court) and we all took an unequivocal position against it. But, like many Indian feminists, I was less than convinced by Udwin's decision to foreground the voices of misogyny—the rapist and his defence lawyers. I wasn't sure what purpose it served; after all, we in the Indian media had chosen not to give the lawyers (one of whom said he would burn his daughter or sister alive were she to have premarital sex) the respectability of a television interview. Did we really need to hear the rapist say, as he did in the documentary, 'You can't clap with one hand—it takes two hands. A decent girl won't roam around at 9 o' clock at night. A girl is far more responsible for rape than a boy'. As abhorrent and sickening as these comments were, what did we expect from a man who had joined four other men and shoved an iron rod inside a young woman's vagina. As Leslee and I debated these issues on a variety of global platforms—I suspect we were now being invited as some sort of latter-day Punch and Judy act—we became friends who were able to have an honest argument and still hug each other at the end of it. At one such conference, Tina Brown's Women in the World Summit in New York, where both Leslee and I had been invited to speak, I got into a minor spat with our moderator, television anchor Norah O'Donnell. She opened our session with a reference to Delhi being the rape capital of the world. I argued that statistically this was simply not true, offering her Amartya Sen's numbers from the *New York Review of Books*. I counter-questioned her: should the Ferguson incident—a high-profile shooting of a young African American—permit me to make a sweeping generalization about the US? Most importantly, I emphasized that the struggle of women was universal. This was a global fight—not a contest between nations and cultures. Udwin revealed that the BBC had deleted the global statistics on rape that she had included in her documentary, numbers that would have reinforced my point. She and I agreed that what the world needed to understand was that the protests that followed the Delhi rape were in fact a moment of hope for India. I tried to explain to a predominantly American audience that the reason they were hearing so much noise about sexual violence in India was because we, men and women, had decided that silence was no longer an option. I ended my comments by saying that I was most troubled by the complicity of Indian lawmakers in allowing marriage to be a licence to rape.

I returned home to find that the video of our conversation had gone viral. It was trending on Twitter and Facebook and, apparently, I had managed to sharply divide people into two camps—those who thought I had been too defensive about India and those who believed that I was absolutely right in calling out the stereotype. For me, this was another instructive experience that no feminist debate could take place in isolation from other existing hegemonies, in this case, the somewhat exaggerated perspective of the white world. I saw no contradiction in being a passionate, unapologetic feminist who could also challenge some of these broad strokes. That our comments had generated such a debate spoke once again to why the Nirbhaya rape and its aftermath was an inflection point in India.

However, the fact that the plight of women has finally begun to make an impression on society should not in any way take away from the fact that the life of the average Indian woman continues to be a war zone. Data released by the NSSO shows that every second woman in rural India walked an average of 173 kilometres in 2012 just to fetch potable water. The 201 hours that this consumed also meant a loss of twenty-seven days' worth of wages annually. This was apart from all the other jobs, inside the home and outside, that these women performed. In my forties, chastened by all that I had seen, I finally understood that for millions of Indian women, survival itself was a battle.

While the war for equality for Indian women will have to be waged on multiple fronts—legal, economic, political—the first conflict zone is the home, where even the best intentioned parents cosset their daughters and give their sons much greater freedom. I know today that the greatest gift my parents gave me, and it must have been tough for them, was to set me free and not wrap me up in layers of protection.

As a parent bringing up a daughter in this essentially misogynistic culture, you will have to fight your own urge to shield her and remain aware that mollycoddling will only stunt her potential. That freedom will have to be given, knowing that when she rides the bus home from basketball practice, she will, every so often, be whistled at, groped, and shoved around or even be coerced into looking at a man who will think nothing of unzipping his trousers in lecherous exhibitionism. It's horrible to contemplate and I can understand why parents fall back on being protective.

The most important change in India today, when it comes to the place of women, is that finally, gender is not a marginal issue. It is no longer confined to the feature pages of magazines or treated as a 'soft' reporting beat by journalists. It is finally at the heart of our conversations and at the centre of our politics. Who knows, tomorrow, we may even see elections being won and lost on the mobilization of women voters.

Till then, for those who still say feminism is impossible to define, I am going to make an attempt. Feminism is about freedom. Ismat Chughtai knew this as a girl growing up in the early twentieth century. Her reminiscences about her childhood are just as true for millions of young Indian women today:

> When I turned twelve my mother dug out an old gharara and told me to make a drawstring for it. 'Your hand will get better at it,' she remarked, placing the needle and thread in my palm. She watched me sew. I felt as if I was suffocating. When I saw

my brothers running after the chickens and climbing trees, the needle would prick me and draw blood. Thankfully, Mother had a lot of housework to take care of. Whenever someone beckoned her I would shove my unfinished handiwork between the folds of the quilts on the shelf. When winter arrived and they were unfolded, my needlework came tumbling down.

Then my mother wanted to teach me how to cook.

'I won't learn,' I insisted.

'Why not?' asked my mother.

'Why doesn't Shahnaz Bhai learn how to cook?' I counter-questioned.

'When he brings his wife home, she will cook for him,' she replied.

'Who will cook for him if she dies or runs away?' I enquired.

Shahnaz Bhai burst into tears at the suggestion that his wife would run away. At this point, my father entered the room.

'Ismat, when you go to your in-laws what will you feed them?' he asked gently after the crisis was explained to him.

'If my husband is poor, then we will make khichdi and eat it and if he is rich, we will hire a cook,' I answered.

My father realized his daughter was a terror and that there wasn't a thing he could do about it.

'What do you want to do then?' he asked.

'All my brothers study. I will study too,' I said.

In the end, whether it was Ismat who was born in Uttar Pradesh or Germaine Greer who is from Australia, these women shone a light for those who were trying to find their way out of the darkness. I read Greer when I was still a teenager. In my middle age her words still ring so true. 'All societies on the verge of death are masculine. A society can survive with only one man; no society will survive a shortage of women.'

Two

THE COST OF WAR

I

HE SPOKE IN brusque, staccato sentences, the matter-of-fact tone in dramatic contrast to the enormity of the moment. To some he would have seemed clinically cold, his face and manner shorn of any obvious emotion. But all I saw was his lack of guile, and the gentleness in his eyes. And, as the roar of guns drowned out his voice to a barely audible whisper, he suddenly seemed childlike and vulnerable. Vishal Thapa, a captain with 16 Grenadiers was twenty-three years old. I was twenty-seven. It was 3 July 1999. This was the first war either of us had experienced.

We were huddled together in the safety of a tiny underground bunker, high in the Himalayas. In a space no larger than a double bed, eight of us—soldiers and journalists—had been brought together by the vagaries of war in a moment of unlikely but intense intimacy. Outside, cloud bursts of orange lit up the skies over the mountains of Drass and Kargil, as Indian soldiers fought to reclaim territory from Pakistani intruders. The silence of the night was broken by the intermittent thunder of the Bofors gun and the sharp snap of the multi-barrel rocket launcher (MBRL) as it catapulted rockets into enemy lines. Every so often, a crackly update would be relayed to us on the internal communication line. In the background, in a disconcerting semblance of normalcy, a decrepit cassette recorder was sputtering out old Hindi movie songs.

The war, which had already been raging for nearly two months, seemed to be entering its final and decisive phase. From the Indian perspective, one of the most important objectives of this part of the campaign was the recapture of Tiger Hill—the strategically crucial mountain peak that loomed perilously close to the national highway that connected Srinagar to Leh.

Marked on the map as Point 5062, Tiger Hill was over 16,500 feet high. Although it was about ten kilometres north of the highway, the Pakistani fortification right on the peak enabled the enemy to dominate large stretches of the road below. Approximately one company of Pakistan's 12 Northern Light Infantry held the feature.

The Indian Army was about to mount a final assault on Tiger Hill. Just an hour earlier, I had been holding my satellite phone up to the sky to try and bring it into signal range. I had been desperately trying to get word to the news desk in Delhi about the imminent assault when I was pulled into the bunker by a total stranger.

This was the age before satellite transmission vans could broadcast live from the front line. Forget iPhones, Androids or Blackberries, even the un-smart mobile phones of the time were blocked across the entire state of Jammu and Kashmir for security reasons. As shells from the Pakistani side poured down on the highway, we were trying to capture it all on our camera—the guns that spat flame into the dark sky; soldiers emerging from the trenches to fire their weapons and then quickly ducking for cover from the instant counter-attack; the fallen bodies that lay unmoving on the tarred road. Nothing in my experience could have prepared me for reporting from the front lines. I remember recoiling sharply the first time I heard the Bofors gun blast its way across the expanse that separated the highway from Tiger Hill. And on TV, people saw me jumping out of my skin. War did not allow for any second takes.

■

That evening in July 1999, the assault on Tiger Hill began from a Bofors gun position; individual guns had been ranged so as to directly fire at the three flanks of the mountain. An intricate fire plan prepared by the 41 Field Regiment provided covering fire to the soldiers of 8 Sikh and 18 Grenadiers who were stealthily moving up escarpments and sheer cliffs from three different directions. Usually, six guns were deployed to provide covering fire to every infantry unit. In Kargil this was increased to eighteen guns. Kargil has often been called a classic gunner's war and the Bofors gun was its mainstay. The gun could fire three rounds in twelve seconds, and it had a range of thirty kilometres in high altitude terrain; 250 of them were deployed at the front line and 250,000 rounds were fired during the fifty-day war. During the Tiger Hill operation alone, 9,000 shells were used. The artillery points had become both the first tier of attack and defence in the war. Field gun positions were now veritable forward posts, inviting attack on themselves as soon as the Bofors gun fired the first round; 80 per cent of the casualties on both sides were from mortar fire.

Writing in *Artillery: The Battle Winning Arm* about the peak period of the war, when each artillery battery fired one round per minute for seventeen days continuously, senior military analyst Major General Jagjit Singh (who started his career in the Royal Indian Navy and saw anti-submarine action during World War II) said, 'Such high rates of fire over long periods had not been witnessed anywhere since World War II… The men at the guns had blisters on their hands from carrying and loading shells and cartridges. Very few of them got more than a couple of hours of sleep in every 24-hour cycle.'

With the advantage of height, Pakistani observation posts had a clear line of vision on Indian gun points. So assault positions had to be shifted as soon as they became vulnerable to counter-attack. As they moved, so would we, jumping on to the back of a Jonga jeep or just darting across the smoke-saturated road, unsure of where it might be safe to halt even for a second, trying all the while to keep pace with the magnitude of what was unravelling before our camera's gaze.

Two hours into what would end up being a thirteen-hour battle, an enemy artillery shell landed close to a 122 multi-barrelled 'Grad' rocket launcher right outside the headquarters of the 56 Mountain Brigade, which had just taken over the sector. With forty rockets stacked upon the back of a single carrier, the Grad was a fire-breathing dragon that spat flames into the sky. In Russian, its name meant 'hailstorm', a fitting appellation, as it hailed destruction down upon the intruders.

Suddenly an enemy shell landed within spitting distance of the launcher. It was time to move to a new vantage point; the commander

of the Grad immediately halted the operation so that the MBRL could
be shifted. Four soldiers had already been killed in a counter-attack
on a gun position earlier and he wasn't taking any chances. Over
the next twenty minutes the battle escalated. The town of Drass
was carpet-bombed by Pakistan. A curtain of grey closed over the
highway as the final acts of the fight to take back Tiger Hill began.

'Run, Run, Run, Now, Now, Now, Run,' shouted out an anxious
voice behind us, and so we did, our bodies bent over, our hands
forming a useless protective cover over our heads, our camera shaking
and jerky, but still switched on and filming, trying to get some of
this across to the news centre, our hearts pumping with adrenalin—it
offered a temporary antidote against paralysing fear. At this point
in the battle I got separated from Ajmal Jami, my cameraman. As
Pakistani shells began to pound the area right around the rocket
launcher, I took shelter behind a broken wall, and frantically worked
the satellite phone. Suddenly, a long arm lunged out and pulled me
back, unfailingly polite even in that life and death moment. 'Ma'am,
you're standing next to an ammunition dump,' said the soldier. 'If a
shell hits the target, this place will explode and you will be finished.'
He waved me towards the shelter of his own underground bunker.

'I need to call my office in Delhi,' I insisted, 'and I have lost my
cameraman, I can't go down leaving him out here.'

He offered to find Jami for me and urged me to hunker down
immediately before I got injured in the shelling. I still had the call
to make but there was no way the satellite phone would pick up any
signal underground. I sat with my legs inside the dugout and the
rest of me leaning out of it, holding the phone outwards. 'I can't talk
long; I'm calling from a bunker,' I said, 'just tell everyone, the assault
on Tiger Hill has begun.' We would spend the next few hours here,
trying to make sense of the latest war between India and Pakistan.

II

'I sincerely hope that they (relations between Indian and Pakistan)
will be friendly and cordial. We have a great deal to do...and think
that we can be of use to each other and the world.'

In August 1947, Pakistan's founder, Mohammed Ali Jinnah,

declared that Partition had resolved the antagonism between Hindus and Muslims and India and Pakistan could now live in harmony. Mahatma Gandhi echoed the sentiment. Both 'fathers' of their respective nations turned out to be grievously wrong.

The partition of India was a bloody and cataclysmic upheaval and the largest forced mass migration of people in the world. Between 1 and 2 million people were killed and an estimated 17 million were uprooted from their homes. The violent rupture proved impossible to heal.

In both countries, many families put locks on their doors but left most of their possessions inside as if they were going on a brief journey from which they would be coming back home very soon. My own family was among them. My grandfather, Krishan Gopal Dutt, a freedom fighter who went on to become Punjab's finance minister in independent India, used to live in a palatial kothi called Pillar Palace in Sialkot, famous for its manufacture of sporting goods. My father was a child of eight when the mob violence spread like a forest fire across both sides of the Punjab province. My grandfather reached out to his friend Chet Ram, the then governor of Jammu, for help in crossing over to the newly demarcated territory of India. A truck with armed guards was sent into Sialkot on the pretext that the governor had to retrieve money from the Imperial Bank (which later became the State Bank of India) in Sialkot. On this truck, my grandfather, dressed only in his dhoti-kurta, left with his family. When he arrived in Delhi, he was penniless and homeless like millions of other refugees.

Decades later, as a college student, I travelled with my father to our ancestral home in Pakistan; its fifty rooms were too expensive to maintain for the family that now owned it—they occupied only one of its residential wings. We had arrived at the house without warning the new owners. Yet, although we were complete strangers, they welcomed us without any questions or suspicions—and having heard our story—handed over the keys of the kothi to us. As we wandered through empty rooms, past bare walls—'the piano was in this corner, your grandmother slept here, that's the fountain made from marble'—I understood for the first time, the anguish that my father, and millions like him, had felt at being displaced in a manner that was so violent, unforgiving and permanent. It was one of only two times I'd seen my father cry (the other time was when his wife died) and it came home to me, in that instant, standing in the abandoned old house in Sialkot, just how deep a wound Partition had carved into the psyche of both countries.

■

Barely two months after Independence, the first military conflict erupted between India and Pakistan when the Pakistani military sent thousands of raiders into the Valley to try and capture it by force and oust the then Maharaja of Jammu and Kashmir, Hari Singh. Apart from its strategic importance, as India's only Muslim-majority state, its staying within the Indian union was a direct challenge to the two-nation theory on which Pakistan was predicated. It would thus remain a perennial theatre of conflict. The first military war between the two nations lasted till January 1949. It ended inconclusively with Pakistan managing to retain nearly 13,000 square kilometres of territory, including Gilgit-Baltistan and Skardu and control over an area that came to be known as Pakistan-occupied Kashmir (PoK). India's forces were able to retrieve two-thirds of the territory that the raiders had tried to occupy. The war of 1947-49 would be the first of four wars between the two nations.

In October 1962 India fought a brief war with China in the only clash that has not been with Pakistan—4,000 soldiers and officers lost their lives and India had to officially give up on Aksai Chin in Kashmir, which had been under Chinese occupation even before the hostilities started. It was a humiliating defeat and India lost face internationally. However, despite the simmering hostility with China that continued after 1962, there was never any real threat of war.

The situation with Pakistan was something else altogether. In 1965 came what would become the prelude to Pervez Musharraf's 1999 Kargil incursions—Prime Minister Zulfikar Ali Bhutto's Operation Gibraltar. Bhutto, then the foreign minister, convinced Pakistani President Ayub Khan to send thousands of Pakistani guerrillas into Kashmir on the assumption that the theatre of war would remain confined to the state. India was quick to open another front on the Punjab border (something the army would also contemplate in 1999). A decisive Prime Minister Lal Bahadur Shastri sent Indian troops across the international border into West Pakistan. A ceasefire was brokered by the Russians in what came to be known as the Tashkent Treaty.

After the 1965 hostilities, in 1971, Prime Minister Indira Gandhi's aggressive support for the Bengali nationalist force Mukti Bahini erupted into a full-blown war, one in which India's decisive victory fundamentally shifted the balance of power in South Asia. Bangladesh was created from East Pakistan. The British historian Percival Spear described Mrs Gandhi's great triumph in the following way: 'Indira Gandhi now bestrode the subcontinent like the winged victory of the ancient Greeks. The spirit of the country was transformed; both she and they had formed a new confidence; the snowy sorrows of 1962 were forgotten...'

Many believe that this was India's moment to reclaim the captured territory of Kashmir from Pakistan and push for a final settlement; India had the advantage as it held more than 90,000 prisoners of war.

Either in a moment of hubris or serious miscalculation, Indira Gandhi agreed to hand back the 93,000 Pakistani soldiers, as part of what came to be known as the Simla Agreement of 1972. Hammered out between Indira Gandhi and Zulfikar Ali Bhutto—who was now the prime minister of Pakistan—the text of the agreement only said that both sides would respect the Line of Control (LoC) 'without prejudice to the recognised position of either side'. They agreed to resolve all disputes bilaterally without third party mediation. Indira told her aides that Bhutto had assured her that he would gradually make the Line of Control into a permanent border but he could not politically afford to put it in writing at this time. The international media heralded the agreement as the beginning of a new phase of peace between the two countries. Nothing could have been further from the truth. The most recent war in Kargil was one in a series of attempts by Pakistan to alter the LoC.

Jinnah's hypothesis about Hindu–Muslim conflict being linked to the larger equation between the two countries had always been simplistic because it failed to take into account the fact that the ongoing hostilities between India and Pakistan were much more than just conflict between Hindus and Muslims. For starters, half the pre-Partition population of Muslims in the subcontinent had chosen to remain in India; eventually there would be more Muslims in India than in Pakistan. The only politician who was prophetic about the future of India and Pakistan was Maulana Abdul Kalam Azad. More than a decade before East Pakistan was reborn as Bangladesh, Azad said, 'It is one of the greatest frauds on the people to suggest that religious affinity can unite areas which are geographically, economically, linguistically and culturally different. It is true that Islam sought to establish a society which transcends racial, linguistic, economic and political frontiers. History has however proved that after the first century, Islam was not able to unite all Muslim countries into one state on the basis of Islam alone... No one can hope that East and West Pakistan will resolve their differences and form one nation.'

By 1999, India and Pakistan were both nuclear-armed nations. Pervez Musharraf, Pakistan's chief of army staff at the time, proceeded with his audacious misadventure in Kargil assuming that India would not engage in a full-scale war because there was always the possibility that it could escalate into nuclear conflict. This was the so-called nuclear deterrence theory. Senior Pakistani journalist Altaf Gohar, who was an adviser to Field Marshal Ayub Khan, has confirmed that a plan to launch a major operation inside Kargil had been on the table at the Pakistani Army headquarters since 1987. But, wary of what the Indian response might be, two Pakistani chiefs of army staff—General Jehangir Karamat and General Mirza Aslam Beg—were not in favour of implementing it. Musharraf, however, calculated that his troops might be able to quickly redraw the LoC, following which global powers like the US and China could be prevailed upon to intervene and prevent the incursion from escalating into a major conflagration. Pakistani infiltrators began sneaking into India between December 1998 and March 1999, bitterly cold winter months when key forward posts had been vacated by Indian troops.

By the last week of April, Pakistani troops had crossed over the LoC and consolidated themselves all along the Kargil sector, ten to twelve kilometres inside India. The Kargil battlefield was now a 200-kilometre-long front at heights between 10,000 and 18,000 feet.

III

'Careful, buddy, you are walking on wire. That's taar there; Duck, Duck, Duck.'

'Oye, company line dena jaldi se.'

'Line toot gayee hai; STD connect kar sakte ho?'

'Sir, one chap injured, sir.'

'Serious, or?'

'He's fine, sir, he's got it on his thigh.'

'That's fine, thigh is okay.'

'Barkha, have you got the phone?'

'Now, they'll start firing helter skelter...idhar udhar sab jagah maarenge.'

'Oh, fuck.'

'Paani kuchh bacha hai (Do we have any water left)?'

From that night in the bunker, scraps of disjointed conversation remain preserved in my memory like voices from a past life—raw, tactile and relentlessly haunting. Inside the bunker, Jami reached out and put some glucose powder on my parched lips. We were on our last bottle of shared water and had to make it last since it was not safe for anybody to leave the bunker and look for more.

The sound of artillery fire had grown a little more distant. The war had moved from the highway to the dark slopes of the mountains where battles at close quarters would determine the final outcome.

As I sat in the bunker and tried to collect my thoughts in order to attain some clarity, I tried to block out the sounds and smells of the war—the sight of a soldier's arm stretched out in despair as his bare, bandaged body was lifted by four people onto a chopper; the unending growl and scream of artillery fire and the smell of death mingling with the chill of an exceptionally cold summer night. The music from the tape recorder began to filter in and I felt afresh the incongruity of hearing music inside the bunker, just when it felt like there would never be music in my life again.

In my coverage of Kargil, beyond the politics of the conflict, what I was really trying to understand was the complex relationship between valour and vulnerability in times of war. These young men— boys-who-would-be-men really—were among the bravest people I would ever meet.

Vishal—the young captain with the gentle eyes—was telling me how a soldier standing on the precipice of death dealt with the fear of the likely fall. He knew that when the night turned to day, it would be his unit's turn to march up into the mountains where men fought and died. He said that he knew his life was destined to be fleeting when he signed up to be a soldier. 'Right now, I can see my entire life race through my head like a short film,' he said, in his characteristic flat tone, as I fought back my tears. 'You see your childhood, your adulthood; you remember your parents, your loves and your fears. And for a fraction of a second you say no. But then, you tell yourself, I have got to overcome it. This is our purpose in life; this is what we were trained for. How can we fail?'

'Aren't you thinking of your home, right now?' asked Vishal, throwing a question I had asked him right back at me. 'That should answer your question.' I had been trying to find out from him whether soldiers in combat had a sense of being undervalued by their countrymen. 'We are not doing this for appreciation. It's the call of duty. We are here, because we have to be here; it's the uniform. And if we do not perform here, it cannot be justified,' he said.

■

The heroism that Vishal and other soldiers who fought in Kargil displayed was perhaps most famously brought into the living rooms of their fellow Indians by Vikram Batra, a soldier with 13 Jammu and Kashmir Rifles. I met him at the base camp in Ghumri in the early days of the war. His was my first major interview with a soldier on the front line. His would also be the first obituary I would write. His men and he had just returned from a successful operation and were trading tales around a shared dog-eared copy of *Cosmopolitan* in a faded white tent that looked like a tiny snowdrop

against the green and brown expanse of the mountains. His smiling
eyes framed by a thick beard, Vikram was rather appropriately code-
named 'Sher Shah'—after the sixteenth-century 'Lion King' eulogized
in medieval Indian history. As he casually flipped through the pages
of the magazine, which seemed oddly out of place in this setting,
he recounted the details of his latest operation with the enthusiasm
and bravado of a teenager. As he and his soldiers moved up the
eastern flank of Point 5140, the highest mountain peak dominating
the town of Drass (thus allowing the Pakistanis direct observation
of Indian targets) they came under fierce artillery and small arms
fire. The enemy troops were constantly firing illumination rounds to
break the cover of darkness under which Vikram's team was moving
up. 'If we had stopped at any point,' Vikram told me, 'we would
have become the target. There was no looking back.' At one point
the Pakistanis intercepted the radio frequency being used by the
Indians and addressed him by his military code name. They said:
'Sher Shah, don't try and come up; you will have a tough time.' The
challenge boomeranged on the Pakistanis and made Vikram even
more determined to rout them. The peak was reclaimed without
any fatalities. Indian helicopters were finally able to fly freely over
Drass. It was a critical turning point in the war. All of twenty-
five, Vikram wore his courage lightly, throwing back his head in
uproarious laughter when I questioned him on fear and vulnerability.
'Yeh Dil Maange More,' he told me with a toothy grin—borrowing
from the lines of what was till then only a popular cola jingle. In
that instant, Vikram Batra became the face of India's self-worth.
His contagious optimism immortalized him as the face of Kargil
just days before he would die, trying to save a fellow soldier who
had come under enemy fire. Much later, his ageing parents would
share his last words as he left for the front. Vikram had told them
that he would either unfurl the Indian flag to mark victory or come
back home draped in one.

■

As the hours went by, the growl of the Bofors gun seemed to drown
out the fire from the enemy lines. A couple of cigarettes and some

nervous chatter had given way to wordless waiting. We did not know then that on the icy heights of Tiger Hill, as soldiers from the Ghatak (assault) commando platoon slipped on some stones, the Pakistanis spotted them and came charging down. What happened next has passed into army lore. The Indians went at the enemy with the sort of ferocity and courage that go beyond the script of conventional battle. To take just one example at random of the numerous instances of astounding valour that played out during the final skirmishes on Tiger Hill, one soldier played dead after he took fifteen bullets. He did not go down. Instead, he tried to wrench off his fractured arm so he could roll down the slope faster and warn his comrades that an attack on the Medium Machine Gun base, just 500 metres below, was imminent.

On the morning of 4 July we gingerly stepped out from the shelter of the mud and earth we had taken refuge in over that endless night. We saw what seemed to be the smoke of a dying fire dancing over Tiger Hill peak. It was 5 a.m., nearly twelve hours after we had gone underground; the sun hadn't risen yet and the guns had fallen silent. 'We've got it now; there's nothing left on top,' said one of the soldiers, 'it should be just a matter of a couple of hours more.'

By 8 a.m., the Indian flag was touching the sky over Tiger Hill. Someone pulled out a tiny silver hip flask and passed it around so we could each take a swig. We stared up at the clouds and took in the warmth of the sun. We all knew that had this battle gone any other way, the outcome of the war could have been very different. Gin for breakfast didn't seem especially outlandish in the circumstances.

IV

As the Indian soldiers began to throw out the enemy from the snow and rock of Kargil and the war entered the final days, they weren't aware that the furious diplomatic activity would also play a part in ending the campaign. In Washington, Pakistan's Prime Minister Nawaz Sharif was to meet US President Bill Clinton on 4 July. As the then Indian Army Chief General V. P. Malik would chronicle many years later, 'About 10 to 15 hours before their meeting we made sure that the whole world came to know about the re-capture of

Tiger Hill, and thus the likely outcome of the war.' In Delhi, Prime
Minister Atal Bihari Vajpayee and his National Democratic Alliance
(NDA) government hoped international pressure would be a force
multiplier. The critical meeting between Clinton and Sharif would
take place after several weeks of diplomatic manoeuvring.

■

Kargil is widely acknowledged as an unprovoked battle that had
been thrust on India, one that Prime Minister Nawaz Sharif would
later insist his army chief, Pervez Musharraf, had plotted unilaterally.
The conventional wisdom has been that nuclear weapons restrained
India's military response and eliminated the option of crossing the
LoC. I decided to try and get at the truth by talking to the one man
who would be able to confirm or deny various theories that had been
aired about the conflict. Brajesh Mishra was the most powerful man
in Vajpayee's government after the prime minister. Mishra was the
PM's principal secretary and also doubled up as the national security
adviser. Mishra, a foreign service officer who had joined the BJP in
the 1990s, enjoyed the complete confidence of Vajpayee much to the
irritation of Home Minister L. K. Advani who thought it eroded his
own authority and influence. In 1998, Vajpayee had entrusted Mishra
with the job of containing global criticism of India's nuclear tests;
in 1999, it was Mishra who was tasked with bringing international
pressure to bear on Pakistan.

'In the eyes of the world, we were the good boys; no one had
supported Pakistan, except China,' Brajesh Mishra told me in a long
conversation in 2012 just a few weeks before he died. 'Crossing the
LoC would have changed that and there would have been immediate
calls from the UN for a ceasefire,' he said. Our interview took place
at his South Delhi residence where he was living a semi-retired life,
although droves of visitors wanting his advice continued to descend
on him (occasionally he would even receive a phone call from the
Congress prime minister, Manmohan Singh).

As Mishra remembered it, when the Cabinet Committee on
Security—which included L. K. Advani, George Fernandes, the
defence minister, and Jaswant Singh, a former army man and the

Minister for External Affairs who would take over the defence portfolio from Fernandes a couple of years later—met for the first time during the early days of the war in May, the option of going across the LoC came up for discussion and was unanimously rejected by the political establishment. Not just that. Even the army's request for air power, first made on 8 May, did not get the go-ahead from Jaswant Singh who was concerned that it would escalate and 'internationalize' the situation.

Air support would become an area of a serious disagreement between the army chief and the air force chief. Air Chief Marshal A.Y. Tipnis turned down several proposals from army headquarters to send armed choppers into the operations arena—insisting on political authorization first. The army was of the view that the use of choppers was an 'in-house' decision. But the air chief wouldn't relent, leading to several volatile and heated arguments between him and the army chief who finally said that he would have to take their differences to the prime minister and the Cabinet. Writing many years later in *Force* magazine about Operation Safed Sagar—the air force code name for its part of the operation—Tipnis was candid about the stormy disagreements between him and the army chief. His main worry about deploying Mi-17 helicopters, he explained, was how vulnerable to attack they would be. He wrote: 'As the helicopters would have to approach enemy locations on the LoC ridge-line from the Kargil Valley, they would not be able to mask their approach and will be visibly picked-up by the enemy well before they come into firing range.'

On 25 May 1999—eighteen days after air power had first been asked for—when the Cabinet Committee on Security met again, the army chief made it clear that his infantry urgently needed the backup of helicopter gunships to soften mountain targets and weaken supply routes to the Pakistani infiltrators. Prime Minister Vajpayee finally acceded. But things were tricky; the permission was conditional on military operations continuing to respect the sanctity of the LoC. A concerned air chief tried to explain that his jets would need to fly from south to north, giving them a turning circuit so small that crossing the LoC would become inevitable. But he was told that the fighters would have to fly from east to west and find a way to remain confined to the Indian side. Describing the circumstances in which Vajpayee finally gave his assent for air power Tipnis wrote, 'In his characteristically laconic manner, he said, "Theek hai, kal subah se shuru karo (All right, start tomorrow morning)." I asked for permission to cross the LoC while attacking targets on our side of the LoC. The PM straightened up in his chair and said firmly, "Please don't cross the LoC. No, no crossing the LoC."' And so began the precision attacks and ammunition drops from the air in an unprecedented use of the air force at 18,000 feet.

The battle on the ground and in the air may have escalated but on 26 May 1999—a day after India gave the thumbs up to air power—General Pervez Musharraf was feeling quite chuffed with how his Machiavellian plan had gone thus far. 'First class,' was his comment when he was briefed on the phone by his trusted chief of general staff, Lieutenant General Mohammad Aziz Khan from Rawalpindi. Musharraf was on an official trip to Beijing and probably thought his hotel phone line was completely secure; this was China after all, a trusted ally of his country. Then again, his indiscretion may have been typical of his garrulous and grandiose personality. On two different occasions—that day, and three days later, on 29 May, his conversations from Room Number 83315 were intercepted by spooks of RAW. The thinking behind his Kargil folly—to use the threat of nuclear conflict and make Kashmir an issue the world would meddle in—was now caught on tape. 'Today for the last two hours the BBC has been continuously reporting on the air strikes by India. Keep using this...let them keep dropping bombs. As far as internationalization is concerned, this is the fastest this has happened. You may have seen in the press about UN Secretary General Kofi Annan's appeal that both countries should sit and talk,' Aziz told his boss. 'This is very good,' said Musharraf. 'Yes, this is very good,' agreed Aziz. The tapes revealed how 'mujahideen' had been used as a cloak for the involvement of the regular troops of the Pakistan Army, offering deniability when needed. The tapes exposed two incontrovertible truths. The operation in Kargil had the full involvement of the Pakistani military and its responsibility could not be transferred to non-state actors. And Nawaz Sharif was clearly being briefed only selectively, and the import and implications of the conflict were being withheld from him by his own army chief.

It was the single most important and audacious coup by India's intelligence agencies since the country had gained independence over fifty years ago. By 1 June, the top leadership of the government had heard the tapes. By 4 June, R. K. Mishra, the journalist turned negotiator with the Reliance-funded Observer Research Foundation and Vivek Katju, a senior diplomat in the foreign ministry, were on a plane to Pakistan for a secret meeting with Nawaz Sharif.

The tapes were played for Sharif to hear; India believed that presented with this evidence, Pakistan would have to back out of the war zone. Sharif listened to the audio recordings in 'astonished silence', one man familiar with the conversation confided to me. Sharif had always maintained that Musharraf plotted Kargil without his knowledge and the tapes brought home to him how he was being manipulated. Later, his father, Mian Muhammad Sharif, told him that to inflict deceit on India and provoke a war was a 'grave betrayal' of Vajpayee's historic trip to Lahore barely three months earlier. Sharif was disturbed by the parental admonition and by the embarrassing truths on the tapes.

V

In May and June, as the war showed no signs of letting up, the Indian military leadership began to draw up secret contingency plans to expand the theatre of the war beyond Jammu and Kashmir. In other words, India's retaliation for the intrusions would most likely not be along the LoC—which had never been officially accepted as permanent by either country—but along the actual, undisputed international border. The states of Punjab and Rajasthan were to be readied as launch pads for a counter-attack. In the army's assessment, if the Kargil peaks were not entirely back in Indian control before the monsoon's torrents drenched the northern plains, any counter-attack would have to wait till after the rains.

In preparation for the worst-case scenario, the army had already fleshed out a 'Six Day War' plan, deploying troops so that the boundary separating India from Pakistan could be crossed in less than a week, if needed. Upset with Vajpayee's public announcement that India had no intention of entering Pakistani territory, General Malik met the prime minister and explained that such absolutisms unfairly restricted the strategic manoeuvrability available to his troops. The army chief was blunt: 'If we can't undo this in Kargil, I will have to attack somewhere else,' he told Vajpayee, making it clear that a new war front could soon be opened in another part of the subcontinent—one that, by definition, involved crossing over. Seeing the need for a more nuanced articulation of the Indian position, that same evening, Brajesh Mishra went on television to say that the approach of confining operations to the Indian side of the LoC held good only for the present. In the meantime, General Malik quietly moved an army brigade from the Andaman and Nicobar Islands to the western border and the navy's Eastern Fleet was moved from the Bay of Bengal to the Arabian Sea.

Even as all these developments took place behind closed doors, India's main effort took place on two fronts—the war on the ground, and a delicately nuanced diplomatic initiative to try and get the Americans to intervene. Pakistan was trying hard to present the dispute around Jammu and Kashmir as a potential nuclear flashpoint so there would be aggressive international mediation. India wanted America to help contain the conflict, but on terms that would be set by India. Washington could not drive hard bargains, especially not on Kashmir. The India–Pakistan equation was still a hyphenated one for the US and India was apprehensive that the classic ambivalence practised by America in all its dealings with countries in the Indian subcontinent would yet again dominate the proceedings.

So when Bill Clinton phoned Vajpayee in June 1999, three weeks into the war, and promised that he was working on Pakistan to pull back its soldiers from Indian territory, a sceptical Indian prime minister—a man who knew how to make masterful use of silence—did not respond. Later, Clinton would say of him, 'that guy's from Missouri big time', after the American state known for the disbelieving demeanour it preferred to adopt when confronted with a tricky situation.

Two days after Clinton's call, Vajpayee sent Mishra, in his capacity as national security adviser, to Geneva, where the American president was to address a meeting of the ILO. From there, Clinton was headed to a meeting of the Group of Eight (G-8) countries in Cologne on 19 June. India clearly wanted intercession from this gathering of the world's most powerful nations. In Geneva, Mishra handed over a secret missive from Vajpayee to Sandy Berger and Karl Inderfurth, both high-ranking officials in the US government. To this day, the contents of the letter have never been released. But Mishra told me that the kicker in the letter addressed to Clinton was the paragraph that warned, 'One way or the other, we will get them out'. 'They were taken aback,' Mishra said. 'Inderfurth pointed to that particular paragraph immediately.' The letter never spelt out what option India was considering. However, the subtext that all bets were now off the table was clear to the Americans. 'Crossing the LoC was not ruled out, nor was the use of nuclear weapons,' Mishra revealed to me, adding that had the American asked him a direct question 'I would not have expanded on what I meant'. Mishra believed that without this letter, Clinton would not have got actively involved. The G-8 countries did not just jointly ask Pakistan to pull its men back behind the LoC; two days later, Clinton sent Anthony Zinni— the commander-in-chief of the US Central Command—to Pakistan. There, Zinni did some plain speaking with Pervez Musharraf. His message was unvarnished—Pakistan's position was untenable and the country stood isolated internationally. When Musharraf pressed for US mediation on Kashmir, Zinni was terse and dismissive. 'My mandate is Kargil, not Kashmir,' the US general said. 'If you don't pull back, you're going to bring war and nuclear annihilation down on your own country.' By now, there was enough evidence to show that, contrary to Pakistan's claims, the armed intruders were not Kashmiri militants, but mainly soldiers of the Pakistan Army's Northern Light Infantry. But Pakistan needed a face-saver, a respectable way to extricate itself from the military mess, and Zinni had none to offer. He returned to Washington without a breakthrough.

For the rest of June, both the war and the diplomatic offensive eddied back and forth. On the ground, the momentum was shifting in India's direction. Just as Indian troops were preparing to take back Tiger Hill, Pakistan's beleaguered prime minister was on the hotline to Washington. On 2 July, Nawaz Sharif pleaded with Bill Clinton for his personal intervention. Twenty-four hours later, at fifteen minutes past five, even as fireballs formed luminous red clouds over Tiger Hill, Sharif was packing his bags to leave for America.

■

The Fourth of July, America's Independence Day, was also a day of liberation in India. The military gains of the victory at Tiger Hill restored the Indian Army's control over the town of Drass and a large section of the national highway. In fact, a different result would have significantly increased the possibility of India executing the till-now-under-wraps Plan B: crossing over into Pakistan from one of the states on the western border of the country. All this while, India and Pakistan had been standing on the precipice of a nuclear exchange. Reclaiming Tiger Hill gave India the space to walk a few steps back from this brink and review strategy. But one push, and it could still be a sharp fall down the cliff. In any case, the mood in India remained grim. There could be nothing celebratory when every victory in the battlefield was shadowed by images of flag-draped body bags and the coffins of men in the prime of their youth being received by ageing, stoic parents who were almost always too proud to cry. The rising number of deaths had only increased the pressure on the government to send either troops or aircraft into Pakistan to snap the supply lines to the well-dug-in camps of the infiltrators.

Pakistan knew this, so did the Americans. The US administration in Washington wasn't having much of a holiday as its officials briefed Bill Clinton on what one aide described as 'the most important foreign policy meeting of his presidency because the stakes could include nuclear war'.

By the time Clinton crossed Pennsylvania Avenue in Washington DC to meet a rattled Nawaz Sharif, his administration had two different drafts of a statement that would be released to the press. What would eventually be transmitted would depend on whether Pakistan's prime minister agreed to pull his soldiers back behind the

LoC or not. That Sharif had arrived in Washington with his entire family had already added to American doubts about whether he had the authority to take a decision on the military operations of his country—perhaps he'd come looking for asylum. American diplomats have published detailed accounts of the negotiations that took place during Sharif's visit to Washington. Clinton wanted to know if Sharif was aware that his military was preparing to launch its nuclear arsenal. When Clinton warned him about the dire consequences that would ensue if 'even one bomb was dropped', Sharif agreed it would be a 'catastrophe'. Sharif denied that he had ordered Pakistan's nuclear missiles to be deployed for launching. In any event, Sharif's attempt to procure a promise of American mediation on Kashmir as a quid pro quo for a military pullback was rejected by an enraged Clinton who likened it to 'nuclear blackmail'. The American president warned Sharif that if Pakistan did not restore the sanctity of the LoC, he would have to release the second of the draft media statements—one that blamed Islamabad for the crisis. Quoting from John Keegan's book, *The First World War*, he warned that the drama of battle never played to script; military operations had a way of taking on a life of their own. If India crossed the LoC, Clinton argued, a 'nuclear war by accident' was a very real probability.

With talks in meltdown mode, both sides retreated for a brief break. A phone call from Clinton to Vajpayee in this interlude elicited mostly taciturn scepticism. By the time Sharif returned for another round of negotiations, a new statement was on the table—one that called for a ceasefire after the Pakistanis were back on their side of the border. Finally, one last sentence was added at the request of the Pakistanis—a promise of 'personal interest' from Clinton to resume the Lahore dialogue process. The reference was to the historic trip that Vajpayee had made to Lahore just a couple of months before Musharraf betrayed India with the Kargil incursions.

The Fourth of July holiday ended with the Americans hoping that they had rescued India and Pakistan from a military morass.

■

The reality on the ground was different. For Vajpayee to convince

the Indian Army to accept the principle of safe passage for retreating
Pakistani soldiers—which was part of the truce that America had
brokered—with hundreds of its own men dead, wasn't easy. When
the prime minister first phoned General Malik with the suggestion,
his shocked reaction was, 'No, sir, no one in my army would let me
do this. It is impossible'.

Malik asked for time to discuss the proposal with the forces. By
now, progress in the Batalik sector, the barren mountains fifty-six
kilometres to the north of Kargil, had given the army a sense of being
in what Malik calls a 'commanding position'. The idea of looking
the other way as the intruders simply hotfooted it back to Pakistan
was unacceptable. When the prime minister called a second time,
he had two questions for his army chief. If no orders were given to
stop firing on the retreating Pakistanis and the Indian Army was to
chase them all the way to the LoC, how long did Malik think this
would take and how many more Indian lives would be lost? The
general said he needed at least a couple of more weeks.

On the front line, no one had any indication that the war
was inching to a close. The soldiers who had sheltered us in the
underground bunker had got orders to get ready for the next assault.
In a moment of sentiment, we had asked if we could accompany
them to the last motorable point before they went into battle. It had
to be absolutely dark before it was safe for the jeeps to drive up to
base camp. As the vehicles were loaded with men and machines,
we hopped on to the back of one, perching ourselves on a bench
much too narrow to fit us all, sticking together for comfort, feeling
the closest we had felt to gut-wrenching panic. Up we went, racing
over sharp rocks and loose gravel, defying the terrain that was trying
to slow us down. We had to be quick as we were driving parallel
to several Pakistani outposts, and darkness did not guard against
the rattle of gunfire that followed us as we drove. In minutes, the
speeding jeep braked to a halt behind a gigantic boulder. We had
reached the point from where the soldiers were to climb upwards on
foot. Strangely, as my colleagues shivered in the cold of the night, a
strange, stinging heat rose from the soles of my feet, rushing through
my veins and hitting my head with the force of a furnace fire. I

stripped off the first layer of my woollens, though we were standing out in the open. The heat felt like it would scorch me, I removed my jacket and stood there in a half-sleeved polo neck t-shirt, hoping to feel better. As I began to babble incoherently, acutely embarrassed about being sick, feeling even more self-conscious for fear of being perceived as someone who wasn't tough enough, somebody bundled me up, flung me onto the backseat of the same jeep we had come up in and drove downhill at breakneck speed to the highway. Later, I was told that I had displayed the classic symptoms of hypothermia as a result of the abrupt jump in altitude. But the fact remained that I had been driven to an inconsequential height; there were soldiers, up there in the mountains, several thousand feet higher, walking on ice without snowshoes, in many cases without bulletproof jackets, lugging light machine guns, finding their way in the dark without night-vision goggles, battling in circumstances where even breathing was a challenge. It was a dramatic reinforcement of why the Kargil battlefield was one of the toughest war zones in the world.

In Delhi, an anxious Vajpayee made a third phone call to his army chief. General Malik finally agreed to the idea of a withdrawal agreement for the Pakistani infiltrators, but one he insisted would have to be 'on our terms and conditions'. By 11 July, the Director General of Military Operations of India and his Pakistani counterpart met at the Attari check post on the Punjab border. At this meeting, India stipulated the framework within which a pullout of Pakistani troops would be acceptable.

Up on the icy slopes of the Himalayas, Indian soldiers were now in the poignant position of having to bury the very men they had fought. Strewn all across the slopes were hundreds of Pakistani dead. Dwarfed by the mountains, the bodies looked even smaller and more forlorn as their country refused to acknowledge the role they had played. As Pakistan had still not officially conceded the involvement of its soldiers in Kargil, its officials refused to take many of the bodies back. The antagonism of battle became more important than the basic decency demanded of a soldier's code of honour. The emotional complexity of that moment was confounding to us. What did it take to bestow dignity and honour upon a man you had been compelled to kill, after struggling up a mountain for two days in the dark, one handhold at a time, weighed down by thirty kilos of guns and ammunition? A man you'd had to kill just after you had seen him fire a bullet that sheared right through the head of one of your comrades.

■

By now, the government in New Delhi made an announcement that it expected the war to wind down within a week. Air operations were suspended and 16 July was set as the deadline for the intruders to make their way back to Pakistan. The announcement was delicately worded for public consumption; so far as the Indian Army's leadership was concerned, it was not giving up the right to attack, should it become necessary.

On the front, the guns had certainly not fallen silent; men continued to die. In fact, on 22 July, just four days before Operation Vijay was declared closed, a troubled army chief had to go back to the prime minister to inform him that despite the agreement between the two countries some peaks had not been vacated. The fighting had continued till the bitter end. Were it not for American intervention, the war would have dragged on even longer and, even more dangerously, would have expanded; it looked set to expand into a much larger theatre of conflict. The deterrence that some argue has been guaranteed by nuclear weapons on either side would have been meaningless without the Americans responding from their own alarm over an imminent Armageddon. And, had that letter from Vajpayee to Clinton in Geneva not indicated India's readiness to escalate the conflict if compelled to do so, America may have remained ambivalent.

The proponents of the nuclear deterrence theory would still argue that because the world cannot afford to even contemplate a nuclear war, India and Pakistan's military options would always be bound by the chains of diplomatic pressure. But, as Kargil revealed, the origin or context of a conflagration, the unpredictable pressures of public opinion, the speed with which global powers respond and the arguments around what constitutes a 'just' war will always have the force to smash all the usual assumptions. And once that happens—just as Clinton told Sharif in Washington in 1999—plans can go awry; the script will write itself. From his experience at the helm in 1999, General Malik argues that 'the effectiveness of a nuclear deterrent depends on the threshold and the threshold is very dynamic'. In other words, in a future conflict between India and Pakistan, if either country were to cross a certain threshold, nuclear confrontation becomes a very real danger. Every point of near-war between India and Pakistan after the Kargil conflict has been white-flagged by American pressure. But the future cannot trust the consistency of past patterns; there are no guarantees that Western intervention will be timely the next time. And there *will* be a next time.

VI

The Kargil conflict was the first battle between India and Pakistan that was captured on television. Although the fighting originated in the remotest reaches of the Himalayas, much of it spilt over onto the national highway that connected Srinagar, the capital, to Leh. Under constant bombardment by Pakistani troops, whose aim was to snap the supply line of food, fuel, ammunition, and winter clothing to the Indian Army and simultaneously cut off the battlefield from the rest of India, the road had been dubbed the 'Highway to Death'. For those network reporters willing to risk driving through a blizzard of mortar fire, past oil tankers up in flames from the impact of the shelling, often through miles of darkness with only the faint illumination of the moon or the intermittent glow of gunfire as a guiding light, this was a chance to bring the war straight into Indian drawing rooms across the country.

For days we just lived on the road, spending long nights crouched in the backseat of our sturdy old Tata Sumo till shells smashed holes through its window and rear and the driver said he could no longer be part of our party. With regular communication lines unavailable, we would ferry our tapes to Delhi on the choppers that flew the dead and the injured back from the front. Initially, wary of the idea of a woman reporter at the front, the army headquarters in

Delhi had feared that my being there would be entirely impractical. I had promised them—and believed it—that I expected no special treatment on account of my gender. Going to the loo was always a quick crouch behind the nearest available rock. I barely noticed that my period came and went, only grateful that I still had a strip of analgesics left over in the cavernous pockets of my Nehru jacket.

Did my being a woman ever influence the way I reported the war? Tough to say, except that the scrutiny made me acutely, and perhaps childishly, self-conscious about displaying emotion or any attribute that could be perceived as a weakness. Our emotions in any case were distorted; either heightened by a volatile combination of adrenalin and empathy or suppressed by the sheer pressure of meeting a news deadline from a war zone.

Personal considerations aside, the television coverage changed forever the way in which we looked at our soldiers and at ourselves as a nation. It would build a new narrative of patriotism; it would force us to confront the horrors of war and it would leave another festering wound in the damaged, dysfunctional relationship between India and Pakistan.

Most importantly, though, it gave us a new set of heroes—our soldiers, who did much to give hope to a bruised and shaken nation.

■

One of the moments from the Kargil War that remain fresh in my memory was the breakfast of eggs and toast—our first meal in days which went beyond glucose biscuits and tea—that I shared with the soldiers I had spent the long night in the bunker with on the eve of the assault on Tiger Hill.

The soldiers shyly showed us photographs from back home, of brothers, sisters, friends and, of course, girls they had hoped to marry. More than one had broken off the engagement as soon as the war began. Martyrdom at the front line was not a wedding gift everyone was prepared to receive.

We spoke and argued about death, about the brutality of war. It was here that I realized how flawed were the assumptions we civilians made about nationalism and war. Journalists, political pundits and in particular war-mongering jingoists could play cheerleaders to conflict from the comfort of their drawing rooms in the nation's cities and towns. But to meet hundreds of young men at the battlefront and talk to them about the possibility of imminent death changed me—and my beliefs—fundamentally. It was entirely possible to be filled with overwhelming admiration for these men in uniform and through their eyes understand that the imperatives of war were different, and that it would always be shadowed by loss.

Major Ajit, whose eyes seemed to wear the marks of a private torment, told me that a soldier's motivation and readiness to die came first from the need to uphold the honour of his paltan, his platoon, his military unit, his regiment—everything else came next. As we were talking, the men who had saved our lives received their orders to move up the mountains and into the battlefield, as at that point the war was still far from over. On a whim I took off the single strand of beads strung around my neck and thrust it into the hands of the soldiers to whom we owed our lives. It was my way of saying good luck. In return, one of the soldiers insisted we keep his dog tag along with a single bullet.

There was no more to be said, and if there was, we lacked the appropriate words. War reporting was conventionally assumed to be about ducking bullets, showcasing military hardware and celebrating courage. But in 1999 it also became about humanizing the narrative of bravery. Our war coverage was all about making Kargil less one-dimensional and to allow for a soldier's portrait to be painted in the colours of both light and shadow.

VII

The Kargil conflict had exposed a woeful moment of underpreparedness—both in the intrusions going undetected for as long as they did and the damage that years of neglect and miles of red tape had done to India's fighting power. And so in Kargil without snow shoes or proper high-altitude gear, Vishal and other first-time troops literally crawled their way up to peaks as high as 18,000 feet, where the temperature slipped to as much as ten degrees below zero to fight for the honour of their platoons and regiments.

They didn't even mutter a complaint when they had to stealthily make their way up the treacherous terrain under cover of darkness without the aid of basic night-vision goggles. Forget weapon locating radars (finally purchased four years after the conflict) there was an acute shortage of basic infantry weapons, bulletproof jackets, and even ammunition. Just three months earlier, General Malik had written to the defence minister with a sense of ominous foreboding, arguing that 'by denying essential equipment, the armed forces would gradually lose their combat edge which would show adversely in a future conflict...' Now, in the middle of the war he struggled to get the ban on the politically contentious Bofors Company lifted, so that guns and spares could be procured. India had to scramble to import 50,000 rounds of 155 mm shells for the Bofors gun from Israel. The bureaucratic red tape that stymied the war effort meant that the army could not engage the enemy as effectively as it wanted to. For example, the gunners wanted to shell the Pakistani military base at Skardu, 170 kilometres away—just across the LoC. But it was out of reach of the Bofors gun, and the only weapon that could have been brought to bear on the target, the Russian Smerch, a rocket launcher, would be held up for another five years. Finally, faced with initial shortages even in fuel containers and lubricants, General Malik declared, 'We will fight with what we have.'

In 2015, almost sixteen years after the Kargil War, a report by India's audit watchdog, the Comptroller and Auditor General, made a startling revelation. India, it said, could not fight a war beyond fifteen to twenty days because of a crippling shortage in its ammunition reserves. The audit, which had been carried out in 2013, said that the stocking of 125 of the 170 different types of ammunition required was not even enough for twenty days of fighting or 'minimum acceptable risk level requirements'. And in half of the categories of ammunition, supplies would last less then ten days.

What this meant was that if there were another war, the cost would be borne, yet again, by men sent to fight a battle not of their making without being equipped for it. This is the tragedy—the cost of war is always unacceptable yet countries act as though it is not. More than 500 Indian soldiers died in Kargil; more than a thousand were wounded. The estimation of how many lives Pakistan lost has fluctuated dramatically from Musharraf's 357 to Sharif's 2,700. For the Pakistani soldiers, the greatest ignominy was to not even be acknowledged by their country; for over a decade, the Pakistani Army was simply not ready to officially accept that its troops were involved. It was only eleven years after the war that Pakistan officially recognized the men it had forced into a mindless conflict; its army website finally listed 453 soldiers killed in 'Batalik Kargil' sector; they were listed in the 'Martyrs' section.

VIII

The stunning beauty of Kargil—the majesty of the bare mountains, the luminous skies of enamelled blue—only served to heighten the wastefulness and tragedy of the war that had been fought there. No one understands this wastefulness more than a soldier who has seen combat. In 2009, ten years after my first exposure to a war zone, I returned to the mountains of Kargil with three men who had carried the painful weight of their own memories for over a decade—Vishal Thapa, whose thoughtful stoicism as a young captain gave context and meaning to the night I spent holed up in the bunker; Vishal Batra, the iconic Vikram Batra's twin who hadn't been able to bring himself to visit the place where his daredevil brother was killed; and Y. K. Joshi, whose leadership as a commander had inspired a spate of Hindi films.

Joshi, now a brigadier with the army, had brought along his seventeen-year-old daughter, not even a teenager in 1999, so she could understand the brutality and horror of what he had seen. It wasn't easy for a father to explain to a young girl why the code of war meant that 'when you are up there your battalion is your family. You think about that; you think about the boys... You think about the (mountain) feature you're going up to. You just don't think about your family. It can't come in between... If I think about that, I can't do this. That's how it has to be.' It was difficult for him to confront his own recollections, none of which had faded with time. Wasn't it just yesterday that he had turned around to talk to Ranbir, the soldier manning the rocket launcher right next to him, and seen a

THE COST OF WAR

bullet go through his forehead, leaving a gaping hole in the skull.

Vishal Batra, a private banker who had once contemplated becoming a soldier, was overwhelmed—like so many of us 'civilians' had first been—by the unvarnished beauty of the mountains. That a war had been fought here was unimaginable to him. As we sat on a rock under a high blue sky and stared out at Batra Top, named after Vikram, as a tribute to his courage, the wind dried our tears, allowing us to cry freely, with only the clouds as witness.

'Yeh Dil Maange More'—Vikram's spontaneous conversion of an ad punchline into a slogan of bravado had made him one of the most identifiable and revered heroes of the war. But when the headlines faded and the cameras retreated, a family was still left behind to cope with the tragedy of loss. That moment when Vikram's pyre had to be lit was the moment Vishal remembers as the one where Death ceased to be an ominous, fearful stranger. 'You know, when we took him for his final rites, the body was taken from the coffin and the tricolour was handed over to Mom. I was holding his body in my hands; it was the first cremation of my life. It was painful. But at that very moment whatever fear I had of death went away.'

In the shadow of the mountains where his brother had been killed, Vishal wrote Vikram a letter, wanting him to know that their shared childhood was what gave him the strength to keep going. He read it out aloud; then, standing in silent salute, left the single sheaf of paper there to be lifted to the skies along with the leaves and the dust.

The quietest among the three men was Vishal Thapa—as reflective and contemplative as he had been ten years ago that night in the bunker. His lens on life had always been unusually clear-sighted. '(This might be regarded as) politically incorrect, but I would just say this much; I don't think any soldier would want a war. It's the developments and the situations, whatever. So basically everybody is just following orders... We kill because of our profession and not by choice, right? If we kill someone, one of ours will also die. So, it's part of a job. Take it or leave it.'

Thapa was now an instructor at the Indian Army's high-altitude battle school. The first time he brought his students to Kargil he couldn't sleep at night. The silent silhouette of the mountain peaks was an auditory shock; in his mind he could only hear the drum fire of bombs and the reverberations of rockets. But once those first impressions faded, he was once again in thrall to the mountains that rose up on every side. He said to me about his time at war: 'I walked away loving the mountains. Mountains don't see the difference in colour, caste, creed, no Pakistan, no India. They judge everybody the same way. They are pure. It's we human beings who mess things up.'

Three

TERROR IN OUR TIME

I

ON CHRISTMAS NIGHT in 2001, at least four people in the United States were in no mood to celebrate. The memory of carols, tinsel, turkey and cranberry sauce had long faded in the face of the mounting anxiety about a possible nuclear war. From her holiday home in Norfolk, Virginia, Condoleezza Rice, the US national security adviser, spent the evening on the phone with Colin Powell (then US secretary of state), Jack Straw and David Manning, foreign secretary and head of national security of the UK respectively. In the White House, President George W. Bush was waiting for an update on reports that India had moved short-range ballistic missiles with nuclear capability to the border with Pakistan. The Pentagon and the CIA had submitted contradictory assessments; the CIA, which Rice believed was 'heavily reliant on Pakistani sources', argued that India was ready to strike; the Pentagon believed the military build-up should be read more as signalling resolve than a call to action. They decided to work the phones to India to buy time and try to stave off the crisis.

In Delhi, the normally unflappable Brajesh Mishra was too agitated to listen to the Americans. Operation Parakram (Valour) was already underway; the holding formations near the international border had been mobilized; the army's strike corps were under orders to move out from peacetime stations in central India to frontal attack positions all along the perimeter with Pakistan in both Punjab and Rajasthan.

The largest deployment of India's armed forces since the 1971 war with Pakistan—more than 50,000 soldiers would eventually line the border—was in response to the most audacious terror attack India had witnessed on her soil this far, one that came within a whisker of taking out virtually the entire political leadership of the nation.

At about 11.30 in the morning of 13 December 2001, India's Parliament was adjourned almost as soon as its members had assembled. Ironically, it was the corruption in the procurement of coffins during the Kargil War—a scandal that had been dubbed 'Coffingate'—that was the subject of raucous, disorderly debate that morning. With no legislative work possible, Members of Parliament retreated to the more informal Central Hall where they did not have to pretend to hate each other. Suddenly the sound of gunshots rang through the air and brought the chatter to a halt. A white Ambassador car, which had escaped scrutiny at the security post on the outer perimeter of Parliament (because of a forged Home Ministry identity sticker plastered across its windshield), was the cause of all the commotion. Inside the car were five men armed with pistols, grenades, spare ammunition, automatic assault rifles and electronic detonators; in the boot of the car was a bomb made from an enormous quantity of ammonium nitrate. The Ambassador was headed straight for the main entrance of Parliament when its path was blocked by the convoy of Vice President Krishen Kant. It was this 'fortuitous circumstance'—as the Supreme Court would later call it in the course of its enquiry into the attack—that stopped the terrorists from getting 'free and easy access' to the Parliament building. Forced to brake, the car crashed into the cavalcade, prompting Kant's driver, Shekhar, to jump out. The men in the Ambassador opened fire and battle was joined. Before all five terrorists were shot dead, they had killed eight security personnel and a gardener.

In its findings, the Supreme Court said the 'firepower was awesome enough to engage a battalion and had the attack succeeded the entire building with all inside would have perished'.

Given the gravity of the attack, India's response to the aggressors was intended to be punitive in the extreme. 'We were within striking distance,' Brajesh Mishra told me, during the long interview that I have cited in the previous chapter. 'The mobilization of troops was to let Pakistan know that we [India] were serious and we were ready to cross the Line of Control.' Mishra understood that such an eventuality—troops entering Pakistani territory—had to contend with the very real risk of Pakistan using nuclear weapons. But 'to not have done what we did would have been to have gone against the public mood,' he told me, looking back at one of his most controversial and much-debated decisions. Nevertheless, he said with satisfaction that Lisa Curtis, a prominent foreign policy analyst had said to him at the time that Pakistan was 'shitting in its pants'.

It fell to Richard Armitage, the US Deputy Secretary of State, to do most of the heavy lifting to defuse the crisis. Armitage, who looked and talked more like a bellicose bouncer than a diplomat, 'pleaded with Vajpayee', according to Mishra, to not take immediate military action. He told Mishra to give President Musharraf a day or two to address India's concerns. 'Don't forget how many Americans there were in the region,' Mishra said, referring to the US troops swarming Afghanistan and Pakistan after the 9/11 attacks earlier that year.

On 11 January 2002, three weeks after the attack on Parliament, India's army chief, General S. Padmanabhan, informed the world that mobilization was complete and that his troops were in position for a full-scale war. 'If we have to go to war, jolly good,' he said, 'if we don't, we will still manage.' Asked about how India would respond were Pakistan to use nuclear weapons, he declared that 'the perpetrator of that particular outrage shall be punished so severely that their continuation thereafter in any form of fray will be doubtful'. The next day, Pervez Musharraf, who had become president of Pakistan after deposing the civilian Prime Minister Nawaz Sharif in a military coup in October 1999, made his famous address promising to shut down terrorism and break the link between the Pakistani Army and Islamic extremists. There was an immediate de-escalation of tension but the Vajpayee administration did not pull back troops from the border. A few months later, when militants hit a residential army camp in Kaluchak in Jammu, killing women and children, Mishra asked the army to get ready for war again. The army chief was not convinced that it was the best time to go to war; he cited the imminent monsoons as one of the obstacles. Ultimately, despite Vajpayee's vow of an 'aar-paar ki ladai'—after a year-long military stand-off, several assurances from Musharraf and aggressive pressure on Islamabad by the Americans, the troops were asked to stand down. Mishra believed India had changed the rules of the game and made the Americans sit up and take notice only because of the mobilization.

But without even going to war, the human cost had been much higher than the Kargil conflict. In 2003, Defence Minister George Fernandes told Parliament that 798 soldiers had been killed in the course of Operation Parakram; many of the deaths occurred laying or removing the one million mines along the border.

■

India—the land of Buddha, Mahavir, Ashoka and Gandhi—imagines itself to be a civilization rooted in non-violence. But the fact that these great apostles of peace belong to India only accentuates the terror that has blighted this land for centuries. Unfortunately, the history, geography, composition and reality of Indian society make terrorist violence almost inevitable. This would be true of any society with similar characteristics—a hugely diverse population that is riven with divisions and inequities. And it is our misfortune that we have rarely been blessed with a strong, non-partisan, non-sectarian leadership that can keep turbulence in check.

In the course of the shaping of the modern Indian state, violence was sometimes used. In *The Philosophy of the Bomb*, Bhagat Singh, and his co-patriots wrote a counter to Gandhi. 'Terrorism is a phase, a necessary, inevitable phase, in the revolution,' they argued, '...it shatters the spell of the superiority of the ruling class and raises the status of the subject race in the eyes of the world, because it is the most convincing proof of a nation's hunger for freedom. Here in India, as in other countries in the past, terrorism will develop into the revolution and the revolution into independence, social, political and economic.' At the same time the revolutionaries of the freedom movement contested the use of the label 'violent' for them, locating their use of force within the larger theme of the pursuit of justice. 'Violence is physical force applied for committing injustice, and that is certainly not what the revolutionaries stand for,' they argued. Little could they have imagined then, as they fought the British, how severely terrorism would come to hollow out India and her sense of security as a nation-state in years to come.

It is beyond the scope of this book to cover all the acts of terrorist violence that have plagued India throughout its history, but even if we look at just the twentieth and twenty-first centuries, the drumbeat of terrorist activity has been steady and has caused much damage.

In 2014, India ranked sixth on the Global Terrorism Index, just below war-ravaged Syria and ahead of Yemen, Somalia, Egypt and South Sudan. The index divided terrorism in India into three categories—Islamist, separatist and left-wing extremist. Officially, the government recognizes sixty-six terror groups in India. While five of them are active in Jammu and Kashmir, with the Pakistan-based Lashkar-e-Taiba (LeT) and the indigenous Hizbul Mujahideen topping the list, more than thirty are operational in the single northeastern state of Manipur; several others are entrenched in Assam, Meghalaya, Nagaland, Tripura, Mizoram in the east and three of them remain threats in Punjab.

We have seen it all—armed militants seizing control of one of our most revered places of worship (the Golden Temple), planes blowing up in mid-air (Air India Kanishka bombing) and prime ministers and chief ministers assassinated by terror squads (Rajiv Gandhi and Beant Singh). Some terror groups could be traced back to flawed politics—like the ascent of Sikh separatist Jarnail Singh Bhindranwale, who was originally propped up by Sanjay Gandhi as a countervailing force to the rival Akalis; others drew sustenance from external enemies or a global community of radicals.

■

In July 2011, thunder and lightning veined the clouds overhead and angry monsoon rains lashed the streets of Mumbai as I waded through mud and water in the city's iconic Zaveri Bazaar. A tangled crisscross of lanes, its 7,000 shops glittered with gold and diamonds in dramatic contrast to its decrepit, crumbling buildings and open drains. Though business was mostly driven by Gujarati merchants in this 150-year-old jewellery souk, it brought together migrants from across India in an economy of interdependence. That morning I had met a vada-pav seller from Uttar Pradesh, a Muslim craftsman from

Bengal and an ebullient trader from Rajasthan.

I was in Zaveri Bazaar because multiple blasts had left Mumbai locked in the all too familiar grip of fear and uncertainty that had begun to shadow the city in the modern era. One of the explosion sites was the khau-galli (eating lane), a bustling street food hub in the interiors of Zaveri Bazaar, where the bomb had been left strapped to a motorcycle. This was the third time in eighteen years that this bazaar was a target for terrorists—the first attack was in 1993, then 2003 and now 2011.

Congestion and commerce both primed Zaveri Bazaar to be an attractive target. Any assault on a market that drove 70 per cent of India's gold business meant damage to the financial nerve centre. Because it was so crowded, it was impossible to fully secure and fatalities were guaranteed to be high. There were other reasons why Zaveri Bazaar drew terrorists. Its inherent cosmopolitanism—even if constructed around the imperatives of economics and livelihood—made it a microcosm of India's pluralism. Historian Sharada Dwivedi has documented how the bazaar stood at the geographical intersection of neighbourhoods that had otherwise become segmented along religious lines. To wear out friendships between Hindus and Muslims, to disrupt the traditional economic overlaps that had kept different communities working together for decades and finally to trigger religious violence, even riots—this was the ultimate terrorist fantasy that played out again and again in bazaars such as this one.

In the late twentieth century, the theatre of terrorist action in India had expanded to areas outside of conflict zones and localized insurgencies—Kashmir, Manipur or Nagaland, for instance—and had become more and more urban in nature; it was India's cities, and the multiculturalism they embodied that were under siege.

Studying how, post 9/11, terrorism all across the world was becoming urban in character, H. V. Savitch, an American expert on urbanization and public policy, explained why. 'The incongruous mixture of growth, density, wealth, poverty and immigration makes... cities primary targets, both as venues of operation and targets of calculation,' he said. In India's case, as I've said, you could add one other word—diversity—of particular interest to jihadist groups who believed they could not just challenge, but disrupt its secular genesis and lock the country into long-term internal strife.

Everyone at Zaveri Bazaar carried a memory that still hurt. Yet, no one had shut shop or moved out because of the recurring terror strikes. Some like Narendra Jain were here all three times, beginning with 1993, when terror hit home. Why have you never thought of leaving this place, I asked him. 'Rozi roti ka sawaal hai, jayenge to kahan jayenge (It's a question of our bread and butter, in any case where could we go)?' he said.

This is what we failed to acknowledge. Every time terror returned to haunt us we tried to seek cover behind that terrible cliché called 'resilience'. Or in Mumbai's case, its fabled stoicism. When people turned up at work the morning after a terror strike, we pretended that our collective spirit had stared down the barrel of a gun and had not blinked.

But truthfully, life carried on because of a strange combination of compulsion and fatalism. For most, their economic condition mandated what they needed to do; others counted on the law of probability and hoped that it was something that happened to other people. Many of us had grown to be strangely fatalistic about terrorism, a consequence of living in a country that was extraordinarily vulnerable to terror attacks.

Which one of us had not said out loud, at some point or the other—while jostling for breathing room on a railway platform teeming with passengers, during the Ganga aarti at the Dashashwamedh Ghat when cycle-rickshaws ferrying tourists and devotees crawled through a crammed alley, or while buying a pair of jeans at an upscale shopping mall where the entire city appeared to have converged, bored and hot, on a summer afternoon—'it would be so easy for someone to plant a bomb here'. Terrorism in India, as we experienced it, was random, unsparing, difficult to foretell, and hence, impossible to protect ourselves against. Sometimes a walk in the park, an evening out with your children—or even just the simple act of crossing the road—could place you in the line of lethal attack. Syed Raheem discovered that in Hyderabad.

When I first met him, he casually took out his left eye and held it up for me to see on the palm of his hand. Just like that. Startled, and unable to look at the hollow, purplish-red socket that was left bare for millions to see on live television, I reached out and tried to cover the raw flesh he had left exposed. 'Please don't do this Raheem Bhai,' I implored, 'please, I know how upset you are, but you shouldn't do this.' We couldn't even look at his damaged eye—he had to live with it.

On a Saturday evening in August 2007, a holiday, Syed Raheem had taken his teenage daughter Chinni out for a treat. They were going to buy a softy ice-cream cone from Hyderabad's much-loved Gokul Chat shop. As he stepped out of the autorickshaw into the heaving crowd, a bomb, triggered by a mobile phone, went off. Almost instantly, mangled metal strips of the ice cream machine that Raheem was walking towards were strewn on the road, alongside bangles, slippers and blood-soaked bodies. Just a couple of minutes earlier, five kilometres away at the open air auditorium in the city's Lumbini Park a bomb had ripped through the middle row of the theatre, flinging bodies into the air. Chinni jumped out of the rickshaw, making her way through the panicked swarm of people trying to run in the opposite direction. A man screamed out for help, his arm was hanging loose from his shoulder; a woman bleeding from a head injury held out her hand, pleading for help. Pushing past both the injured and the dead who lay on the road, she kept going, desperate to find her father. When she finally found him, he was lying on the ground, badly injured, with a long, sharp piece of metal embedded in the cornea of his left eye. Pieces of shrapnel, they would later discover at the Osmania Hospital, had pierced his skull.

Raheem, who used to be a commercial painter, was blinded in one eye and barely able to see with the other. Now, six years later, unemployed, angry, bitter and broken, he wasn't willing to be just one more forgotten statistic in the numerical grid of India's terrorism victims. When he pulled out his eye in front of the TV camera to reveal the sunken pit that lay beneath, he was showing us all what we failed to see once the blaring headlines had faded—the impotent fury of the survivors, who were forgotten about as soon

TERROR IN OUR TIME

as the outrage had taken place.

It is hard to see when things will get better. With two hostile countries, both nuclear powers, as neighbours—Pakistan in the north, China in the east—terror travels easily across the border. For decades, Pakistan has used terrorism as a weapon in its strategic arsenal, pushing in men it has called 'mujahideen' into the Kashmir Valley, armed and trained in camps controlled by its spy agencies. Chinese intelligence, while not overtly aggressive, has lent support, financial and organizational, to militant groups in the Northeast.

Over the years, and especially after Osama Bin Laden's audacious strike on the twin towers in New York, American pressure mounted on Pakistan to shut down factories that manufactured and exported terror to India. This marked the beginning of what came to be known as the 'Karachi Project'. The anti-India intelligence infrastructure was shifted to the port city in the south of Pakistan where, instead of Pakistani guerrillas, disaffected and radicalized Indian Muslims (not from Kashmir, but from states as varied as Karnataka, Uttar Pradesh and Maharashtra) were preyed on in a recruitment hunt to create a generation of proxy warriors.

It illustrated what Admiral Dennis Blair, the former director of US National Intelligence, called a Pakistani strategy to 'use militant groups as an important part of its strategic arsenal to counter India's military and economic advantages'. The Karachi Project took this a step further—the militants were now not only Pakistani but Indians as well, creating an inter-connected terror network that transcended borders and created an enemy both within and without.

Pakistan had previously argued that its fostering of Kashmiri insurgents was linked to its support for a cause it believed intrinsic to its nationhood. But this had nothing to do with its favourite 'core issue'. Classic conflict zones—Punjab, Kashmir, states of the Northeast—were no longer the most vulnerable to extremist violence. A new script was being written for the changing theatre of terrorism with freshly cast protagonists that helped Pakistan's shadowy non-state actors disown their role.

Under the Karachi Project discontented young Muslim men from India were smuggled into Pakistan via a third country—

Nepal—trained in the UAE and then sent back to India to execute attacks. Because they were Indian citizens they were able to embed themselves deeper into the system without suspicion. Groups like the LeT continued to be the handlers of these operatives. But because they were Indian it offered Pakistan perfect deniability and disassociation. As far back as 2000, LeT chief Hafiz Saeed had warned of a 'third round of jihad' against the enemy. The Kargil incursions were described as the 'first round' in this 'holy war' against India; suicide squad attacks on military camps in Kashmir were dubbed the 'second round'. 'Very soon we will be starting the next round,' announced Saeed, India's most wanted terrorist who functioned with impunity from across the border. This is how the Indian Mujahideen (IM)—the most dominant and lethal home-grown terror outfit—came to be born, with the Lashkar playing the part of godfather.

Named after 'Bhatkal', their hometown in coastal Karnataka, brothers Riyaz and Iqbal (born with the family name of Shahbandari) and their follower Yasin Bhatkal (born Mohammed Ahmed Siddibappa) were the founders of the Indian Mujahideen. Its first 'manifesto' was released in 2007 shortly after it bombed courthouses in Lucknow, Varanasi and Faizabad. Emailed to newsrooms across the country it spoke of 'wounds given by the idol worshippers to Indian Muslims... If you want to be a successful person in India then you should be an idol worshipper and kill Muslims.'

Tapping into a siege mentality and constructing a narrative of perennial victimhood for Muslims and themselves as righteous avengers, this and subsequent 'manifestos' repeatedly referenced cataclysmic events in India's recent history—the demolition of the Babri Masjid in 1992, the Gujarat riots a decade later. Its proclamations repeatedly targeted the judiciary, 'Supreme Court, High Court and the lower courts and all the commissions' for letting down Muslims. In 2011 there were explosions outside the Delhi High Court.

Scholar Stephen Tankel, who spent years documenting the rise and fall of the IM, called it 'an internal security issue with an external dimension'. He also argued that the 'primary indigenous jihadist threat' was created as a result of 'endogenous factors, specifically communal grievances and a desire for revenge', but became 'more lethal and resilient...thanks to external support from the Pakistani state and Pakistan- and Bangladesh-based militant groups'. Pakistan's essential aim of propping up this domestic insurrection was an attempt to destabilize India from within.

What was bewildering to me was the absence of focused anger by Indian society at large at the repeated attacks by terrorists, and the inability of our intelligence and security networks to stop them.The 26/11 attacks would finally rouse the country out of its apathy but until then, our 'acceptance' of terror was passive in the extreme. This was brought home forcefully four months before the 26/11 attacks.

■

On 25 July 2008, at Ahmedabad's civil hospital, policemen lit incense sticks and bowed in prayer; women squatted on their haunches to scrub the blood off the floors and the body of a man lay abandoned in one corner of a desolate corridor.

In a new chapter in India's long tryst with terror, for the first time ever, a hospital, and the doctors, medical workers, nurses and patients inside, had become the target. The civil hospital, frequented by those too poor to afford private medical treatment elsewhere, was among the locations of the twenty-one synchronized blasts that tore through Ahmedabad that day. That evening an ambulance had driven into the hospital's trauma ward, its siren blaring—most people thought it was ferrying a patient—and then there was a gigantic explosion. Later, police believed a suicide bomber was inside the ambulance.

Even children had not been spared. Inside the ICU I met Yash Vyas, all of ten years old, who was asking the doctors where his parents were. He was in acute pain and shivering. On the bed beside him was his elder brother, Rohan, who doctors said was not likely to survive. The children had come to meet their father, Dushyant, who worked in the hospital's cancer wing as a technician. He had been teaching the kids how to ride a bicycle in the hospital grounds when the explosion took place. When I met the children their father's body had just been wheeled out of the mortuary. Their mother was too distraught to break the news to them. In the same room, another father had just identified his son—his body blown to bits—by his earring.

Stretchers usually deployed to lift patients into the safety of the hospital were today soaked in blood. Students who had not yet earned a medical degree were doubling up as doctors because so many of their seniors were wounded.

This was the most brutal image of terror the country had yet been exposed to. And yet, it would be another four months before India decided to get really angry about terrorism. I always wondered why. Was it because the attacks in Mumbai would bring home terror to the upper middle class—to 'people like us'? Or was it because it was the most audacious assault India would ever see?

II

On the night of 26 November 2008, on a rare evening off, I was lying in bed watching episodes of *24*, utterly gripped by the espionage and counter-terrorism series that the somewhat intelligent part of my mind recognized as even less believable than the 'action'-hero Hindi movies of the seventies. Each episode of the series spanned twenty-four hours of a single day in which all manner of disastrous occurrences were averted by the hero with testosterone-drenched implausibility. But it was still enjoyable to suspend disbelief for an hour or two and lose oneself in a universe where Agent Jack Bauer could be relied upon to pull the world back from the brink of disaster. There were suitcase nukes, chopper chases and men slithering down ropes and crawling up walls in dimly lit passages where danger lurked in the shadows. Gunfire punctuated the dialogue like commas and colons. And, of course, Bauer never missed a shot.

I heard a ping on my work email. It was about a shoot-out in Mumbai. Initial reports suggested an internecine gang war. I continued with my lazy TV fix for the evening thinking it was a local Mumbai story which would be reported by the bureau there. But within an hour of the first shot fired in Café Leopold just after 9.30 p.m., from the scale of the attack and the manner in which targets across the city were being hit it was clear that this was a terror strike. That ten men could bring a city to its knees and lock it down in a seventy-two-hour siege; that this was an attack that would leave India's systemic incompetence and inadequacy on embarrassingly naked display; that this was going to be our equivalent of watching two planes blaze straight through the twin towers and knowing that your country could never be the same again—all this was still in the future.

As I began to track the tragedy, I learned that two of the ten Pakistani terrorists (later identified as Ajmal Kasab and Abu Ismail) had been on a killing spree at the city's main railway station, the Chhatrapati Shivaji Terminus (CST). Kasab wore grey cargo pants, a blue t-shirt with Versace printed on it in white and strode around jauntily, an assault rifle slung around his shoulder as casually as his duffel bag. If it weren't for the weapons he was wielding he would have looked like a young tourist; the much-taller Ismail wore all black, a shiny plastic jacket over crumpled pants. They used hand grenades and AK-47s to shoot more than fifty people and wound a hundred others. They were able to wander through the railway station unchallenged for almost ninety minutes until police reinforcements arrived. They then moved to Cama Nursing Home, adjacent to the station. Three of Mumbai's top police officers, including the head of its anti-terrorism squad (ATS), Hemant Karkare, were on their trail. With him were encounter specialist Vijay Salaskar and assistant commissioner of police, Ashok Kamte.

Transcripts of wireless communication with the police control room record that at twenty-nine minutes past ten that night, the police station closest to the nursing home sent a message saying, 'Two terrorists from CST are walking towards Azad Maidan.' Half an hour later the message confirmed that the terrorists had reached their target. For those thirty minutes Kasab and Ismail walked unhindered. Every moment of theirs was tracked in that interlude between the train station and the nursing home but no strike teams were diverted to stop them before they entered the nursing home. In the aftermath, an analysis of the painstakingly detailed text messages, phone calls and walkie-talkie communications would highlight the criminal collapse of the command and control response of the Mumbai police.

It was now a little after 11 p.m. Spooked by the fictional, yet suddenly too-close-to-the-bone images of bombings and assassinations on my screen, I shut down the laptop and got myself a ticket on the first morning flight from Delhi to Mumbai. Like millions of other Indians I couldn't do much more that night except watch the chaos unleashed by the terrorists on one of our great cities.

Kasab and Ismail had taken nurses and patients hostage at the nursing home and taken up positions on its terrace. A series of messages from Sadanand Date, additional commissioner of police, would later reveal plaintive cries for reinforcements, commandos and SWAT teams to help contain the situation at the nursing home. But even after 11.30 p.m., despite heavy firing and injuries to police officers—two inspectors were unconscious on the floor, Date had been shot in the leg—no reinforcements arrived. The Pakistanis hurled a final grenade in Date's direction and made their escape from the terrace of the nursing home. Date lay injured, waiting for help that never came; finally he called a friend on the police force who came and took him to the emergency room.

It was somewhere around the time that Date had been battling Kasab that Hemant Karkare and his team also arrived at the nursing home. Not because they had been dispatched to help Date, but because by following the trajectory of the attacks, they had heard about the gun battle at Cama.

Records of the communication between Karkare (code-named Victor on the wireless channel) and the control room show he made an urgent call for intervention. The Mumbai Police headquarters was only a few blocks away. Karkare kept messaging about the need to encircle the building so Kasab and Ismail couldn't make their escape. He asked for quick response teams and army commandos to be rushed in. 'Noted'—was the reply from the control room.

No support teams arrived on time. With nobody to stop them, Kasab and Ismail calmly walked out of the front entrance and hid in a thicket in the adjoining lane. Karkare, Kamte and Salaskar were in a Toyota Qualis barely a hundred metres from where the terrorists were hiding. Suddenly, the terrorists opened fired on the police vehicle. As the shooting carried on, Kamte jumped out of the car and fired at the bushes where the terrorists lay hidden. He succeeded in injuring Kasab who took a bullet in his hand.

But it was an unequal battle. The bulletproof vests that the officers wore had been purchased several years earlier, and were only good enough to offer limited protection against 9 mm bullets. They could not withstand AK-47 fire. One year later the police authorities would have to explain to the courts why they had issued substandard protective gear to their personnel. Their explanation was less than satisfactory. Apparently, they had never anticipated a 26/11-like threat. But they couldn't explain why the jackets were purchased even after the police officer vetting them had specifically warned, in writing, how obsolete they were, unable to even guard against fire from 7.62 mm self-loading rifles (SLRs). The officer had also noted that the jackets were heavier than the norm—5.9 kg against the much preferred 3 kg weight. His report was ignored by his superiors and money was paid to the vendor on advance dummy bills, carefully kept below the spending limit so the chief minister's office did not need to sign off on them.

With no one to run point on their operation, equipped with low-grade vests and weapons, and in the absence of a coherent or clear reaction from the central control room, the police officers did not stand a chance. They were pulled out of the Qualis by the terrorists and left to die on the streets. Kasab and Ismail settled into the front seat of the vehicle and sped away. This was a few minutes after midnight, according to police records. No ambulance or help came for at least the next forty minutes. Salaskar was still alive when the dying policemen were finally taken to the hospital; he was declared dead at one in the morning. Had medical assistance come earlier he may well have lived.

Even more strangely, by the time Hemant Karkare's body was wheeled into Mumbai's J. J. Hospital, the vest that had failed to save him mysteriously went missing. The police chief would later argue that the five bullets that killed Karkare went through his shoulder blade and so the quality of the bulletproof jacket was irrelevant. A sweeper would testify to finding the blood-soaked vest; incredibly he did not throw it away but alerted a nurse to its existence. Karkare's widow Kavita would devote the remaining years of her life—she died a few years later from a brain haemorrhage—to uncovering the mediocrity and malpractice that had killed her husband.

For the next sixty hours, in a complex, sequential operation, the Pakistani terrorists launched multiple attacks on different locations, dividing themselves into four assault teams, three with two members each and one with four members. High mobility was central to the tactics of the terrorist attack; they moved swiftly from target to target to overwhelm the security forces and create an impression of being in greater numbers than they actually were.

However, one year later, J. K. Dutt, the chief of the National Security Guard (NSG)—the elite commandos who flew in from Delhi to flush out the terrorists and saved hundreds of lives—told me that there might have been more than ten men involved in the siege. Explaining that the number of terrorists had been corroborated by matching them to the number of weapons recovered after the attack, he said, 'When I contacted a senior official in Delhi to find out how many terrorists we had to account for, I was told that I had to account for ten AK-47s. We had nine: two had been got by the local police, two at the Oberoi, two at Nariman House and three over here... It was only three hours later as our NSG dog went around looking for unexploded grenades that it sniffed out the tenth weapon lying under a lot of soot and carbon.' Dutt worried that the method of tallying terrorists by the number of recovered assault weapons may not have been perfect; he thought there could have been more gunmen hiding in plain sight among those trapped inside the hotel. 'We passed on to the local authorities that since the information is that some of them may have been staying as guests, you have to screen the hostages very carefully.'

Apart from the automatic rifles, the terrorists were armed with 9 mm pistols, eight to ten hand grenades and improvised explosive devices. Each bomb was assembled using high-impact RDX, digital timers and a 9-volt battery. Two were left behind in taxis and killed the unsuspecting passengers who rode in them. The last bomb was only recovered on 3 December, from the luggage of the dead and the injured at the CST railway station. Luckily, its timer had malfunctioned.

Dutt confirmed to me that at one point his commandos made the terrorists an offer to surrender, both at the Taj and at the Oberoi; to capture a terrorist alive could have meant the unearthing of a wealth of intelligence about the terrorists and their handlers. He said the offer, made face-to-face, was met with invective in Punjabi. The men had come to kill and be killed.

Muslim groups in Mumbai refused to allow their grounds to be used to bury the bodies of the terrorists. For the next twelve months, until the investigations were completed, the corpses of nine terrorists lay embalmed in a mortuary at the J. J. Hospital, after which they were buried at a secret location. The only terrorist captured alive, Ajmal Kasab, was executed in 2012; his body was buried within the precincts of Pune's Yerwada jail.

The NSG chief believed the 26/11 attacks could not have been possible without local support. Mumbai's police commissioner, Hasan Gafoor, said something similar, and then hastily retracted his comments after they provoked an uproar. But Dutt was firm. 'Given how well the terrorists seemed to know their targets, either they had advance teams for reconnaissance or local support that guided them to their targets.'

The missing link however was not Indian; he was American.

■

Monster. That was the word Rahul Bhatt, gym owner and son of film director Mahesh Bhatt, used to describe David Headley, the man with the differently coloured eyes, one blue, one brown. Rahul met Headley, the son of an American mother and Pakistani father, through Vilas, a gym instructor Headley used to work out with at a fitness centre Bhatt owned. 'He was a true-blue, walking, talking Yank,' Rahul told me when I caught up with him and Vilas in Mumbai to figure out how they could not have known that the guy they hung out with every Sunday for a movie or a quick bite was the man behind the Mumbai attacks. Eerily, the nickname Rahul had for Headley was 'Agent'. Astonishingly, the two men didn't seem to have a clue as to Headley's true identity.

Headley, who was once an undercover informant for the US Drug Enforcement Administration (DEA), scouted five Indian cities for potential terror attacks and provided intelligence to the men who terrorized Mumbai on 26/11. Yet, when the United States refused to hand him over to India, only allowing Indian sleuths to interrogate him on their turf, suspicions mounted over whether he was a CIA operative gone rogue. The Indians had unhesitatingly given the FBI access to interrogate Ajmal Kasab and the initial American reluctance to even permit a meeting between Headley and Indian investigators appeared to hide something.

There were many missing pieces to the Headley puzzle. Headley was on the FBI radar for over a year before he was arrested in October. In fact, he was already under surveillance a month before the 26/11 attacks. Why was this information not passed on to New Delhi at this time? How did Headley manage to make a trip to India in April 2009, five months after the Mumbai attacks, without India having a clue that the FBI was keeping watch on him? That Headley's half-brother was an official in the public relations office of the Pakistan prime minister has made Indians wonder just how much Pakistan knew.

Eventually David Headley pleaded guilty to all twelve charges of being a part of the LeT's 26/11 Mumbai terror plot and admitted to receiving training in terror camps in Pakistan. That the plea bargain he worked out with the American authorities ensured that he would not get the death sentence confirmed the suspicion in India that he was some sort of valued asset for American intelligence—or perhaps knew too much. It was ironic that Ajmal Kasab, a foot soldier in 26/11, was executed and David Headley, a mastermind and conspirator was able to live.

■

The 26/11 attacks changed the discourse about terrorism in India, forcing a slew of reforms in a security set-up that had become flabby and careless. But a cover-up of the multiple lapses—in the bureaucracy, the police, the political establishment and the disconnected architecture of national security that allowed every organization to function in independent silos—would come to be part of 26/11's untold, unexplored story. Unlike the United States where a comprehensive commission of enquiry probed what made the 9/11 strike on the World Trade Centre possible, the Congress-led government in New Delhi was quick to rule out the need for such a probe, saying it already had all the facts it needed. Some perfunctory political punishment was meted out; the sartorially fixated home minister, Shivraj Patil, resigned his job as did the Bollywood-obsessed chief minister of Maharashtra, Vilasrao Deshmukh, who took movie director Ram Gopal Varma on a terror tour of the Taj hotel.

But oddly the bulk of public angst, at least among the middle-class TV-viewing segment, was reserved for the media. What was it about this television coverage that so rankled a section of the citizenry, while drawing generous praise from others? Was it that the journalists—I among them—were not in control of the story, or was it that there was something about the nature of the attacks themselves that had unleashed a typhoon of urban rage?

Quite apart from the fact that it brought home, again, the frequent thanklessness of being a television journalist—you could spend days in perilous situations without food or sleep but still return to a volley of feedback steeped in hatred—I was curious to understand what these responses revealed to us about the changing response to terrorism.

What collective nerve had the attacks touched that suddenly none of the old rules applied? When I took my place, by turns opposite the Oberoi Hotel and the Taj, jostling with not just other camera crews but also the bhel-puri wallah for a little patch of space, I had already been covering terrorism and violence in society for a long time. Apart from years of experience both at the border and within the Kashmir Valley, I had reported on countless encounters and explosions in cities as varied as Jammu, Varanasi, Delhi and Mumbai. In these situations, we had often chronicled the despair and anguish of relatives—mothers, sons, and sisters—sometimes through wordless images, at other instances with spot interviews. We all drew our own red lines of course—no thrusting of mikes in the faces of survivors or grieving families, no ambulance chases, utmost circumspection about how graphically you could show a body that had just been blow up by a bomb and so on. What was different about the public response to the media, during and after 26/11, was the fact that this was the first time we were being individually and collectively criticized for the

job we were doing. Why was this so? Why was it palatable to these
viewers for the mother of ten-year-old Yash Vyas to speak to us in
a cramped public hospital in Gujarat just hours after her husband
died and while her son was still battling for his life in the ICU, and
not okay for the husband of journalist Sabina Saikia to walk up to
me in Mumbai and ask to be on my live broadcast, just in case his
wife was still alive inside the Taj and watching the news? Like so
many other distraught family members who waited with us in those
seventy-two hours in Mumbai, her husband wanted his voice to be
heard by his wife and by all the people watching. Perhaps talking
about his loved one would serve to alleviate the panic just a little
rather than just helplessly waiting for whatever outcome there was
going to be. Perhaps he wanted his beloved partner, the person who
was possibly on the verge of death, to be humanized, understood
intimately and celebrated, before she became just another forgotten
number on the list of those killed.

None of the angst about television coverage came from the
families we met; those who were outraged on their behalf were not
living their horror, they were watching the news from the distant
and safe comfort of a TV monitor.

Afterwards I heard some snide comparisons made between the
US media and ours. People asked why we couldn't be more like the
American networks had been while reporting on the 9/11 attacks—no
stake-outs at hospitals where the injured were taken, no interviews
with heartbroken husbands or mothers and no mention of the dead,
just sanitized studio talking heads. The United States, under President
George Bush, also banned the images of military coffins that came
home from his ill-chosen war in Iraq. Explaining the government
censorship—mutely complied with by TV stations—the *Washington
Post* had written in a 2003 op-ed: 'Since the beginning of the Vietnam
War presidents have worried that their military actions would lose
support once the public glimpsed the remains of US soldiers arriving
at air bases in flag draped coffins.' Big networks did not fight the
decision in a country where the First Amendment on free speech is
considered sacrosanct; it did not dwell on funerals and the suffering
of the families that had been left behind either. The point I'm trying

to make is that the supposed restraint displayed by the US media in recent times has had a lot to do with political imperatives rather than any self-imposed curbs rising out of some moral code. And, in any case, hasn't the same western media today opted to showcase the haunting photograph of a dead Syrian boy washed ashore on a Turkish beach to underline the humanitarian refugee crisis unfolding in a war zone torn asunder by the Islamic State (ISIS)? They have, in a break from their self-censorship of grief during 9/11, also interviewed the father of the boy who was trying to emigrate with his family to Canada, when their boat capsized. The photograph drew instant comparisons with Nick Ut's Pulitzer Prize winning picture of a nine-year-old Vietnamese girl running naked, tormented by the scalding burns of a napalm attack. Both these photographs were graphic and disturbing but they also reinforced the power of the single image that becomes too strong to turn away from.

Most Indians have shared the photograph of the three-year-old Syrian boy on their Twitter timelines and Facebook pages. But how would TV viewing classes—who were already apoplectic about us interviewing families and friends—have reacted to a similar image of a dead child killed in the Mumbai terror strike? Television never broadcast such an image but we faced a violent backlash nevertheless.

By contrast—and with the cushion of a few years separating the trauma of the Mumbai attacks from our information-saturated age today—our viewers did not complain when a ten-year-old girl stood in salute at her soldier-father's funeral when television broadcast the funeral ceremony live or when the teenage son of an assassinated police officer on duty in the Maoist-controlled forest promised through a flood of tears that once he grew up he too would don the uniform. We did not ask for the censorship of these raw emotions because psychologically they made us feel better about our future; perhaps they tapped into our need for hope and our search for heroes.

Less explicably, the same upper echelons of society who complained about privacy and dignity not being preserved in television's coverage of the Mumbai attacks, were not disturbed by images of a poor man threatening to immolate himself so he could get an unresponsive administration's attention or by the public spectacle of a farmer's suicide at a political rally in Delhi. Why were public responses so different both before and after 26/11? And what happened to laments about privacy and dignity when, a few years later, the chatterati vicariously lapped up every single personal detail in the sordid murder saga of Sheena Bora, in which the high-society businesswoman Indrani Mukerjea was the prime accused, coverage that was often so tawdry that it even embarrassed most of us in the fraternity.

When the two planes crashed into the twin towers in New York and brought them down, the image that remained embedded in our heart was that of the unidentified 'Falling Man'. Taken by Richard Drew of the Associated Press it showed a man who plunged to his death from the North Tower, where he and hundreds of others were trapped with no chance of surviving. When the *New York Times* published the photograph the next morning, it was labelled 'exploitative and voyeuristic', words that would be all too familiar to us seven years later. The photograph was deemed so controversial it was struck from the record only to reappear several years later.

When I look back at 26/11 that sense of despairing helplessness was just as disturbingly encapsulated by a single image. From the windows of the Oberoi-Trident hotel people were holding up scraps of paper and cloth, stationery, napkins, whatever they had, for the cameras to capture. Handwritten on these was the single silent scrawl—'Save Us'. They waved down at us as if to say, don't let us die. In the alley behind the hotel, friends and lovers stood close together and trained binoculars at the glazed, unbreakable glass to see if they could spot one of their own at the windows.

While these poignant scenes were playing out, throughout the city (as well as the country) the tornado of urban rage was picking up strength. Members of the public were hitting out—first at the politicians, then at the media and then at anything and everything that stood in its path. The anger was inchoate and unfocused. In contrast, the families of those trapped inside the hotels were quiet, philosophical, broken from within but stoic on the outside. Perhaps it was because those watching 26/11 unfold on the television inside their homes were gripped by a fear of the unknown and the realization that the alien now lived in their backyard, whereas those waiting outside those hotels had come together to form a wider community of shared grief. They wanted to talk, they wanted to be heard, they wanted a human connection at a time which was isolating as it was frightening. Those watching, however, probably wanted to be calmed and reassured about their own safety; every story that made them feel otherwise made them angrier with us.

Later I understood the rage against the media a little better. Until 26/11 every time bombs ripped through the bazaars of Delhi or Ahmedabad or Jaipur, it was still largely the poor of India who were the targets of terrorism. Middle-class India had never complained about how we reported on those crises. But 26/11 was too close to the bone in a way that it would never have been had, say, only CST—the main railway terminus—been targeted by Kasab and the other terrorists. This was now about 'people like us' and the Indian middle class did not want to be reminded, in the graphic way that TV coverage was capable of, that they too could be bruised by random, destructive violence. The anger grew out of the feeling that they were no longer safe. We, the media, reflected the class gap too. The only time CST, where most of the victims were from the poorer sections of society, really figured in television coverage was to show the CCTV images of Ajmal Kasab entering with a knapsack and a gun slung from his shoulders. Those who died at the railway station barely got attention.

■

Is India safer after 26/11? Have we fortified ourselves well enough that such an attack cannot happen again? Although in the wake of the tragedy, our security grid and systems were put under the scanner and numerous recommendations made, in actual fact we are not much better off today. While it is probably impossible to ever make India completely terror-proof, it is ridiculous to see how little improvement has been made in the systems we have in place to deal with terror. In 2011, when serial blasts ripped through Mumbai, I met the then chief minister of Maharashtra, Prithviraj Chavan. What he told me about our state of preparedness was frightening. For the first fifteen minutes after the bombs went off he was unable to contact his seniormost officers because the mobile phone circuits got clogged. 'Networks got congested. I could not contact the chief of police, I could not contact the DG police,' he told me, 'until we organized wireless apparatus and came online.' Three years after the Mumbai attacks no one had thought of giving key police officers satellite phones so the communication lines could always be open. Chavan also revealed that a proposal to procure 5,000 CCTV cameras—often the most critical evidence gathering mechanism—had been gathering cobwebs because no officer was willing to sign off on the file and clear it. Corruption controversies had engulfed recent government procurements and no one was willing to get embroiled. Chavan agreed that 'bureaucracy had trapped the proposal'. He also revealed his unhappiness at the fact that the all-important portfolio of home affairs—the nodal counter-terrorism ministry—had been given to his ally, the NCP, instead of to the chief minister. 'Decision making takes time,' he conceded, 'it's very difficult.' Yet, again the narrow calculation of political survival—in this case to keep the ruling alliance going—had been privileged over decisions that involved human survival. Terrorism, and the debates around it, would always be tragically politicized in India.

III

In the sixteenth century, Panipat was a dusty little village in the north Indian plain that would witness one of the most famous battles ever fought in medieval times—when the Mughal emperor Babur defeated the much larger force of the Lodis ranged against him through the brilliant use of artillery. Two more decisive battles would be fought in Panipat. In the sixteenth century, Emperor Akbar defeated King Hemu, and in the eighteenth century, Ahmad Shah Durrani was victorious against the Marathas. Today, Panipat is an untidy town that straggles along NH1, and is mainly known for its Pachranga pickles and as the country's single largest centre for the manufacture and sale of blankets and carpets.

In 2007, war came to Panipat again, when the Samjhauta Express (a train that was also called the Friendship Express), which ran two times a week between India and Pakistan, was bombed by terrorists. The bodies littered throughout the wreckage of the train were so scorched and disfigured that it was impossible to separate Indian from Pakistani among the dead. Tubes of Fair & Lovely, embroidered juttis or khusas as they were called across the border, a kaajal stick, a teddy bear; the simple belongings of ordinary folk, whether from Delhi or Lahore, were poignant reminders of the violence that had taken place.

The bombs went off just before midnight as the Samjhauta Express was passing through Panipat. The improvised explosive devices were packed into suitcases that detonated in two of the unreserved coaches on the train. Later, police would discover two more suitcase bombs that did not explode. After the explosion the train continued to hurtle onwards, with some of its carriages wreathed in flames. As the driver was unaware of the explosion that had taken place, the train showed no signs of slowing down, even as fire began to engulf sleeping passengers. People began screaming and banging at the windows and doors as they tried to flee, but the bombs and the fire had jammed the doors of the two bogies in which the explosion had taken place. When the train was finally brought to a stop and the dead were counted and identified, it was discovered that sixty-eight people had been killed, most of them Pakistanis.

Pakistan's foreign minister, Khurshid Kasuri, was to arrive in India for talks in four days. Most believed, even in Pakistan, that this was a typical attempt by groups like the LeT to destabilize that dialogue. Pakistan's President Pervez Musharraf declared that he would 'not allow elements that wanted to sabotage the ongoing peace process to succeed in their nefarious designs'.

Little did anyone know in the immediate aftermath of the blasts that this would soon become the most sensitive—and for India, the most embarrassing—example of Hindu extremism or right-wing terror. It added an entirely new dimension to the conventional narrative around terrorism and while it did not take away from the rising concerns about Islamist fundamentalism, it queered the domestic political pitch like never before. We had seen enough instances of fundamentalism among the loony fringe of Hindu extremist groups but the Samjhauta bombs were the first instance of an organized Hindu terrorist conspiracy.

The National Investigative Agency (NIA) would soon charge-sheet Swami Aseemanand, once the head of the Rashtriya Swayamsevak Sangh (RSS)-affiliated Vanvasi Kalyan Ashram in the Dangs district of Gujarat, as a key accused in the Samjhauta blasts as well as the terror attack that took place later that year at the venerated Sufi shrine of Ajmer Sharif. Aseemanand would later be granted conditional bail among charges by the Opposition that there was an unofficial go-slow on all cases which could be classified as Hindu terror, an allegation that the NIA chief Sharad Kumar rubbished in an interview to me. Yet the NIA decided not to challenge the bail. Nine months after the court granted him bail, Aseemanand remained in prison because he was also an accused in the Ajmer blasts of 2007.

In another terror strike—the Malegaon blasts of 2008—a serving army officer, Lieutenant Colonel Srikanth Purohit, also a member of right-wing group Abhinav Bharat, was arrested and listed among the main accused by the Maharashtra anti-terror squad. The ATS documents placed in court quoted Purohit as lamenting how weak Hindu groups had become. Even the Shiv Sena and its legacy of anti-Muslim politics was not 'strong' enough for Purohit, according to the Mumbai police. 'In the daytime they shout slogans about protection of Hindus and at night they sit with Muslims and deal in illegal activities,' Purohit told other members of the Abhinav Bharat. In this case too, there was criticism of the government's response to Hindu terror. Rohini Salian, the public prosecutor in Maharashtra quit her job alleging that she was under government pressure to go 'soft' on the perpetrators.

Political scientist and critic of the BJP, Christophe Jaffrelot, while acknowledging that Hindu terror did not pose the same sort of threat as Islamist groups to national security, argues that the history of Veer Savarkar threw up its own clues to this particular brand of terrorism. 'As a young revolutionary Savarkar created the first Abhinav Bharat society in 1905. The movement drew its name and its inspiration from Mazzini's Young Italy, but was also influenced by [Thomas Frost's] *Secret Societies of the European Revolution*, a book dealing mostly with Russian nihilists,' he argued.

In its own defence, the right-wing BJP said the very phrase 'Hindu terror' was one designed by the Congress to please the 'Azamgarh constituency', a snide reference to a district in eastern Uttar Pradesh from where several young Muslim men had been recently implicated in terror cases. With the issue of terrorism becoming dangerously politicized between hyperbole and denials, in 2013, things reached a head when the BJP threatened to boycott any public function attended by the then home minister, Sushil Kumar Shinde. Shinde, an otherwise affable Congress politician, was widely seen to be out of his depth in the home ministry. It was his influence as a Dalit politician that is believed to have been the reason that he got the portfolio. This was a development that again showed how poorly India's battle against terror was being conducted. It was ridiculous to discover that the front line ministry in charge of counter-terrorism was being handed out like a prize to whoever was seen as influential, rather than choosing the minister on account of his or her expertise in national security. This time, Shinde—who had previously given himself a certificate of 'excellent' in an interview to me on the very day the country's power grid collapsed—had provoked the BJP into reacting. He had accused the RSS and BJP of running 'training camps' to incite 'Hindu terror'. Shinde had always had a reputation for being a bit of a bumbler and for committing verbal faux pas. For instance, in 2012, he had suggested that the then Prime Minister Manmohan Singh was unaware of the decision to hang Ajmal Kasab. And, sure enough, after an uproar in Parliament, in this case too, he denied the words attributed to him and hastily retracted them.

'There is no such thing as saffron terror,' announced BJP MP and journalist Chandan Mitra, who supported his claim by arguing that there were only two kinds of 'organized' terrorism—left wing and jihadi. The Congress—wary of a political backlash—was unprepared to take a strong position on whether it believed in the existence of 'saffron terror'.

'Some Hindu groups on the fringe may be involved in retaliatory attacks,' Mumbai's former police commissioner, M. N. Singh, told me, naming two: Sanatan Sanstha and Abhinav Bharat. But he believed their influence was restricted to pockets of Maharashtra and Madhya Pradesh and thought they lacked the capacity for widespread, organized terror. Nevertheless, they remained a danger to national security. In 2015, members of the Sanatan Sanstha were accused of murdering Professor M. M. Kalburgi, a respected teacher and rationalist. Sameer Gaikwad, a member of the Sanstha, was subsequently arrested for the murder of Govind Pansare, a veteran left activist.

A BJP lawmaker in Goa called the Sanatan Sanstha a 'terror group' that must be banned by the centre, but Chief Minister Lakshmikant Parsekar ruled it out, saying the group could not be held responsible for one man's action. Even more puzzling was why the hard-line group was not clamped down upon despite a 1,000-page dossier on it sent by the then Maharashtra chief minister to the centre at a time when his own party was in power.

The sad truth about India is that sectarian tendencies always have the potential to turn into overtly terrorist actions. This is true of both Hindu and Muslim radicals. I met Milind Joshi Rao, a portly, cheerful spokesperson for Abhinav Bharat who said without flinching, 'We do believe in a Hindu Rashtra. But that's because we believe no one can be more secular than Hindus.' So what does the Abhinav Bharat stand for, I persisted. 'We stand for making this country truly pro-Hindu. Why can't we say like John Howard said in Australia about Christians, that in this country Hindus are the majority and so this country will run on the principles of Hinduism?'

Before investigative agencies began to suspect right-wing Hindu groups for their role in the terror attacks in Malegaon, Ajmer, Hyderabad and on board the Samjhauta Express, a series of wrongful arrests were made in almost all of these cases, implicating young Muslim men who were later found to be innocent. In Hyderabad after the strike on the historic Mecca Masjid, as many as seventy men—all Muslims—were arrested and kept in illegal confinement. I met one of these men, Syed Imran, a few months after his acquittal. Initially he was charged with storing at his house the RDX used to set off the bomb; no such explosive was ever found. 'Do you know they even said I spent ten years training in Pakistan?' asked Imran incredulously. To my astonishment, he said this not just without a trace of rancour but with a bemused smile. 'I studied in a Kendriya Vidyalaya in Hyderabad, then enrolled to become an engineer. The police had access to all my records, how could they level such a bizarre allegation against me?' And yet, Imran ended up spending eighteen months in jail, where he was frequently tortured with electric shocks. Imran told me life after his release from prison had been even tougher than the time he spent behind bars. 'The police still stop by at my house from time to time and harass me with strange questions. I had to go to court to get permission to complete my engineering degree. And after that, it's been a nightmare getting a job,' Imran told me. The acquittal had not erased the stain that the initial charge of terrorism had left on his resume; he was viewed with suspicion by potential employers. 'And yet,' Imran said, 'for everything I've gone through, I still call myself a proud Indian.' Inside prison, Imran said, he had been stripped naked and beaten by cops who wanted him to confess his links to the Lashkar-e-Taiba. 'I have never stepped out of Hyderabad; I know nothing about the Lashkar. Yet they didn't believe me. I am a patriotic Indian. But I was not treated as one, was I?' Imran had one question for those who said there was no equivalence between Islamist terror groups and Hindu terror groups—M. N. Singh had suggested that violence by radical Hindu groups was driven by the need for retaliation to jihadist terrorism—'If I retaliate for what was done to me, won't I be immediately branded a terrorist?' Apart from the glaring question of injustice, if the purpose of terrorist strikes was to damage the amity between Hindus and Muslims and rupture India's diversity from within, every such fake terror case—whether from incompetence or prejudice—had the potential to alienate young Muslim men from the mainstream. This too would come with its own dangerous implications, especially given the changing face of global terrorism.

On the other side of the ideological and political trenches was the spectre of the Islamic State. Unlike in the West, where people were leaving in the hundreds to join ISIS in Syria, in India intelligence agencies believed that there were only about a hundred young boys whom they had to keep under surveillance. A senior RAW official told me that by his calculation less than twenty had already crossed over; another thirty to forty had been stopped just before they intended to and had been brought back from countries like the UAE before they were lost in the fog of terror. The remaining were those who had been identified as potential terrorists. Four of the southern states of India—Kerala, Karnataka, Andhra Pradesh, Telangana—and in the west, Maharashtra, were the centres of recruitment for ISIS in India. Arif Majeed, a young twenty-two-year-old engineer from Kalyan near Mumbai, was the first identified Indian to join ISIS along with a group of three friends he had met on Facebook. Injured in the war, Majeed turned tail and fled to Istanbul where he contacted the Indian embassy. Take me home, he told them. His friends stayed back.

Typically the profile of men who were susceptible to the ISIS deathtrap was like Majeed's—young, educated and urban—either lower middle class or middle class. Contrary to popular assumptions, not one of them had studied at a madrassa, the traditional Islamic schools sometimes viewed as breeding grounds of orthodoxy and radicalism.

But the RAW officer had an interesting poser. 'We must ask ourselves why all these years, even though Afghanistan is much closer to us not a single Indian Muslim went to join the "jihad" there. Iraq and Syria are someone else's war; so why are people going at all?' All these years, the officer pointed out, the Indian Muslim had shown no linkages to the global ummah; home-grown jihadists had been more moulded by domestic grievances in India. The officer believed that in an increasingly polarized environment, with the internet opening the gates to a universe that could not be monitored, India had failed at building an effective counter-radicalization message. 'Extremism, in my opinion, is a bigger threat than terrorism. Hindu and Muslim radicals are feeding off each other. We need to be intolerant about intolerance.'

IV

'If you don't want the poor to be attracted to terrorism, if you don't want young men to kill, then first of all, the government needs to deliver governance and basic rights to those who live in the most backward, undeveloped areas.'

This was no platitude dished out by a vote-seeking, politically correct politician. Nor was it an attempt at punditry by an analyst or a journalist. The words were important—not just for the common sense they conveyed, cutting through a noisy fractious national debate with simple clarity, but because of who was speaking them. That they came from the young widow of a police officer who had just been assassinated by the Maoist rebels who took him hostage made them extraordinary.

If she was angry or bitter—and she should have been—you couldn't tell. Her hair was pulled back from her face as tightly as her grief was withheld from public display. Her face, free from make-up or any other adornment, save a tiny black bindi, was glistening in the light, almost like a halo.

I met Sunita Induwar in January 2010, four months after her husband's body was found in a ditch on the highway between Ranchi and Jamshedpur. His head had been severed from the body in a Talibanesque decapitation. A note written in red ink and nailed to a nearby tree declared that the recent killing of a comrade by security forces had now been avenged.

But she made no mention of the grisly beheading that had compelled her ten-year-old to vow that just as soon as he was old enough he too would become a police officer and kill the men who had murdered his father.

Instead, in a country which lived from headline to headline, abduction to abduction and massacre to massacre, she was focused on, somehow, stopping more bloodshed.

'In these areas, there is no literacy, no education,' she said, her tone, steely and firm, yet soft. 'Terrorists are able to lure young men by gifting guns and making other promises.' Francis Induwar, still only in his thirties, was an intelligence officer who was kidnapped when he went to meet an informant.

But his wife was not asking for the army to be unleashed against the Maoists or even for unequivocal condemnation by public intellectuals. Her loss was personal but her comments were gentler than those of the home minister at the time, P. Chidambaram, who had called for civil society to answer for their sympathy for left-wing extremists, charging it with 'tying down the hands of the security forces'.

■

The homespun movement of armed rebellion led by India's Maoists, also known as Naxalites (after the first left-wing uprising in the village of Naxalbari in West Bengal in 1967), was described by former Prime Minister Manmohan Singh in 2006 as the country's 'single biggest internal security threat'.

Controlling what is known as India's red corridor and vowing to overthrow the state, their fiefdom ran all the way from Nepal down to southern India and from the east to the country's central regions. More than 200 districts in several states of India were impacted by Maoist groups whose literature claimed that 'the seizure of state power should be the goal of all our activity'. Indian intelligence officials argued that Naxalites were financed and armed by China but the Maoists who operated from remote tribal districts and forest areas positioned their terrorism as a home-grown class war and an 'armed struggle' seeking to rectify social and economic inequities. Successive governments—despite many demands from within to the contrary—had declined to use the military against Maoist insurgents, distinguishing their violence from that of the secessionist threat in areas like Jammu and Kashmir or the Northeast, where the army had been deployed for decades. Such distinctions aside, the Maoist insurgency was no less dangerous than any of the other violence that the state had to contend with. As the terrorists menaced rail tracks and primary schools, and even entire police stations, the red corridor became more dangerous for a police or paramilitary soldier than duty in Kashmir. In 2014, rebels in the red zone were killing more men in uniform than in all the other insurgency areas together. Terrorism in the red corridor remained India's most unaddressed and dangerous fault line, as it challenged the very legitimacy of Indian democracy. And it was tougher to pin on an external threat.

'Even yojanas [government schemes] don't reach the people they are meant for. Let's say a hundred rupees is allocated for a programme, only ten rupees from it will reach the citizen,' Sunita said, flagging rampant corruption, leakages and inefficiencies in the system. 'If there was access to education, if the public distribution system for rations worked, if the deprived were looked after, we could stop this.' She was proud of her teenage son's decision to become a police officer but she understood that the challenge ran deeper. She knew that what had happened to her husband would happen again. And again.

Locked into battles of ideology and politics, India's Maoist conflict was already its longest war within. And yet, in the absence of any policy consensus for decades, it was a battle we were set to lose. Public responses were usually of three kinds. There were those who romanticized the Naxals as do-gooders whose armed struggle had given a voice to the poor; they condemned their violence but saw the state as the oppressor and the Naxals as the generals of an army of the victimized pushed into battle by inequities of class.

On the other side were those with the hard-nosed view that you could only talk about 'development' after you had reclaimed large swathes of land dominated by Maoists. Chidambaram, for example, told me that he was in favour of air support for operations against the insurgents, a demand he said was echoed by the security forces and five different chief ministers. But reflecting the dangerous divide within, he confessed to a 'limited mandate' as home minister in being able to prevail upon his own government to grant this. He said he had made a pitch to the Cabinet Committee on Security, where his proposals were shot down by party colleagues A. K. Antony and Pranab Mukherjee. 'I have tried to convince them,' he told me in comments that would erupt into a huge political storm, 'I will go back to try and revisit that mandate. I have already spoken to the prime minister.'

And then there was the third approach—one of sheer casualness and ineptitude—best embodied by politicians like Shivraj Patil, Chidambaram's predecessor. To my utter incredulity he once said to me, 'Do you know how many people die in road accidents every year?' to underline his bizarre claim that traffic accidents were more fatal than killings by armed insurgents—so why worry. Frighteningly, it was while addressing a conference of India's top police officers that Patil as home minister argued that the Maoist threat was exaggerated and asked that no 'fear psychosis' be created. At the same conference, his boss, the prime minister, had just described left-wing violence as India's biggest internal security threat. The dissonance trivialized the gravity of the issue.

Sunita Induwar's cogent articulation of the Maoist challenge cut through the chaos of these contradictions. It was the perfect middle ground that could have brought the extremes closer to the centre.

■

The genesis of the armed uprising among the peasantry can be traced back to pre-independence India. The British strategy was to solidify control by winning over the high caste, local elites. Landlords and revenue collectors were co-opted to be allies and mediators. A new tax policy gave the zamindars full control over land and wrested away the right of the peasant to the soil he tilled. With no ownership rights over what was cultivated, poor farmers were reduced to being bonded labour. Historian Sumit Sarkar has a subaltern narrative of who drove the revolt against the colonialists. Writing about the need for a 'history from below' he argued that Pax Britannica was challenged in a series of revolts by people 'predominantly lower class in social composition'. The most militant uprisings even then were by tribal communities who in the opinion of anthropologist and historian K. Suresh Singh, 'revolted more often and far more violently than any other community'.

In a prelude to the contemporary fault line that runs through modern India's forest areas inhabited by tribals and often 'controlled' by Maoists, the Adivasis of the late nineteenth century fought attempts by the imperialists to channel the forest wealth for themselves. Today, there are tribal movements against mining behemoths like POSCO and Vedanta. And just as the Dongria Kondh community in eastern Orissa successfully convinced the highest court of India that corporations could not mine the Niyamgiri Hills—considered the seat of God by their clan—without the consent of the local population, so too in the 1890s did Birsa Munda, a firebrand tribal revolutionary lead his people against 'intruders' in what would come to be the separate state of Jharkhand. As effigies of the British Raj were burnt, his protest did not even pretend to be non-violent. His slogans included the vow that 'guns and bullets would turn to water'. Munda became a legend among his people, kept alive through folk songs passed down the generations.

Through the length of British rule, peasant and tribal movements took the shape of violent mutinies, against not just the foreigners but also the Indian land-grabbers and rentiers who had dented their economic rights. Finally, it was in independent India, in 1967, that their restiveness got christened 'Naxal' after the hilly area where Charu Mazumdar called for an armed struggle along the lines of Mao Zedong's communist revolution.

Today, of course, though Maoist and Naxal are words used interchangeably in popular parlance, the China reference has little contemporary resonance; Beijing itself has abandoned revolution for 'market socialism'.

But the Maoist threat remains chillingly real. Forty thousand square kilometres of territory and 2,000 police stations in 223 districts are affected by the ultras either partially or substantially. And the state's efforts at combating this threat have only been partially successful. It has also continued to repeat mistakes that were made elsewhere when it came to tackling terrorism. The creation of a private militia—the Salwa Judum—mirrored the error of using counter insurgents (Ikhwanis) to fight militants in the Kashmir Valley. In both cases, the result was similar: a slew of extra-constitutional killings and a deepening of the alienation among the local people. In 2005, in response to the brutality of Maoist violence, Congress leader Mahendra Karma formed the Salwa Judum—which means 'peace march' or 'purification hunt' in Gondi. It began with an innocuous procession led by Karma, but supported by the BJP as well, against the Maoists' diktat prohibiting tribals from collecting tendu leaves. It soon evolved into a vigilante group, sponsored by the state to forcibly flush out tribals from Maoist controlled areas and force them into other states or special camps. It was not unusual for the militia to recruit teenage boys as young as fifteen and sixteen. The vigilantes were called Koya commandos or Special Police Officers and paid a paltry Rs 2,000 a month. They conducted violent raids, pushed out tribals to relief camps, did combing operations and fought alongside the security forces. Soon they began plundering and looting Adivasi villages, misusing the arms they were permitted to carry. There were complaints of rape and murder. Before 2011 when the Supreme Court shut it down as illegal, several thousand tribals had been displaced by the Salwa Judum from their homes and shoved into camps they did not want to stay in. In 2013, almost the entire leadership of the Congress in the state of Chhattisgarh was wiped out after Maoists attacked their motorcade, blew up two cars and opened fire. In the convoy was Mahendra Karma, the founder of the Salwa Judum. In May 2015, his son Chhavendra Karma started a new anti-Maoist militia. Is this Salwa Judum Part 2, he was asked.

'Yes, you can say that,' he replied.

It was astonishing that it was left to the victims of Naxal violence to drive home the gravity of the challenge. Sumer Singh, a paramilitary officer, lost his younger brother to a massacre in Dantewada in 2010. He told me that people like his brother became statistics that were forgotten the day they died. 'Yeh bhi kisi ke bache hain. Who thinks about the family, the five children who are left behind without a father?' he said angrily. In a startling admission he said that when the jawans were sent deep into the forests to fight the Naxals they often did not even have basic knowledge of the topography. They were, literally, cannon fodder.

'Hamne sub kuch kho diya hai ab ham chahte hain ki kisi tarah iss ka ant ho (We have lost everything. We just want this [Naxalism] to end somehow),' he told me, breaking down in tears. 'If there is illegal mining, if tribals are being denied ownership of their resources, if the state is not governing as it should and that is what is pushing people into violence, why should we, the soldiers, pay the price for that? That is the state's responsibility; not ours.'

And yet Naxal violence, like so many other aspects of terrorism in India, remains dangerously politicized and is not treated with the seriousness it deserves.

Playing politics with terror, no matter of what kind— home-grown, external or Maoist—is exceptionally dangerous.

Former RAW chief Vikram Sood warned, 'There is a lot of politics in the insurgency. But no state can afford to have this much politics in counter-insurgency.'

Four

IN THE NAME OF GOD

I

CHARRED AND BLOODIED beyond recognition, the body showed signs of a final struggle—mouth open and one hand outstretched in an unanswered plea for help or maybe mercy. The head lolled sideways on the tarred road and the legs were brutally parted. For the man or men who had done this, murder was not enough. Rape was the preamble to the final murderous assault.

The truth, in this instance, was too graphic to be telecast. But on that March evening in 2002, we kept the camera rolling for the sake of documenting the horror; at the time we weren't aware that sexual violence would become the near invisible leitmotif of the Gujarat riots.

Before the small milk van in which the woman was travelling was overturned and set alight, it had been carrying a group of forty villagers trying to escape a rampaging mob. We rushed to the spot when we got news of the massacre but we were too late. There was no one there but the woman, whose name we would never know, lying on the road. By the side of her body the aluminium handles of overturned milk cans gleamed through the orange of the flames that were consuming the van.

Later, at the local police station, we would meet someone else who had been in that vehicle. She had managed to escape. Only just. Sultani was a waif-like young woman of eighteen, her voice a whisper, her eyes drained of all emotion, her head draped in a thin muslin dupatta that she clung tightly to, as if it were her only remaining shield of protection. When the armed mob descended upon the van, pushing it over and setting it on fire, its occupants had clambered out and run in every direction, many of them towards the nearby river. Sultani fell behind with her three-year-old son Faizan. The rioters tore her clothes off and one by one they raped her. What she remembered vividly was the sound of her baby crying, unable to comprehend the specifics, but instinctively aware that something terrible was being done to his mother. Sultani fell unconscious and her rapists took her for dead. It was the only reason she was still alive.

Two months later, when I met her for the first time, she had decided to try and file a criminal complaint against the rapists. I watched aghast as this traumatized young woman was made to recount her story to a group of constables—all of them male. Even the presence of a television camera made no difference to the pot-bellied men as they gawked and sniggered at her. The police argued that they had already received multiple complaints about the 'tempo incident' and to register a separate FIR for rape would not be possible. 'After all, if a shopping centre is burnt down,' offered the deputy inspector, smiling contemptuously, 'we won't take down hundreds of different FIRs from individual shopowners. The incident is one; the mob is one. Only a single FIR needs to be filed.' Across the state, this method of clubbing cases together would effectively render rape almost invisible. And this, despite the fact that numerous women who had been brutally violated, who had lost everything—their homes, their families—were bravely coming forward to tell their stories.

Before she made it to a relief camp, one woman walked 300 kilometres over twenty-four days, her two children with her, sometimes hiding in the fields, at other moments pretending to support the marauders by chanting 'Jai Bajrang Dal' to get safe passage past them. Another wrestled with a mother's dilemma: her twelve-year-old son was the only witness to the rape and murder of his elder sister. She wasn't willing to put him through the trauma of testifying. When we met Ayub Pathan and his mother Hasina she told us that her child had slipped into an abyss of silence from which she could not pull him out. He had barely spoken in weeks; not since the day he had had to recount the horror of what he had seen when hiding from the rioters, along with his four cousins, all younger than him. When the mob came for his family, the kids ducked for cover behind tall grass from where they saw Ayub's sister, Afsana, and ten other family members being shoved around and then stripped to their skin before being sexually assaulted and pushed into the village canal, one by one. Hasina had made ten failed attempts to register an official case with the police. The cops demanded an eye-witness account—in this case that could only come from her traumatized, pre-adolescent child—and that was something she just could not do. This was the moral quandary for aid workers and activists—in many instances children were the only living witnesses who could testify to the truth.

Eventually, the cases of some of the brutalized women—like Bilkis Bano—would go on to make national headlines. When I first met her at a relief camp in Godhra, Bilkis sat on a thin plastic sheet under a flickering gaslight, swathed in black, her broken arm in a cast. That evening she was unable and unwilling to put words to the nightmare that still haunted her. Not once did Bilkis cry as her friend told us what she had been through. First, her forty-year-old mother was raped; then the men lunged for her two sisters, followed by her sister-in-law. Finally, it was her turn. She was gang-raped by three men she recognized from her village. That she was three months pregnant made no difference to them as they flung her down, ripped her clothes off and took turns assaulting her, bruising her back, breaking her arm, leaving her praying for the relative mercy of death; praying for anything but this. But the worst was not over. Her three-year-old daughter, Saleha, was killed by the mob as Bilkis lay battered and bleeding.

Later, she and her husband, Yaqub, would ask for their case to be shifted outside Gujarat in order to secure a successful conviction against the culprits, but not before fighting threats and intimidation to withdraw the complaint or accept that they would never be allowed back in their village. They would find a way to tell their daughters why they spent so much time in the courts and why they were on the news every evening. They would name their newborn after their firstborn who was murdered in 2002.

∎

Rape survivors are often stigmatized and shamed by a cultural mindset that seeks to transfer blame from perpetrators to victims. But when sexual abuse becomes a tool of mob violence, it is a different matter altogether. These women were not embarrassed; they did not seek silhouettes and shadows to crouch behind; they wanted no false names or hidden identities. But, in the toxic, highly charged post-riot environment, their accounts were subsumed by the larger volatility of national politics.

On the floor of Parliament, the NDA Defence Minister George Fernandes fell back on the past to rationalize the present, 'Yeh jo sara rona roya ja raha hai, ek ek kahani bata kar, jaise yeh kahani pehli baar desh mein ho rahi hai. Ki kahan ma ko maar kar pet se bacche ko nikala, kahan ma ke saamne uski beti ke saath balatkar hua, kisko aag mein jalaya gaya. Kya yeh sab pehli baar ho raha hai? Kya 1984 mein Dilli ki sadkon par aisa nahin hua tha (Why are people building a narrative of sob stories as if this is happening for the first time? Is this the first time that a pregnant woman has been killed; her foetus ripped out? Is this the first time that a daughter has been raped in front of her mother? Is this not what happened on the streets of Delhi in 1984)?'

In that year began the tragic bookending of the Indian debate on secularism with two unspeakable pogroms. From that time onwards the 1984 riots in Delhi that took place on Rajiv Gandhi's watch and the 2002 Gujarat riots that took place on Narendra Modi's watch would be used to checkmate one another in what might be called the chessboard of competitive communalism. And secularism, the foundation of the republic, fashioned out of our astonishingly diverse society, would find itself challenged again.

II

I was thirteen the year Prime Minister Indira Gandhi was assassinated by two of her Sikh bodyguards as she stepped out on the gravel pathway of her garden, her firm, brisk stride abruptly halted by the thirty-one bullets aimed point-blank at her abdomen. Only one missed its mark; twenty-three went right through her, seven were trapped inside her body. When we were sent home early from school we didn't quite understand what had happened. No one said much in the school bus. Although a holiday had been declared that day—31 October 1984—none of us celebrated. We were frightened. The roads were deserted, Delhi was absolutely silent—yet, we could subconsciously feel the gathering of the violent forces that would soon rip through it.

When we reached home and settled down in front of the television, the public broadcaster was still not ready to tell the country that Indira was dead. All India Radio was playing film songs. But the word was out on the street. BBC Radio was the first to begin reporting that Indira Gandhi had been killed. Restive crowds gathered outside the All India Institute of Medical Sciences. As the motorcade of President Giani Zail Singh arrived at the hospital, stones were hurled at the Sikh Congressman who had famously outdone fellow sycophants by offering to sweep Indira's doorstep, if 'Madam asks'. That was the first hint that no one was going to be spared. 'Khoon ka badla khoon se lenge (There will be blood for blood)', the crowd outside the hospital roared, their call to arms building up to a crescendo, as they declared vengeance on thousands of innocent people who had nothing to do with the death of the prime minister.

At home, doors were being latched; we were told to stay put and not venture out. Our parents and neighbours spoke in worried, hushed tones, as they phoned relatives and friends. My mother's sister was married to a Sikh; as a child I would tie my long hair up into a knot on my head to play the part of a 'sardar' to look more like my cousins. My father's closest friend was Sikh. 1984 scarred us all.

In my neighbourhood—originally a refugee colony created for post-Partition migrants from Pakistan—there was a very high concentration of Sikh families, many of them shopkeepers, automechanics or local electricians. News was trickling in from the local bazaar that shops belonging to Sikhs were being set on fire and razed to the ground. They were lucky, given what was happening elsewhere in the city. Men wearing turbans had become targets for homicidal rioters. Gurudwaras where people had sought protection were surrounded by men armed with giant kerosene cans. In buses and on trains, Sikhs were dragged out by their hair and burnt alive in front of helpless, and sometimes complicit, spectators. Entire colonies were widowed. In less than four days, almost 3,000 people were killed.

The rioters were in control of the capital. Eyewitnesses would later testify that the hunting packs were exhorted to kill by assorted Congress politicians who would go on to become ministers and chief ministers in the ruling establishment. Rajiv Gandhi, who had become prime minister after his mother's death, inducted party colleagues like H. K. L. Bhagat and Jagdish Tytler into his Cabinet despite credible allegations against them. The national elections that had followed two months after the carnage became the perfect setting for majoritarian muscle flexing in the capital. H. K. L. Bhagat, often called the 'Old Fox' of Delhi politics and identified by witnesses as one of the Congressmen who incited the mobs, won with the highest margin in east Delhi. This was the area which had seen the largest number of killings in the capital.

Police officer Ved Marwah, a former Delhi police commissioner who was appointed to conduct the first enquiry into the 1984 pogrom, argued that in most places the mob was made up of no more than twenty to thirty individuals who could easily have been contained had the military been alerted or had the cops just done their job. But he found case diaries in police stations left blank. Officers had clearly refused to even register cases, leave alone pursue them. Marwah discovered that the police had simply abandoned vulnerable areas in the city, giving the rampaging mobs untrammelled freedom to kill. Later, when he tried to conduct an enquiry into the role of police officers who had displayed such a gross dereliction of duty, they took him to court.

It is now well known that despite the existence of a large military cantonment within the capital, the military was not deployed during the crucial forty-eight hours after Indira Gandhi was assassinated. Former Prime Minister I. K. Gujral asked Delhi's Lieutenant Governor P. G. Gavai to send in troops but found no takers for his suggestion. Celebrated Sikh writer Khushwant Singh said he felt like a 'Jew must have in Nazi Germany'. When he tried to reach the country's Sikh president, Giani Zail Singh, he was advised to move into a friend's home till the trouble passed. Not everyone had that option. Cartloads of petrol cans were ferried across the breadth of Delhi, seventy-two gurudwaras were incinerated as policemen stood by idly, not even bothering to use the lathis they wielded. Deposing before the Nanavati Commission, one of the multiple enquiry committees subsequently set up to investigate the riots, Major General J. S. Jamwal (the commanding officer of the Delhi area in 1984) said his men were standing by 'in readiness' but the executive orders to move in didn't come till two days later, by which time seventy-two critical hours had elapsed.

For the next three decades, the victims of 1984 would be knocked around from court to court, their tragedy lost in a maze of criminal cover-ups and judicial delays. In 2013, the government informed the Lok Sabha that 442 of the 3,163 persons arrested had been convicted; there wasn't a single politician among them. Even the charge sheet prepared by the police on 8 April 1992, implicating Congress leader Sajjan Kumar in a murder case—he was repeatedly named by witnesses and victims—was not placed before the court for two long decades. By 2013, Kumar was acquitted on what H. S. Phoolka, a crusading lawyer for the victims, would call 'fudged records and the protection of the Delhi police'. Phoolka charged that the police officer who kept the charge sheet locked away in a dusty file never to see the light of day had been rewarded with a promotion.

On 12 August 2005, twenty years after the riots, the then Prime Minister Manmohan Singh offered his regrets. 'I have no hesitation in apologizing to the Sikh community. I apologize not only to the Sikh community, but to the whole Indian nation because what took place in 1984 is the negation of the concept of nationhood enshrined in our Constitution.'

Justice, however, was another matter.

■

In the age before private television came into being, Doordarshan, the public broadcaster, censored and controlled by the government, was the only network in India. And so, 1984 was the pogrom that was not on television. This aspect differentiated it in a critical way from the aftermath of 2002 when a still-young television industry made it impossible for murderous men to hide from the omnipresence of the camera. In many other ways, though, the two pogroms were eerily similar. Both were methodical in their madness while masquerading as 'spontaneous' expressions of violence. So precise and targeted were the outrages committed by the rioters that when bazaars were burnt, every shop that did not belong to the community under attack—Sikhs in 1984, Muslims in 2002—was left unscathed. Both set out to punish people entirely unconnected to the original sins of the perpetrators—the assassins of Indira Gandhi in 1984 or those who torched the Sabarmati Express in 2002. In both, the mobs which murdered went about their business without fear of the law because of the political patronage they seemed to enjoy. Worst of all, thousands of lives could have been saved both in 1984 and eighteen years later, in 2002, had the governments in power acted swiftly to contain the riots by directing the police to do their job or by calling in the army without delay.

III

Nearly two decades after 1984, Gujarat's moments of shame and murder lasted about the same amount of time as the pogrom that had preceded it—seventy-two hours. What apologists described as a spontaneous upsurge of violence in response to the carnage on the train was in fact the consequence of a lethal combination of acts of omission and commission. Within hours of the incineration of four coaches of the Sabarmati Express at Godhra on 27 February 2002, in which fifty-nine people died, prominent local functionaries of the Vishva Hindu Parishad (VHP) and the Bajrang Dal—both affiliates of the loosely organized right-wing Hindu Sangh Parivar—began mobilizing their cadres and exhorting them to take 'revenge'. The protagonists and patrons were different but the slogan was exactly the same as in 1984—'khoon ka badla khoon'. History was condemned to repeat itself, not as farce, but as tragedy.

Most of those dead on the train were kar sevaks returning from Ayodhya, where the BJP had long campaigned for a 'Ram Janmabhoomi' mandir. The president of the Sadhu Samaj, Gopal Nand, called upon Hindus to unite in retaliation and demanded to know why twelve hours had passed without 'action' against the burning of the train. Busloads of loyalists began moving into nearby districts to spread the word. By the night of 27 February, the attacks on innocent Muslims—bystanders at a railway station, shopkeepers, villagers on the run—had begun. Just after midnight, there was in fact specific intelligence warning of possible riots as the bodies of those who had died on board the train at Godhra were being brought into Ahmedabad, escorted by Jaideep Patel, the state unit president of the VHP. Its office-bearers went ahead and announced a state-wide bandh, one that provided them greater cover for the free movement of both arms and men. But there were still no preventive detentions or crackdowns, there wasn't even a curfew ordered till the next afternoon, even though a mob of 3,000 had gathered outside Sola Hospital to which the bodies had been brought in a macabre funeral procession.

Across the state, it was the same story. The police either refused to get involved or in some cases sought reinforcements of troops that were dispatched far too late to quell the rampage. In the hours after the horrific attack on the Sabarmati Express, the police control room in Ahmedabad was overrun with wireless messages warning of communal mobilization and asking for more men on the ground. All day and night on the 27th, as the bodies of the murdered kar sevaks were brought back to Ahmedabad—a decision that arguably contributed to the conflagration—state intelligence officers kept alerting the administration to the perils of what could follow. No specific early action was taken on their inputs. Did the Gujarat pogrom (in which almost 1,000 people, mostly Muslims, were killed) take place because of the abdication of responsibility, misjudgement, incompetence, or other acts of omission or commission?

The city's police commissioner P. C. Pande, would later defend the delay in placing legal restrictions on people gathering together by arguing that 'circumstances did not exist to warrant the imposition of curfew... And any hasty decision would have led to panic in the city'. 'Panic' does not even begin to describe what happened as a result of that specious theory. Vigilantes flooded the cities and villages drowning all reason or compassion in a deluge of hatred.

∎

When we began the ninety-kilometre journey on the highway that
connected Vadodara to Godhra—where it all began—we were the
only car for miles on end. The otherwise humming four-lane freeway
that ran all the way to Indore and Delhi was lifeless. Tragic signposts
marked the trail of mob violence—an open packet of salt, a broken
bottle of ketchup, an overturned cart, shards of glass, a burnt-down
shed. The men and women whose sources of livelihood had been
plundered were missing. They had either fled to safety or had been
killed.

Up ahead in the distance, clouds of soot hung in the clear sky.
A factory had been set ablaze. A few kilometres from the fire, a
couple of policemen leaned lazily against the single barricade on the
road, unapologetic about their determined lack of intervention. This
was the industrial township of Halol, a major hub of manufacturing
companies. As we made our way through the ashes and debris of
wood and metal, we found that factory after factory owned by
Muslims had been systematically attacked by the arsonists. At a
scrap-metal centre, we missed the mob by a few minutes. Distraught
workers told us that a band of about a hundred men had descended
on the factory because four of those who had died on the train at
Godhra had lived in the neighbouring area. The police had not
responded to calls for help in the past forty-eight hours. The villagers
would stay up at night, forming a small circle of protection around
their families—but preparing for the worst.

Many of the aggressors had no personal connection to the
tragedy at Godhra. But the politics of hate touched them all—
perpetrator and victim. The violence was simultaneously senseless
and perfectly controlled. It never got its targets mixed up.

At a car-manufacturing unit in Halol we walked straight into a
bunch of looters who started to run as soon as they saw our cameras,
but then began to enjoy the attention as we pursued them to enquire
whether they had started the fire. 'Kaun baat karega, madam, kaun
baat karega (Who is going to talk to you)?' they said tauntingly,
daring me to follow them as they hastily left the scene of the crime.
The complete absence of the police—the army was not called out
until three days after the violence had broken out—had created an

anarchic free-for-all. Thugs were able to saunter in and steal from the burning factories whatever the rioters had not already destroyed. Such was the sense of impunity the rioters enjoyed that a group of young men on motorcycles led us from one scene of destruction to the next without being the least bit afraid or apologetic.

As we got closer to Godhra the air was thick with tension. The roads were no longer deserted; every 200 metres, small bands of men waved down cars and passers-by, hammering on the windows and windshields of vehicles with their long wooden lathis, forcing them to come to an abrupt halt. What you said next would determine whether it was to be a moment of redemption or retribution. The 'open sesame' answer to get past the blockade was to make sure you weren't from the 'wrong' religion. 'Hindu ho kya? Jaane do, jaane do Hindu hain yeh,' said one man forcing his head halfway into the car and staring at each one of us in turn as if he were endowed with superhuman powers to detect the presence of 'unacceptable' faiths. In that moment, I took a deep breath, tried to keep my voice steady and not betray the burst of revulsion and panic I felt welling up inside me. In other circumstances, my answer to the question—What's your religion?—would have been, 'I am agnostic and multicultural, but areligious'. At this time, to make it past the mob unscathed, there was only one good answer.

Next to me, my cameraman, Ajmal Jami, sat absolutely still, a quiet matter-of-factness masking all his other emotions. We had just lied about his religious identity to the thugs who had stopped us. I wanted to apologize to him, but right now safety was our only imperative.

We were waved past the first barrier, suspicious eyes still following our car. Not everyone made it through. On one side of the fortification were scores of trucks that hadn't been able to move ahead for the last two days. Most of the drivers were Muslim, and many of them had tried to disguise any obvious giveaways of their faith. One of them was sporting a long tilak on his forehead.

As we drove onwards we saw the first police van we had seen in eight hours. The angry crowd surrounded it and for a moment it seemed as if they would pounce on the van and demolish it with the weapons they carried. We accosted the police officer as he negotiated with the men to allow his vehicle right of way. 'Aren't you going to help all the people trapped on the highway because of the violent crowds?' I asked him. 'See, it is very problematic, but it's their problem. What can I do?' he mumbled, eager to get away from my camera. 'Are you saying the police are helpless to do anything about this situation?' I persisted. 'See, I am helpless because I have been sent for other duties. This is not my lookout.'

On the highway, as we approached the last town short of Godhra, blazes began to mark the journey with the consistency of milestones. Swarming crowds brought our car to a halt every few hundred metres, the sticks and stones now replaced by swords and petrol bombs. News was coming in of thirteen residents having been burnt alive. Just ahead, the field was strewn with bodies, torched beyond recognition. We stared quietly at the bottles filled with inflammable liquid in the hands of the mob milling around us, their rag wicks just waiting to be lit, wondering if it were possible to move any further. The responses of the men were brazen when I asked who had given them the petrol bombs. 'We have made them for our safety,' said one, trying to stare me down. Sensing trouble, local reporters bundled us into their car and we made a run for it. At the wheel was a Hindu right-wing sympathizer who at first thought his connections on the street would get us through the chaos. But after a couple of kilometres he said it was advisable to turn back—he could provide no guarantee for our safety.

It was my first experience—as a journalist and as an adult—of religious conflict. Since this was also India's first 'television riot', and given the sensitivities involved, the rules were not immediately clear. For instance, according to an archaic press council advisory, naming religious groups during a conflagration of the kind we were witness to was to be avoided. But to omit mentioning the community under siege—whether in this instance or the many riots that had come before—would have been sanitizing the truth.

To broadcast details as the camera caught them had its own perils. Footage was often up-linked live back to headquarters in Delhi; when it aired there were consequences we could not always anticipate. At a burning factory on the highway, a page of the Quran lay crushed under overturned furniture; as the wood caught fire, the flames spread across the white and black calligraphy on the page turning it to ash. The visual was no longer than a few seconds in a long loop of destruction caught on tape. Yet, it had only to be telecast once for the potentially disastrous impact it could have on an already tense environment to strike us. As violence spread from district to district, we felt as duty bound to prevent the situation from worsening as we were to chronicle it. It was pressure of the kind I hadn't experienced before. Every sentence, every interview, every camera angle had a possible fallout.

Rumour was the 'weapon of mass destruction'. An unverified article in a local newspaper claimed that some Hindu women had been kidnapped from the Sabarmati Express at Godhra. A day later the same paper reported that the bodies of two of these women had been recovered with their breasts cut off. The police categorically denied the incident—both the abduction and the savagery—but by now, the falseness of the report notwithstanding, the dishonoring of Hindu women had become an immovable truth in the public imagination. The specifics of the rumour varied, but as it spread from village to village, the story became the stuff of folklore and an emotional rallying point for macabre retaliation. Eyewitnesses in Ahmedabad's Naroda Patiya neighbourhood, among the worst hit during the riots, later testified that when the mobs came they were brandishing not just bricks and swords but also copies of the newspaper with the incendiary banner headline. Two days later, the same paper published a retraction. But it was much too late. The state was engulfed in an inferno of violence.

In March 2010, the then Gujarat Chief Minister Narendra Modi was interrogated for over nine hours in two separate sessions by the Supreme Court monitored Special Investigative Team (SIT). He was being questioned after a complaint filed by Zakia Jafri, widow of former Congress MP Ehsan Jafri, who had been killed in the riots. She alleged that the chief minister was also answerable for the violence. Zakia said her husband made repeated phone calls for help, including one to the chief minister's office—Modi denied receiving any such call. In his final moments, Ehsan told his friends and family, 'No help will come.' As Zakia looked on in speechless horror, her husband was dragged out of the house, stripped and paraded naked. Witnesses would later say his limbs were chopped off before he was burnt alive. His body was never recovered.

Sixty-nine people were killed in Ahmedabad's Gulbarg Society, where the Jafris lived. In the same housing society, a young Parsi boy of thirteen, Azhar Mody, got separated from his parents, Rupa and Dara. Rupa's last memory of her son is him holding on to her hand before she passed out from the smoke of many fires. For years she hoped he might still be alive. 'My son loved trains, maybe he hopped on to one', she would tell journalists. Azhar's story would inspire the Bollywood film *Parzania*—the film was banned in Gujarat.

Eventually, the final report filed by the SIT, which was headed by former CBI director R. K. Raghavan, exonerated Modi. In fact, it suggested that Jafri may have provoked the rioters. 'It may be clarified here that in case late Ehsan Jafri fired at the mob, this could be an immediate provocation to the mob, which had assembled there to take revenge of Godhra incidents from Muslims,' the report said. It also asserted that Modi never invoked the Newtonian principle of 'action and reaction' to justify the Godhra violence and the pogrom that it sparked off. Instead, the report concluded that the chief minister's comments were in specific reference to Jafri. 'In his interview the CM has clearly referred to Jafri's firing as "action" and the massacre as "reaction",' it said.

There was no legal case against Modi in any of the riot cases and now the clean chit given to him by Raghavan's SIT was the ultimate vindication of his innocence for his supporters. Many BJP leaders would repeatedly point out that Modi had been chief minister for only four to five months before the violence erupted; the real power, they argued, was wielded at that time by Praveen Togadia, the rabble rousing extremist of the VHP. Subsequently, as Modi consolidated his political hold over Gujarat, Togadia—who had been one of his biggest challengers—would become marginalized.

In 2012, a court convicted Maya Kodnani, a BJP legislator, who served as Gujarat's Minister for Women and Child Development between 2007-2009, to twenty-eight years in prison for her role in inciting riots in the neighbourhood of Naroda Patiya—a massacre in which ninety-five Muslims were killed. It also found thirty-one other people guilty, including Babu Bajrangi, a leader of the Bajrang Dal.

Just like Rajiv Gandhi had with Tytler and Bhagat in the elections that followed 1984, Modi allowed Kodnani to contest the elections of 2002 from the same constituency in which she was later found responsible for mass murder.

By the time Modi was ready to run for PM, the riots had ceased to be an electoral issue. In fact, the Opposition too rarely brought it up. If a journalist asked Modi why he had not considered apologizing for the killings that took place under his administration, the chief minister's eyes would harden into a cold, withering gaze. 'Hang me if I am guilty, what purpose does an apology serve,' he told journalist Shahid Siddiqui in 2012, 'but if I am not the culprit the media and others should apologize.'

IV

The national media, in particular the English language press, became an object of enduring hatred in Gujarat during, and well after, the riots. In the minds of the average Gujarati, it was we, the journalists, who were seen as 'anti-Hindu' and 'anti-Gujarati'.

Much before Narendra Modi was embraced at the national level by the urban middle class and the who's who of the business community as a tough, no-nonsense, super-efficient, pro-growth administrator, at the state level he was shrewd enough to tap into the widespread ire at Gujarat's reputation being sullied by biased 'outsiders'. He emerged as the assertive guardian of Gujarati 'asmita' (pride), routinely invoking the injured self-respect of 'five crore Gujaratis' in a narrative that conflated the media's criticism of arsonists and killers with the entire state and its people being viewed in a negative way.

That Modi was a masterful politician first became evident in the state election campaign that took place just a few months after the 2002 riots. Playing into the primordial impulses of pride and resentment, he blurred the battlelines by smartly constructing an artificial enemy—the army of hypocritical 'secularists'—who were being held back at the gates of Gujarat by one man—himself.

For Modi, the 'Hindu Hriday Samrat' (Emperor of Hindu Hearts)—a prefix first used for the Shiv Sena's Bal Thackeray—secularism was in fact the chink in the opponent's armour. On the battlefield, the tactician in him took aim at this weak spot, jeering, mocking and assaulting it when needed. Not since the veteran BJP politican L. K. Advani had coined the phrase 'pseudo-secularism' in the eighties and nineties to challenge the conventional construct of secularism would one man so successfully overturn the entire debate around it.

If Advani fused caste restiveness with revivalist politics to make the Ayodhya temple movement a symbol of resurgent Hindu pride, exactly ten years later, in post-liberalization India, Narendra Modi welded economic aspirations and technology to narrowly-defined cultural-rootedness and muscular self-confidence to unleash a new assault on traditional secularism—which in the realm of politics was largely associated with the Congress party.

Even Atal Bihari Vajpayee's suggestion that Modi at least offer to resign—which he made at the BJP conclave in Goa held barely a month after the 2002 riots—made no difference to the latter's political ascent. He went from victory to victory, taunting opponents and critics who attacked him with cutting asides about the secularism stick they had used to beat him with.

My sense of Modi then was that he loved going to battle. In a deft 'othering' of all those who had been disparaging of him, the Gujarat chief minister did not just sneer at the criticism that came his way, he actually appeared to relish the polarizing impact he had on public opinion.

This was well before he would rebrand himself for the prime ministerial campaign. In 2002, and for several years after that, Modi intuitively understood that what made him unpalatable to his opponents consolidated the following of his supporters. For Modi, it was both pleasurable and useful to have an 'enemy'.

In July 2002, just four months after the riots, his penchant for getting into combative confrontation combined with a sharp electoral instinct made him dissolve the assembly and call for early polls a good eight months ahead of schedule. In that charged political environment he knew that the majority of Gujaratis felt they had been defamed by hostile outsiders. They certainly didn't see him as the villain, they saw him as their saviour.

The Election Commission, headed by the soft-spoken but steely James Lyngdoh, declined to give its go-ahead. Lyngdoh was worried about both law and order in a fragile post-riot environment and also the need to rehabilitate riot victims who had been displaced from their homes and were living in relief camps. The Election Commission was to oversee an especially delicate election in Jammu and Kashmir later that year and was already overstretched with anxiety.

Narendra Modi asked his friend, the lawyer turned politician Arun Jaitley, to build his case before the Election Commission. Surprisingly, because Jaitley could usually charm his most fervent antagonists into seeing his point of view, the meeting went terribly. He first argued on a point of law and then quoted super-cop K. P. S. Gill, adviser to the Modi government, as a supporter of the cause of early elections. Lyngdoh snapped that Gill was not relevant to the discussion. The exchange took a controversial twist when Lyngdoh declared that his decision was complicated by the fact that Modi's was a 'discredited government'. An apoplectic Jaitley got up in anger and stormed out of the meeting, but not before telling Lyngdoh that his language was biased and blatantly political.

Modi could not have been especially worried. In Lyngdoh's resistance, he had found yet another illustration of the secular conspiracy—it was ammunition for his campaign. The elections were to finally take place in December, but itching for an I-told-you-so moment, Modi took out a Gaurav Yatra (Procession of Pride) across the state which rolled out from the Bhathiji Maharaj Temple in the state's Kheda district.

In 2013, when he was readying for his national debut as a candidate for the post of prime minister, Modi, in an unobjectionable and welcome statement, said that his definition of secularism was 'India first'. He would reinforce these sentiments later in Parliament by saying that the only holy book for his government was the Constitution, the only prayer, welfare for all.

But in 2002, in those four weeks of his Gaurav Yatra, Modi's idiom of political assertion was rather different. In his speeches, Lyngdoh was now referred to as 'James Michael', a loaded reference to the chief election commissioner's Christian faith. At Bodeli, near Vadodra, he fell back on the inflammatory messaging that got the crowds all excited: 'Some journalists asked me whether Lyngdoh has come from Italy. I said I don't have his janam patri, we will have to ask Rajiv Gandhi. Then they asked, "Do they [Lyngdoh and Sonia Gandhi] meet in church?" I said maybe they do.' As the standoff between the two threatened to spiral out of control, it was Prime Minister Vajpayee who had to finally jump in with a terse statement asking that both 'high constitutional authorities'—the chief election commissioner and the Gujarat chief minister—must be given equal respect.

At another public rally, he mocked Sonia Gandhi's foreign origins but also poured scorn on Hindus embarrassed to embrace the symbols of their own faith. He jeered, 'I ask my Congress brothers if it is wrong to say "Jai Shri Ram" in this country. If you don't say it here, will we have to go to Italy to say it?'

Though Modi was basically attempting to position himself as a culturally proud Hindu who was a staunch nationalist instead of a religious chauvinist, his speeches in those four weeks—especially coming against the backdrop of the riots—would subtly arrange Pakistan, Muslims, 'psuedo-secularists', the Congress, and the media, all in one sentence. Across the border, Pervez Musharraf's criticism of the Gujarat killings only strengthened Modi's argument that the negative commentary on the riots by the media and a host of others was a perfidious assault on the self-worth of his people. Presenting the elections as a choice between supporting Pakistan and being nationalist he repeatedly referred to the Pakistani President as 'Mian Musharraf', warning him that five crore Gujaratis would not hesitate to chop off the hand that pointed a dirty, defamatory finger at them. The choice, for the voter, was effectively offered as one between Modi and Musharraf and nationalism and treachery. Once these battle lines were drawn, secularists were the adversaries whose language echoed that of India's opponents. 'The songs which Sonia Gandhi and some

English TV channels were singing about Gujarat have obviously been heard across the border,' Modi would roar at election meeting after election meeting. The crowds would cheer him on, and chant in unison, 'Dekho dekho kaun aaya, Gujarat ka sher aaya (Look who is here, it's the lion of Gujarat).' In the Gujarat of 2002, secularism was not just disparaged as the preoccupation of the urban elite, it was also being portrayed as anti-national. And journalists, especially the ones who came from Delhi, were the main culprits.

A few months later, when the election results pronounced an emphatic victory for Modi, a group of men belonging to the VHP turned on the journalists standing on the road outside the party headquarters. My colleague Deepak Chaurasia, then with the TV channel Aaj Tak, and I were pushed around and slapped. BJP workers finally pulled us free of the mob, rushed us inside to the safety of party headquarters and helped us climb down a drainpipe running along the exterior of the building and into the refuge of a back alley—such was the intensity of hatred among the extremists for journalists who had reported on the riots.

The more he was criticized, especially outside Gujarat, the more Modi's popularity grew. At his rallies, thousands of his supporters enthusiastically wore plastic masks crafted in his image. The patriarchs of the party, Advani and Vajpayee, were swiftly overshadowed. For his followers there was now only one leader. From Hindutva, the Gujarat chief minister's politics evolved into Moditva, with the man becoming indistinguishable from the message.

Ironically, as the years went by and Narendra Modi won three successive elections in his home state, it was often the hardliners within the wider Sangh Parivar whom he antagonized. And then, as his ambitions for national power crystallized, he began to craft a new, fiercely individualistic brand of politics that welded administrative efficiency with a testosterone-rich toughness of style. Appearing to shed the dead skin of Hindutva politics, he began to focus almost exclusively on growth rates, infrastructure and industrialization. On national security, though, Modi remained as absolutist as before. For his supporters, here was a decisive leader who was also a modern, neo-right challenger to the historical dominance of left-liberalism

in the political discourse. To his critics he remained intolerant of
dissent and a purveyor of fundamentalist politics.

V

Today, when the dominant feature of our political discourse is
religion, it is useful to remember that many of the ideas that are
being contested today first originated in the minds of thinkers
who were neither Hindu, Muslim, nor even Indian. Writes the
great Indian historian Romila Thapar in her latest book, *The Public
Intellectual in India*: 'The colonial focus on religion as the pillar of
Indian identity to the near exclusion of other identities, and the later
endorsing of this notion by extremist religious politics, has led to our
unquestioning acceptance of the colonial construction of who and
what we are.' She goes on to explain that many of the theories that
are used today 'to explain and justify our definitions of identity...
were initially fashioned by colonial writers to suit colonial policy and
were the colonial brainchild of the nineteenth century.' She points
out that the two-nation theory, for example, with its 'insistence on
the innate hostility between Hindus and Muslims' was the work of
James Mill, just as it was Colonel H. S. Olcott of the Theosophists
who first propagated the theory that 'Aryans were indigenous to
India and took civilization from India to the West', a theory that is
now being used by Hindutva supporters, 'but with no reference to
the colonial view where its origins lie.' Many of the sectarian and
divisive ideas of the colonialists were seized upon by Hindu and
Muslim ideologues and politicians to opportunistically pursue their
own goals. But fortunately for our country and its ambition to be
a plural, inclusive society at the time of Independence, one of the
fundamental ideas on which the modern Indian state was founded
was of course secularism, an idea that is being fiercely contested
and redefined today.

Interestingly, the word 'secularism' was not part of the country's
Constitution until the Indira Gandhi-led government enacted the
42nd Amendment in 1977, changing the description of India in
the Preamble from a 'sovereign democratic republic' to a 'sovereign,
socialist secular democratic republic'. An examination of the

constituent assembly debates around the Preamble reveals an early ideological fault line among the men and women who were the architects of the republic. Their feisty, sometimes acrimonious debates reflect an unresolved argument that has persisted in modern times. How does a state establish itself as a reliably secular entity in a multi-religious society? By subsuming religious identity as part of a larger national identity and by placing an equal distance between the state and all religions or by admitting that such a distance was impossible in a republic like India and pushing the state to respect all religions equally? As the founders of independent India argued over whether a reference to God should be included in the opening lines of the Constitution (H. V. Kamath's amendment was defeated 68-41) and whether the freedom of worship was the same as the freedom to practice, several of them argued in favour of a model that would be uniquely Indian. K. M. Munshi, for instance, underlined that Indian secularism would have to recognize 'a people with deeply religious moorings. At the same time we have a living tradition of religious tolerance...'

Mahatma Gandhi and Jawaharlal Nehru, the two most influential leaders of the time, were both fierce advocates of tolerance and pluralism. However, Nehru's approach was to leave religion entirely out of the political discourse, while Gandhi was comfortable using it as a tool of political mobilization. Unlike Nehru's essentially atheist humanism, Gandhi—both religious and reformist—pursued the ideal of a syncretic society that borrowed from all faiths. 'I swear by my religion. I will die for it. But it is my personal affair. The state has nothing to do with it. The state would look after your secular welfare but not your or my religion,' said the Mahatma who famously dismissed Jinnah's two-nation theory as an 'untruth... Hindus and Muslims of India are not two nations.'

■

It is indisputable that the campaign by the Hindu right wing to build a temple to Ram in Ayodhya on the site on which a sixteenth-century mosque called the Babri Masjid stood was the single most successful element in the BJP's first bid for electoral power. Ayodhya has been at the centre of a political and religious dispute for decades. The Babri Masjid was a mosque built in 1528 by a Mughal general called Mir Baqi. Hindu groups have argued that the site is the birthplace of Lord Ram and that before the mosque, there was a temple there. In September 2010, sixty years after the dispute went to court, the Allahabad High Court, in an 8,500-page verdict, said the land should be divided between Hindus and Muslims with two of the three-member bench recognizing the site as the birthplace of Ram 'as per faith and belief of the Hindus'. In May 2011, the Supreme Court said the High Court judgement was based on a 'fundamental error' and put a stay order on the judgement, taking the dispute back to square one. The facts are well known but bear brief recapitulation.

In the nineteenth century, following communal unrest, the British authorities designated a separate area near the mosque for the Hindus to conduct religious ceremonies. Soon after Independence, in 1949, an idol of Ram was smuggled into the mosque; following Muslim protests the Babri Masjid was then locked up. The dispute over the mosque simmered on until the 1980s, when the VHP began an agitation, backed by the BJP, to build a Ram temple in Ayodhya. L. K. Advani, the BJP leader with prime ministerial ambitions (he got as far as deputy prime minister in Atal Bihari Vajpayee's 2002 NDA government) became the face of the movement in 1990 when he launched a rath yatra to raise support for the construction of the temple. The Babri Masjid was eventually demolished on 6 December 1992, in the presence of Advani, Murli Manohar Joshi and a host of other senior BJP leaders.

The breaking of the mosque had terrible consequences, and it unleashed a swathe of destruction throughout the country. Over 2,000 people died in the riots that were directly sparked off by the demolition in December 1992 and January 1993—in Mumbai, Ahmedabad, Kanpur and elsewhere. Then came the 1993 serial blasts in Mumbai which killed hundreds more. The Liberhan Commission, which investigated the razing of the Babri Masjid and called it 'one of the most abhorrent acts in the history of India', held Advani and Joshi, among others, as being responsible for the demolition.

But the Congress also played an insidious role in creating the circumstances that led to the demolition of the mosque. Though Rahul Gandhi once grandly claimed that the mosque would never have been brought down had a member of the Nehru-Gandhi family been at the helm of government, it was his father, Rajiv Gandhi, who on the request of the VHP first ordered the locks on the Ram Janmabhoomi–Babri Masjid complex to be opened in 1985. And in 1989, with one eye on the elections, it was Rajiv who sent his home minister, Buta Singh, to participate in the 'shilanyas', or the symbolic temple foundation laying ceremony, at a site near the Babri Masjid but outside of what he understood to be the disputed site. After his assassination in 1991 it became the responsibility of Narasimha Rao to safeguard the mosque from demolition. The Liberhan Report said Prime Minister Rao and his government were 'day-dreaming'; his own party colleagues and those who met him in the days leading up to 6 December say his inaction was deliberate. Veteran journalist Kuldip Nayar even went so far as to suggest in his memoirs that Rao 'sat at a puja when the kar sevaks began pulling down the mosque and rose only when the last stone had been removed'.

This impression that Rao didn't just display naiveté but that he was consciously indecisive is reinforced by journalist and politician Shahid Siddiqui. He had been in a meeting with Rao and Congress leaders where he had angrily urged them to do something about the situation. 'I was so angry with the inaction of Rao in preventing the demolition,' Siddiqui told me. Hours later, after the dome of the mosque had been destroyed, he and Rajesh Pilot proposed to the prime minister that another dome could be airlifted to the site and placed on whatever walls of the structure remained standing. 'We thought at least that we could be making a powerful symbolic statement that we intended to preserve the structure as a mosque.' Although Siddiqui and Pilot waited patiently for the helicopter which was supposed to fly in the dome, it never came. 'We were told it had developed a technical fault.'

■

On the back of its Ayodhya movement, the BJP—from being a party of little consequence (it won only two seats in the 1984 general elections, although its showing might have been somewhat better if Rajiv Gandhi hadn't been the beneficiary of a massive wave of sympathy following his mother's assassination)—became the third largest party in Parliament in the elections in 1989 (after the Congress and Janata Dal) winning eighty-five seats. It could be argued that Advani's Ayodhya campaign would not have delivered the electoral dividends that it did if some other factors had not been in play. The first, of course, was that the Ram temple movement became as successful as it did in the 1980s because of widespread dissatisfaction among the middle class, in particular those belonging to the upper castes after the announcement that the recommendations of the Mandal Commission would be implemented. Prime Minister V. P. Singh accepted the 27 per cent job quota in government institutions for Other Backward Classes (OBCs) in addition to the affirmative action that was already in place for the Dalits and Scheduled Tribes. Singh's actions triggered a widespread anti-reservation stir in many of India's cities. The BJP capitalized on the unrest by presenting itself as the party best placed to serve the interests of the Hindu middle class. Advani managed to successfully portray the Hindu middle class as the unfortunate victims of vote bank politics. From Mandal to Mandir was but a short step.

Advani's calculated move was aided by the cynical politics of the Congress after its electoral victory in 1984. For example, it is unlikely that his Ayodhya movement would have got the sort of traction it did had the Rajiv Gandhi government not reversed the Supreme Court judgement in the seminal Shah Bano case. In 1985, Shah Bano, a sixty-two-year-old destitute Muslim woman and mother of five, filed a case in the Supreme Court seeking maintenance from her ex-husband. The court, citing provisions of criminal law, ruled in her favour. The provisions were seen to be an interference with Muslim Personal Law by sections of the Muslim clergy. By 1986, the Congress, worried about an electoral backlash, used its majority in Parliament to overturn the ruling, leading to the resignation of Arif Mohammed Khan, a Muslim minister in the government who had passionately supported the verdict. In the next few years, the Congress would take a series of decisions that would discredit its claims to secularism.

By the summer of 1989, the BJP's national executive endorsed the demand for a mandir in Ayodhya and charged the Congress with 'callous unconcern' towards what it called 'majority sentiment' in the country. In October 1988, a decision by the Rajiv Gandhi government that would forever polarize the free speech debate made India the first country in the world to ban Salman Rushdie's *The Satanic Verses*. Author and political scientist Christophe Jaffrelot has pointed out that Rajiv's keenness to appease both Hindu and Muslim extremists was lethal. 'From the Shah Bano case to the opening up of the Masjid on VHP's request to launching his election campaign from Faizabad calling it Ram's land, he was playing Hindus against Muslims and vice-versa,' he said. It played right into the hands of the BJP.

From that point onwards, despite a few electoral reverses, the BJP continued its inexorable rise to absolute power at the centre, culminating with Modi's massive electoral victory in the 2014 general elections.

■

Even more damaging to the Congress's attempt to portray itself as secular is the fact that some of the worst communal conflagrations in India's history have taken place when the Congress has been in power. The Nellie massacre of 1983 where 5,000 people, mostly Muslims, were killed; the 1987 Hashimpura massacre in which 40 Muslims were killed in cold blood; the Bhagalpur riots of 1989 (in which the victims were predominantly Muslim); the Hyderabad riots of 1990 (where both the Hindu and Muslim communities suffered a large number of fatalities); and the Surat riots of 1992 (where again the victims were largely Muslim) all took place with Congress chief ministers in charge.

The absolute failure of Congress governments to uphold the principles of natural justice in all of these massacres has forever sullied the conversations around secularism in India. Most worryingly, it has made Indians cynical; is any party in our country genuinely secular? Or are the differences only of degree, circumstance and opportunity? When violence takes places in states governed by so-called 'secular parties'—take the most recent riots in Muzaffarnagar in 2013 (that resulted in the death of forty-six Muslims and sixteen Hindus) in which the socialist Samajwadi Party was seen to have played a key role—it permanently dents their credibility to then oppose Hindutva politics.

In March 2015, sixteen accused policemen were acquitted of their involvement in the Hashimpura massacre, making minorities even more cynical about the promises of justice from secular parties. The case dated back to 1987 when riots had erupted in Meerut. Men from UP's Provincial Armed Constabulary (PAC) dragged out young Muslim men, most of them poor daily wagers and weavers, drove them to the Upper Ganga Canal in Ghaziabad instead of to the police station, and threw them in one by one. V. N. Rai, who was superintendent of police in Ghaziabad, wrote a chilling account of how the police—who described Meerut as a 'mini Pakistan' and held the Muslims solely responsible for the violence—had behaved.

'Every survivor who hit the ground after being shot at tried hard to pretend he is dead and most hanged on the canal's embankments with their heads in water and the body clutched by weeds to show to their killers that they were dead and no more gunshots fired at them. Even after the PAC personnel had left, they lay still between water, blood and slush. They were too scared and numbed even to help those who were still alive or half dead.'

When the perpetrators of such a massacre walk free—or when both Samajwadi Party and BJP leaders are held responsible for fomenting riots (as they were by a judicial panel investigating the Muzaffarnagar violence)—claims to secularism become no more than a fierce battle of contestations.

•

In Mumbai, I met Girish and Tahir—both fathers of dead sons, one Muslim, one Hindu, one a victim of the 1993 Mumbai blasts, another of the 1992–1993 Mumbai riots. I met them both just a few days after underworld don Yakub Memon was executed in 2015 for his role in the 1993 serial blasts. They quietly listened to each other's anguish, strangers bonded in instant intimacy by the essential sameness of what they had experienced.

Hanging Memon may have brought symbolic closure to the 257 people killed in the 1993 blasts, but the memory of those violent years lingered on in the collective consciousness of the country—especially because the events of 1992 and 1993 had a significant effect on how secularism would thereafter come to be perceived. For me, Tahir and Girish illustrated how and why secularism had come to be regarded as a two-faced entity, deployed selectively as a political weapon and, just as easily, sheathed and put away when convenient.

Bundled up in the pocket of Girish Mehta's trousers was a young boy's school tie. It's the last memory he has of his son and he carries it with him wherever he goes. On the morning of 12 March 1993, thirteen-year-old Tejas told him that he wanted to go outside and play cricket. School had let out early and all his friends were planning to meet at Mumbai's Shivaji Park. It was just another day and the family went about its normal business. A few hours later, Girish heard that a bomb had gone off in Zaveri Bazaar. 'The building where I worked shook violently, I thought it was an earthquake. Then I heard that there had been a blast.' Soon, he realized the enormity of what had happened—a series of coordinated bomb blasts had hit the city in multiple locations from Century Bazaar to the Bombay Stock Exchange. Worried about his boy, Girish rushed home. His brother and he spent the rest of the day looking for Tejas, walking from parks to train stations, from building to building, through the ravages of the explosions. Tejas was nowhere to be found. The next morning at Mumbai's Poddar Hospital, Girish's friend saw a corpse that looked somewhat like Tejas. It was hard to tell because the body was so severely burnt that the bones were exposed. All that had been left untouched by the explosives was his young innocent face. And the tie around his neck. 'I washed what remained of him with Dettol. I told the doctors, this is my son, my Tejas,' Girish told me when we met, his voice still trembling, twenty-two years after his son was killed. Now all he had to remember him by was a maroon tie.

Tahir Wagle's son, Shahnawaz, was seventeen when he was killed in the aftermath of the Mumbai riots that preceded the serial blasts of 1993. Shahnawaz tried to display his student identity card to the cops who had come to round up the young boys in the neighbourhood, kicking and pushing them around with their rifle butts. His mother was watching helplessly from the balcony. Suddenly, one of the constables grabbed Shahnawaz and turned him around, held his .303 rifle to his head and shot him dead. The police never accepted the Wagle family's version of events and refused to register a formal complaint. The ageing husband and wife devoted the rest of their lives running from court to court in the hope of elusive justice for their dead son. The Justice Srikrishna Commission—set up to investigate the riots in which more than 900 people were killed—had described the Shahnawaz shooting as 'cold blooded murder'. Even now, years later, the recommendations of the Srikrishna Commission have never been officially accepted let alone acted upon by the Maharashtra government.

Justice B. N. Srikrishna, a man who lived away from the public glare, but never pulled his punches, told me that the 'state did not prosecute those accused in the Mumbai riots with the same zeal as they did Yakub Memon'. A hundred people had been convicted for their role in the blasts; by contrast, only three people were found guilty for inciting violence during the riots. Justice Srikrishna did not disagree with the death sentence for Memon, who he felt was 'given the fullest opportunity of defence'; he was only dismayed at the partial and selective application of justice. In his report, Srikrishna had likened Bal Thackeray, the chief of the ultra right-wing Shiv Sena, to a 'virtual General' during the riots, but he was just as scathing about the Congress–NCP government on whose watch the violence had taken place. 'I do not buy the theory that the riots were inspired or that they occurred spontaneously. The response of the state was remiss. There was hardly any serious investigation, even in cases where there was enough prima facie evidence,' he told me, resigned to the fact that no party, neither the BJP, nor the Congress, was ever going to take action on the findings of his report.

■

'If I were to write *Sholay* today, I'd have to write it differently, wouldn't I?' said Javed Akhtar, one of India's best-known screenwriters and lyricists, referring to his cult film. He said this in all seriousness in the course of a conversation we were having about the assassination of three elderly rationalists in three years—Narendra Dabholkar (sixty-seven years old), Govind Pansare (eighty-one years old) and M. M. Kalburgi (seventy-six years old)—and what it meant for freedom and secularism in India. Pansare had been targeted for challenging the conventional narrative around Shivaji and suggesting that the great seventeenth-century Maratha warrior king's rule had been inclusive towards Muslims. In the same week that I met Javed in September 2015, musician and composer A. R. Rahman, a devout Muslim, had been served with a fatwa for composing the music for the Iranian film *Messenger of God* directed by Majid Majidi. In a stirring response to the fatwa, in which Rahman described himself as 'part traditionalist and part rationalist', he posed a counter question to those who had targeted him: 'What, and if, I had the good fortune of facing Allah and He were to ask me on Judgment Day: I gave you faith, talent, money, fame and health…why did you not do music for my beloved Muhammad film?'

The two incidents—the murder of rationalists and the attack on Rahman—brought home the sad truth of an increasingly intolerant and toxic environment in the country, where individual liberty was under siege.

Investigators believed that there was a pattern and a common connection to all three murders; all three men had been targeted by Hindu right-wing groups for their scepticism and questioning of ritualistic religious practices. 'India was once known for its tolerance and the elbow room it gave to free thinkers, especially when compared to countries in its neighbourhood, like Pakistan and Bangladesh. Now, it seems instead of them learning from us, we are learning from them,' Akhtar said to me. 'In 1975, *Sholay* had a very innocent scene where Dharmendra hides behind an idol and talks to Hema Malini and she thinks "bhagwan" is talking to her. Today, if I were writing *Sholay* all over again, I would not write this scene. Because I know that there are so many people who will claim to be outraged. There was another film called *Sanjog* that told the story of Krishna and Sudama through film songs; today somebody would object even to that.'

Akhtar, a self-professed atheist, believed that India had been a freer country in some ways forty years ago. He had always been an outspoken critic of fundamentalism among Muslims, often inviting the wrath of clerics and the more conservative Muslim politicians. Today, he believed, that Hindus were showing the signs of orthodoxy and intolerance that had once been typical of the practitioners of conservative Islam. 'I have always respected the kind of liberal values that Hindu society has, the kind of space it has always given to people who are not very reverent. It's tragic that instead of these Muslim groups learning from Hindu groups, these Hindu groups are learning from Jamaat-e-Islami.'

Well-known Hindi author Uday Prakash, best known for his book *The Girl with the Golden Parasol*, was also on the same television show I was presenting. Uday had just returned his Sahitya Akademi award—the highest national honour for literature—to protest the murder of Kalburgi. He was the first of dozens of prominent writers who had returned awards or made strong public protests over the stifling of dissent and free speech and growing sectarian intolerance. One of the objections to Kalburgi from religious groups had been that he had quoted Jnanpith award winning writer U. R. Ananthamurthy in one of his speeches. Ananthamurthy had written that as a child he had urinated on the Devva stone in the village to rid himself of the fear that the deity had superpowers. Ananthamurthy's account of his childhood experiment was in a book that had been in print for eighteen years. But it was only when Kalburgi repeated the story at a public programme that it erupted into a major controversy. After Kalburgi's murder, a local Bajrang Dal member in Karnataka—a state governed by the Congress—had said on Twitter that he had got the 'dog's death' he deserved.

Invoking Ambedkar and Buddha, Uday Prakash said that the Hindu tradition had always made space for people who challenged faith. He shared his own story about how he had, in a fit of rage, broken all the idols in his house when his mother died of cancer. 'Today, will they kill me for it? We are scared now,' Uday told me, 'we have begun to censor ourselves.' Another prominent writer who returned her award was Nayantara Sahgal, niece of Jawaharlal Nehru, who said she was standing up for the right to dissent. 'I am a Hindu, a believing Hindu,' she told me, 'and it saddens me and infuriates me more than anything else the mockery that Hindutva has made out of Hinduism. It has reduced it, shrivelled it, to a kind of nightmare. Millions of Indians like me who are Hindus reject Hindutva.' The award wapsi, in turn, reopened all the old debates about the double standards of secularists. Why had writers not returned their honours after the 1984 riots, supporters of the BJP demanded to know. And so, here we were back to the bookending of injustice, where no outrage can stand on its own without being compared to other, just as horrific, injustices.

Hamid Dabholkar, the son of Narendra Dabholkar captured in a single sentence the tragedy of 'secular' politics in India: 'The pain of the common citizen in this country is that we are crushed between a party that is programmatically communal and another that is pragmatically communal,' he said, to the applause of the audience. 'That is the only difference I see between the BJP and Congress.' Hamid's father had been murdered in Maharashtra when it was governed by the Congress–NCP coalition; he found them uncommitted about taking a clear position and pursuing justice for his father. Hamid pointed out that the Congress had refused to ban the Sanatan Sanstha—the right-wing group being investigated in Dabholkar's murder—even when presented with incontrovertible evidence.

He explained that unlike many other rationalist groups, his father had taken a 'neutral stance' on matters of faith. 'We don't tell people to abandon religion and God, we only encourage them to question it.' Quoting Veer Savarkar, regarded as the ideological hero of the RSS, Hamid argued that Savarkar had questioned the cow being a holy mother, calling for humanism to be shown to it more because it was a useful animal. 'Do you want to shoot him too?' he challenged. Politics in the name of the holy cow would surface in the ugliest way possible, when a few weeks later, Mohammad Akhlaq, a village blacksmith, was lynched with bricks and lathis by a mob in Dadri in Western Uttar Pradesh over rumours that he had slaughtered a cow and stored beef in his house. 'Does the rule of law apply or not in this country?' asked Hamid, displaying extraordinary courage. 'This is not an attack on an individual; this is an attack on Reason. You may have killed my father; you can't kill an idea'.

The paradox in the country today is that while, on the one hand, there is a rising tide of intolerance committed by what some call the radical fringe (Romila Thapar is more forthright. 'The violent fringe are terrorists, let's call them that,' she told me), on the other hand there is an indifference towards some of the most contentious issues of the not-so-distant past. For example, when the Allahabad High Court delivered its Ayodhya judgement, the only people who whipped themselves into a frenzy were the politicians. So, are we entering a new period where the old disease of sectarianism will be kept in check by the new mantras of development that Modi is fond of promoting (and that won him his prime ministership), as well as by the advent of a watchful, aggressive social media and ubiquitous TV coverage? Or are we going to see the mainstreaming of religious politics and its practitioners—voices that were once only heard on the margins and are already much more voluble today? All one can say with any certainty is that the secularism that will survive into the future will be Gandhi's brand of secularism rather than Nehru's. In a country where religion is threaded into the fabric of society and culture, the only thing we can hope for is a way of living that respects all faiths and does not deny faith altogether.

VI

We began with 2002, and I'd like to end this chapter with some of the more positive lessons that I learned from that calamity. The one thing that gave me hope was how organic secularism was to the everyday lives of people, before it was tarnished by political divisiveness. Back in Vadodara, among the many Muslim-owned storehouses burnt down was one belonging to the largest wholesale timber supplier to Hindu crematoriums across the state. When we met Mohammed Salim, the owner of the warehouse that made and sold the material ('aakhri samaan') for the 'Hindu last rites ceremony', he proudly showed us around, pointing out the wood that is precisely cut three ways to carry the earthen pot, even as he held up pipes (used to craft the stretcher that carries the dead) that had been burnt by the mob. He explained with pride that this had been his family's profession for years; the historic economic interdependence of various religious communities made his embrace of secularism calm, philosophical and unquestioning. 'Hum rozi roti inse hi kamaate hain, inse bhed-bhaav rakh khar hum kya karenge. Hum apna kaam karenge, uska phal Allah humein dega (We earn our living from them, there's no question of any prejudice or hostility. I will continue to do my work. I'm sure Allah will recognize that),' he said.

Opposite Vadodara's Swamy Narayan Temple we met Nusrat Bhai—the city's most famous kite maker. 'Our Hindu brothers, especially those who come to pray at the mandir, have always bought kites from us,' he told me. 'Our business depends on them.' In the backstreets, Muslim women and children would work through the day, threading the string used to fly the kites during the Hindu festival of Makar Sankranti, while the men handled the production and sale of the kites. The annual burst of colours in the sky was also a rainbow of shared histories.

Whether it was the Ganesh statues used during the Ganpati puja or bindis and bangles, they were all made and sold by Muslim craftsmen and shopkeepers. The motor workshops and small factories ravaged by the rioters may have been owned by Muslims, but nearly all of them employed people from both communities as labourers and mechanics. One such businessman, Abbas Kothari, expressed his anguish about the meaningless and waste of the destruction that had been visited upon him. 'We belong to the Bohra community and have three factories dealing in plastic. All three got burnt and looted in the recent riots. The irony is that the rioters didn't realize that there are more than 200 Hindu workers' jobs at risk. In our factory we have fifteen Hindu families living on the premises and on our payroll we have only one Muslim worker—the watchman. We came to know later that the fifteen families had protected him from the rioters.'

Salim, Nusrat and Abbas's stories bear out the contention I have made that the future of secularism in this country will need to be founded on this idea of inclusiveness and respect for all faiths. Many of us were shaped by an automatic and often unexamined Nehruvian discomfort with all things religious or ritualistic. I would include myself among those who grew up wary of religion, always opting to leave unanswered the column in forms and surveys that sought to know which faith you practised. It was only with the wider exposure that journalism brought that I realized that life in the confines of a liberal bubble had closed my mind to a deeper understanding of the social dynamics of my country. The pursuit of an ideal that would never allow religious identity to divide people had made me dangerously acultural. It was time to get rooted in a liberalism and secularism that was inclusive and celebrated the plural and multi-religious reality of India.

■

Ten years after the riots, I returned to Gujarat to meet some of those I had first met in the shadow of violence. In Ahmedabad I met Bharat Panchal, an autorickshaw driver attached to a private school in the city. Bharat's wife, Jyoti, had been among the kar sevaks returning from Ayodhya to Godhra, when the S-6 coach she was in was set on fire. Since then Bharat's life had moved on. He married a neighbour and friend, Bela, who was carrying the scars of her own tragedy. Bela's mother-in-law was also among those killed on the Sabarmati Express and her husband died in violent street clashes three months later. But Bharat harboured no hostility or rancour. He told me that every morning, as freshly scrubbed little children clambered into the back of his rickshaw, he thought of the kids whose parents had been killed in 2002. He said he was haunted by the thought of their growing up without the nurture and love of their parents. His healing, he told me, was now through the bonds he had built with the children he ferried to school. 'Main aapko bataana chahta hoon ki mere saath zyada tar Muslim bacche hain aur unke ma baap ne kabhi nahin yeh socha ke main Hindu hoon (I want you to know that there are many Muslim children whom I drop to school everyday. Not once do their parents say that I am a Hindu so they don't trust me or vice versa. And the kids really love me),' he told me proudly.

Another survivor from the Sabarmati Express was undertaking a personal journey that he hoped would deliver him from a troubled past into a more peaceful future. Satish, an understated businessman, his wife Mangla, and their daughter Archana were also among those trapped inside a burning coach on the morning of 27 February 2002. As clouds of smoke filled the coupe, Satish had used his hands and feet to wrench open the three-rod window, pushing his daughter out to safety. In the ensuing chaos, he was separated from his wife. He would never see her again, nor was he ever able to locate her body. But a decade later, Satish had decided that he needed to make his daughter's happiness the focus of his life—he was making the same journey that he had on that fateful day, but this time in the opposite direction, from Vadodara to Lucknow and beyond. There was a fitting symbolism in embarking on new beginnings on the anniversary of a deep loss. 'Grief and happiness are co-travellers in life's journey,' he said reflectively, explaining that he was headed to Uttar Pradesh for his daughter's wedding. 'She was just ten-twelve years old when she was trapped inside that train. I wish her mother were alive today to see this day. Jo hua, woh insaniyat ke khilaf tha, mera yeh hamesha manna raha hai (Whatever happened, first at Godhra and then the riots that followed, both went against the grain of humanity).'

In Vadodara, I had to make a stop at the home of J. S. Bandukwala, one of the few people I had met in the course of my career who led his life on Gandhian principles. Professor Bandukwala, a twinkly-eyed nuclear physicist, had made his home in a colony with a mixed religious demographic, a conscious decision to defy the creeping ghettoization of the urban landscape in Gujarat. In 2002, he was with his daughter Umaima, when a 300-strong mob of rioters attacked their home. They made a narrow escape with help from their Hindu neighbours. The myth of 'spontaneous' violence was once again busted—the vandals who came for the professor, first pelted stones and smashed his cars; when they could not force open the gates of his apartment, they returned the next day with reinforcements. The neighbours who had dared to help did not escape the rage of the mob either. 'I don't know where this is going to end,' he told me, when I interviewed him in 2002, still gentle of mind and spirit, 'they were physically assaulted just for helping me out. At one stage I even considered stepping forward and telling them if you want my life, take it, but don't harass others.' Even though it had only been hours since he had been forced out of his home, he spoke without anger, without a trace of bitterness as his young daughter sat by his side in a friend's balcony, holding back her tears. Umaima was engaged and soon to be married to a Gujarati Hindu she had fallen in love with. Inter-faith romance was no cataclysmic event in this household; what frightened them were the invisible and seemingly indelible lines that were being drawn to demarcate communities. 'These extremists, they want that no Muslims should live in Hindu localities and no Hindus should live in Muslim neighbourhoods,' said Bandukwala, who was also among the first to call the attack on the kar sevaks at Godhra 'absolutely barbaric. The viciousness on both sides is what frightens me'.

Ten years later, the professor told me he had become more, not less, religious since 2002. This surprised me. I would have imagined that once religious fault lines ripped apart the life he had known and left him vulnerable, he would have turned more cynical.

Instead, the professor, now considerably older, greyer and wiser, said he drew strength from the fact that Umaima was happily married to Maulin, the man she had been engaged to when the riots broke out. They live in the United States, committed to the idea of maintaining a multi-faith home. 'Umaima has a Quran and also the statue of a Hindu goddess gifted to her by her mother-in-law. Every morning, she worships the goddess and then kisses the Quran. This is the pluralism we have to build. I know many of my Muslim friends don't agree with my choices. But we are living in a diverse society. We can't let Pakistan develop over here.' He spoke of the pressure on him in the aftermath of the riots to force his son-in-law to convert to Islam. 'I told them that would be wrong. Instead, they should both practise the best of both religions. You may think I am exaggerating but I believe Umaima's marriage to Maulin was a way of Allah telling me that you have to join hands with Hindus and build the bridge that Gandhi wanted us to.'

Five

A CHRONICLE OF KASHMIR

I

THERE WAS A distinct chill in the air in Delhi on the morning of 31 December 1999, and it wasn't due to the wintry weather alone. A little over a thousand miles away, in Kandahar, Afghanistan, the lives of 190 Indians on board the hijacked Indian Airlines plane, IC 814, were hanging by the thread of a decision that would come to haunt the Indian government and the then Foreign Minister Jaswant Singh for years to come. Singh was getting ready to escort three dreaded terrorists, who had just been released from prison in Jammu and Kashmir to Afghanistan in exchange for the safety of the passengers and crew. The mood outside the high-security Indian Air Force-managed technical area of Delhi airport (where journalists were being kept at a safe distance) was tense.

It was then that I spotted a battered Maruti van approaching the gate. As it slowed down for security checks at the multiple barriers that had been set up, I discovered that it was carrying food for the officials inside. I used the few seconds available to plead with the driver to let me hop on. Sitting at the back between astonished food vendors and boxes of squishy sandwiches, I managed to make my way in past security. I reached the aircraft just as Jaswant Singh was climbing the steps of the Boeing 737. Eight officials from the intelligence agencies and the foreign ministry were already on board. Next to the plane was parked a jeep. Inside were the three terrorists, their faces completely masked.

I soaked in the details. It was a week earlier, on 24 December, that IC 814 was hijacked and the conditions set for the release of the passengers. The identity of the men had not yet been officially released. Brajesh Mishra—who was both principal secretary to the prime minister and the national security adviser at the time—would tell us who they were only after the plane was airborne. By this time the journalists outside the gate had begun calling every high-ranking bureaucrat they knew to protest my presence inside the security perimeter. Mishra made an anxious call to my bosses.

Determined to take my chance, I implored the minister to let me accompany him to Afghanistan, offering to leave my camera behind if that made taking me along more viable. I begged, I tried everything I could to somehow climb those steps to the aircraft with him. But in his firm yet gentle baritone he told me I must leave. Minutes later, Maulana Masood Azhar (who in less than two years would plan the attack on the Indian Parliament, mentioned in the previous chapter), Omar Saeed Sheikh (who would go on to kidnap and decapitate journalist Daniel Pearl in 2002), and Mushtaq Ahmed Zargar (or 'Latram' as he was known in the Kashmir Valley where he had three dozen murder cases registered against him) were taken out of the jeep. They were the last to emplane. In many ways, their flight to freedom would, in the months and years to come, change the very nature of insurgency in the Kashmir Valley.

∎

'The minute we gave in, India became a soft state,' an apoplectic Farooq Abdullah, who was chief minister of Jammu and Kashmir during the hijacking of IC 814, would tell me later. He had phoned L. K. Advani, the then home minister, to vehemently oppose the release of the terrorists. 'Yeh desh ke saath gaddari hai (This is a betrayal of the nation),' he told Advani. Farooq's impression was that Advani himself was not comfortable with the decision but if that were the case, Advani did not let on. Threatening to resign, he told the state's governor, Girish Saxena, that he could not continue as chief minister if the men were released from Jammu's Kot Balwal prison on his watch. 'Hindustan ka janaaza niklega (This is as good as taking out India's funeral procession),' he shouted at the governor. Finally, A. S. Dulat, India's RAW chief at the time (and Farooq's golfing buddy) was dispatched to the state to convince the chief minister that this was the only way to save lives. It was five hours before Farooq relented. But not before giving them a dire warning. 'We were already weak; now we are finished.'

So began a new and bloody phase of militant violence in Jammu and Kashmir. Four months later, a seventeen-year-old student from downtown Srinagar, Afaq Ahmed Shah, the quiet, somewhat reclusive son of a teacher who had dreams of becoming a doctor, drove a stolen red Maruti laden with explosives into the high-security barrier of the army headquarters in Badami Bagh, blowing himself up at the entry gate. It was the very first suicide attack in the Valley and Masood Azhar's recently launched terror outfit— the Jaish-e-Mohammed—was quick to own responsibility. Previous 'fidayeen' squads who stormed security installations employed a hit-and-run strategy, leaving themselves a fighting chance of making it out alive. The Lashkar-e-Taiba (LeT), which had first unleashed these attacks, stopped short of endorsing suicide as a battle tactic because of the disapproval of taking your own life in Islam. But when Afaq blew himself up, he became the Valley's first human bomb, forfeiting the option of survival the moment he accepted the mission. Masood Azhar, now ensconced comfortably in Pakistan, was back in business.

On Christmas day that same year, the Jaish ordered another young suicide bomber to strike at the army barracks in Srinagar. This time, when the bomb exploded, six soldiers and three Kashmiri students returning home for Eid were killed. The *Zarb-i-Momin*, a weekly mouthpiece for the Jaish, eulogized the twenty-four-year-old bomber from Birmingham, Mohammad Bilal, and called him a 'martyr'. This was proof that the attempt by the militants and their sponsors to internationalize the Kashmir issue by locating it within the larger global 'jihad' was beginning to make headway. The homespun separatist insurgency of the late eighties and early nineties was moving firmly into the control of foreign hands, simultaneously transforming in nature from the political to the religious. Over the next few years, in graveyards across the Kashmir Valley, I would see tombstones commemorating 'fighters' not just from across the border in Pakistan or Kalashnikov-rich Afghanistan, but also from as far away as Sudan and Libya. With the conflict now lurking in the deep shadows of global terrorism, it was often impossible to isolate the enemy.

Reporting from the state in those years—my lifelong obsession with Kashmir began in the mid-nineties—was to live from crisis to crisis until the only thing your mind could play back was a constant barrage of violent or threatening memories. Curfew at the onset of dusk, silent, empty streets, the silhouette of a suspicious soldier who yelled at you to identify yourself in the gathering dark, the crash of explosions shaking you violently from your sleep, buildings burned to the ground to smoke out terrorists, dismembered limbs and shattered bodies strewn on the cratered ground, the flat report of pistol shots and the rattle of AK-47s mingling with the keening of the bereaved and the screaming of the wounded—the only constant about everyday life at the time was brutality and death. Morning after morning I would run out of the hotel room, often still in my pyjamas, because a grenade had been thrown into a crowded bazaar or an improvised explosive device had been triggered to blow up a military convoy or because paramilitary forces had opened fire on a village procession. So accustomed did I become to daily trysts with violence and tragedy that it was the relative 'normalcy' of Delhi that would disorient me whenever I came home.

Strangely, the great beauty of India's most spectacular state only reinforced the depth of its relentless suffering. The undulating hills, the blaze of the saffron fields, the apple orchards and the walnut trees, the luminous blue of the sky, the water turning to green translucent ice on the Dal Lake, the poetry of the chinar's changing colours—all this splendour made the absence of tranquillity all the more poignant. The horror of militancy on the one hand and the monumental mistakes and violations by the state on the other left many ordinary Kashmiris imprisoned between the battle lines. There is no doubt that much of the terror that ravaged Jammu and Kashmir emanated from across the border, but several grave wounds to the body politic were self-inflicted as well.

The brazenly rigged 1987 elections spawned a host of secessionist movements and militants. These included Syed Salahuddin, the chief commander of the Hizbul Mujahideen, who had contested elections in Srinagar and is said to have won, only to find his opponent declared victor. His polling agents included Yasin Malik and Javed Mir, who would go on to take up arms, train in Pakistan and found the Jammu and Kashmir Liberation Front (JKLF). Over the years the blunders only multiplied—a result of apathy, misjudgement, denial and, sometimes, wilful arrogance in the responses of successive governments to Kashmir's unresolved problems. A slew of fake encounters, abductions and disappearances, the notorious rise of armed counter-insurgents (or Ikhwanis as they were locally known), the absence of visible or swift justice in cases of blatant human rights violations—all these added to the emotional alienation of the Valley's inhabitants from Delhi.

II

'We were Kashmiris,' says the opening page of the autobiography of India's first prime minister, Jawaharlal Nehru, written from prison in 1935. Two hundred years earlier, Nehru's Kashmiri ancestor, Raj Kaul, a famous Sanskrit and Persian scholar had migrated from the mountains to the plains. The Kauls adopted the surname 'Nehru' after the family took a home by the edge of a 'nahar' or canal. Nehru's formative years may have been moulded by Allahabad in Uttar Pradesh, where he was born, and later Harrow and Trinity in England, where he was educated, but the son of Motilal and Swarup Rani Thussu, held his Kashmiri Pandit ancestry close to his heart. After spending a summer there in 1940, he felt the inexorable pull of the Valley. 'Kashmir calls [you] back, its pull is stronger than ever, it whispers its fairy magic to the ears. How can they who have fallen under its spell release themselves from its enchantment?'

In 1946, soon after Mahatma Gandhi had pressured Sardar Patel and Acharya Kripalani to withdraw from the race for Congress president—even then, it was known that the chosen leader would also be independent India's first prime minister and Gandhi's preference was clear—Nehru decided to travel to Kashmir to support his friend Sheikh Abdullah who was, at the time, being held in prison by Maharaja Hari Singh, the then ruler of the state.

Nehru had rallied behind Abdullah's Quit Kashmir Movement

to replace the Dogra royalty with a popular government. It was not the most opportune time to offend the maharaja. Only the princely states had the option of not going under the surgical knife with which Sir Cyril Radcliffe would make multiple incisions in the heart of undivided India, and Maharaja Hari Singh had not yet decided whether Jammu and Kashmir would stay with India or Pakistan. But Nehru was undeterred by the possibility of antagonizing the king. Defying a ban to enter the state, Nehru travelled to Kashmir and was arrested and sent back at the border.

A year later, just two weeks before independent India's 'tryst with destiny', its prime minister-to-be was still fixated on Kashmir. 'Between visiting Kashmir when my people need me there and being Prime Minister, I prefer the former,' Nehru said in a letter to Gandhi. Sardar Patel would later describe some of Nehru's interventions in Kashmir as 'acts of emotional insanity'. Kashmir can have that effect on you.

A month later, in September, the prevaricating Maharaja Hari Singh made an offer of accession to India for the very first time. Nehru stunned him by making the deal conditional on the release of Sheikh Abdullah from jail. The maharaja refused.

Finally, in what would become Pakistan's classic modus operandi for decades to come—sending well-armed infiltrators into Indian territory and then denying their existence—on 22 October 1947 thousands of Pathan tribesmen, backed by the military in Rawalpindi, invaded Kashmir, looting, pillaging and capturing vast tracts of land, including Muzaffarabad and Poonch. Launched from Abbotabad (where sixty years later Osama Bin Laden would be captured and killed by the Americans), the militia invasion was code-named Operation Gulmarg. It would be Pakistan's inaugural proxy war in India. The details of the operation were revealed by Major General Akbar Khan whose job it was to plan the covert incursions. In his book, *Raiders in Kashmir*, Khan confirms that he prepared a blueprint for battle titled 'Armed Revolt In Kashmir' which was planned as early as late August 1947, just after the British had played midwife to the birth of the two nations.

Within two days of the invasion, as the militia took control of

Baramulla and was marching towards Srinagar, panicked telegrams from Hari Singh began to arrive in Delhi appealing for troops. On 26 October 1947, Maharaja Hari Singh signed the instrument of accession to make Jammu and Kashmir a state of the Indian union.

By now, the Pakistan-backed marauders were just seven kilometres short of Srinagar's airport. Field Marshal Sam Manekshaw—India's most celebrated soldier who was then a young colonel in the Directorate of Military Operations—made a presentation to the Cabinet, arguing that Kashmir could be lost forever if troops were not rushed in. In Manekshaw's recounting, Nehru still dithered. He was concerned about world opinion and wondered aloud to his colleagues if it might not be wiser to first consult the United Nations. An indignant Sardar Patel, already exasperated with Nehru's sentimentalism about Kashmir, snapped, 'Jawahar, do you want Kashmir or do you want to give it away?'

'Of course I want Kashmir,' Nehru snarled in reply.

On the morning of 27 October 1947, Dakotas from the No. 12 Squadron of the Indian Air Force, along with dozens of planes requisitioned from privately owned companies, airlifted the 1st Battalion of the Sikh Regiment from Delhi's Safdarjung airport.

The newly born nation's army would spend the next fourteen months waging war against a people who had until recently been countrymen. More than 1,000 soldiers of the Indian Army and 1,990 men of the Jammu and Kashmir state forces died in battle. However, despite the best efforts of the limited force that had been rushed to take on the intruders (several battalions of the army had to be held back to defend Punjab and military operations in Hyderabad), nearly 37 per cent of the original area of Jammu and Kashmir could not be retrieved. Muzaffarabad and Giligit-Skardu fell into Pakistani hands.

■

Since its stormy entry into the Indian union, multiple political protagonists have emerged that hold the key to the state's future. There are the Valley-based parties like the National Conference and the People's Democratic Party (PDP), the Congress—a national party that has some presence in both Jammu and the Kashmir Valley—and the BJP, which has never held a seat in Kashmir but has always been rooted in Jammu. There are also the small Ladakh-based parties that remain unconnected to the larger dispute but see their future within the Indian union. And finally, there are the separatists primarily represented by the Hurriyat Conference—disparate players, with different ideologies all in pursuit of an elusive peace.

III

'For God's sake we are not asking for jihad like some of these Hurriyat fellows. I don't bluff people, I don't lie.' Farooq Abdullah spoke as always with a rhythmic cadence, his voice rising and falling with dramatic effect. It was July 2000, and we were sitting on the sprawling lawns of the chief minister's residence in Srinagar just after he had steered a radical resolution for autonomy through the Jammu and Kashmir assembly with a stunning two-thirds majority. The report prepared by his party, the National Conference, asked that the state's autonomy be restored to its pre-1953 position when New Delhi only had control over three areas—defence, external affairs and communication. 'There is no turning back now,' he thundered with a flamboyant flourish, typical of him.

As a member of the National Democratic Alliance (NDA) and an ally of Vajpayee, Farooq's autonomy gambit had thrown the centre into a predicament. What he was asking for went against the grain of the BJP's core ideology. Other, more extremist, partners in the coalition, like the Shiv Sena, were already asking for Farooq to be dropped from the NDA. BJP members had worn black bands during the autonomy debate in the assembly and tried to shout him down in protest. Farooq thumped the tables and shouted back. 'We are not Pakistani, we are Indian. What we are asking for is within the Indian Constitution.' Was he just play-acting, I asked him. Surely he knew that the RSS and the BJP were never even going to consider the proposals? 'Let the BJP decide, do they want to be leaders or followers,' he shot back.

What was striking was how, in so many ways, history was repeating itself.

In August 1953—the year that Farooq wanted to turn the clock back to—his father, Sheikh Abdullah, was stealthily dismissed and thrown into jail for several years on charges of sedition in what came to be known as the Kashmir Conspiracy Case. Though the orders to sack Sheikh Abdullah as Wazir-e-Azam (prime minister) came from Karan Singh, Maharaja Hari Singh's son and heir who had been appointed the Sadr-e-Riyasat (president) in 1952, Nehru supported the decision. His intelligence chief had persuaded the Indian prime minister that the leader he saw as a fellow secular nationalist and called his 'blood brother' was now working against India's interests.

'From a position of clearly endorsing the accession to India, he had over the last few months moved into an entirely different posture,' wrote Karan Singh, who had ordered Sheikh Abdullah's removal.

Just a year earlier, in July 1952, Nehru and Sheikh Abdullah had signed what had come to be known as the Delhi Agreement. They had agreed on a detailed set of terms that gave Jammu and Kashmir special status, including vesting the residuary powers of the legislature with the state and not the centre. But now all communication between them had broken down.

■

In a 1948 speech to the United Nations, Sheikh Abdullah, the most formidable political leader the state of Jammu and Kashmir had ever seen, made a blistering defence of the accession to India. Lashing out at Pakistan for sending its raiders into the state, the self-styled 'Sher-e-Kashmir' (Lion of Kashmir) roared, 'I had thought all along that the world had got rid of Hitlers...but from what is happening in my poor country I am convinced they have transmigrated their souls into Pakistan... I refuse to accept Pakistan as a party in the affairs of Jammu and Kashmir. I refuse this point blank.' Two years later, however, Sheikh Abdullah had begun to question the credentials of Indian secularism and lament what he saw as economic discrimination against Muslims in the newly born republic.

Although he had always rubbished the idea of a merger with Pakistan, Sheikh Abdullah began to talk about the possibility of an independent Kashmir which could enjoy the same status it did before the accession. Soon after he changed his stance he was jailed and dismissed from office and was not able to lead the state for another twenty years. His unceremonious and forced exit would be the first in a series of similar undemocratic interventions from Delhi, blunders that would vitiate the state's future. The Sheikh's clash was not just with Nehru but, closer home, with the Praja Parishad of Jammu, a new political party representing the interests of Jammu Hindus, led by men like Balraj Madhok, who went on to become the president of the Bharatiya Jana Sangh (the precursor to the BJP). With its slogan of 'Jammu Alag Karo' (Separate Jammu) it sought to end the Muslim dominance of Sheikh Abdullah and wanted a complete integration with India without any exemptions of law.

Jammu and Kashmir is the only state in India permitted to fly its own flag alongside the national flag and also the only state to have its own constitution and separate penal code. This was part of the special arrangement under Article 370 that had formed the basis of its accession to the Union of India. It is these constitutional privileges enabled by the state's special status that led Shyama Prasad Mukherjee—the Bharatiya Jana Sangh founder, member of Nehru's first Cabinet and vocal supporter of the Praja Parishad movement— to famously proclaim, 'Ek desh mein do vidhan, do pradhan aur do nishaan nahin chalenge (In one country, we cannot have two constitutions, two leaders and two flags).'

During the Praja Parishad uprising, protesters would pull down the state flag from government buildings and replace it with the Indian flag. In one of many missives to Nehru, Mukherjee wrote, 'If India's constitution was good enough for the rest of India, why should it not be acceptable to Jammu and Kashmir?'

Over the years, many of these distinctive powers were whittled down. The centre was given the power to dismiss an elected state government in case of a breakdown in law and order, the nomenclature of the heads of the state were changed from Sadr-e-Riyasat and Wazir-e-Azam to governor and chief minister respectively, and hundreds of union laws were made applicable to Jammu and Kashmir through a series of constitutional amendments. Nevertheless, exceptional prerogatives remained with the state.

Now, just like his father had five decades ago, Farooq appeared to be on a collision course with the RSS on the issue of greater autonomy for the state. 'Name one Hurriyat leader who has ever stood for India, can you name even one?' He smiled when I suggested he was being overdramatic. 'We are with India, Barkha, they are with Pakistan or for independence,' he said, expounding on why his call for autonomy was the only effective antidote to their slogans of 'azadi'.

Farooq Abdullah was hard to read. Excitable, passionate, impetuous and colourful, he was as much at ease cavorting with Bollywood heroines as he was talking about terrorism and foreign policy. He had a knack for the Kodak moment; he thought nothing of suddenly diving into the cold waters of the Dal Lake to enliven a tourism meet. One day, in the interiors of the Valley, I asked an ageing village man what he thought of the chief minister. 'Voh to disco hain (He is like disco),' he replied, in the most accurate summary I have ever heard of Farooq's kaleidoscopic and idiosyncratic personality.

Farooq spoke Kashmiri, Punjabi, Dogri, English and Urdu, and was unchained by worries about how people would perceive him. He was a master at using humour to deflate tricky questions. As a young reporter who was on the Kashmir beat for decades, I got to know him quite well and was often at the receiving end of his frivolity.

As happened to all high-profile reporters on the front line, slanderous whispers would follow me and I was used to hearing that I had married or was in a relationship with this or that powerful Kashmiri leader to explain how I got my stories. I had learnt to laugh this nonsense off. Farooq must have heard the silly, malicious jokes as well. One day, during the 2002 elections which would depose the National Conference after twenty-seven years in power, I accosted Farooq and his son Omar as they emerged from a polling booth after casting their votes and asked them to respond to persistent rumours—I used the Urdu word 'afwah' for rumour—about rising friction between father and son. As Omar prepared to launch into a serious rebuttal, Farooq interrupted him with, 'Afwah to yeh bhi hai ki hum tumhare aashiq hain, afwah se kya hota hai (Rumour also has it that I am your suitor, what does rumour have to do with anything)!' he said with a big smile, stumping me on live national television. It was classic Farooq. Father and son were, of course, a study in contrast. Farooq's spontaneity and earthiness made it far easier for him to connect to ordinary people than his son, Omar. Omar, the third generation of the Abdullah family in politics, was a much more emotionally reserved figure than his father, or grandfather. At the same time, Omar, a hotel management graduate who his father would have preferred to stay out of politics, was regarded as the more sober, level-headed and politically correct of the two.

Neither ever spoke publicly of any disagreements but in the 2008 elections I got a sense of some tension between father and son. On the night of 28 December, when the results were to be declared, I was in Srinagar, sitting close to a kangri heaped with burning coals, trying to keep warm as we broadcast live from Nagin Lake. Farooq Abdullah strode in, dressed in a beige phiran and his signature Karakul hat. The National Conference and the Congress party were all set to form the next government in a coalition but Farooq looked grim and slightly irritated. As we analysed the results the conversation shifted to who would lead the government. 'Am I looking at the next chief minister of Jammu and Kashmir?' I asked, waiting for the politically correct replies that usually followed such questions. 'Yes, Inshallah, you are,' he said without a moment of hesitation. 'Is that categorical?' I asked, taken aback by the certainty of his response. 'Absolutely categorical,' he said cutting my question short, 'the party has already decided.'

Within minutes of the interview airing, my phone rang. It was a senior party leader who worked closely with Omar Abdullah. 'Yeh to tabahi ho gayi (This is a disaster),' he said, sounding agitated and confused. 'What have you done?' The party had contested the election with Farooq as the official chief ministerial candidate. But now that the results were in, those closer to Omar saw this as his chance. The Abdullahs needed Congress support to form the government, and rumour had it that Rahul Gandhi had one condition—that Omar, and not his father, be the CM. Farooq declaring that the job was his to take had created a awkward situation and Omar's team was anxious. Nobody knows what transpired that night. Did the father and son have a heart to heart? Did the Gandhis give Farooq an ultimatum or did they offer him something better? The next morning

Farooq Abdullah told the media that he would much rather sit in Parliament than move to the state assembly. 'Father and son can never have differences,' he announced airily.

Of course Farooq's autonomy report, endorsed by the state assembly, was never considered for discussion by any government at the centre. The disregard with which it was treated by both national parties in Delhi made the redundancy of committees and reports and interlocutors and working group discussions abundantly clear to the Kashmiris. Nobody at the centre followed through on anything they had promised.

■

History was condemned to repeat itself in far too many ways in the Kashmir Valley. Just like his father's elected government had been dismissed when Nehru was prime minister, in 1983 Nehru's daughter Indira backed a split in the National Conference that brought down Farooq's government. Farooq had told friends he thought the years Indira brought his government down to be the worst years of his life—even worse than the challenges of militancy. He would tell his friends the story of how he landed in Saudi Arabia for the Umrah soon after his government fell—to find that his luggage was missing. Indira, he suspected, had ordered the intelligence to spy on him and rummage through his bags. The man who engineered the coup would end up being the second pillar in Kashmir politics, along with his fiery daughter Mehbooba. But at the time Mufti Mohammad Sayeed was only the president of the Jammu and Kashmir Congress. Farooq would never forgive him because the split in the party was not just political, it was also personal—the man Mufti had propped up to lead the breakaway faction was none other than G. M. Shah, Farooq's brother-in-law.

Eventually, Mufti would become a Cabinet minister in Rajiv Gandhi's government, part ways with the Congress to join the V. P. Singh uprising, become India's first Muslim union home minister, return briefly to the Congress during the Narasimha Rao years, and then leave it all behind to form his own party in 1999. Once considered New Delhi's voice in the Valley, Mufti now leads the

PDP, widely regarded as borderline separatist in its politics. In 1989, while he was union home minister, his daughter Rubaiya was kidnapped by militants. Despite that, as well as several attempts on his life by separatists, Mufti was soft on insurgents, insisting that his government's 'healing touch' would extend to all—separatists and families of militants included.

Mufti's other daughter Mehbooba, a law graduate from Kashmir University, is the only member of the second generation of the Sayeed family to become a force in politics. She described herself as someone who had come to politics by accident and contested her first election in 1996 upon her father's advice. Soon, it was Mehbooba who travelled door to door, village to village, braving threats, wading into crowds to build a connection with people, especially women. Outside the Valley, she became controversial for her frequent visits to the families of militants who had been killed. 'They are dead now,' she would tell me, 'why should their children be punished?' In a conservative society, she became the first woman to head a political party and emerged as a popular campaigner for civil rights. She was sometimes regarded with wariness in Delhi because of the shrill political positions they thought she took. But I must say that I found her gumption and guts admirable. A divorced single mother to two daughters, she forged her own path and through sheer energy and focus was able to build a mass base for a relatively new party that, unlike the Abdullahs, had no advantages of dynasty or legacy.

In comparison to her political opponents, she was more like Farooq than Omar; she could be volatile, sentimental and sometimes theatrical. In 2004, she stormed into a polling booth and dramatically lifted the veil of a woman she believed was a bogus voter. As luck would have it, I was in the same booth when this happened and our cameras caught the flare-up. The woman fled without voting and later told journalists that she had veiled herself because she felt safer in a burkha from militant threats (they wanted the polls to be boycotted). As the footage played nationally Mehbooba was irritated with me; she believed I had overdone the story to embarrass her. But we remained in regular contact through the ups and downs of Kashmir politics. As I got to know her, I discovered that beneath the fire and brimstone was a laid-back, regular young woman with a wicked sense of humour.

I still chuckle when I think of our conversation right after the dramatic elections of 2002. She told me how Omar had dropped by to meet her to offer congratulations. He apologized, she said, for coming empty-handed and remarked that he should have at least brought a cake or something. 'Never mind, Omar,' she recalled telling him, 'tum bhi koi cake se kum ho kya (You are no less than a cake)!'

The Muftis emerged as a force to reckon with in the Valley and raised the slogan of 'self-rule', taking Farooq's autonomy demand several steps further. Their politics was antithetical to everything the BJP stood for so no one could have ever predicted that the two sides could come together in possibly the most unlikely coalition Indian politics had ever seen. Yet, after the mandate of 2014, when Jammu voted overwhelmingly for the BJP, and the PDP led the tally in the Kashmir Valley, the only alternative to a dangerous vacuum was for these ideological enemies to forge a partnership.

'We are like the North Pole and South Pole,' said Mufti Mohammad Sayeed with a smile, when the negotiations between the two sides to draft a common minimum programme of governance were still on. I met Mufti in a government guest house in Mumbai in early 2015, more than a month after the results were out but a government had not yet been formed. Although Mufti was an old-school politician with a propensity to digress into rambling stories, today he was absolutely focused on one point. There would be no PDP–BJP government if there was any move to scuttle Article 370 which gave Jammu and Kashmir its special status. 'All we are asking for is that they [BJP] commit that the present status—we aren't even calling it a special status—not be altered in any way. We cannot compromise on this,' he told me. And what if they didn't agree? 'Then perhaps they can try and form the government with someone else. I am not desperate to be chief minister. As former home minister, everyone knows I am Indian by conviction. We are negotiating with the BJP out of conviction not compulsion... I hope Prime Minister Modi understands that this is a great opportunity and one that is not likely to come again.'

Notably, in the state elections of 2014, the BJP vision document made no mention of doing away with the state's special status, nor did Prime Minister Modi's campaign speeches bring it up. Despite the seasonal political rhetoric around Article 370 no national party, including the BJP, is likely to push for its abolition. To start with, scrapping it would need not just a constitutional amendment in Parliament but a subsequent ratification by the state's assembly. And no Valley-based party can afford to tamper with what has come to be a symbol of the closest the Kashmiris may ever get to sovereignty.

So, Mufti had his way on Article 370. And when the new state government was sworn in on 1 March 2015, in the presence of Prime Minister Modi, both the state's flag and the national flag flew in the foreground in an ironic reminder of what was no longer possible to change.

IV

The truth and lies of Jammu and Kashmir's reality reminds me of Akira Kurosawa's masterpiece *Rashomon,* in which a crime is recounted by all those connected to the event. Each telling of the tale is contradictory, yet equally plausible, casting doubts on the absolute singularity of Truth. Any chronicle of Jammu and Kashmir is marked by the Rashomon effect—what I mean by this is that to attempt a reasonably accurate portrait of a complex reality one has to always work with various versions of the truth. The propensity to see the challenges faced by the state in stark black and white has led to the insurgency either being romanticized by ultra-left sympathizers, who always cast the Indian armed forces in the role of the enemy, or misunderstood by ultra-nationalists who believe that a combination of firmness and force can eventually do in Kashmir what was done in Punjab in the eighties during the Khalistan militancy years. Neither approach does justice to the multiple strands of truth that tie together its reality.

The real misfortune is that sorrow and pain have become instruments in a competitive narrative of 'Our suffering vs. Their suffering'. Even grief has become a subject of political polarization. Mourning the loss of innocent lives and seeking justice for them is qualified again and again by the ifs and buts of politics, the divisions of ideology, the weight of history and the deep fissures in social and religious amity. But, when the coffin comes home, the father of the teenage boy killed by a tear-gas shell fired by security forces and the father of the young soldier pumped with bullets by terrorists at the border—share the same feelings of loss and heartbreak.

The postcards I collected from Kashmir were not of a sun-dappled Dal Lake or pristine snow on the ski slopes of Gulmarg or red chillies and walnuts laid out to dry on the gleaming thatched roofs of storybook cottages in rice fields. My collection was a chronicle of corpses and coffins, too many to count, too many to forget. Burials and funeral pyres, slogans and street processions, bombs and blood, grief and gore came to be the collage of memories I carried of a state that I still found hauntingly beautiful, made somehow more achingly real by (as Yeats would say) the 'sorrow of its pilgrim face'.

The violence I had seen had shockproofed me. In April 2005, as the Srinagar to Muzaffarabad bus was to be flagged off, I was present when militants took over the city's tourist centre. I watched the police burn it entirely to the ground to smoke out the attackers. Before that I reported on the assassination of a regional politician who was blown to smithereens by the force of the explosion that killed him. The bomb had thrown parts of his body into the branches of a giant tree, a sight that would haunt my dreams.

There was the crushing sorrow of seeing an eleven-year-old daughter hold back her tears, her slender back arched and her head held high as she bid a final farewell to her heroic father, Colonel M. N. Rai, with his regiment's war cry. Colonel Rai was shot by terrorists who misled him into believing they wanted to surrender. Just a day earlier he had made his mark as the youngest officer to be recognized with the Yudh Seva Medal, a prestigious gallantry award. The next morning, he was dead. His Whatsapp status read like a premonition: 'Play your role in life with such passion that even after the curtains come down, the applause doesn't stop.' It was impossible not to be moved deeply by the extraordinary family of three brothers—the colonel was the youngest—sons of a government school principal in Kalimpong, who all became decorated soldiers.

On the day of his funeral, I met his elder brother, a commandant with the Central Reserve Police Force, also honoured with a bravery medal for containing a terror attack by the LeT on Jammu's Raghunath Temple. He said he would want his brother to be remembered for two things, for his valour of course, but also for his humanity and the attempts he made at building emotional bridges with the people in the Valley. I was struck by the fact that he wanted to emphasize his brother's compassion as much as his courage. It is this benevolence and generosity of feeling that is sometimes in short supply in our national conversation about the state, perhaps understandably choked by the enormity of the grim daily battle against bombs and bullets. Incendiary remarks from Pakistan-backed separatists like Syed Shah Geelani, who brazenly described the men who killed Colonel Rai as 'martyrs', only deepen the collective hostility of the rest of the nation towards Kashmir.

I have seen the insurgency in Kashmir through the eyes of the remarkable, ever-optimistic Indu Mukund, a widowed mother to a three-year-old daughter, who caught the imagination of the country when she strode up to the dais to receive the Ashok Chakra from President Pranab Mukherjee at the Republic Day parade in January 2015. That day during an interview with her, I read out a love poem she had written in memory of her husband. 'I know this for sure, one day I will meet him, I know this for sure... And he shall give me that warm hug of his, I know this for sure, and I will not complain that I can't breathe, I know this for sure, you can hug me, hug me all you want.' She didn't want to recite it herself because she feared it might unlock the floodgates of loss and longing. Why was it so important for her not to betray any emotion, I asked. After all, who would not appreciate what she had gone through? 'It's important that India should see the man Mukund was, not my sorrow. It's what he would have wanted,' she said recounting how her husband had first evacuated civilians from the target house in a village of south Kashmir, and then moved towards eliminating three militants holed up inside, crawling on his stomach through the last lap of the operation, even when bleeding profusely. It was impossible not to be overcome with sadness when you saw the home video on the major's Facebook page, now run by friends and family. His daughter Arshea on his lap, her hands wrapped around his neck, father and daughter were singing aloud to the words of iconoclastic Tamil poet Subramania Bharati.

'Fear I have not, fear I have not,
Even if the entire sky breaks
And falls on my head even if they judge me as the worst,
Fear I have not, fear I have not.'

This was one powerful and defining aspect of the twenty-five-year-old conflict in Kashmir. Yet, I have argued, often without success, that it does not in any way diminish our gratitude for the heroism of our men and women in uniform to also be sensitive to the injuries of genuine injustice.

Take, for example, the experiences of the Valley's 'half-widows', women who live in the twilight zone of not knowing whether their husbands are alive or dead, forever asking the same question—when will he come back home, will he ever return? I would often see these women stream into the ancient Sufi shrine of Makhdoom Sahib in the foothills of Hari Parbat, their hands outstretched in prayer. They came here for solace, the hope of salvation and for a moment of peaceful solitude. One of the images that came to characterize the conflict was of grief-torn women sitting cross-legged on the floor, clutching faded photographs of the men who had disappeared, sometimes the only material memory they had of them, holding them up for the visiting cameras, hoping that media attention could somehow, magically, deliver a homecoming. Their husbands had evaporated into the ether of conflict. The uncertainty was so much more difficult than the certitude of death. Years had passed, yet they waited, both helpless and hopeful, for a knock on the door, borrowing perhaps from the words of the fourteenth-century mystic poet Lal Ded, 'Ill or well, whatever befalls, let it come. My ears will not hear, my eyes will not see. When the Voice calls from within the inmost mind, the Lamp of Faith burns steady and bright, even in the wind.'

The women mostly blamed custodial disappearances and in some cases, militant groups, for their men vanishing. Most of these disappearances took place in the first decade of the conflict; by the mid-2000s, an altered security environment and sustained campaigns by human rights groups saw a steep decline in such complaints. But, by now, an estimated 1,500 women had no reason but the irrationality of hope and the absence of bodily evidence, to believe that their partners were still alive. Neither widows, nor wives, their tragedy was compounded by the fact that religious leaders had issued diktats prohibiting remarrying. Often in the prime of their youth they found themselves facing a future of uncertainty and emptiness. In March 2014, the clerics finally relented and said that half-widows could remarry after a waiting period of four years, but for many this decision came too late.

I met Shamima when she was only twenty-five. Her husband, Shabbir, had already been 'gone' for seven years. A midnight knock on the door by a unit of the Rashtriya Rifles proved to be dire. 'My heart still says he is alive,' she said softly, her head bent in sorrow, her wide-set eyes blank and tired. We were sitting together on the cold floor of her kitchen. In one corner, she'd put milk to boil on a small kerosene stove placed precariously atop a frayed rug with bright pink roses. Next to it sat her young daughter Bisma, dressed in an over-sized phiran, frowning in confusion at the presence of strangers in her mother's home. The girl had been only forty days old when her father was taken (her brother Naseem had been three). Shamima had told her children their father was away on work in Jammu; every year she would tell them he would be back the next year. 'I lied to them,' she confessed in haltingly spoken Hindi. 'I said he would be back in five years. When five years were up, my son asked me when he would be back. I said six or seven years. When seven years ended, I told them Papa called from Jammu and said he'd be back after the eighth year.' When Shamima brings out her husband's framed photograph to show us, the only form in which his daughter has known him all these years, Bisma burst into tears. A child knows when her mother is using the crutch of untruth to somehow walk around loss.

In the one-room tenement that was home to a joint family of eight people, Shamima's father-in-law, Ghulam Ahmed Gazi, a small-time shopkeeper, spread out numerous documents and affidavits across the floor of the tiny house, a testimony to the endless search for his son. A candle flickered on the kitchen ledge; a gas lantern provided some supplementary light as we pored over his papers in the dimly lit room. His face lined by age and grief, Gazi said he had spurned the offer of monetary compensation ordered by the state's Human Rights Commission. Until he saw a body he would not believe his son was dead. 'I told them I don't want your one lakh rupees. I will sell my house and give you that money, just give me my son back,' he said, as his grandson reached out and placed his tiny hand on Gazi's gnarled, wrinkled fingers. Gazi told me his wife slipped into insanity soon after her son disappeared until death mercifully released her from pain. Now he spent sleepless nights worrying about what would become of Shamima when he passed on.

Collapsing into inconsolable sobs mid-sentence, his hand reached out and clasped mine. 'Mujhe yeh gham kha raha hai ki in bachchon ka kya hoga. Inko sirf upar wale ka aur mera sahara hai. Raat din mujhe yeh hee gham khaye ja raha hai (These children have no one but God and me as their support. What will happen to them when I die? This worry is eating me up inside. Who can say if their father will ever come back? Who knows if he is alive or dead)?' As Gazi broke down, his grandchildren leaned forward to comfort him, one using the sleeve of her phiran to wipe his tears, the other wrapping his arm around him. Shamima worked wordlessly in the kitchen, barely looking up.

This haunting image of personal tragedy should have evoked a humane response from observers, especially in the rest of the country, but sadly there were so many other elements muddying the picture—the violence, the terrorism, the lies, the untruths—that these victims did not even receive basic human compassion. This attitude mocked our mouthing of the statement that Jammu and Kashmir was 'an integral part of India'.

Equally, I watched with dismay as the worst militant attacks failed to evoke widespread condemnation or outrage within the state. No one took to the streets in protest when guns and bombs snuffed out the lives of countless soldiers, political workers, politicians, or even civilians. The violation of human rights rightfully triggered angry marchers and international op-eds calling for justice and due process but even mass killings by militants saw no overt chest-beating in the Valley. Not even when a hundred people—most of them civilians and pilgrims—were killed in a single day, in August 2000, in six coordinated attacks attributed to the LeT. Today, lulled into denial by the promise of 'normalcy', it's easy to forget those sinister days. But if you were there, and saw as I did, body after body propped up on ice slabs at Srinagar's Bakshi Stadium, with incense sticks being furiously lit to fend off the stench of death, you wouldn't forget that easily. It was among the bloodiest twenty-four hours that the state had witnessed, beginning with blind firing at an Amarnath Yatra camp about ninety kilometres from Srinagar. At another location, seven migrant labourers were woken up from their sleep and shot one by one. Across the tunnel, in Jammu, members of a village defence committee were gunned down. The line of violence zigzagged across the state, finally ending with seven members of a surrendered militant's family being killed in north Kashmir. No part of the state was spared the bloodshed. Yet, for years, global media continued to describe these killings as attacks by 'gunmen' in 'disputed Kashmir'; the shift in Western perceptions of Kashmir's tragedy, when the attacks began to be described as terrorist acts, only came about after the twin towers were brought down by Osama Bin Laden and his cohorts in 2001 and then too, not always. And Western observers were not the only ones at fault. In a society desensitized and hardened by constant violence, where death had become almost routine and thus unremarkable, the most frightening outcome was the failure to empathize. If local sentiment steered by separatists often fell woefully short of basic compassion or unequivocal condemnation, public opinion in the rest of India often dismissed grave human rights violations as the inevitable collateral damage of conflict.

■

It was in 1994, that the Association of Parents of Disappeared Persons was first formed. Its leading light, Parveena Ahangar, a woman of indomitable spirit, often said that nothing but death would stop her search for her son Javed who was picked up by security forces at the age of seventeen during a raid and never returned home. In 2011, a police team of the state's Human Rights Commission re-opened the debate on disappearances of people like Javed with its investigation of unmarked graves in north Kashmir. A survey of graves in four districts and at thirty-eight different locations led the commission to conclude that 'there is every possibility that unidentified bodies in various unmarked graves may contain bodies of enforced disappearances.' The report went on to say that as per the local police, the bodies were of unnamed militants handed over to villagers for burial. However, without exhumation and DNA sampling, the panel concluded, it would be impossible to identify and categorize with certainty the 2,000 plus bodies buried in various graveyards. Yet, the conclusions of the commission barely made the national headlines.

To map the geography of the commission's enquiry you had to head out north from Srinagar past the town of Baramulla towards the border villages of Uri near the LoC. Soft dappled light shimmered on the rice fields. The gentle gurgle of the Jhelum river guided us along the mountain curves. Three hours later, off the main highway, a winding smaller path led us to the village of Boniyar, overlooking the community graveyard. Only a handful of graves—six, to be precise— had tombstones and epitaphs, more than two hundred were nothing but slabs of blank stone waiting for history's witnesses to inscribe their tale. In some cases, there was just a mound of mud thrown over the body that lay six feet under. The ageing grave-keeper, Atta Mohammed, had buried all those brought to him over many years, without asking too many questions. But what he had seen kept him awake at night even decades later. He spoke of families who came to the graves looking for sons, fathers, brothers, husbands; he had no answers to give them. 'Burying bodies has begun to damage my health,' he told me. 'Hum kamzor ho gaye hain, aankhon ki roshni chali gayee. Raat ko neend nahin aati. Jab hum sote hain to hum in logon ke saath hote hain. Lekin inka chehra dekha nahin jata. Yeh sab khoon hai (I have become old and weak; the light has gone out of my eyes. At night I just cannot sleep. When I try, I see myself with all these men I have buried. But I can't even look at their faces. All I see is blood, blood everywhere).' As Atta Mohammed recalled bodies that had been brought to his graveyard—some dismembered, missing an arm or a leg, one with the entire stomach absent—he would lapse into sudden silence as he recounted the horror of what he had had to witness; it was too painful, even today, to put words to it.

Less than an hour away from Atta's graveyard, in another interior hamlet, I met a brother and a sister whose hopes had been rekindled by the Human Rights Commission report. Roshana and Ishtiyar sat close together with their mother wordlessly listening in, and told me about their father, an ordinary shopkeeper who went to work one morning in 1991 and had been 'missing' ever since. The siblings were infants then. As they grew older, finding their father became their life's mission. 'Every time I read something in the newspaper or see someone protesting, I feel a new hope rising within me,' said Ishtiyar, his eyes downcast in silent admission that the hope was irrational. 'When we haven't seen a body, why should we believe he is dead?' argued Roshana. 'We can dream, can't we?' In the initial years after his disappearance, the children say, their mother was too over-burdened and grief-stricken to pursue a legal case. When the children were older and the family approached the police they suggested it was time to declare him dead as he had already been gone for seven years. Staring down at her clenched hands, Roshana said, 'But I keep thinking he will walk in through that door any day...' What was ordinary for others was hurtful for them. 'Kissi ko bhi main "papa" pukarte huye sunta hoon to mujhe bhi lagta hai dil mein ki main papa bolun. Kyon ki maine zindagi mein kisi ko papa nahin bulaya (When I hear anyone calling out "papa", I too feel the urge to say it. In my life, I have never been able to use that word),' said a forlorn Ishtiyar.

But this being the Kashmir Valley, the torment of the family did not end here. Roshana and Ishtiyar's sister, Yasmin, was also killed in mysterious circumstances. When their father vanished Roshana was just over a year old, her brother not even three. As Yasmin grew into young adulthood, she led the family's search for their father, making countless trips to the local police stations. One evening, in a terrifying echo of what had happened to him, she went out to meet someone and never came back. A month later, in the dead of night, there was a knock on the door. A voice ordered them to keep their lights off and listen carefully: Yasmin was dead, her body had been buried two kilometres from their house. The family believe Yasmin may have been targeted because her frequent visits to the police could have led militants to (wrongly) assume that she was an informer for the security forces. 'We are trapped between both sides,' Ishtiyar lamented.

In several pockets of north Kashmir, similar tragedies were to be encountered. In one village of Kichama district in Baramulla, residents only had to glance out of their windows to see unmarked graves scattered in the wilderness behind their homes. The Human Rights Commission report estimated that there were a hundred unidentified bodies in this small patch alone. Though it had been investigated and compiled by a team of their own colleagues, the Jammu and Kashmir police were infuriated by the report. S. M. Sahai, a high-profile officer, argued that the revelations were 'nothing very new'. Insisting these were the corpses of men who tried to travel into Pakistan for training in militant camps he told me, 'Fact is that people while crossing the border were killed. A large number of them were from Pakistan, so a large number of them will remain unidentified.'

The government was angry at the description of these burial grounds as 'mass graves' in sections of the international media. Kashmir is not Cambodia, Chief Minister Omar Abdullah argued. Human rights activists did not deny that within these unmarked graves could be victims of militant violence, or indeed even militants themselves. Hidden away beyond the apple orchards in a remote mountain hamlet with rundown hutments I met one such family. When the only earning member of their home 'disappeared', they suspected a militant group had abducted him, but it was impossible to protest or speak out. 'If the army or police pick up a young man, there is some law you can invoke, an institution you can rally against. Whom do you protest against in a situation like this?' asked one young man I met. 'Agar hum awaaz uthayenge koi banda humare ghar aakar humko bhi mar dalega (They would have killed us too, so we kept quiet).' So, like much else in Jammu and Kashmir, the truth about the unmarked graves was certainly not absolute. What made it truly unfortunate was that few were concerned about it in the rest of the country. This was especially true of the government at the centre. Within the state the authorities continued to argue over exactly how many people had gone missing, when and under what circumstances. But the debate was meaningless to families where time had failed to bring the glimmer of hope or the certainty of heartbreak. When I met them, the women in these homes would wrap their arms around me and cry without inhibition even before they knew my name. It's almost as if for them every visitor from outside was a bearer of some news, any news that would seal the open-ended sorrow of their lives.

There were countless stories, like those of Shabnam's brother Manzoor who was just nineteen in 1997 when he was bundled into a car by security personnel and never seen again. He had been walking home after picking up some milk and vegetables for his three sisters. When I met her in 2011, Shabnam had searched the prisons of Jammu, Delhi, even Rajasthan, for any sign of her brother. With the only earning member gone, there were days that the girls literally starved because there was no money at home. Now Shabnam had learnt tailoring and stitched clothes to support her family. She hadn't given up on her brother.

■

In many ways the most tragic aspect of Kashmir's sorrow was that even the mourning for a dead child was not free from ideological politics.

In May 2002 terrorists targeted a residential army camp in Kaluchak in Jammu. Unarmed women and infants were pumped with bullets by men who stormed into the family quarters. In the intensive care unit of the city's main hospital were toddlers, some as young as two years old, strapped to tubes and wires. From behind the glass I looked on helplessly at Surya, a baby girl who was not yet three, her tiny face precariously held together by surgical stitches. Shrapnel had pierced through her lower jaw and ripped it open. Her

left hand had taken a bullet and was missing two fingers. Doctors
said it was a miracle that she had survived at all. In the adjoining
room was nine-year-old Preeti who had taken a bullet through her
chest. The oxygen levels in her brain had fallen and she was rambling
incoherently about an uncle who had pleaded, 'mat maro, mat maro'.
At the cremation grounds I saw the body of Havaldar H. S. Chauhan
brought out in olive greens and placed on the pyre beside that of
his thirty-year-old wife and fourteen-year-old daughter. An ageing
father who could barely walk performed the last rites. There was
also Havaldar R. K. Yadav who had come to say farewell to his
comrades but not before burying his four-year-old son. Six of the
seven pyres lit that morning were of women who had been killed
trying to shield their children from bullets.

Back at the army camp, bloodstained school bags, orphaned dolls,
a toddler's pink lace dress were testimonials to lives cut short. At
Nirmal Kaur's home, the smashed photo frame of her two teenage
children, Amandeep and Jitendra, lay on the floor. One of the three
terrorists who had infiltrated the camp came charging into her house,
chasing her right into the tiny bathroom where she ducked behind
a metal bucket. As they shot at her, she screamed, her kids heard
her cry for help and started shouting in panic as well. The terrorist
turned his gun on the children and killed them. In another home
an unarmed havaldar, Manjit Singh, wrestled with the gunmen but
could not save himself or his family. One of his children was two,
the youngest just two months old.

Children and women, not defined as combatants by any code of
war, had been at the epicentre of the Kaluchak attacks. Yet beyond
stock condemnations, there was no outcry in the global media, no
marches of solidarity, no moments of silence, and no mass protests as
there would be several years later for the Peshawar school massacre
in Pakistan.

Even grieving dead children came with disclaimers and qualifiers
in the vitiated atmosphere of Kashmir. Almost a decade later in
2010 when more than a hundred young boys died on the streets
of Srinagar after violent clashes between those pelting stones and
armed police and paramilitary, there was once again unwillingness

in the rest of India to see the boys as victims of excessive force and poorly handled crowd management despite the clear asymmetry of power in the confrontation.

The real story in that season of death was waiting to be told not so much on the empty curfew-bound streets of Srinagar but inside the over-burdened hospitals where the children of conflict were strapped to hospital beds.

I met nineteen-year-old Munir Ahmad from the frontier district of Kupwara who was battling injuries from two bullets, one in the thigh, another in the ankle. A higher secondary student, he didn't deny that he was part of a stone-pelting crowd. But when we met him, there was no bluster or sloganeering or uncontrolled rage. He whispered to us that he dreamt of being a schoolteacher. Munir could have been faulted for being a participant in the street violence, but there were far too many children I met in hospital whose only fault was that they had been at the wrong place at the wrong time.

Fifteen-year-old Amir Ashar was leaving the local madrassa when a gunshot ripped open his leg and dislocated his hip. Halfway through recalling what happened to him, he stopped mid-sentence, his speech taken hostage by the trauma of the memory.

The youngest victim was all of nine—Sameer Ahmed, who died during a funeral procession for one of the young men who had been shot. The last march drew thousands of protesters onto the streets and the police said Sameer had been crushed in the stampede. His family said he had been beaten to death. No matter which narrative you believed, that summer of unrest was a national crisis. Omar Abdullah, the chief minister, has often described those two months as his most difficult. Children and teenagers had become the face of the Kashmir tragedy.

In fact, the two-month-old conflagration had begun with the death of seventeen-year-old Tufail Mattoo who was walking home from tuition, his books still in his hand, when a tear-gas shell accidentally hit him and split open his skull. He died instantly. His family had been planning a big celebration for his birthday that month. Now, all the windows of his house in downtown Srinagar were framed with giant sheets of white paper with 'Wake Up' scrawled over them. It was a call for justice by his parents; Tufail was their only child. His wise father, Mohammad Ashraf Mattoo, even in that moment of personal tragedy, spoke to me of how every such incident would only draw more young men armed with stones onto the streets. 'These boys are young; some of their ideas may be half-baked. But if these things happen, of course they will be angry.'

The paramilitary and the police defended their actions by pointing to the broken windows of their bulletproof vehicles. One man's jaw was smashed and his teeth broken, another was in danger of losing his eyesight after a stone hit his cornea.

Four years later, while travelling through Jammu and Kashmir for the state elections, I went back to Tufail's house. In his room, several shelves were lined with textbooks—Tufail loved to read, even his school bags had been framed for posterity. Under a giant portrait of the young boy, his ageing father and I sat cross-legged on the floor and over salty tea and bread spoke about him. Mattoo had decided not to vote in any election till there was some punishment for those who had done this to his son. 'Do you still believe in the system,' I asked? 'Yes, I still believe. This is a chance. It's a golden opportunity for India. Justice is not just about human rights: it's about democracy.'

V

In October 2010, just as the blustering, bombastic former president of Pakistan, General Pervez Musharraf, had launched his own political party and declared that he would return to Pakistan (as it turned out, he was placed under house arrest right after his return), I met him in London where, protected by the Specialist Protection Unit of the British police, he had lived in exile for four years in a three-bedroom apartment near the city's Arab quarter. We spent an hour talking in a well-appointed drawing room that had, along with Persian rugs and leather chairs, on proud display a framed picture of him on the cover of *Time* magazine with a headline that read: 'The Toughest Job in the World'. He did not hesitate to take absolute credit for a Kashmir peace formula that had come to be the informal frame of reference in all discussions on India and Pakistan's troubled relationship. The broad contours of what was sometimes called Musharraf's four-point formula were something like this: Borders would not be redrawn, the LoC would become the de facto boundary but it would be a soft and porous border. There would be increased autonomy on both sides of the LoC and a joint mechanism for some areas like tourism and culture. The Pakistanis pushed for demilitarization as well—a sticking point for the Indians. 'Let me tell you, very proudly, these parameters are mine,' he said boastfully, but in this case truthfully. 'I realized when I was talking to everyone on the Pakistani side, on the Indian side, that the dispute is Kashmir. What is the solution? Not one of them ever gave me a solution. So that set me thinking.'

Revealing that both countries had almost sealed the deal Musharraf said, 'You ask me how close we were? We were as close as drafting the final agreement.' I pressed him for more details. Were drafts physically exchanged on both sides? 'Yes, of course, through the back channel.'

Praising Manmohan Singh for his 'sincerity and flexibility', Musharraf insisted that had he remained at the helm of government in Pakistan both countries could have moved towards signing a final pact on Kashmir. Minutes later, we got locked into an ugly argument about the Pakistan-sponsored Lashkar-e-Taiba terror attacks on Mumbai in 2008. 'From our point of view anyone who is fighting in Kashmir—your part of Kashmir—is a mujahid who is fighting for the freedom and rights of the people there,' he said without apology or embarrassment. 'Using acts of terror that don't even spare women and children?' I retaliated, unable to keep my composure. 'I think we are going to enter into a discussion where you won't prove anything; I also won't prove anything,' he said tersely. The tension was palpable and was proof that Musharraf's confidence about India and Pakistan 'resolving' Kashmir was severely misplaced. Not because his peace model was unachievable but because in a post 9/11 and 26/11 world, Kashmir was no longer the most central or intractable issue between the two countries—terrorism was. As a journalist I would always try to be as impartial and as objective as I could be on whatever issue I was covering but as an Indian and as a human being there could be no countenancing of terror, and terror attacks on India and Indians. When a former president and army chief of Pakistan spoke of the LeT's 'popularity with the public' and argued that 'to handle and deal with them requires some finesse' as Musharraf did with me, it was impossible to not get worked up.

For India, the terrorism unleashed by shadowy Islamist militant groups like the LeT and the Jaish should have been the cue to call for a review of a Kashmir policy that has over the years always failed to seize the moment with the more moderate and indigenous elements of the insurgency. The diminishing of the JKLF, for instance, is not necessarily a cause for celebration when you consider how pan-Islamic extremists, most of whom are foreigners linked to global terror networks, have completely hijacked what was once essentially a local uprising. Unlike now, in the early years it was easy for journalists to meet and interview various JKLF militants without fear of reprisal or violence. One of the JKLF's chief commanders, Yasin Malik, was a scrawny twenty-year-old, who may have become a model instead of a militant had the elections of 1987 played out differently. Malik and his three friends became the first group (named HAJY after their initials) in the Valley to cross over into Pakistan for arms training. By 1990 he was in jail and in 1994, citing inspiration from the books he had read on Gandhi and Mandela, Malik announced a unilateral ceasefire and gave up the gun.

At the entrance to Srinagar's locality of Maisuma, where Yasin Malik lives today, the barbed wires and security bunker are vestiges of a past steeped in violence. An environment of perpetual protest and the frequent street clashes between police and young men here have earned it the newspaper sobriquet 'Kashmir's Gaza Strip'. The crowded, densely populated bazaar selling everything from spare parts to spices can empty out in seconds in times of trouble and curfew calls by separatists. My abiding memory of Malik's home is of the effervescence of his three sisters, the relative silence of his father (who was a bus driver for the state government) and Malik's own brooding intensity that perfectly complemented his uncombed hair, unkempt clothes and stubborn argumentativeness.

All my conversations with Malik took place well after his militant years were over, and as I interviewed him several times, it was sometimes difficult to believe that this wiry, untidy bearded man had directed that bombs be thrown at the city's Central Telegraph Office or subsequently masterminded the kidnapping of Rubaiya Sayeed to push for the release of jailed militants. He was also charged with the murder of five unarmed air force officers, the first such direct attack on the armed forces. His early release from prison in 2002—on grounds of his 'deteriorating health'—was hugely controversial given the gravity of charges he faced. It was clearly a gamble calculated to revive political activity in the violence-ravaged Valley. At the time, the JKLF enjoyed mass popularity and was the only group that stood for independence—the 'third' option—instead of accession to Pakistan. Still, no attempt was made by the government in Delhi to draw the JKLF into the dialogue process. Islamabad, by contrast, was swift and brutal in moving to decimate the JKLF whose independence motto was anathema to the Pakistani establishment. It propped up the pro-Pakistan terror group—Hizbul Mujahideen—to displace Malik and his men and to destroy their networks of support. It would have been an opportune moment for India's intelligence agencies to engage with the relatively less religious and malleable separatist politics of the JKLF. Instead, the JKLF was allowed to crumble under a focused offensive from counter-insurgents armed by India as well as targeted assassinations by the Jamaat-trained, more lethal cadres of the Hizbul Mujahideen. Malik's public rejection of the gun had already split the JKLF down the middle. Now, targeted by both India and Pakistan for very different reasons, it was gasping and spluttering for survival. Over the years, the JKLF found itself more and more marginalized. Many of the old warriors of the Valley who had survived, became small-time shopkeepers or traders in an effort to make an alternative life for themselves.

On the other side of the border, in Rawalpindi, not far from Pakistan Army Headquarters, I once met a soft-spoken, nondescript young man who was a salesman in a shop selling data cards for mobile phones. As we got talking I discovered he was from Srinagar, a former militant with the JKLF, fatigued and worn out by years of relentless violence. He was keen to return, but unsure of the risks that might await him back home. Some of his co-conspirators from a past life had taken the plunge and returned after the Omar Abdullah government announced a new rehabilitation policy. But since not one of them had taken the official government-approved route back into India—choosing to escape the ire of Pakistani intelligence by sneaking in from Nepal instead—they were not entitled to any of the benefits the policy offered. They had been disillusioned in Pakistan but were languishing upon their return to Kashmir.

I was in Muzaffarabad reporting on the much-publicized trip of the Hurriyat Conference to Pakistan-occupied Kashmir (PoK) and saw how stunned the security establishment was when Yasin Malik warned them not to romanticize militancy. It was definitely a strategic error for India not to negotiate with the JKLF at the right time; its collapse marked the ascent of Pakistan's jihadist fundamentalists, most of whom had no previous roots in Kashmir, taking control of the insurrection, as the original insurgents lapsed into lives of retirement or irrelevance. One former militant told me the missed opportunity by Delhi had only fortified the power of the gun, because those who had surrendered it had been abysmally weakened. 'We all decided on a ceasefire but since then we have lost 600 of our workers. They wanted an amicable solution but they have been killed only because they don't have a gun,' he said pointing to the more deadly nature of militancy now. 'Earlier there used to be firing or ambush, now it's become so bad that they take 125 kg of explosives and blast it on the roads, not caring who dies. It's become ugly. It's moved away from Kashmiris to international agencies that have their own vested interests. Call it pan-Islamic, call it fundamentalist, but in reality if the issues aren't solved this will just carry on.'

■

It is outrageous of course that those who are culpable of murder and terrorism should lay claim to amnesty. If the spirit of justice demands accountability and punishment for soldiers when they violate the law, it is contemptible to argue that militants should be absorbed back into the mainstream without being made to legally account for bloodshed. But in Jammu and Kashmir the complicated challenges of war and peace have seen thousands of surrendered militants turn informants and renegades for the state, this time armed with an official licence to kill. Others have fallen quietly into the anonymous crevices of ordinary lives. And several have joined political groups, either mainstream or separatist. It is this last category that ends up slipping between two stools, viewed as treacherous by India and traitors by Pakistan, if they dare to talk peace. Like Shahid-ul-Islam, former militant and lawyer and present-day separatist who narrowly escaped an assassination bid by throwing burning coal at two men who had come to meet him right after he delivered a public speech calling for 'peaceful dialogue'. Islam's years as a commander of the Hezbollah (he trained in an arms camp in Afghanistan) helped him spot the pistol concealed under the bulky phiran worn by one of the men. In Srinagar, where he is now an aide to Mirwaiz Umar Farooq—the Hurriyat Conference leader and main cleric of the city's Jama Masjid—he told me how difficult it was for the young Kashmiri men of his generation to extricate themselves from the terror trap they were ensnared in. 'Sometimes people used to tell me this is not your cup of tea, you are not fit for it,' he said, during an expansive interview, his sunglasses perched fashionably on his head. 'Ajeeb lagta tha, kissi ek mahaul se nikal kar bilkul doosre mahaul mein jaana. Lekin aur koi chara bhi nahin thha, wapis ja nahi sakte thhe (It was strange to be in an environment I had never been exposed to but at the time I didn't think there was any looking back possible).' The first generation of Kashmiri militants had all had some exposure to mainstream politics. Shahid's grandmother was a committed National Conference worker, his father a sports instructor who had taught Omar Abdullah at high school and bitterly opposed his son's embrace of the gun. When he left the house for PoK to make his way into the training camps of the Harkat-ul-Ansar in Afghanistan, his heartbroken father told him, 'Since you refuse to listen to me, you are not my responsibility anymore, now you are Allah's amanat.' Shahid was arrested in 1997 and though he is still an active political separatist, admits that rank outsiders have taken charge. 'Revolution needs its own children. If it goes out of your hands, you can't do anything, you are helpless. That's what happened to us.'

VI

Whether you commit to the idea of India or remain a secessionist, in Jammu and Kashmir a career in politics is a likely pact with death.

Sakina Itoo, once the only woman minister in the National Conference government, was just twenty-five when her father, the state's former revenue minister, was shot dead at point-blank range as he made his way home from the evening namaz. She was studying to be a doctor and reluctantly took his place in politics. Since then, she has been the victim of the most number of attacks on any politician in the Valley. Undeterred, she campaigns during every election in the remotest parts of rural Kashmir. On these journeys, she's had explosives planted on the route of her motorcade, been shot at, ducked grenades and lost count of the number of times an attempt has been made to take her out. In one such attack, two of her bodyguards died saving her. In another, a young woman, a passer-by, was killed when police exchanged fire with militants determined to plant a mine in the path of her convoy. 'My house is always under attack, sometimes they throw grenades, sometimes they fire at me,' Itoo said to me during the assembly election in 2002 during which she was the victim of four militant attacks in ten days. 'If my security had its way, I would not be allowed to step out. Once they kept me house-bound for four days. I told them I was not ready to stay locked up inside,' Itoo said, her face betraying both fear and strength. 'I said this will not do. I can't give up politics and just sit at home. Baad mein Uparwaale ki marzi, what is destined for me will happen anyway.' Did she not miss the relative safety of a more ordinary life, I asked her. 'What I miss are the small things. As a student, I used to love going to a theatre and watching a movie. Now I can't do anything like that. Being in politics here has finished my personal life.'

■

If the willingness to engage with the electoral process in Jammu and Kashmir can literally be a deadly choice, across the ideological divide, the readiness to talk peace can be just as fatal. Seventy-year-old Abdul Gani Lone, a dove among separatist hawks, discovered that the hard way. I remember being there at the precise moment he was slain.

It had been an annual summer ritual for twelve years now. A procession led by Mirwaiz Umar Farooq to commemorate the day his father, the separatist politician Maulvi Mohammed Farooq, was shot. For years, government agencies argued that Umar's father had been murdered by militants because they believed he was in covert negotiations with Delhi. Umar bristled at the explanation. 'It's really difficult to believe that when we see what followed the assassination,' he retaliated, recalling how paramilitary forces had fired on the several thousand people accompanying the final march to the burial grounds. 'There was firing at his funeral procession, sixty-five people were killed, the whole situation of Kashmir changed with that single event, but they have still not come out with the facts.'

As the cavalcade of cars and buses crept its way through the narrow lanes of downtown Srinagar, supporters of the Mirwaiz, old women and young children among them, showered rose petals and almonds on the twenty-eight-year-old separatist whose father's violent death had pushed him from being a computer engineer into the muddy waters of state politics. Soon, we were firmly in separatist territory, the grounds where the Mirwaiz's father was buried were known in this part of the city as a 'martyrs' graveyard'. It's here that militants and separatists alike were brought after their deaths. The media interest in the rally was because of its timing: Prime Minister Vajpayee was arriving in Srinagar the next day and the BJP government had been making a serious effort to get the Hurriyat Conference to the dialogue table. Little did we know that history was about to repeat itself in a bizarre and frightening manner. The unrest began when a group of young men, barely a handful among the few thousands who had gathered, began to raise slogans in favour of Pakistan. Chaos erupted as a fist fight broke out in the crowd, with the men finally being chased out of the grounds. This was a time when the Hurriyat Conference, the twenty-three-separatist-party conglomerate, was badly riven by a clash of ideologies and personalities. As things quietened down and the Mirwaiz began his speech, Lone was on stage with him.

Over many years of reporting the conflict, I had got to know Lone rather well. His chequered career in politics began with the Congress; during the initial years of militancy in the nineties his newly floated People's Conference briefly had its own armed wing; a decade later he was taking on the ISI and Pakistan and condemning the intrusion of jihadi mercenaries and foreign militants. In 2000, I had travelled to Pakistan to report on the wedding of his son Sajjad to the daughter of Kashmiri separatist Amanullah Khan—the cross-border wedding diplomacy was seen as a major political story. But once the song and dance had subsided what really grabbed the headlines was Lone's unsparing condemnation of foreign militants who he said were not welcome in the Valley. At a tea party with President Pervez Musharraf, Lone told him that Kashmiris were exhausted and could not be expected to fight indefinitely.

Perhaps these were the words that claimed his life. The rally at the Eidgah grounds was drawing to a close and along with other journalists we were heading towards the stands where our cameras were positioned, when we suddenly heard the sound of firing. Panic-stricken people began to run in different directions, one man suggested that maybe the shots were some sort of gun salute in memory of the Mirwaiz's father. Another confirmed that two men wearing uniforms, their faces masked, had merged into the crowd before one of them pulled out a gun. For a brief moment, my cameraman who was on his first ever visit to Kashmir, was paralysed with shock. 'Roll,' I shouted, pushing him in panic, 'roll!' urging him to start filming. Right in front of us bodies were being heaped into the back of a car that was speeding away to the nearest hospital. As news of Lone's assassination spread, I ran out of the grounds, racing my competitor from a rival network to the closest STD phone booth; mobile phone networks were still disallowed in the state.

The assassination, said Vajpayee, as he arrived in Jammu later in the day, was because Lone had spoken for peace. His daughter, Shabnam Lone, told people who had come to condole his death to refrain from crying. 'Look at his face,' said Shabnam, holding back her own flood of tears, 'it does not show fear, it shows knowledge. He knew the assassin had come, but he wasn't scared. Look at him, it's as if he is just sleeping.'

That evening, his distraught son Sajjad broke down in tears of rage and blamed militants, Pakistan's spy agency, the ISI, and Hurriyat hard-liner Syed Shah Geelani for his father's murder. When the Pakistan-leaning Geelani arrived at the residence to offer his condolences, mourners and supporters physically threw him out of the house in full gaze of the waiting cameras. By next morning, whether from pressure, fear, or simply self-preservation, Sajjad retracted his accusation blaming it on his emotional fragility. Instead, he targeted the state government of Farooq Abdullah for not providing his father adequate security cover. But from that moment, he began his rather lonely voyage towards the promise of democracy, fielding proxy candidates in the polls of 2002 that took place just a few months after his father was killed. By 2014, he was an elected member of the legislative assembly, fending off the label of 'traitor' that ironically came from equal and opposite directions. Many of his own people charged him with 'selling out' after his much-publicized meeting with Prime Minister Narendra Modi and his praise for the BJP. Others in the rest of the country thought his antecedents made him inherently perfidious. The initial isolation of someone like Sajjad once again underlined the biggest error in India's Kashmir policy—the failure to reach out and grab the hand that was being tentatively offered.

Among the first separatists to unequivocally condemn all loss of life in Kashmir, Sajjad Gani Lone called upon 'the liberal and emancipated silent majority...to isolate the hawks'. Like his father, he took on the militant-recruiting expeditions by jihadists, telling his people to beware. 'Yeh log jo aap ke paas aate hain aur aap ko bolte hain ki humein ek baccha de do, shahadat ke liye, Lone sahib ki kasam, yahan jo khoon behta hai, is khoon ko bhi ye log bahar bechte hain (These people who come to you and say give us a child for martyrdom, I swear on Lone sahib, they will sell your blood for their own agenda).' Yet, for years, no one in government bothered to engage formally with Sajjad, not even when he wrote a lengthy vision document for the state as he continued to experiment with electoral democracy. In 2014, when he finally took the plunge and joined hands with the BJP, he defended his decision by pointing out that it was the only national party that had bothered to communicate with him in over a decade.

VII

Among the many strands of the Kashmir story that are worth remarking upon is the one where, in the mid-1990s, instead of trying to rehabilitate surrendered militants, the government decided to use them to form a pro-government militia that would be deployed to battle the insurgency. Operating on the 'it-takes-a-thief-to-catch-a-thief' principle, the government encouraged these men to use their months of training in militant camps across the border to now turn the tables at home. The much-feared Ikhwanis (Arabic for 'brothers'), as they were known, killed hundreds of militants and provided crucial intelligence in anti-terror operations as members of the special operations group (SOG). But with the unfettered freedom to retain arms and weapons, a power they were often accused of abusing, they came to be as notorious and reviled among many Kashmiris as they were powerful.

Kukka Parrey—at first a folk singer on Radio Kashmir, later a militant, an Ikhwan, and finally a legislator—was the best known of the gunmen who were co-opted by the government. In the nineties when he first turned trooper for India's forces, you would find cryptic and coded references to him in radio frequency conversations: 'This is Bulbul,' the message would go, 'ask Koel what song he is singing tonight.' Bulbul was a military intelligence officer, Koel a veiled reference to Parrey.

The strategic community gave Parrey and his men credit for helping the army decimate the Hizbul Mujahideen cadre effectively using their insider understanding and competitive guerrilla tactics. Police officers credited the Ikhwanis for creating a security environment that enabled the 1996 elections. But along the way these counter-insurgents went beyond the grasp of the law. They illegally felled and sold timber, their men would extort money from shopkeepers, vendors and bus drivers at checkpoints, and they were charged with a spate of extra-judicial killings. Finally, because violence always begets violence, Parrey was assassinated in 2003 by militants of the same Hizbul Mujahideen that he had taken on. His family furnished letters to show that his many pleas for greater personal security and a bulletproof vehicle had been ignored. But so unpopular was Parrey by the time he was killed that he was buried in the backyard of his own home instead of being allowed a place in the village graveyard.

The Ikhwanis would argue that as they steadily outlived their utility they became the forgotten army. On the other hand, ordinary Kashmiris would say that they had never been brought to justice for the atrocities they committed. As with most other things in this conflict-swept state, both statements were true.

Until the early 2000s, it was not uncommon to see Ikhwanis walking through the streets of Anantnag with AK-47s slung casually over their shoulders. At the time there were still an estimated 3,000 surrendered militants who had been allowed to retain their weapons. Most of them were on the temporary payroll of the special task force of the state's police on a fixed salary of Rs 1,500 per month.

I spent some time at the headquarters of the south Kashmir Ikhwan and as I interviewed a man who still called himself 'chief commander', his henchmen spread out in a protective ring around him. Some stared down at me from the roof where they stood guard. Their rifles, pistols, automatic guns were casual extensions of themselves. Every single one of them protested what they saw as a defamation campaign against them. The disagreement over whether they were victims or villains was evident during the watershed elections of 2002. Chief Election Commissioner James Lyngdoh— widely credited with having delivered the first fair and free election in several years—officially called for a lockdown on the uncontrolled movement of Ikhwanis on polling day. They were allowed to vote, but only on condition that they left their weapons at home. Lyngdoh went on record to say that 'there are people who have surrendered their arms and come over to this side. But the public perception is that they have been misused for other purposes...'

But as violence escalated in the next phase of the elections, the Jammu and Kashmir police chief blamed it on the confinement of

the counter-insurgents. The utilization of these renegades in anti-
terror operations, without subjecting them to the normal rules of the
game, was a decision that proved to be more tactical than strategic.
It would have some quick short-term gains but several long-term
repercussions that were extremely damaging for peace in the Valley.
They should either have been disarmed and provided with regular
employment or recruited as full-time, legitimate soldiers of the
army. The unleashing of unregulated armed militia further broke
down trust among an already alienated people. The failure to create
any other role or economic incentive for those who were willing to
surrender left them disenchanted as well as vulnerable to militant
violence. In the netherworld they came to inhabit, these men became
hate figures for both ordinary Kashmiris and the militant groups
they once trained with.

Before he was killed in 2003 in a targeted terror strike, another
Ikhwan, Javed Shah, spoke to me candidly of his many avatars. He
had been a police constable, and later a Pakistan-trained militant.
Soon after, he joined the ranks of the state's counter-insurgents. He
finally ended up as a politician who also edited his own Urdu daily.
Shah admitted that some of his 'boys' had been guilty of extortion
but argued that they had no dependable source of income. He blamed
the government's flawed policy for leaving surrendered militants with
few options. 'We are heroes, you know,' he said to me. From which
film, I asked, jokingly. 'Like Shah Rukh Khan,' he said. 'Which film
of Shah Rukh's?' I asked, now interested in the self-image he was
drawing. 'You know that film, *Anjaam*?'

I hadn't seen it. He elaborated, 'In *Anjaam*, Shah Rukh Khan
pleads with Shivani to tell him once, just once, that she loves him.'
'So no one says that to you,' I pushed him to open up more. 'Koi
nahin karta. Na maa, na baap, no koi ladki (No one loves us. Not
our fathers or mothers, nor any women. Even our neighbours call
us traitors),' he said, his voice cynical and resigned.

Most worryingly, the Ikhwanis warned that many of those
who had surrendered could end up returning to militancy because
of shrinking options. Mehbooba Mufti, the leader of the People's
Democratic Party whose political slogan was the promise of a 'healing

touch', said the absence of 'normal' options for a young man who wanted a second shot at life were so minimal that in many ways 'he had become a suspect forever'. There were only two options that a surrendered militant had, she told me, 'Join a government agency and pick up the gun or return to militancy and pick up the gun.' One of the first decisions of the Mufti government, when elected in 2002, was to disband the special task force of counter-insurgents and merge them into the regular police force. But by this time the brutalities the Ikhwanis were blamed for had mounted and, as far as ordinary people were concerned, they remained grossly unpunished.

Every honest election made an attempt to lift the shadow of the gun. But sometimes the ironies were staggering. In 2014, when the critically-acclaimed but contentious Bollywood film *Haider* portrayed Kukka Parrey on celluloid, in real life, his son Imtiaz was gearing up to contest assembly elections in Bandipora, his father's hometown where the very mention of his name still provoked fear and anger. Sitting by Parrey's grave, Imtiaz argued that history had been unfair to his father, while conceding that in today's Jammu and Kashmir, battles would have to be won and lost by the ballot unlike the years that his father lived through when it was the gun that wielded power. 'If my father's legacy were only about violence, why would so many big leaders endorse me; why would I be as famous as I am?' he asked as I persisted with questions about his father's infamous past.

A short walk away from where I was sitting with Imtiaz, people were queuing up to vote in sub-zero weather, the serpentine line making its own powerful statement about the redundancy of the boycott that had been called by the separatists. But in that same row of people was haunting evidence that the Valley's past was still an open wound. One of the voters at the polling booth was a man called Abdul Rashid. He pointed to a patch of grass close by—the exact spot where his brother had been shot dead by Parrey's band of renegades during the tumultuous years. He is still fearful of talking openly in public about it. At his home, he breaks down under the weight of that memory. Holding a photograph of his brother's bullet-ridden body, he wept. 'My brother did nothing, he was an innocent man.'

As he spoke, a small group of angry men entered the courtyard and started shouting angry slogans urging Rashid not to vote. But Rashid said he was counting on his vote to be an instrument of change. Both Imtiaz and Abdul Rashid—perpetrator and victim—were seeking a departure from a violent past in yet another reminder of how many destines are interlinked by conflict in this state.

VIII

Often forgotten by the media, paid lip service to by politicians in every election, and on the periphery of global attention, the Kashmiri Pandit community has every reason to be embittered. Their history, and with them the fate of the Valley, changed forever on 19 January 1990. This was during the first stages of militancy and there were reports of an imminent attack on the Pandits. Local mosques began asking them to leave their homes. On that night, thousands of Kashmiri Pandit families packed up and left in what would be the beginning of a mass exodus.

The Valley's separatists have always blamed the state's governor at the time—Jagmohan—for engineering a divide between the Hindus and Muslims as part of the strategy to crack down on the calls for 'azadi'. The Pandits themselves rubbish that theory. They were pushed out at gunpoint, they say, after communal threats and targeted killings. Decades later, more than six lakh Pandits remain dislocated and uprooted from their cultural and linguistic moorings, unable to return home and unable to feel at home anywhere else. In the immediate aftermath of their banishment, a majority of families were pushed into migrant camps where they lived for years in makeshift plastic tents and one-room tenements. Their memories of where they came from had photographic detail, infused with colours and textures and smells. But their children, they have always worried, will be strangers in their own land, never having known the idea of home. Like with the partition that separated Pakistan from India, many of those fleeing thought their departure was temporary. Some left in a panic without taking any belongings. One man I met had come away with only a picture of the Kheer Bhawani temple but told me his mind would not permit the peace of forgetting.

Refugees in their own country, most families in migrant shelters were dependent on the few thousand rupees they got from the government. But more than their economic future it was their identity that was at stake. Because of dismal living conditions in the camps, lack of privacy, and late marriages, the displaced Pandits were now worried that their numbers would dwindle. 'Our sons and their wives sleep in the same room as us. We don't complain. But are we cattle to be herded together like this?' asked one elderly migrant. A National Human Rights Commission report in the early 2000s backed this fear. 'There is a serious erosion in the normal sexual functioning of Kashmiri Pandits living in migrant camps...a fall in birth rate is a natural consequence.' Even where there was economic comfort, the scare of cultural decimation was very real.

Shakti Bhan, a prominent gynaecologist at a private hospital in Delhi, said she earned more now than she possibly would have had she not had to leave. 'It's about identity. I feel rootless,' she said to me, her anguish punctuated by bursts of anger. Bringing up children in an unfamiliar milieu meant that as parents they sometimes overcompensated to help their kids assimilate. 'Your identity is your language,' she said bitterly, 'now I live in Delhi and I speak English, Urdu, Punjabi and teach my children the same. So where is our identity? I think a day will come when the Kashmiri Pandit will exist only in name.'

■

In Srinagar's Habbakadal area, once the throbbing centre of the flourishing Pandit community, where an estimated 30,000 families used to live, there are now barely forty such households. A Ganesh temple stands as a lone witness to what once was. Otherwise it's like taking a walk through the ruins of the past. There are several abandoned homes that are empty and locked up, others that were once owned by Pandits have been sold, occupied by the security forces, or taken over by squatters. On one of my many visits there, I saw a solitary vulture perched atop a burnt wooden beam that must have once held up a house. The narrow alleys were still and lifeless; the bird seemed to be feasting on the carcass of history.

There are now less than 3,000 Pandits left in the entire Valley, the numbers a grave challenge to the plurality of 'Kashmiriyat', which the people have always claimed defines them culturally. Their decision to stay on was extraordinary for the times they lived in. Among them was one of Srinagar's best known doctors—S. N. Dhar and his wife Vimla. In the summer of 1992, Dhar was kidnapped by the militant group Al-Umar, and spent eighty-three days in captivity. The rickety Fiat the doctor drove up and down the boulevard was the same car the militants had bundled him off in a decade earlier. In his personal diary, which would later be published as a book, Dhar wrote, 'There was an acute sense of shame and betrayal. "Why me?" I often wondered. The initial days were full of anguish and fear.' After he was freed his family and friends urged him to leave, maybe move to Delhi where he had a lucrative job offer or America where could live comfortably off private practice. But Dhar refused, this was home, he said, he couldn't imagine being anywhere else.

Vimla spent those eighty-three days her husband was gone living on prayer, but her trauma was about to be compounded. One morning she woke to the news that Sharda Peeth—the school and research centre her family had run for generations—had been razed to the ground by militant groups. Hundreds of schools were burnt during those years of senseless violence. But Sharda Peeth was special, it was run by a Hindu trust in one of the city's poorest Muslim neighbourhoods. Its library housed rare Persian and Sanskrit texts and manuscripts that had now all been reduced to ashes. Heartbroken, but determined, Vimla did not let the school shut down for even a day. She created a makeshift room with tin sheets and classes resumed almost immediately. But her husband's diary entry spoke the bitter truth. 'Images of a bonfire sent a shiver down my spine. There were hardly any Hindu students or staff in the school. We had hoped it would be spared. But we had committed a grave mistake in understanding the magnitude of this mad violence,' he wrote.

As the split between the Muslims and the Pandits grew wider, a 'separate homeland' became the demand of Pandit groups who organized themselves into a party called Panun Kashmir. Panun in

Kashmiri means 'our own'. They argued that the state should be split into four parts, Jammu, Kashmir, Ladakh, and Panun Kashmir—a union territory for the Pandits that would club regions north and east of the Jhelum River.

Even when militant violence declined significantly, the Pandits said a homecoming could not be considered unless they were promised separate enclaves. The Muslims said the Pandits must live as they always did, assimilated and together. For, by now, personal friendships notwithstanding, political beliefs had come to be polarized along religious lines.

It wasn't just Kashmiri Pandits but other religious and cultural minorities as well, be it the Sikhs or the Punjabis, who carried within them that strange mix of constant yearning and rage towards their homeland. The filmmaker Vidhu Vinod Chopra returned home only briefly during the shooting of his film *Mission Kashmir*. When the plane touched down on the tarmac and Vidhu disembarked, setting foot in Srinagar for the first time in years, he knelt on the cold tar and kissed the earth. 'I miss the seasons, the hawa, the taste of the air I used to breathe,' he told me. His ageing mother had accompanied him because she wanted to find her home before she died. A small handheld camera filmed her search for her house. Inside everything was gone—the blankets, linen, silverware—but her puja room had been left absolutely intact. 'Maybe if the Pandits had taken up guns, we would have also been heard,' declared Vidhu.

Wandering through the back alleys of Habbakadal, I met Ghulam Mohammed Abdullah, a local photographer, born and brought up in the area. Wiping the dust off long-forgotten images from a time when the Valley was still Bollywood's Switzerland, he pulled out a photograph of Shashi Kapoor. Then, excitedly, he dug out some more photographs, this time of the Amarnath Yatra. 'I used to take photographs mostly of Pandits, their weddings, their pilgrimages. Now those times are gone,' he said, cradling his granddaughter in his lap and plying us with cups of salty tea. Abdullah took out a bunch of silver keys and beckoned us to follow him. He led us into one of the derelict structures, past a metal gate, and up some wobbly stairs. For fourteen years, he told us, he had safeguarded the house of his Pandit neighbour. He described it as his amanat, a treasure of an old friendship given to him by God for safekeeping. Though he controlled access to the house, and it was unlikely that anyone would ever return to claim it, he said he would never rent it. He wanted us to go back to Delhi and tell the Pandits we knew that their temples were safe. 'Mandir ki hifazat karna hamara farz hai, iss tarah hum Panditon ki rakhwali karte hain. Voh chale gaye. Yeh hamari badkismati hai aur unki bhi (It's our duty to protect their temples, that's our way of protecting the Pandits. They had to leave. That is their misfortune and ours),' he said his eyes welling up with tears. One day, he said, one day they may come back because 'duniya umeed par kayam hai—the world lives on hope'.

IX

As journalists we had become weary witnesses to carnage and conflict but there was also that one time when we were not the storytellers, we were the story. In August 2000, a temporary ceasefire by the Hizbul Mujahideen had just been withdrawn after the collapse of the first round of formal talks between the militant group and the centre. Independence Day was just a few days away. This was usually a time when security was tightened; this year it was even heavier because of the meltdown in the only concrete negotiations to have ever taken place between the highest levels of government and any indigenous militant group. The BJP was in power in Delhi, always strident and hyper-nationalist on Kashmir when in the Opposition, but much more innovative, bold and ready for risk when in power than the Congress had ever been. If there was a strategic mistake made in the first real peace talks it was the haste and enthusiasm to go public with them and convert the moment into a premature press conference. When the Hizbul militants arrived at Srinagar's historic Nehru Guest House wearing ominous black masks, I remember thinking that the moment was filled with possibility, but also grave danger. I dug out my reporter's diary from that day; notes I scribbled down at the time use one word to describe the image of India's home secretary standing shoulder to shoulder with the Hizbul Mujahideen—'surreal'. Hailed as a breakthrough before a detailed roadmap for reconciliation was ready, the initial euphoria dissipated swiftly when from his protected perch across the border, the Hizbul chief, Syed Salahuddin, set a deadline of 8 August for negotiations to be concluded, and warned that his group's ceasefire would be withdrawn if Pakistan was not involved. The demand was outrageous and the stage was set for a violent confrontation. Two days after the peace talks collapsed and the ceasefire was dead came a day that none of us who report from the state would ever forget.

In a craftily designed attack, militants first threw grenades at security forces outside the city's State Bank branch. The bank was situated close to Srinagar's Residency Road, where most media had their offices. As the reverberations were heard across newsrooms we ran out in the direction of the explosion. This was our reflex reaction formed over the years—hear bomb go off, drop everything, pick up camera, run, report, run back. We all knew that there was an inherent risk to our lives and yet whether we were dedicated professionals or danger junkies or both, nothing so far had prepared us for our community actually being singled out for assault. The grenade attack was nothing but a booby trap, a distraction designed to lure a large number of journalists to one site where an improvised explosive device had been planted in a white Ambassador car and fitted with a timer for maximum impact. It detonated with a roar as we charged towards it. There were screams, then blood and mutilated bodies everywhere. The *Hindustan Times* photographer Pradeep Bhatia had sprinted the fastest among us. He now lay dead on the street, his camera by his side. Another photojournalist, Fayaz, was covered in blood and sobbing. I cradled him in my arms, tears rushing down my face, as I tried to pull him to safety. For a moment, the rest of the scene receded into a blur—the sirens, the shouts for help, the retaliatory firing by shell-shocked security forces. I just sat on the crowded street holding Fayaz tight, rocking him.

When the bodies were counted, eleven people were dead, twenty-nine injured, among them eight journalists. There were worries that one of them, Irfan Ahmed, was so badly injured he could be maimed for life. Intelligence agencies believed that although the strike was timed to coincide with the collapse of talks with the Hizbul, it was actually the Pakistan backed Lashkar-e-Taiba that was responsible for it. That night after I had filed my report—because that still had to be done—I took the phone off its hook in my hotel room. My family and my colleagues were all calling repeatedly, insisting that I fly back to Delhi the next morning. I refused. One of our own had just been killed, we couldn't be cowards and leave. There was no question of it. On the cold floor of the room, I sat with my friend Muzamil Jaleel, one of the several outstanding Kashmiri journalists I had gotten close to. I poured myself a small glass of Old Monk and Coke and we shivered just a little bit, unable to find the words we used so swiftly for other moments when we were not directly in the firing line. In that moment I felt some fear, but acute sadness as well. I felt the loneliness of the conflict reporter bonded to her area of work by an unspeakable emotion, an attachment that perhaps only others in the same situation could understand.

We were battered and bruised but we had survived. Those who had enabled the now-dead talks between the Hizbul 'commanders' and the centre would pay the price over the next few years. One by one, all the significant militants who had participated in the direct dialogue with the government were eliminated by their own brethren who accused them of being sell-outs. Not one was spared. Fazul Haq Qureshi, the low-key separatist, who had been the principal mediator and negotiator on the back channel between the two sides had firmly declined the offer of government security. He said before there was a larger plan for rehabilitation no separatist or militant could afford to be seen as appropriated by the government; that would be more life-threatening. And, as it turned out, he was chillingly right. Underlining the peculiar uncertainty of his efforts at bringing militants to the table, he said the men who were part of the talks had ceased fire but had 'neither surrendered nor dropped the gun yet.' They were waiting for a fuller understanding of what lay ahead for them. This remained the conundrum for every government looking for lasting peace. An amplified, hysterical, mass-media fuelled narrative of what was patriotic and what was treacherous only further shrank the space for manoeuvrability. On the other side, those who contemplated a life without the gun also battled labels of traitors and deserters. Qureshi himself came under a life-altering militant attack and quietly faded away from political life.

The intricate reality of the state means that there are many simultaneous and seemingly contradictory truths; the inbuilt volatility of the situation creates pressure to take sides and be boxed in by simplistic labels of for and against. If you feel empathy with or admiration for the men in uniform who have over the years battled both venom and violence, dubbed 'occupiers' by separatists in a conflict that was not of their making, you are instantly called a jingoist and a status-quoist. If you speak honestly about the emotional alienation in the Kashmir Valley or condemn any violent subversion of the law or extra-judicial killings you are classified as treacherous and anti-national. It was rare to have both labels foisted on the same person—that privilege was mine. During the floods that submerged Srinagar in 2014, I was vilified by young Kashmiris for praising the military's mammoth rescue operations; they accused me of running a public relations campaign for the army, privileging the stories of soldiers over those of local volunteers. But on social media, I was mocked—as I still am every day—for my non-existent Kashmiri husbands and my softness for separatists. I was apparently both a hyper-nationalist and a seditious traitor. It didn't bother me; Jammu and Kashmir had been a more profound journalism school than any Ivy League institution I had attended. Its beauty, its scars, its hostility, its warmth, its danger, its tragedy had all enveloped me, and provided me with a lifelong attachment to the place. I could only be grateful for the learning.

X

Pakistan's obsessive-compulsive Kashmir disorder and the use of terrorism as a strategic extension of state policy have locked India into decades of conflict in Jammu and Kashmir. As I've said earlier, some of the blunders have been ours. We have missed opportunities and lost trust where faith could have been easily built. Among the biggest mistakes that I have witnessed in two decades was the staged encounter at Pathribal. Presented to the world as an operation that had eliminated the perpetrators of one of the worst massacres in recent history, it ended up being the ruthless murder of five innocent civilians wrongly linked to the mass shooting of Sikhs in the village of Chittisinghpura.

The year was 2000. It had only been a few months since President Bill Clinton had intervened and read Pakistan the riot act on withdrawing their remaining infiltrators from Kargil. Now as he was about to touch down in Delhi the visit was already being hailed as a turning point in Indo-US relations. I was in Srinagar keeping an eye out for imminent trouble. Fresh from covering a war on the front lines, I was not unused to death and coffins and the heartbreak of those left behind. But I had never been exposed to what I was about to witness next. The sight of thirty-six bodies, all Sikh men, draped in white sheets and spread across a village courtyard splattered with bloodstains and littered with broken shoes chilled every sense. This was a meticulously plotted massacre designed to draw Clinton's attention and internationalize the Kashmir problem.

We had driven out three hours from Srinagar to the interior village of Chittisinghpura in south Kashmir. When we got there helicopters were hovering over the village. On the ground a maze of jeeps, ambulances and soldiers formed a wall around the site of the carnage. Even from a kilometre away, we had been able to hear the women weeping, their cries rising in a crescendo of pain. But now the sound of their pain was drowned out by the wave of sickness and panic that rose within me. At the entrance to the gurudwara, I saw the bullets that had pierced the wall. The men had been separated from the women and children, lined up with their backs pressed to the wall and shot at point-blank range. Their murderers had masqueraded as an army patrol, dressed in battle fatigues and claiming to be on a combing operation. They came bearing not just AK-47s and grenades but also alcohol. 'Their "commanding officer" was very polite and spoke in soft Urdu,' recalled Nanak, the night's only survivor, his voice shaking as he spoke. As gunshots raked the ground and bodies collapsed into lifeless heaps, one of the shooters threw his head back and laughed. 'This is our way of playing Holi,' Nanak recalled him saying.

The terror attack was clearly aimed at driving a wedge between the Sikhs and the outlying Muslim majority neighbourhoods. That morning, those who had survived were already debating leaving. As army and police officers waded through the grieving crowds, they were almost lynched. Angry slogans were raised against them; the villagers wanted to know why they were not provided enhanced security if trouble was expected to coincide with the Clinton visit. The police freely admitted that they had been taken by surprise; they had never expected the Sikhs to be targets of mass violence.

Five days after the slaughter, there was a dramatic announcement. In the presence of Union Home Minister L. K. Advani (who was also the deputy prime minister at the time), Anantnag's senior superintendent of police, Farooq Khan, declared that the butchers of Chittisinghpura had been eliminated. An identical statement was released in Delhi by Home Secretary Kamal Pande. The perpetrators were revealed to be five terrorists from the Pakistan backed Lashkar-e-Taiba. According to the official account, a local milkman, Mohammad Yaqoob Wagay, had guided the killers to the homes of the Sikh villagers. Wagay's arrest had led the security forces to the terrorists, said Kamal Pande, commending the forces on a job well done. In the Jammu and Kashmir assembly, Chief Minister Farooq Abdullah hailed the quick crackdown as a major success.

If it weren't for the torn scrap of a maroon sweater this may have been where the story ended. The sweater was how Raja Begum was able identify the charred body of her twenty-five-year-old son, Zahoor Ahmad Dalal. The body was recovered with 98 per cent burns. Zahoor had left home for a walk and never came back. In fact, it would transpire that Zahoor was not the only civilian who did not make it back home that evening. Within a five-kilometre radius of Pathribal in Anantnag, four others had also gone missing around the same time that the anti-terror operation was being hailed as a huge breakthrough. Agitated relatives spilled on to the streets of south Kashmir, with the village women leading the march, to demand news of the whereabouts of their sons and husbands. Compounding the escalating and entirely self-created crisis, the police and paramilitary shot at a procession of 2,000 protestors who were petitioning for an independent enquiry into the mysterious disappearances of five innocent men. Nine persons were killed even as the police maintained that the firing had started from within the crowd. Later, a judicial commission, headed by Justice S. R. Pandian, firmly rejected that theory, instead faulting the police for the use of excessive force and a failure to take the protests seriously. As public anger mounted, the Farooq Abdullah government was forced to order the exhumation of the bodies said to be of the five Chittisinghpura terrorists and order DNA tests to verify whether the killings of the five missing civilians had been staged to manufacture a 'successful' conclusion in the Sikh massacre investigation. If it seemed that the credibility of the administration could not possibly fall any lower, the worst was still to come. The forensic tests were fudged, the DNA samples had been tampered with. When the news of the manipulation came into the public domain, Mohammad Yousuf Tarigami, the only Marxist legislator in the assembly and an unfailingly polite, unflappable politician told me, 'We talk of rebuilding the confidence of the people, but I am ashamed to say—forget that distant dream. Today, we have washed away their trust.' A furious Farooq Abdullah, now forced to apologize for the botched investigation in the assembly, announced that the CBI would be taking charge. 'I want justice. I really cannot understand why people don't want the honest answers,' Farooq told me in an interview.

Twelve years later, in March 2012 when the CBI filed its charge sheet, it made for harrowing reading. The bureau wrote of the 'tremendous psychological pressure to show quick results' after the Sikhs were mowed down by militants in Chittisinghpura. It charged the security forces with plotting a 'criminal conspiracy to pick up some innocent persons and stage manage an encounter...' It listed in gruesome detail the mutilation of the five bodies, almost beyond recognition. So if Zahoor had died of burns, according to the CBI report, 'Bashir Ahmad Bhat's body was with half of [the] skull, face distorted and unidentifiable'. Some of the information was too incendiary to be used in real time reporting. The charge sheet said that 'Mohammad Yousuf Malik's body was without head, neck and upper one-third of the left side of the thorax'. The extensive burn injuries, it argued, were evidence that 'the encounter was stage managed with a view to obliterate the identity of the killed persons'.

For years after the report was made public, the CBI and the Ministry of Defence were entangled in a legal battle with one pushing for penal punishment and the other arguing that the Armed Forces Special Powers Act provided for immunity against prosecution of soldiers engaged in security operations, unless specifically ordered by the central government. The army stood firmly behind its officers arguing that they had moved forward on intelligence provided by the police. It pointed to diary entries at the local police station which indicated that it was on the orders of the Anantnag SSP Farooq Khan that a team of the SOG was dispatched for a 'secret operation'. But in his testimony Khan disassociated himself from the encounter by saying that though 'police representatives had accompanied the army, they had not necessarily taken part in the shoot-out'. It was Khan who had first made the statement to the media that the militants responsible for the Chittisinghpura massacre had been eliminated. Asked how he justified the announcement, Khan told the enquiry commission that his comments were based on a briefing by the army, adding that 'army operations are always led by their officers'. Khan, who had earlier received a president's medal for gallantry, contested his suspension from the force, and once exonerated by the CBI report, was reinstated. The army officers were tried by a military court of enquiry, but in 2014, fourteen years after the CBI told the Supreme Court that the Pathribal encounter killings 'were cold-blooded murders and the accused officials deserve to be meted out exemplary punishment', the army closed the case against them, concluding that the 'evidence recorded could not establish prima facie charges against any of the accused persons'. And that was that. By 2015, Farooq Khan, the police officer at the centre of the controversy, had joined electoral politics. The Pathribal case had been reduced to a footnote.

■

'It will have blood, they say. Blood will have blood. Stones have been known to move and trees to speak.' Macbeth's tormented admission on being revisited by the ghost only he could see could well have been written of Kashmir's cyclical violence that allowed episodes like the Chittisinghpura massacre to take place.

Though an arrested Pakistani militant from Sialkot, Suhail Malik, told the *New York Times* in an interview from prison that he had been a member of the killer squad sent by the LeT to massacre the Sikhs, the staged killing in Pathribal, the manipulation of DNA samples—all these hurt India's otherwise strong case on the carnage of Chittisinghpura. The state's credibility was not the only casualty, conspiracy theorists were suddenly emboldened to question the official account of the bloodbath itself.

Several years after the headlines had faded, Farooq Abdullah, now union minister in the central government, revealed that he had wanted a judicial probe into the massacre, 'but vested interests scuttled the move'. With that hyperbolic flair typical of him he also said he was writing a book that would address what he believed to be the truth. 'This should only be opened after my death,' he whispered while addressing a Sikh group in Srinagar. No one knows if the book was ever written or whether that was merely a dash of rhetoric that Farooq was known for.

XI

The younger generation in the Valley has been shaped entirely by the harshness of two decades of turmoil and violence, growing up for the most part without exposure to a daily dose of religious diversity. An unintended consequence of this social change, combined with the impact of foreign terror groups like the LeT and the Jaish, has been the creeping ascent of radicalism among sections of the Valley's young men. This radicalism has been largely uncommented on, there remains an element of denial about it. Of course their sentiments still remain firmly located within the context of ethno-nationalism rather than a global Islamic movement. And it is pertinent to point out that while the sighting of the odd ISIS flag in the Valley creates huge media interest, of the young Indian men who have gone to fight alongside the Islamic State in Syria, only one is from Kashmir—the rest are from cities like Mumbai and Hyderabad.

But the radicalization is a real concern, and there has also been a simultaneous increase in social conservatism dictated by religious orthodoxy once unknown among Kashmiri Muslims. The reality is contradictory and confusing. At one level are the women who have defied the archaic stereotypes and judgements that imprison their gender in other parts of the country. In the Valley, divorce is not frowned upon, nor are late marriages. As a single mother to two daughters, Mehbooba Mufti has emerged as an extremely popular and dynamic politician. One of the city's most beloved high-school teachers, Qurat-ul-Ain, has been a passionate advocate of personal liberty. She got divorced twenty-five years ago when it was still unheard of, bringing up her daughter single-handedly. She says people have offered nothing but 'love and moral support'. When I first met Dr Hamida Naeem, a professor of English at the university, she introduced herself as 'Kashmir's original feminist'. 'I got married late because I had one condition and it was that I would be marrying one person, not an entire family,' she said, defiant in her rejection of the expectations that are made of women after marriage. All the Kashmiri women I have met, poor and rich, educated and illiterate, have remained strong and indomitable in the face of violence and tragedy.

Yet, there was also a time when a shadowy militant outfit that no one had ever heard of—the Lashkar-e-Jabbar—tried to force a dress code, warning women to observe purdah or face the consequences. While some women did choose the burqa, it has never been an authentic part of the Kashmiri tradition. Typically, a Kashmiri woman will dress in a short phiran and a scarf wrapped around her head and knotted at the nape of her neck. If she is young she may substitute this with the dupatta of her salwar kameez. The sudden diktat ordering women to go behind the veil spread panic and fear in those months, more so because it was a command from a group whose antecedents no one could trace.

The dress code was openly challenged by women from different political ideologies. As a member of the state cabinet, Sakina Ittoo said women would not accept force or pressure, especially from those coming into Kashmir from 'outside', alluding to Pakistan-backed groups. Pointing to how the wife of General Musharraf had dressed on their visit to India, Ittoo underlined how there was no hijab or purdah or even a dupatta framing Ms Musharraf's face. Only one woman welcomed the violent threat to impose purdah and that was the pro-Pakistan insurgent Asiya Andrabi who issued a written statement saying, 'we are indebted to those courageous men who have started a campaign for the veil in Kashmir and made us realize that we are Muslims. Let us take a pledge that as long as our souls are in our body we will adhere strictly to the Islamic dress code'. Professor Hamida Naeem rubbished Andrabi's claims to represent the women of the Valley. 'We are liberal by nature, not rigid. We have always followed the golden mean.' She challenged the very reality of the Lashkar-e-Jabbar. 'I am suspicious of the whole thing. We have never heard of it, it seems to be some kind of fabrication, the figment of someone's imagination.' But she admitted that the threat had been successful in creating an environment of alarm. 'I have seen that college girls are especially scared and some of them have tried to stitch these abayas or burqas. But I think women should stand together and while remaining wedded to their customary clothes, they should withstand this coercion, they should not kneel before it.'

When I tried to elicit the responses of ordinary women I hit a wall. Many were too fearful to speak their minds. Others admitted to a conservative backlash and admitted that while they may have worn trousers growing up, as adults pants were a strict no-no. At a high school for girls in the heart of the city, they sought safety in numbers. They agreed to speak to me provided I addressed my questions to the entire classroom and not to individuals. I polled the room: those who think this campaign to enforce purdah through violence and threats is unjust, please raise your hand. Every single hand shot up, it was the strongest chorus of opposition I had seen so far. Yet there were covered heads and faces shrouded by veils in a classroom where teachers said this was not the case till just a few weeks ago. The girls admitted that much as they wanted to fight the decree, they were scared that someone would come and fling acid at them. Defiance could be deadly.

When my interview with the courageous young women of Kashmir aired on television, there were unforeseen and startling ramifications for me as well. I discovered that an incensed Lashkar-e-Jabbar had issued a fatwa against me, warning that I would not be safe if I returned to Kashmir. The fatwa got play in national newspapers the next morning and I confess that I felt rather unsettled. But I knew I could not yield to this intimidation. Women and young girls with no protection had braved the threats to talk to me; there was no question of my opting out of the debate. I vowed to return to Srinagar the same week. Intervening in the controversy was the young Mirwaiz who boldly declared that there could be no fatwas on the entry of people into the state and that I was welcome just like everyone else.

XII

Until the floods of 2014 ravaged the Kashmir Valley and converted it into a sea of rubble and debris, tourists were scrambling for selfies on the boulevard, shikaras were festooned with fairy lights, hotels were booked out and posh golf holidays in Srinagar and adventurous skiing expeditions in Gulmarg were much in demand. Many casual observers of Kashmir point to these trends and argue that the situation has changed dramatically for the better in the state once called the world's 'nuclear flashpoint' by Bill Clinton.

At one level, they have. Militancy in Jammu and Kashmir has come down. Three consecutive state elections, starting with the path-breaking one in 2002, have taken place transparently without any controversy around manipulation or coercion of voters. The most recent one saw a historic turnout; more people voted in Jammu and Kashmir in 2014 than had in the last twenty-five years. Most significantly, mainstream politics has made space for a soft-separatism and sub-nationalism within the bounds of the constitution. Slogans of 'greater autonomy' and 'self-rule' are now debated by elected representatives within the state assembly, further reducing the political clout of hardline azadi seekers. Erstwhile separatists like Sajjad Lone have jumped into the hurly-burly of politics with his Pakistani wife Asma Khan, daughter of Kashmiri separatist Amanullah Khan, joining the campaign trail. Ironies abound as curfewed nights, blocked mobile phone services and the staccato of intermittent gunfire become yesterday's reality, seemingly replaced by more contemporary aspirations, where bakeries and cafes are now brimming with young Kashmiris.

But to anyone who knows the state closely, conflict is still simmering beneath the surface and can easily boil over. What was once a regional disagreement between Jammu and Kashmir has turned religious as the gap continues to widen between the different parts of the state. In times of tension it is not uncommon to see street protests from a younger, more hardened generation of educated men, their fists wrapped around stones, punching the air in anger and full-throated revolt, their rebellion cast in the same image as the Intifada of Palestine. It hasn't helped that the police and paramilitary forces are yet to learn how best to control the fury of volatile but unarmed crowds. It was just two years after the 2008 election, also hailed and celebrated as a milestone in the state's journey toward 'normalization', that more than a hundred boys were shot by security personnel during clashes in which bullets were used to counter stones. It took not just a peace missive by an all-party delegation, but the additional intervention of the otherwise pro-Pakistan separatist Syed Shah Geelani to return a measure of calm on the streets. Geelani made the startling revelation that Chief Minister Omar Abdullah had sent his political adviser to him as a secret emissary.

The Islamization of what has been a strictly political problem is a real possibility, especially in the age of the internet when propaganda by reactionary groups is both cheap and effective. If the emotional distance between Delhi and Srinagar continues to widen we run the risk of pushing young men into the embrace of pan-Islamic forces. In seeing Kashmir only as a national security challenge—which it also is—without building trust in the institutions of our democracy, we are only making it easier for religious fundamentalists to grow roots. Every mistake that violates the rule of law and denies accountability strengthens conspiracy theorists and enables Islamist influences to fill the vacuum the promises of democracy should have occupied.

You only have to follow the story of Burhan Wani—who at the young age of twenty-one became one of the most wanted Hizbul Mujahideen commanders of the Valley—to know what could become the new face of militancy. Just some years ago, Burhan had scored 90 per cent marks in his school exams; now clad in western casuals, he addresses his generation of Kashmiris through video clips or audio packages vowing to 'unfurl the flag of Islam on Delhi's Red Fort'. He dropped out of school just days before his Class X examination. Pictures of him in full battle fatigues have gone viral online and the local police forces believe that he has single-handedly recruited thirty young men, many of them educated, into militancy in south Kashmir. Some say Burhan, a cricket lover and the son of a school headmaster, took to militancy after his brother Khalid was assaulted during the 2010 unrest. Khalid and his friends were stopped at a security check post where one of the police officers beat him up.

The question is whether a different, more imaginative, approach by the state may have prevented Burhan from picking up the gun. And how many more Burhans are there in the towns and villages of the state just waiting to be pushed into the clutches of radicals?

∎

The scars of the Jammu and Kashmir insurgency have often been measured by body bags and coffins and by statistics and sorrows. What's tougher to understand and easier to forget is the impact of this continuous, unabated violence on the deepest recesses of the mind. In many ways the full horror of how the violence is unsparing to the sanity and mental stability of everyone who comes in its path—man, woman, child, soldier, renegade, militant—is best understood by a visit to Srinagar's only psychiatric hospital. Long after the headlines have faded, it is here in the damaged landscape of the mind that the real stories are to be found.

The numbers are telling. In 1990, when the insurgency first erupted, only 1,762 people were diagnosed with mental disorders. After a decade of inexorable violence, those numbers shot up to 38,696. Behind these figures was the fatigue, mental and emotional, of a people both battered and bruised. This was their private hell, one that remained invisible to the cameras and the public gaze, this was the loneliness that came with the feeling that you were losing your mind.

At the hospital we met Mushtaq Margoob, the state's most famous psychiatrist, a soft-spoken doctor who had devoted his life to shepherding people through the cobwebs of the mind with a messianic zeal. He allowed us in on the condition that we would not reveal the identity of the patients we met. Whether azadi-seekers or counter-insurgents, soldiers or secessionists, children or adults, men or women—in different ways, they were all haunted by the mental imprint of the bloodshed they had seen.

We met a young girl, still in her teens, who saw a stray bullet kill her father. For years, the doctors said, she had slumped into a wordless depression that took away her will to live. 'She has been suffering very badly,' Dr Margoob told us. 'Her father was killed eight years ago. But she saw his mutilated body and ever since that time she completely withdrew from social and other activities. She refused to go to school. Finally she refused to eat her meals.'

Then there was the elderly man who had been trapped inside the venerated Hazratbal Shrine during the month long siege in 1993. He was among the 170 civilians held hostage by militants who were in the midst of negotiating a safe passage with the army that had surrounded the dargah. Venerated by Muslims because it was believed to house a holy relic of Prophet Muhammad (a hair from his beard), in those years it had become a haven for militants who believed no government could afford a repeat of an Operation Blue Star style storming of a place of worship by its army. Though the man we met at the hospital eventually came out unhurt, it took a few years for him and his doctors to understand that the scars were emotional. 'He says that he had gone there to pray and thought that Allah had decided his time had come,' Margoob explained. 'He still thinks he will never recover and that there is nothing in this world for him.'

Analysing why the trauma here was different from that of a mental hospital in any other part of the country, Margoob wrote, 'Beginning in 1990 the whole population was abruptly exposed to severe stress arising from mass destruction of life and property, overwhelming fear and uncertainty. It is well documented that exposure to this kind of stress means more and more apparently normal people suffer from palpitations, insomnia, anxiety disorders, hysteria, depression and even major disturbances.'

Other doctors at the hospital explained that almost every single patient they had treated had at some stage been witness to a violent death. They would not come immediately in the aftermath of the incident for treatment. In fact it would usually take another smaller incident of violence, for instance, a grenade blast that they saw on television, to trigger the panic that had been lying dormant.

In the land of pitched battles, both political and militaristic, the hospital was a sad but effective equalizer. When the demons struck they were unsparing; there were no favourites, no exceptions. At the entrance we met a group of men in police uniform lining up alongside ordinary civilians. 'I suffer from depression,' admitted one, talking about how troubled and restless he feels, adding hastily, 'I shoot quite well. I stood first in the competition between eight units. It's just that I get tense sometimes.' A group of security personnel at the hospital that morning were from Tripura in the Northeast where they had seen their own share of conflict. The Valley, they said, was their toughest assignment. They spoke of jawans pulling out their guns and turning the rifles on themselves. Why were we hearing about such incidents so often, we asked. 'Problems at work, there's a lot of tension,' explained one soldier.

Every morning there were so many people at the walk-in clinic of the hospital that people would spill over onto the streets. Many had made the trek from far-flung interior villages. There were not enough doctors to cope with the swelling numbers. Margoob calculated that there was only one psychiatrist for every 200,000 people in the state.

Even in the crowd their haunted eyes gave away their inner turmoil. Waiting his turn was a young boy of fifteen with a vacant look on his face who had come to Srinagar from hundreds of kilometres away. When he spoke, it was in barely audible whispers. 'I have headaches, I feel dizzy.' And then, after a pause, 'I consumed poison,' he said, his tone betraying absolutely no emotion. Dr Vinay Bhat who was treating him told us that this was not uncommon. 'Every day in the emergency we tend to at least two to three suicides.' The irony, of course, is that Islam forbids the taking of one's own life. And yet, here in violence-torn Jammu and Kashmir, insecticides—used to keep the Valley's lush apple orchards in bloom—which are inexpensive and easily available have become the favoured tool of suicide.

We asked the young boy what had driven him to attempt killing himself. 'I used to feel scared,' he said softly. What were you scared of, I asked. 'Ghosts.' Why were you scared of ghosts? 'I thought they would kill me.' This was a state where the gun had become the ghost and there was nothing friendly about its fire.

In the worst years of violence when the city would shut down at sunset and the security environment did not permit tourism or any other commercial activity, many young boys fell back on drugs as recreation. Brown sugar, heroin, even cough syrups had become the emotional crutch to cope with the nothingness of existence.

Down the corridor in the hospital we met a woman who broke down in tears. More than a decade ago she was interrogated by the Ikhwanis. Her son was also taken away for questioning and has been missing since. Her doctor, Maqbool Dar told us, 'She feels sad most of the time. She also feels acute restlessness and is unable to sit at home. Whenever anybody knocks on the door her heart starts beating faster, she starts palpitating.'

In Jammu and Kashmir, post-traumatic stress disorder (PTSD) was not the affliction of adults alone. Dr Margoob had surveyed orphanages across the Valley to find that 40 per cent of the children he spoke to were suffering. Many of them had major depressive disorders especially those who had lost one parent before the age of eleven. 'Because of loss of [a] social support network which chronic conflict is known to cause, many of these young traumatized children landed up in orphanages,' Margoob's paper argued.

At one such orphanage for young boys I met Aijaz and Shahnawaz, who had become the best of friends. Aijaz was the son of a militant, Shahnawaz's father had been shot by militants. 'I want to run very far away when I see a gun,' Shahnawaz said. His buddy agreed. We asked the two boys what they dreamt of becoming. 'We want to help the poor,' they both said shyly.

Six

OF POLITICAL DYNASTS,
JUGGERNAUTS AND MAVERICKS

I

IN THE WINTER of December 2013, just as the BJP's star was ascending on the political horizon, I received a surprise call from Priyanka Gandhi Vadra. It was unexpected because, while we had exchanged more than a few text messages over the years, I was not in regular journalistic contact with her. This was partly because she was not in active politics and partly because the Gandhis were famously inaccessible and media-averse. Once we were beyond the niceties she proposed a freewheeling interview with her brother Rahul Gandhi, the vice president of the beleaguered Congress party. He had been elevated to the post that year, nine years after he first entered Parliament in 2004 at the age of thirty-four. The general perception was that he had taken too long to step up to the plate; now everyone wanted to know whether he would finally lead his party's campaign in the elections of April 2014.

Priyanka told me candidly that I would not be the only broadcast journalist to get the opportunity but added that I'd definitely be the first. This was a potential scoop—Rahul had never gone on television to take questions before. She wanted me to come by her brother's Tughlak Road residence for an informal chat so we could discuss logistics and schedules.

A couple of days later, I was shepherded into an anteroom done up in minimalist style. I had been a journalist for two decades but this was only the second time I had been here—the first time I was part of a larger media group, for an off-the-record meeting in which we didn't get beyond the side lawns of the house. Priyanka walked in dressed casually in a skirt and black tee. Her laid-back vibe had always been a charming contrast to the relatively stiff and aloof personalities of both her brother and mother. I suspect I had been considered ahead of other TV journalists because four years earlier my televised interview with her in Amethi had gone well.

In 2009, when we sat down to talk on the lawns of the guesthouse where she was staying, Priyanka was still idealized in the larger public imagination. She was charismatic, photogenic and stylish without being fussy or precious in any way. She came across as a people's person in politics. However, I had always felt her spontaneity—suddenly hugging a village woman, affectionately pulling her mother's cheeks on stage at an election rally, wading through crowds while shrugging off her security—was marked by inner turmoil and unvoiced angst.

For a country that had only known her until then through photographs in newspapers and short clips on television, she remained an enigma. So when she opened up to me in that very first full-length interview, and spoke publicly of both private and political issues, people were absorbed by what she had to say. They wanted to know her better. Criticisms of her husband Robert Vadra's contentious business dealings had not yet dented her brand. She disarmed me because she spoke without any guile or sophistry and I was unused to that in interviews with politicians, where the truth was often obscured by platitudes or deflected by spin.

The part of the interview that drew the most attention was her reason for making a quiet visit in March 2008 to a prison in Vellore to meet a member of the Liberation Tigers of Tamil Eelam (LTTE), the terrorist squad responsible for the assassination of her father. He was killed in May 1991 when a suicide bomber blew herself up after touching his feet. 'In the beginning, when my father was killed, I didn't realize it, but I was furious. I was absolutely furious inside. I was furious not with particular individuals who killed him, but I was furious with the whole world,' she said, her calm tone in contrast to the wrath she had admitting to feeling.

Yet, she disagreed with the media narrative of her 'forgiving' Rajiv's killers. She had a startling challenge of the very notion of victimhood. 'The minute you realize that you are not a victim and that the other person is as much a victim of the same circumstance as you, then you can't put yourself in a position where you are anyone to forgive someone else. Because your victimhood has disappeared.' She added later in the interview: 'People ask me about non-violence, I think true non-violence is the absence of victimhood.'

As we continued to chat, she confessed freely to 'one moment of terror' in 2004, just after her mother had led the Congress party to an unexpected victory, dislodging the popular Prime Minister Atal Bihari Vajpayee. Elaborating on the days right before Sonia famously invoked her 'inner voice' to turn down the sycophantic Congressmen who wanted her to take the country's top political job, she said she had peeped into her mother's office and seen, 'Laluji and everybody surrounding her and saying you have to be prime minister... I had this one moment of complete terror and I burst out crying.'

At the time of this conversation, Sonia Gandhi was the most powerful politician in India. In 2005, I had asked Sonia whether Rajiv would have been surprised to see her leading the party. 'No, maybe, not,' she had laughed. And then came the revelation. 'He was very keen that I fight an election when he was alive. Of course I resisted it...he always felt that (though) I used to make a fuss in politics and all that, I could certainly manage a constituency. So, I think, perhaps, he would not be that surprised.'

From Priyanka's perspective, though, her mother's decision to embrace politics was totally counter-intuitive. She had envisaged Sonia retiring to a cottage in the hills, spending her hours reading and gardening. 'People ask why she joined politics. She explained it in one simple sentence—I can't look at the photos in this room if I don't. These were the photographs of my father and my grandmother. She went completely against her grain to do this.'

The young woman whose broad forehead, sharp nose, sari-draped frame and firm stride had drawn many parallels with her formidable grandmother had often been described as more naturally suited to public life than her brother. 'There was a time when I was a kid, when I was about sixteen or seventeen, when I thought that this is absolutely what I want to do with my life...the question has existed for me since I was fourteen,' she admitted. Growing up as Indira Gandhi's grandchild—'I did idealize my grandmother, I grew up in a household where she was the head and she was an extremely powerful woman. Not just politically powerful, she was a powerful human being to be around'—had confused her sense of self. It took her a while, she explained, to separate the strands of who she actually was and who she imagined herself to be because of Indira's overwhelming impact on the family.

She told me it was during the 1999 election, when she had to decide whether she was actually going to run for Parliament that she had made up her mind not to get into active politics. 'Actually I went for Vipassana meditation. I was so troubled by the fact that I didn't know my own mind, I just disappeared for ten days of meditation to better know my own mind, rather than what other people wanted of me.' Ten years later, she was insistent that apart from the seasonal forays into her brother's and mother's pocket boroughs 'this is not for me'. Defying public perceptions she described herself as 'personally, a complete recluse', much more so than Rahul. 'I'm very happy living my life the way I am. I think there are certain aspects of politics I am just not suited to.'

■

That interview took place in 2009. Now, as I began to prepare for the interview with Rahul in early 2014, much had already changed. The polls had begun to forecast a clear victory for Narendra Modi, the BJP's prime ministerial candidate in the general elections that would take place in April. Priyanka had suddenly and unexpectedly taken full control of the entire Congress campaign. Her life so far had been mostly about baking, bringing up her two kids, pursuing photography (an interest inherited from her father), studying to complete her masters in Buddhist Studies, working on a book about her mother—and of course, periodically helping her brother and mother with their parliamentary constituencies in Uttar Pradesh. Now she was calling the shots on every campaign decision. From spin-doctoring to selecting candidates, even the party's strategy meetings had shifted to her Lodi Estate residence.

So what had happened to her oft-stated disinterest in electoral politics? Priyanka told a friend that she had not been able to sleep for five straight nights thinking about the prospect of Modi as prime minister. She also believed that Modi—who had taken several swipes at her husband Robert—would come after him and his business. Contrary to persistent Delhi gossip about trouble in their marriage, she was absolutely and totally in love; Robert was definitely her blind spot. Their detractors sometimes spoke of him as her 'Asif Ali Zardari'—a reference to Benazir Bhutto's husband who came to be known as 'Mr Ten Percent' because of corruption allegations. But she saw him as a victim of the political battle between the Congress and the BJP.

Robert himself was hard to read. Though he was initially a Facebook 'friend' of mine, we did not know each other well beyond the cursory exchange of hellos at large gatherings. His friends insisted that he was a down-to-earth, unfussy guy. I wasn't so sure that description fit his flamboyant and loud persona, figure-hugging t-shirts and beefed up body. Before the surfacing of accusations that he had made his wealth off sweetheart business deals enabled by political influence, Robert even contemplated joining politics. In an interview to me in 2012, he did not rule it out saying he would think about a political career, 'the day I feel that I can make a difference for the people, and the people would like me representing them, and it's a complete focus; because I feel you can't do two things, business or something else and politics. I want to do it for the right reasons and make a difference. That calling will come at some stage, I feel.' Curiously, on that same day, Priyanka told reporters that Robert was a 'happy businessman' and he was 'not interested' in entering politics.

Priyanka was enormously protective of Robert. Some months after the 2014 election was over—when I and other members of the media criticized him for the tantrum he threw when an ANI reporter quizzed him about his dubious business dealings (the reporter had door-stepped him at a gym opening and Robert had snarled back, 'Are you serious?' summoning his security guard to delete the footage from the reporter's camera) he sent me a message on Facebook informing me that he had decided to 'unfriend me'. 'Get a life', he told me in his irate message and that was the last time I ever heard from him. I suspect that little incident is what would change the friendliness of Priyanka's dealings with me.

All this lay in the future. In the run-up to the election, Priyanka was fully involved in the 'Halt Modi' attempt of the Congress. She told people she met that if Modi won and his government pursued a case against Robert she would reconsider her decision not to run for Parliament. And though she officially denied any such plans word was that she had already volunteered—though she was probably just thinking out loud—to run against Modi in Varanasi.

'No one in my family would ever stop me from contesting an election. My brother, mother and husband would whole-heartedly support me if I wanted to contest,' she told me in 2014. 'My brother has expressed to me many times that he thinks I should contest.'

The enmity between Narendra Modi and the Gandhi family was not merely ideological or political; it was visceral and often deeply personal. While the rhetoric used against political opponents is always overstated and often ugly, the exchanges between the Gandhis and Modi had always been of an entirely different order. In 2004, while campaigning in that year's national election, Modi taunted Sonia's foreign origins while he was on the stump by likening her to a 'Jersey cow' and her son to a 'hybrid' bacchada (calf). During the 2007 Gujarat state elections, Sonia called Modi 'Maut Ka Saudagar' (Merchant of Death), alluding to his alleged role in the Gujarat riots of 2002.

There were no across the aisle moments of brief friendliness or social civility in Parliament—at least not until after Modi became prime minister. The Gandhis were friendly enough with other BJP politicians. For instance, BJP leaders Arun Jaitley and Sushma Swaraj had shared some moments of cordiality with Sonia, despite their political combativeness. Right after the 2014 elections, when Jaitley was hospitalized for surgery, Sonia picked up the phone and called his wife Dolly to enquire after him. Sushma Swaraj had moved well past the shrillness of her 2004 election threat to shave her head if Sonia Gandhi ever became prime minister and was frequently photographed with her, chatting amicably. As Opposition leader she had even offered respects at Rajiv Gandhi's samadhi. (This was well before a controversy in the cricketing world in 2015, involving businessman Lalit Modi, would sour relations between the Gandhis and Swaraj.)

The rift between Modi and Sonia and her children went beyond political differences. In some ways, both tapped into the other's political and psychological insecurities. Beyond the overt ideological clashes, especially when Modi was still Gujarat chief minister, the Gandhis epitomized the culture of entitlement that had treated people like him as unwelcome outsiders. They were the anglicized sophisticates who had been born into power and affluence in contrast to his own humble origins. With his slogan of 'Congress Mukt Bharat' (that aimed to make the Congress party an irrelevance) Modi was determined to overthrow the political royalty of the Gandhis. He was the citizen who had come to take a kingdom.

Apart from the stated ideological differences, the Gandhis were unused to Modi's brand of confrontational politics; so far even Opposition leaders had been awkwardly polite around them. Modi's contempt for them, on the other hand, was undisguised—he once called Sonia 'Pasta Ben'. His consecutive victories in Gujarat made it impossible for them to ignore him. But trapped between offence and defence, they were unsure about how to tackle him.

Sometimes they worried that they made him stronger every time they attacked him directly. During one of the Gujarat state elections, photographs of Sonia and Rahul Gandhi simply went missing from Congress election posters and banners so as to not draw direct comparisons of style and personality between them and Modi. On the other hand, there were times they would lurch in the opposite direction and make direct, personal attacks, such as dragging his marital status into the campaign—these would often boomerang on them. In this battle, they didn't know whether to duck his precisely targeted sniper shots or retaliate with mortar fire. Modi had changed the rules of war and the Gandhis—certainly the daughter—understood that even in victory he would be an inscrutable opponent to formulate a strategy against. Had Modi not been the BJP's prime ministerial candidate—had it been, say, Rajnath Singh or L. K. Advani—Priyanka would not have jumped headlong into the campaign of 2014.

But here we were, listening to the self-professedly 'reclusive' sister urging her brother to begin talking more to the media. Or so, I thought. When Rahul Gandhi ambled in, his terrier Piddi at his heels, I got the distinct impression that he was more persuaded than willing when it came to being interviewed. His party had just been reduced from three terms in power in the political capital to an embarrassing single-digit presence in the Delhi state assembly. But if he was dismayed or nervous about either the recent defeat or the imminent debacle in the general elections (that exit polls were prophesying), he betrayed few signs of that anxiety. The electoral rise of bureaucrat-turned-crusader Arvind Kejriwal had already occupied the alternative democratic space that he had long wanted to grab. Yet he spoke casually, confidently and somewhat complacently about his plans for the future.

In the notoriously fickle drawing rooms of Delhi, I had often heard Rahul being described as not-too-bright (in far less charitable terms). But the few times I had spoken with him I had thought otherwise. He was well read, respectful of academic expertise, and keen to meet specialists to mine their minds. His problem was not that he had read too few books—it was that he had a clinical, statistical approach to a profession that was often about instinct and human connections. He was like a man looking for the exactitudes of mathematics in the mysteries of poetry. His ways befuddled many of his own party colleagues. In Congress circles there was the hilarious story of the Punjab Member of Parliament who thought the only way he'd get Rahul's attention was if he sent him a regular supply of research papers. So he hired a group of MBA students just to draw up documents that he could send to Rahul. He didn't understand a word of them—something he freely admitted to—but he had given the researchers standing instructions. 'Write about issues like malnutrition. That's what he likes.' Of course Rahul never got back.

In some ways, he was like his technocrat father Rajiv who had been forced into politics as a rank outsider without any understanding of either his own party's power dynamics or that of the system at large. Except that, unlike his father, whose career had had its genesis and abrupt end in violent assassinations—first that of his mother, then his own—Rahul had the luxury of several years of authority without any responsibility. He neither became a minister in the government, nor took charge within the party.

Amartya Sen, the acclaimed economist, had a telling story about Rahul. Once over dinner in Delhi, Sen told me that when he was Master at Trinity College in Cambridge University, Rahul came to meet him, apparently on Sonia's advice. In Sen's recollection, Rahul—who studied at Trinity under the name of Rahul Vinci—'was not interested in politics at all'. Nor did Sen believe at the time that the young man was suited for it. The impression of his lack of interest in his profession and his unsuitability for it persisted over the years amid whispers that it was his mother who had insisted on him entering politics over his more charismatic sibling in order to sustain the family legacy.

In contrast to his mother, however, who was advised by old-style back-room strategists who were much more instinctive than studied, Rahul Gandhi's aides seemed to be detached, America-returned analysts who weren't exactly sure of what to make of the rough and tumble world of politics. His mother relied especially on the subtle political cunning of Ahmed Patel, her political secretary, who kept a low public profile, but virtually ran the party from the small, covered annexe verandah of his Delhi residence. Ministers of the UPA government used to vie to get an appointment with him; during Cabinet expansions they would worriedly call different journalists and ask us if 'AP' had given any hints about what 'Madam' had in store for them. AP, or Ahmed Bhai as he was universally referred to, had friends in every party. In political circles, it was widely known that it was his phone calls to a section of the BJP that had stopped that party's leadership from creating a storm over the issue of Robert Vadra's business deals in Parliament in 2011. (It was eventually not the BJP but Arvind Kejriwal who would question Robert's business dealings at a press conference a year later.) Patel, who slept in the morning and worked by night, also made it a point to keep in regular touch with journalists, handing out dribs and drabs of gossip and information to keep us engaged. His boss,

Sonia Gandhi, may not have been media-friendly, but her political secretary was acutely aware of how the media worked and would sometimes test possible public reactions to party decisions by leaking information in advance to journalists.

By contrast, Rahul's chief of staff, the St Stephen's and Wharton educated Kanishka Singh, or 'K' as he was more commonly known, was as opaque and inaccessible as the man he worked for. Forget talking to journalists, older party leaders resented him for being a hurdle to their being able to meet with Rahul; weeks could go by before most of them could get an appointment. Other key members of his team—whether it was Sachin Rao or Mitakshara Kumari—all had the right pedigree and degrees (Harvard, MIT and Oxford) but clearly lacked the emotional quotient needed to pick up the pulse of the people.

I listened to Rahul expound on his alternative model for the Congress while his sister sat by his side on the sofa letting him dominate the conversation, occasionally looking up with a smile. He did not deny the malaise in the Congress was severe enough to make it almost moribund. The rot within, he suggested, needed surgical excision—'open heart surgery' was the phrase he used—and repair. It was almost as if he planned to raze the party to the ground and then rebuild it. He said he didn't agree with half the things the Congress leadership said and did. His comments were confusing. Was he suggesting that he did not see eye to eye with his mother or just her band of advisers? Or that the institutionalized resistance to change was so entrenched in the Congress, admittedly a status-quoist organization, that even he, the would-be king of the fiefdom, could not issue a firm diktat for change? This helplessness, whether feigned or felt, was unconvincing.

I'd heard this a couple of years earlier as well, in 2012, during the assembly elections in Uttar Pradesh when Rahul had fronted the campaign with unflattering results. At the time, as I've said earlier, a small group of us had been invited for coffee—which was being dispensed from a Café Coffee Day machine placed on the pocket lawn of his house. In response to our questions on why he did not build a more permanent, grassroots network in India's most politically significant state, one from which his father, grandmother and great-grandfather had made their way to the prime ministership, he had claimed an absence of authority to take his own decisions. He said he had expressed a wish to run as the Congress candidate for the post of chief minister—an attempt to prove that the party's commitment to the state was serious and long-term—but the 'higher' authorities wouldn't hear of it. So he quietly fell in line.

Now, in 2014, just a few months before what would be the biggest electoral wipeout for his party since its inception well over a hundred years ago, he was clearly distancing himself again—at least in private—from the Congress way of doing things. I asked him whether he was ready to take Modi head-on by becoming his party's official candidate for prime minister. There was a moment of awkward silence and a quick look exchanged between the siblings before he replied saying that the decision had been left to people 'more senior' than him—in other words, his mother. Eventually, of course, the party would avoid the direct confrontation with Modi; his mother decided that Rahul would not formally run for the post of prime minister.

As Rahul spoke to me of lowering the entry barriers for politics and empowering MPs with real authority to frame policy—he could be quite garrulous in private—I got into an argument with him over the evident contradictions in his formulations. These went well beyond his (until then) tardy attendance and glaring lack of participation in Parliament. He spoke of democratization but represented entitlement, he speechified on creating a level playing field but was the only one who did not even have to compete for a spot on the team. I argued that Kejriwal had already appropriated one of his pet slogans—to make politics a professional option for regular, middle-class folk.

Kejriwal and he were almost exactly the same age—youthful men in their early forties. Yet, their journeys were a study in contrast. Kejriwal's trajectory was that of any young man or woman from a middle-class family who was industrious and well-educated. He had competed hard to secure admission to the prestigious Indian Institute of Technology (IIT), and had then moved on to a career in the bureaucracy before spearheading the Right to Information campaign for greater transparency and an anti-corruption crusade before joining politics. Only the last part—politics—was atypical of tens of thousands of Indians like him.

Kejriwal's life stood for everything Rahul claimed to be, or more accurately, wanted to be. But the circumstance of birth alone cast him in the role of political dynast rather than liberal democrat. I asked Rahul why he did not do something more dramatic (and democratic)? Why didn't he declare, for instance, that there would be a vote for the post of party president and he or his mother would not be among the candidates? Surely, he needed a radical fix if he wanted to compete with the badge of proud self-made-ness that bonded the otherwise different personas of his principal opponents, Narendra Modi and Arvind Kejriwal?

He had no convincing answer. He believed that if his family vacated the leadership position the Congress would splinter. 'If my mother and I were to leave for the hills tomorrow, the party will not survive,' he told me. He made this seemingly arrogant statement in a perfectly dry and matter-of-fact voice. Opting out, he said, was not an option for him or his mother, at least not in the near future, not until there were fundamental structural changes to the party. He may well have been right but it spoke to a grim reality. A party that still treated one family as veritable royalty, no matter if it was the adhesive that held them together, was out of sync with changing, contemporary India. It's not that other parties were not replete with dynastic leaders—in particular, many smaller regional parties, like the Shiv Sena, Samajwadi Party and Akali Dal, were effectively family-owned companies—but Rahul's two principal challengers, Modi and Kejriwal, had no political sugar daddies. Their extraordinary journeys resonated with the average Indian whereas Rahul's offered no points of easy identification.

When I met him Rahul appeared to already know that the Congress was not going to win the election. Their ten years in power, from 2004-2014, had been marred by corruption, controversy and a crisis of leadership. Curiously, I got the sense he was almost looking forward to electoral defeat—so he would finally get the opportunity to recast the party in a mould that he had designed. There may have been other reasons he was unconcerned about the disaster that loomed ahead. Either it was because he had no idea of the scale of the loss; or it was because he had worked out that even if Modi were in power for a decade, he would only be fifty-three years old at the end of that period. He had the subconscious arrogance of a man who had age on his side and who took it for granted that he would be prime minister one day.

They would never have admitted to it, but it was this right-to-rule mindset that would prove to be fatal for both the party and its first family. The Congress was the last to wake up to the currents of change that threatened to sweep it away. For forty-nine of India's sixty-eight years of independence, the Government of India had been a Congress government. On the eve of the 2014 elections, the party's long years in power had lulled its leadership into believing that they were indestructible, that nobody could threaten them beyond a point. The Modi juggernaut that swept the 2014 polls would soon dispel this notion, and show them how wrong they were.

■

It was under its most powerful prime minister—Indira Gandhi—that the Congress party's institutional decline began. The political dominance of the Indian National Congress was derived from India's freedom struggle. Founded in 1885, it began as a political movement. Its influence expanded when Mahatma Gandhi took the battle for independence to the British; the organization he fronted, and was the mainstay of, was soon everywhere in the mind and soul of India. Jawaharlal Nehru, like thousands of others, joined the Congress in response to Mahatma Gandhi's call. Even after independence was won and the Mahatma was murdered by Nathuram Godse, the Hindu zealot with links to the RSS (between 1930 and 1934), and the Congress became the party that ruled India, it was anything but a family firm; it was democratic and made plentiful room for spirited dissent. Like India itself, the Congress party was a patchwork of personalities and ideologies.

Today, sycophantic phrases like 'high command' are used

by Congress workers to describe its central leadership, and chief ministers are appointed from Delhi by a tiny cabal of decision makers. Then, even towering personalities like Nehru had to contend with the demands of strong provincial leaders, especially those known famously as the 'Syndicate', who in turn guaranteed votes and ensured that the electoral dominance of the party remained unchallenged. Nehru called the Congress an 'agent of historic destiny', but even he understood that for this high ideal to be a reality he had to be pragmatic and make peace with the relative political independence of the state satraps. It may have restricted the centre's authority but it allowed for a certain efficiency and stability in governance.

All this was well before the age of coalitions and fractured political mandates of the late twentieth century. For several years after Independence, Indian politics was defined by one-party dominance. Yet, as political scientist Rajni Kothari has captured in his seminal work, *Politics in India*, within the Congress 'System' there was plenty of open disagreement—this did not allow the leadership to become authoritarian. Kothari explains how in the years between 1947 and 1967 it was within the Congress, and not between the Congress and Opposition parties, that the major debates of Indian politics took place. All strands of opinion, from the left to the right, found voice in a party that was then a microcosm of the country. This plurality within the party not only made it more representative; according to Kothari, it also 'provided flexibility and sustained internal competition'.

In his classic study, W. H. Morris Jones echoed this argument by pointing out that Congress leaders were so (simultaneously) diverse and dominant that Opposition parties had been reduced to playing the role of pressure groups whose best hope was to address themselves to 'like minded groups' within the party. In other words, in some ways intra-party democracy ensured that the Congress was both the ruling party and the main Opposition. And from all these differences and heated arguments would emerge a centrist consensus for governing India. After Nehru's death in 1964, Rajni Kothari said, 'Nehru's life-work was not so much of having started a revolution as of having given rise to a consensus.'

That changed in 1967 just after his daughter Indira first became prime minister. Just a few months earlier the Syndicate, whose influence had risen during Nehru's dying years, had chosen her as the party chief in the mistaken belief that she could be controlled. She upset every calculation by going over the heads of the regional bosses and splitting the Congress in 1969. She nationalized banks and scrapped the privileges doled out to the country's erstwhile royalty. With her brilliant use of the 'garibi hatao' slogan she lurched to the left of the political spectrum and sought to speak to the poor voter directly without her political fortunes being mediated by provincial strongmen. The creation of Bangladesh and the defeat of Pakistan in 1971 further consolidated her electoral triumphs. But her personal ascent was accompanied by the weakening of the party organization. The Syndicate was routed; state governments now got their (marching) orders from the prime minister's office in Delhi. Her misuse of President's Rule—the imposition of central rule in the provinces by throwing out elected governments—was the clearest example of her growing authoritarianism. In the early years after Independence, during the tenures of her father and his successor Lal Bahadur Shastri, President's Rule was imposed eight times. During the periods when Indira was prime minister, from 1966-1977 and from 1980-1984, President's Rule was imposed forty-eight times. She began to see the freedoms enshrined in the Constitution as an obstacle to her self-aggrandizement. Her decision to impose the Emergency and curb basic freedoms was the culmination of this process. She may have been the party's 'strongest' prime minister but it was she who gave birth to India's first non-Congress government. After her defeat in 1977, the Janata Party alliance, an unlikely coalition of socialists, right-wing groups and farmers, led India for the next two years.

Interestingly, though Priyanka reminded people of Indira, she told me that it was her brother who had taken after her. 'His understanding of politics is really very good, much better than he is given credit for. And that, I think, comes from our grandmother.'

■

In case you're wondering here's what happened with my 'exclusive' interview with Rahul. Some time after Priyanka had first broached the idea, we set up a time, date and a venue. Producers, lighting boys, set designers were dispatched to discuss and finalize camera settings. Black cloth was bought to block the sunlight beaming through the windows of Delhi's Jawahar Bhawan, the chosen venue. Then came the first postponement. Let's do it after the big decision (whether or not he would officially be the prime ministerial candidate), his sister said to me. Then the second set of dates was locked in. And later the third.

Finally, and mysteriously, the interview was given to my competitor at Times Now whose otherwise rambunctious persona was oddly mild-mannered during his conversation with Rahul. Embarrassing questions about his brother-in-law's contentious land deals were not asked. Rahul still flunked the interview and became the butt of a million Twitter jokes and social media memes. What's revealing is that his minders thought he did well. On the evening the interview aired on television, by way of an apology, I got a call from one of Priyanka's aides. She wanted me to come by and interview Rahul the next afternoon. But I was requested to record and embargo the airing of the conversation by a week. Why, I asked, by this time absolutely furious with the unprofessionalism I had experienced. 'We want the full impact of the first interview to play out,' she said, utterly oblivious of the disaster it had been. It was only after the gigantic backlash on social media that Rahul's team realized how poorly he had performed. At three that morning I woke up to a beep on my phone: 'Mr Gandhi has been called for an urgent meeting, we will have to postpone the interview', the message read.

II

In February 2012, I met Nitin Gadkari for a breakfast interview at his residence in Delhi. Gadkari, a portly, cheerful leader was, at the time, president of the BJP. Being from Nagpur—where the headquarters of the RSS are—his influence was seen to derive directly from his closeness to the Sangh. Over poha and sabudana khichdi— Gadkari was an unabashed foodie—we had a long freewheeling conversation. Often seen whizzing about on the streets of Nagpur on his two-wheeler, Gadkari was an old-school politician, politically incorrect and unflappable in the face of the most awkward questions. I remember being taken aback when he freely admitted on a television show, just after he had become a union minister, that he'd flown in a chef from Mumbai at a salary of Rs 50,000 per month to cook his favourite Maharashtrian dishes. When the bookkeeping of his business group was under the scanner he was pugnacious and combative. He never avoided a question.

This morning, however, one of my questions made him uncomfortable. I asked him whether as party president he saw Narendra Modi's defiantly staying away from the campaign trail in Uttar Pradesh (where elections were imminent) as an act of 'indiscipline'. Modi was furious with Gadkari for giving Sanjay Joshi—a man he hated—the role of managing the UP polls. Modi had fallen out with Joshi after a fierce power struggle in the nineties and blamed him for his virtual banishment from Gujarat to Delhi back then.

Now the tables had turned. A few months ago, Modi had already boycotted the party's national executive meet in protest. He had made it clear to the party seniors that he would not address any rallies—in what was the most critical state in the country for the BJP's electoral fortunes—unless Joshi was sacked. Gadkari fumbled for words to explain Modi's absence. Unable to come up with a plausible explanation, Gadkari revealed that he and Modi had not even been communicating on the issue directly. Instead, they were talking through a go-between—Balbir Punj, a veteran party leader. A few months later Gadkari had to capitulate. Joshi was removed from the party's decision-making body and Modi finally deigned to attend a BJP conclave in Mumbai. The primacy of the Gujarat chief minister was evident. He was able to challenge the authority of both the RSS and the party leadership because he knew, and they knew, he was their only passport to seize power in Delhi.

•

For Rs 600 you can now take a day-long tour of Vadnagar—a nondescript town in north Gujarat's Mehsana district made famous by its most famous resident, the Indian prime minister, Narendra

Modi. Organized by the state's tourism corporation, the tour is called 'A Rise from Modi's Village'. It begins in Ahmedabad and includes a stop at Modi's simple, one-storeyed ancestral home as well as the railway station where Modi used to help his father sell tea from the age of six. You can, if you wish, also drop by at the Vadnagar Prathmik Kumar Shala where he studied and meet former classmates who recount childhood stories about Modi. The package throws in a mineral water bottle and a traditional Gujarati lunch for free and even offers a visit to the Sharmistha Lake where Modi used to swim every morning before cycling to school and where his childhood adventures included learning how to 'catch a crocodile'. The tourism corporation's website describes the railway station as 'the most unforgettable place' in the context of his humble origins and his extraordinary journey from Vadnagar to Race Course Road in Delhi. The very existence of the tour, reported to be a big hit, points to the cult status Modi has achieved in the eyes of many of his countrymen, an unusual achievement for an active politician. It also showcases the political leitmotif of his life that he has used to good effect—the struggle from poverty to power.

Three years after India attained independence, Narendra Modi, the third of six children, was born to Damodardas and Heeraben in a lower middle class family which belonged to the 'ghanchi-teli' caste, traditionally a community of oil-pressers included in India's official list of Other Backward Classes (OBC).

At the age of seventeen he left home to join the RSS, where he rose through the ranks. In 1987 he joined the BJP and soon became a key office-bearer of its Gujarat unit. In an irony that neither men could have forecast, among his earliest high profile assignments was the organizing of L. K. Advani's Ram Rath Yatra from Somnath to Ayodhya. It was Advani who elevated him to the rank of national general secretary. This was several years before the guru–shishya relationship that Advani and Modi had initially settled into would collapse.

Interestingly, other than Deve Gowda—and after him, Modi— India's prime ministers have mostly been upper-caste Hindus from north India. This clearly represented a social skew but if Modi believed that he didn't say much about it. In fact, throughout the election campaign of 2014, there were only a couple of moments when he made mention of his caste antecedents. One of these was in Uttar Pradesh when he was craftily able to make Priyanka sound like she was slighting his caste. During the campaign's final moments, Modi took the war to Amethi, the home turf of the Gandhi family and the parliamentary seat that Rahul represented. Here, while campaigning for BJP candidate Smriti Irani, he castigated Priyanka for saying, mockingly, 'Who?' when asked by reporters whether Rahul needed to worry about Smriti. Terming it her 'ahankar' (arrogance) Modi bellowed, 'I will tell you who she is—she is my younger sister,' immediately raising the political importance of Smriti within the party superstructure. At his rally he matched Priyanka jibe for jibe and made a reference to Rajiv Gandhi as well.

When Priyanka criticized him for 'neech rajneeti', referring quite obviously to what she alleged was the 'low level' of political discourse he was engaging in, Modi seized the swipe and converted it to his political advantage by suggesting she meant his caste. Referring to his birth into a 'lower' caste community, he said: 'You can insult Modi as much as you like but do not insult the lower castes. I was dubbed a tea-seller as if I have committed a crime. I have sold tea, not the country...'

But mostly his emphasis, during that campaign, was not on caste but on economic aspiration and the promise that a better life need not be proscribed by poverty. He shifted the political pivot of modern Indian politics from the narrative of noblesse oblige to the dreams of the neo-middle class by framing the argument in terms of merit and anti-elitism.

When Modi stood up as the son of a tea vendor, wearing his modest origins like a badge of honour, and spoke about pulling people out of poverty, he sounded authentic and sincere in a way that Rahul, who also talked incessantly about changing the lives of the poor, could not. His main opponent's lineage provided Modi with the perfect opportunity to mock Rahul as the 'shehzada' or prince who had 'grown up in five-star hotels'; he would say in speech after speech that as Rahul had never experienced poverty he would never understand it.

But the Congress failed to grasp the import of why his personal story was compelling. When Congress MP and senior party leader Mani Shankar Aiyar smarmily taunted Modi for being a 'chaiwallah' who would 'never make it as PM in the twenty-first century' his jibe perfectly captured the collision between the old angrezi elite and the new India seeking to dislodge it. 'Dosco', 'Stephanian', 'Cantabrigian'— the labels on Aiyar's resume were typical of his pedigree. His clipped English and easy wit enlivened posh living rooms where women draped in tasteful tussars and men in fashionably casual khadi kurtas animatedly debated politics and the state of the world over good French and Italian wine, Russian vodka and imported cigarettes. In this instance, Aiyar's barb about Modi only reinforced the image of the Congress as classist and feudal. And, although the Congress let it be known that it did not agree with the remark, and that Rahul disapproved of it as well, the rebuke did not seem particularly severe; hours later, at the same party conclave where Aiyar had snootily offered to make 'some room for Modi if he wants to come and distribute tea' he got a personal shout-out from Rahul who praised him from the podium for his commitment to grassroots democracy.

The controversy was illustrative of how the ground was shifting beneath the feet of India's erstwhile elite and transforming old-style politics. If it was once a calling card to be a member of India's closed circle of influence, today it had become a political liability. Modi took on Ivy League-educated Finance Minister P. Chidambaram with his swipe, 'Hard work matters more than Harvard' while Kejriwal constantly referred to himself as a 'chhota-aadmi', a small man battling corporate giants. Never before was being shut out of the cozy coterie of the 'Dilli Durbar' better for a politician's public image as it was now.

If the rise of assertive caste-based politicians in India had been the first challenge by the subalterns to the upper-caste, hierarchical status quo, this was the second wave of social revolt. If Kanshi Ram, Mayawati, Nitish Kumar, Lalu Yadav and Mulayam Singh Yadav were among the social engineers of the first phase—most of them schooled in an old socialist tradition—in this moment of churn, Modi and

Kejriwal were, in very distinct ways (and as it would turn out, with very different measures of success) tapping into the resentments and aspirations of a post-caste (but not necessarily post-religion) middle India. Of course, both found a reasonable number of supporters among the traditional elites as well, but apart from the personality-centric strategy of their campaigns, these two disparate men had this in common: like characters from a Fitzgerald novel, they had both positioned themselves as untainted 'outsiders' to a culture corroded by corruption, clubby parties and cliques that protected each other.

In 1956, social scientist C. Wright Mills first examined this incestuous organization of political power and social influence in his influential work, *The Power Elite*. 'There is a kind of reciprocal attraction among the fraternity of the successful—not between each and every member of the circle of the high and mighty, but between enough of them, to insure a certain unity,' he wrote in words that could have been used just as accurately to describe the India which came into being after the economic liberalization of the 1990s. Ushered in by Prime Minister Narasimha Rao, and his finance minister, Manmohan Singh, liberalization resulted in sweeping change everywhere in society. Wrote Mills: 'Members of several higher circles know one another as personal friends and even as neighbours; they mingle with one another on the golf course, in the gentleman's clubs, at resorts, on transcontinental airplanes and on ocean liners. They meet at the estates of mutual friends, face each other in front of the TV camera or serve on the same philanthropic committee; and many are sure to cross one another's paths in the columns of newspapers, if not in the exact cafes from which many of these columns originate.' Before 1991, the circle of power and influence was limited to the old political families, storied business houses and the royals. After economic liberalization, the circle widened, and a few more rich and powerful circles were added to the existing one. Think of the '100 most powerful' lists published annually by glossies and even serious newspapers (and the bruised egos of those who get bumped off them) and you realize that what Mills wrote about America in the 1950s was very true of India in the twenty-first century. It was this elite that Modi sought to disempower by appealing to the millions who were shut out of these charmed circles—the lower middle-class and the poor.

When Modi spoke at rallies or to journalists of a childhood steeped in poverty as the son of a father who sold tea and a mother who washed utensils in the more upscale homes of the neighbourhood, he was successfully able to fashion himself in the public perception as a genuine mascot of the working class. As a thrice-elected chief minister he connected the dots between the 24x7 electrification programme in Gujarat and his own experience of growing up without the guarantee of electricity at home. An underdog, but never a victim, his own political journey was meant to encourage others to pull themselves out of their socio-economic exigencies.

If Orwell's *1984* had chronicled how 'throughout recorded time and probably since the end of the Neolithic age, there have been three kinds of people in the world, the High, the Middle and the Low', the 2014 general elections in India were challenging the rules of the old social order. Until this moment, the political class had wooed the rich and patronized the poor, forgetting for the most part to engage the middle. Now, whether it was Kejriwal's muffler or Modi's mojo this was the election of Everyman, and Rahul seemed embarrassingly like the raja who had gatecrashed the revolution.

The undercurrent against the chosen few may have primarily been an urban phenomenon. But given that more than 30 per cent of India was already urbanized—a number projected to rise from 340 million people in 2008 to 590 million in 2030—no party could afford to ignore the middle class or the burgeoning neo-middle class anymore. Winston Churchill may have been able to quip that the 'best argument against democracy is a five minute conversation with the average voter', but after decades of a top-down democracy that was almost feudal both in its dependence on the benevolence of the ruler and its exclusion of the average person from the dominant discourse, the class and cultural walls that insulated India's elites from the rest was about to be brought down.

Narendra Modi was among the first to understand that 'people like us' could no longer condescend to 'people like them'.

Positioning himself as the latter he repeatedly stressed his absence of 'insider' status in the rarefied corridors of power in the capital, even underlining it much later in his first Independence Day speech as prime minister. Corruption, uninspiring leadership, and policy paralysis—these aspects of the Congress decade in government were only partial explanations of the Modi victory, the pushback of millions against entitlement, elitism and privilege was at the centre of the churn that he harnessed brilliantly to his advantage.

∎

Until the very end, when Modi thundered home to a massive victory—winning more decisively than any politician had in thirty years—there were attempts by party colleagues, some public, some covert, to block his ascent. Murli Manohar Joshi would whisper to journalists about how 'autocratic' Modi was. Sushma Swaraj was miffed at the sudden prominence given to Modi's troika of spokeswomen—Nirmala Sitharaman, Smriti Irani and Meenakshi Lekhi—which she felt was designed to dilute her profile in the party.

Nevertheless, in September 2013, party president Rajnath Singh formally announced Modi's name as candidate for prime minister. Even after that announcement, while nobody had the guts to say it out loud (faced with the prospect of irrelevance in a one-man party), many were hoping for a victory that would be modest enough to 'manage' Modi. What may have seemed like innocuous political optics acquired new meaning in the context of this silent power struggle within the party.

This included Rajnath Singh. In 2011, Narendra Modi had refused to wear a skullcap offered to him by a Muslim leader, thereby setting off a huge outcry. So when Rajnath Singh, in the run-up to the 2014 general elections, chose to wear a skullcap at an ancient Sufi shrine in Lucknow, he was sending out an implicit message that nobody missed. Shia Muslim leaders heaped praises on Rajnath; comparisons were made to former BJP Prime Minister Atal Bihari Vajpayee whose charm won him friends and voters in unlikely corners. Within the BJP there was fevered speculation—was this Rajnath positioning himself as a more acceptable face for the post of PM were the BJP to fall short of a majority and need to hunt for allies? Of course, that was not to be.

It was only L. K. Advani, the original Hindutva mascot and once the patriarch of the 'Parivar', who was ready to openly take on the might of Modi. Other anti-Modi forces within the BJP quietly coalesced around him. As we have seen in an earlier chapter, there were interesting parallels in the political evolution of Advani and Modi. Initially, the electoral popularity of both was shadowed by a cataclysmic event that they were held responsible for—by concerned public opinion if not the courts. Advani was blamed for his role in the demolition of the Babri Masjid in 1992 and Modi was held accountable for the Gujarat riots of 2002 that happened on his watch.

Three decades earlier Advani was to the BJP cadre exactly what Modi was today. When the party made a dramatic jump from two seats in Parliament in 1985 to eighty-five seats in 1989 it was largely because of Advani's aggressive Hindutva campaign. Both men were fundamentally shaped by the RSS as 'pracharaks' but had, later in their careers, tried to distance themselves from Hindutva and recast their political identity for wider acceptability. Advani's attempts at reinvention came at a large cost—he was forced to resign as the president of the party after he praised Mohammed Ali Jinnah on a trip to Pakistan. Modi, by contrast, had reasonable success (at least in the early phase of his prime ministership) in branding himself differently. The controversies would come later. But his promise of a development-centric government had gone down well with industrialists, the aspirational middle class and young, first time voters looking for change. He was able to shed the labels of the past much quicker than Advani.

While many leaders in the BJP waged covert wars in the shadows against their prime ministerial candidate, there was one BJP leader of national consequence who remained unflinching in his support for Narendra Modi. That leader was Arun Jaitley, although, in many ways, he was very different from the Gujarat CM. A wealthy, gregarious, easy-going lawyer turned politician, Jaitley was, as the Punjabis in his family might say, a 'yaaron ka yaar' or a friend among friends. An early morning walker in Delhi's Lodi Garden, where the city's powerful converge, he was known to carry packed samosas and chai for anyone who wanted to join his morning durbar. He enjoyed a good argument unlike his friend Modi. His constant lament was the absence of wit in parliamentary debates, and when he cracked a good joke he was fond of repeating it to friends and journalists and chuckling over it again.

Again, unlike the man who would be PM, he did not hold grudges, and did not cut you off if you were critical of his actions. On more than one occasion, I had disagreed with him on matters related to Jammu and Kashmir. He would rib me in a good-natured way about it. One day, when I had a sore throat while reporting from Srinagar, he quipped that 'the Hurriyat had lost its voice'. Because he did not take disagreements personally, of all the politicians in India, Jaitley was definitely the best liked by journalists. This again was in sharp contrast to Modi who, since 2002, had had a friction-filled and antagonistic relationship with many in the media.

Jaitley was also the perfect antidote to the cultural conservatism that Indians still associated with the BJP. He was, for example, the only BJP leader to take a position supporting the decriminalizing of homosexuality. A suave, well-networked denizen of the power elite in the capital, Jaitley in many ways was Modi's voice in Delhi before the 2014 election. That he lost his own election in Amritsar, the first time he was running for popular office, would do nothing to reduce his influence in the capital which remained unmatched despite the bitter and vocal resentment of other (one-time) Modi supporters like editor turned politician Arun Shourie.

But, like Indira Gandhi before him, the Modi campaign had rendered old party machinations and rivalries redundant. In a modern variation of Jean Jacques Rousseau's philosophy of direct democracy, Indira and Modi did not want their sovereignty mediated by party structures and parliamentary representatives. Instead, much like American presidents, they sought to portray themselves as regular individuals who drew their power directly from the people.

It's because this characteristic of Modi's was such a powerful dimension of his win that seven months into his term the symbolism of the monogrammed pinstriped suit he wore on his day out with the visiting American President Barack Obama created such a furore. A gift of indeterminate cost (whispers that its value was at least Rs 3 lakh were denied by the Gujarati businessman who presented it), the suit seemed to herald the gentrification of Modi and went against the grain of the 'I'm just like you' image that he had used to such great effect in his ascent to power.

Coming as it did ahead of a key electoral contest in Delhi, it sat in uncomfortable contrast to the shabby but immediately identifiable muffler that the Aam Aadmi Party (AAP) chief Arvind Kejriwal was always seen wearing. The muffler was anything but chic (in fact, it was the butt of many a joke), but borrowing from Modi's tactic of proudly embracing an absence of sophistication (as evidence of a humble background), Kejriwal's team started a self-deprecating but trending Twitter hashtag about the muffler and converted the scruffy black wrap—always worn over one of only two sweaters, maroon or blue—into a badge of honour. #Mufflerman was to the Delhi state elections of 2015 what #Chaiwallah came to represent in the parliamentary elections of 2014.

Eventually the suit that Modi wore was auctioned for charity and raised over Rs 4 crore but in the perceptional battle between monogrammed pinstripes and shabby mufflers it was obviously the underdog that got the popular thumbs up. Of course, there was also a certain amount of class snobbery in criticizing Modi for wearing an expensive suit in a way that Rajiv would never have been for wearing Gucci shoes. Yet, this was not an argument over aesthetics or the clash of old wealth and the nouveau riche. It was about losing the-little-guy-who-made-it-big status, of appearing as Goliath instead of the David figure that had won Modi the general election. The 'suit' stuck as a metaphor for the same elitism that Modi had revolted against.

In those weeks before the Delhi election results would embarrass the BJP I had a long conversation with a member of the RSS, the organization that had shaped and influenced Modi since he was eight years old. The Delhi state elections were being held just a few months after the big national win and it was expected that the image of the prime minister as an all-conquering hero, combined with the entire Cabinet being marched out into the battlefield, would result in an

OF POLITICAL DYNASTS, JUGGERNAUTS AND MAVERICKS   235

easy win. Because the BJP had invested so much political capital in the elections, the subsequent defeat was especially discomfiting. The RSS ideologue I met predicted a certain defeat for the BJP in the state elections and whispered conspiratorially to me about how the government was losing its grip on the narrative. Known for its ascetic and spartan values, the RSS, he said, was especially upset about the 'suit'. 'Pagalpan tha (it was madness). What were they thinking?' He went on to complain about how the RSS had been shut out from decision-making by a 'coterie around Modi'. Pointing to the choice of policewoman turned corruption crusader Kiran Bedi as the BJP's chief ministerial candidate he said the RSS preferred the more low-key but dependable and controversy-free Dr Harshvardhan but its counsel was ignored. 'We have warned them, you will get less than twenty seats and it won't stop at Delhi.' As it turned out, the BJP clocked only three wins in a state election that saw the AAP win an unprecedented sixty-seven out of seventy seats.

■

At first Narendra Modi confounded most of his critics, especially those who were afraid he would usher in an era of hardcore Hindutva politics. As soon as he was elected prime minister he prostrated himself at the entrance to Parliament on his very first day there, repositioning himself as a supplicant at the temple of democracy. Worshipping at the altar of Parliament made for a powerful image and was entirely unobjectionable. As he bent his head down and kissed the steps, seemingly oblivious of the jostling cameras, yet offering them the perfect picture, he was also challenging conventional ideas about secularism, as he had many times before. The semiotics was of prayer but the idol was democracy. The image seemed to drive home his point that in a multi-faith, pluralistic country like India, where religion and culture could often be inseparable, the language of the sacred would always be more effective than the sanitized secularism of his political opponents.

There were other signs that showed that Modi would not be easily categorized. The same man who had mocked the UPA government for feeding 'chicken biryani' to Pakistani dignitaries while Indian soldiers were being killed at the LoC had shown courage and statesmanship by inviting Nawaz Sharif to his swearing-in.

It appeared at the time that we would be seeing more of what we had seen during his rule in Gujarat. There, his repeated electoral triumphs had emboldened him to centralize power, take bold decisions, and begin marginalizing extraneous influences, especially those with an overtly sectarian flavour. At the centre too, as he pursued his developmental agenda, unveiling initiatives like 'Make in India' that sought to woo foreign direct investment (FDI), especially in the manufacturing sector, and a relentless touring schedule through dozens of countries where he sought to rebrand India as a dynamic nation that was seeking to make its mark on the world stage, it appeared that he would be staking a claim to a place in the centre-right spot of the political spectrum. He had been voted in on the promise of achhe din—better days. The young voters who overwhelmingly preferred him to his much younger rival Rahul Gandhi had no patience with controversies that arose out of the Hindutva agenda, and did not identify with social or religious conservatism.

As his initial moves as prime minister kept people guessing, it was difficult to predict what sort of rule the country would experience. It wasn't as though everything was in Modi's hands, as had been the case in Gujarat, once he was firmly in the saddle. But what couldn't be denied was that whoever ruled a country as diverse and difficult to govern as India had inevitably been nudged towards the centre. During the years that Atal Bihari Vajpayee was prime minister, from 1998 to 2004, the BJP had already planed down the angularities of its Hindutva project, partly because of Vajpayee's own gentle, consensual approach and partly because it needed to keep other parties inside the tent. Though still tagged as 'Hindu nationalist', especially by the Western press, the Vajpayee-led BJP government pretty much inhabited the ideological centre, making it possible even for Farooq Abdullah, the leader of India's only Muslim majority state, to be a partner.

However, unlike Vajpayee, who had had to keep a coalition together, Modi's absolute majority freed him from the need to temper ideology. Among a section of his supporters, expectations mounted that his was going to be India's first truly right-wing government. But they all defined 'right' differently.

Historically, as we have seen, a good portion of the political right had once existed within the embrace of the Congress, especially during the freedom struggle and in the early years of the country's independence. The Congress at the time was capable of accommodating all manner of ideological expressions, including those of centre–right cultural conservatives. Madan Mohan Malaviya was both a founding member of the Hindu Mahasabha and a proud Congressman. Three weeks before Mahatma Gandhi's assassination in 1948, Sardar Vallabhbhai Patel—with whom Advani and later Modi would display a certain affinity—had invited leaders of the RSS to join the Congress, describing them as 'patriots' who would need to be 'won over by Congressmen with love'. The murder of the Mahatma changed all that. While no allegation against the RSS was ever pursued in a court of law, the fact that his assassin Godse had had links with the organization led Patel to blame it (and the Hindu Mahasabha) for creating an environment 'in which such a ghastly tragedy became possible'. He banned the RSS but lifted the clampdown in less than two years. But it was clear that the days in which the right wing could be an intrinsic part of the Congress were numbered. Soon after, in 1951, Shyama Prasad Mukherjee founded the Bharatiya Jana Sangh as the political wing of the RSS. This was the earliest avatar of the BJP.

Ten years later, in 1961, came the short-lived centre–right politics of C. Rajagopalachari's Swatantra Party—an anti-communist, non-socialist, secular, progressive party that was sympathetic to the markets and free enterprise. Which version of 'right-wing governance' was Modi going to choose for himself? As we know, his supporters included those who hoped he would usher in their long-held dream of a Hindu Rashtra, and others—the young and aspirational, industrialists, free-marketeers and, but naturally, readers of Ayn Rand—who hoped he would be a twenty-first-century hybrid of Ronald Reagan and Margaret Thatcher.

Would Modi be compelled to 'outgrow the RSS' just as President

Obama had had to outgrow the Church—a theory first posited by well-known economist Jagdish Bhagwati, a self-confessed admirer of the prime minister? Or would he, as the ever-provocative Subramanian Swamy asserted, never be able to escape the compulsion of his early personal and political upbringing? When I tweeted the highlights of what Bhagwati had said to me, including his likening the various Hindu sectarian controversies that had begun to plague Modi's tenure as prime minister at about the time I interviewed him to a 'virulent disease', the backlash from Modi's right-wing supporters was furious. And, when Bhagwati suggested that the prime minister would have to put space between his office and the RSS, he faced the wrath of known ideologues of the right. One of them, a professor of history, wrote to me to say 'even Narendra Modi would dislike this argument. He is an honest swayam sevak. Every swayam sevak is grateful to the mother organization'. A senior newspaper journalist tweeted me to say: 'Advice is free. Bhagwati telling Modi to leave the RSS is like a girl's family asking the boy to leave his parents.'

■

After the promise of his early days in office, it appeared that some fears of Modi's trenchant critics were coming true. Except that the sharpest criticism (and expression of disappointment) was coming from some of his own prominent supporters. Columnists like Tavleen Singh, for instance, an admirer of the prime minister and a journalist with a pathological dislike of the Congress, warned the government repeatedly in her writings and television appearances that the majority of Indians who voted for Modi had not voted for Hindutva. She said again and again that 'Hindutva fanatics' were 'blackening' the prime minister's image. But the surround sound of inflammatory politics and extremist statements had begun to drown out all other attempts by the prime minister to hit the high notes. The headlines that Modi would have liked, such as India's assertive pitch for a permanent seat at the United Nations' Security Council or those that spoke about his meetings in Silicon Valley, where the world's most influential CEOs lined up to meet him, began to be interspersed with less flattering ones about the stifling of free expression, the murder of rationalists and the lynching of Akhlaq in Uttar Pradesh because he was suspected of storing beef in his house. What was more disturbing—and bewildering—was how much leeway many of those spouting sectarian nonsense were given. The worst offender in some ways, because of the importance of the position he held, was the government's culture minister, Mahesh Sharma, a doctor turned first-term MP. (The other minister who was often in trouble for making incendiary statements was minister of state for external affairs, V. K. Singh.) When Sharma appeared on one of my shows and spoke about ending 'cultural pollution'—an ominous sounding prelude to cultural 'cleansing'—an RSS ideologue who was also a participant on the same show whispered to me that 'Modi is going to be furious with him. He will probably tell him to never appear on TV again'. And yet, Sharma continued to make cringe-worthy remarks that would have been laughable for their absence of logic were they not in fact dangerous given the office he represented. Sharma would even describe the much-loved former President Abdul Kalam as someone who was a nationalist 'despite' being a Muslim.

Yogi Adityanath, another vitriolic parliamentarian would often make speeches full of invective. He warned that Hindus would 'organize themselves' and 'people who try to defame the symbol of Hindutva will have to pay the price for this'. Not only was he allowed free rein, he once opened a debate on the Communal Violence Bill for the BJP in the Lok Sabha.

Every now and then the BJP leadership would let journalists know that the prime minister was furious and the motormouth MPs had been put on notice. But a few weeks would pass and they would be back at it again. Given his early moves as prime minister to move away from overtly sectarian politics, one would have thought that ministers like Sharma or MPs like Adityanath would be publicly rebuked, if not sacked from office. Instead, there was never any direct comment from the prime minister and only generalized statements of disapproval from party spokespersons.

Why, for instance, did the BJP give such a long rope to the Shiv Sena in Maharashtra—undoubtedly a weaker partner in the coalition?

The Sena had embarrassed not just the government, it had shamed India with its acts of violent hooliganism against visiting Pakistanis—authors, artistes, even cricketing officials—disrupting meetings and unleashing ugly ink attacks. While ministers like Arun Jaitley were swift in their condemnation, the prime minister himself did not reveal his 'mann ki baat', on this or on a variety of other incidents that in fact should have worried him greatly.

I have always felt, in the many years that I have observed him, that Modi's ambitions are personal not ideological. His political career may have had Hindutva roots, but it was clear to me that if he needed to abandon these in the pursuit of a political legacy, he wouldn't think twice. Given Modi's amplified sense of self and his well-earned satisfaction at having reached where he has, it would not be an exaggeration to say that what guided him was probably the desire to go down in history as one of the greatest and longest serving prime ministers the country had ever had. But this could hardly be possible if his government remained mired in sectarian and divisive controversies. Why was Modi not reining in right-wing extremists in a visible way? Was he reining them in at all? It was hard to explain how a government that was voted in at least partially on the strength of its effective messaging and communication had lost control over the development narrative so soon. Was it incompetence, ideological confusion or simply a mild contempt for a liberal media that the BJP had in any case always seen as biased?

∎

These questions become even more relevant when you think of Modi's pragmatism, and ability to constantly confuse those who think they have figured him out. I remember a high-voltage controversy that Modi seized hold of to his advantage. This took place in 2013. A day before the then Prime Minister Manmohan Singh and Nawaz Sharif were scheduled to meet during the annual United Nations summit in the US, I landed a breakfast meeting with Nawaz Sharif at the spiffy New York Palace Hotel.

Sharif's authority had not yet been diminished by Pakistan's overweening military. When I had met him just four months ago in the sylvan sprawl of his mansion in Raiwind, an hour from Lahore, he was a man in command of his nation. As peacocks preened on the vast expanse of green that encircled the roof to floor glass windows of the gold and rust drawing room and phalsa juice was brought out in long-stemmed glasses—still basking in his impressive electoral majority, Sharif had told me that, as prime minister, it was he who was the 'boss' and not the army chief. For a man who had been pushed into exile a decade earlier by the then army chief, Pervez Musharraf, these were rather brave and risky words. But then Sharif had matured as a politician, working quietly with Benazir Bhutto when she was alive to restore a semblance of democracy to his country. When she was assassinated, he gave me a seat on his private plane to her funeral in Sindh and I could see how genuinely devastated he was.

During Asif Ali Zardari's turbulent years in power he had had several opportunities to bring him down but he opted to remain a responsible Opposition leader. Now, back as prime minister of Pakistan for the third time, he was confident of ruling effectively. In his interview with me, hours before he was sworn in as PM, he spoke of his desire to visit India 'whether invited or not' and repair the broken threads of the 1999 war. The Manmohan Singh government wrote to him with an open-ended invite just hours later. While Sharif never did visit India while Manmohan Singh was prime minister, the two men had agreed to meet in America on the sidelines of the annual United Nations summit.

Over many years of reporting from Pakistan I had got to know Sharif reasonably well and he spoke to me with a degree of candour and informality. He wanted an understanding of how his domestic politics back home were being appraised in India. He told me he had the go-ahead, from both the government and the army, to offer India the much talked about 'most favoured nation' status to boost trade ties. But he was unsure of making the announcement while an outgoing prime minister—whose authority seemed to be waning— was at the helm in Delhi. He told me it would mean investing a lot of political capital for minimal return. By the end of our informal chat he said he had decided to save the breakthrough for the new government in India.

Naturally, I was keen to get him on record and asked him if he would consider a short television interview. Sharif said he would think about it, but only after I joined him downstairs in the hotel coffee shop for breakfast. Sharif was always extremely hospitable and, like all Punjabis, excellent food for him was the centrepiece of any good conversation. Once he got to know you he was also garrulous—a raconteur who lapsed into earthy Punjabi or Urdu while spouting dialogues from his favourite film, *Mughal-e-Azam*, or recounting allegories, fables and jokes, which he did often to make a larger political point.

At the table, I found myself joining a large Pakistani delegation which included the country's national security adviser at the time, Sartaj Aziz, and the foreign secretary Jaleel Jilani, whom I knew from his days at the high commission in Delhi. I was seated at the corner of the table right between the prime minister and the redoubtable Pakistani journalist Hamid Mir. By now, restless and more interested in a possible scoop than the eggs and freshly cut fruit spread out before me, I once again asked Sharif if he would consider stepping out into the hotel lobby where my cameraman and producer were waiting for me. Mir overheard and immediately interrupted to complain that no Pakistani journalist had been granted an interview by Manmohan Singh and argued that it would be most unfair if an Indian were to land an interview with Sharif.

The conversation at the table shifted to the rather sensitive subject of the Punjab government in Pakistan, headed by Sharif's brother Shehbaz, funding the Jamaat-ud-Dawa (the patron group of the Lashkar-e-Taiba). During his meeting at the White House, Manmohan Singh had already brought up the 'handsome financial support' by Pakistan's provincial government to schools, hospitals and mosques linked to the Jamaat headed by the mastermind of the Mumbai attacks, Hafiz Saeed. In his talks with the US president, Singh had described Pakistan as 'the epicentre of terror' and 'the major wild card in the region'. Obama had called the LeT a worldwide threat. Washington's public reprimand came on the heels of twin terror strikes in Jammu in which ten people had died.

Officials at Sharif's table launched into a complicated and unconvincing rebuttal of India's charge arguing that the state machinery had taken over the management of the madrassas and dispensaries and that they were no longer controlled by Hafiz Saeed. At this point Sharif, turned to me and asked, rhetorically of course, why India felt the need to take its complaint to the United States when the leaders of both countries were scheduled to meet each other anyway.

I explained, as best as I could, that there was enormous political and public pressure on the government to halt the recent dialogue with Pakistan because of unabated terrorism. Any leader, in particular Manmohan Singh—who was often accused of being soft on Pakistan because of his own pre-Partition links of birth and ancestry—would have to publicly underline that it was not business as usual. And besides, with America feeding Pakistan millions of dollars in military aid—more than $700 million that year alone—wasn't Big Brother already a part of the equation?

Sharif persisted. Couldn't Manmohan Singh have brought India's grievances and concerns directly to him? At this point he suddenly lapsed into a mix of Punjabi and Urdu and said the week's developments reminded him of a story. He related the tale of a dispute in a village between a woman and a neighbour. I can't say I understood every single word but the gist of the story went something like this: the warring parties approached the village Qazi with prayers to intervene in their dispute. Listening to them the cleric's advice was that you should seek blessings for yourself but not complain about others or seek 'baddua' (malediction) for them. From what I understood, it was a strictly figurative, non-literal tale with the message that disagreements were best resolved without third parties intervening. It appeared that he had basically repeated himself in a more metaphorical way to argue about the need for Pakistan and India to negotiate directly rather than use the US as an intermediary. As a journalist who had seen bigger problems break down talks between India and Pakistan, I didn't pay too much attention.

Already distracted by a looming deadline I once again pressed Sharif for an interview. This time he relented and I left the table hastily to organize the logistics. Later, among the other remarks he made on camera, Sharif called Manmohan Singh a 'good man' whom he would like to welcome to Pakistan for a 'long overdue visit'. Chuffed with my scoop, I dashed out of the hotel to uplink the footage to New Delhi for the prime-time bulletin.

A few minutes later my phone began beeping frantically. I saw that there was a flood of tweets, mostly by supporters of the BJP and other journalists, asking me whether Nawaz Sharif had pejoratively called Manmohan Singh a 'dehati aurat' (village woman).

The controversy was started by Hamid Mir who had filed a news report based on our informal breakfast conversation. He had not only claimed that Manmohan Singh had been compared to a village woman, but he said the comments were made in my presence.

I was both furious and taken aback. There had been no such phrase used for the prime minister while I was at breakfast except for the brief anecdote about the village dispute that had been a metaphor for something else altogether.

It was late night in India by now and social media had just picked up the story. Sensing trouble—because I've seen how even a misplaced comma can mean a full stop in Indo-Pak talks—I picked up the phone and called officials in both the foreign ministry and the prime minister's office and recounted in detail what had transpired.

The officers I spoke to were sanguine; one wondered if it was Hamid Mir's intention to sour the bilateral, another asked whether he was just irritated that I had scooped the interview with Sharif. They were going to inform Manmohan Singh about what had happened and would get back to me if they needed any clarifications.

The diplomats were of the opinion that Twitter hysteria among some users did not need to influence the government's response. By now even Mir had tweeted that 'nothing derogatory' had been said by Sharif about the Indian PM. It would have ended there were it not for what happened next.

I fell asleep, exhausted after an unexpectedly harrowing day only to be woken up in the middle of the night by incessant calls from Ruby, my producer in Delhi. 'Have you seen what Narendra Modi has said about you at his recent rally?' she asked.

Elections were only eight months away and the BJP's prime

ministerial candidate was in fine fettle. In a deft political move that reinforced his nationalism and made the incumbent leader look weak and humiliated, he roared from the stage that India would not tolerate its PM being insulted. 'How dare you address my nation's prime minister as a village woman? We can fight with him on policies but this we will not tolerate. This nation of 120 crore people will not tolerate this insult.'

In his address was also a message for me. 'The journalists who were sitting in front of Nawaz Sharif when he was insulting our prime minister should also answer to the people of my country. Journalists who were having sweets with Nawaz Sharif when he was abusing our prime minister, calling him a village woman, I would expect them to refuse the sweets and walk out.' Modi had not named me but since I was the only Indian journalist present at the breakfast and I had already acknowledged that online, there was no ambiguity about who his message was directed at.

I jumped out of bed, made myself presentable, hailed a cab in the pitch dark and made my way to the hotel where the cameras were up and ready for me to go live. In two decades of being a practising journalist you get used to controversy stalking you, but this was new even for me. Never before had I been injected into the electoral battle between a prime minister and his main challenger.

On social media I was being abused and hounded in the vilest terms for supposedly not standing up for India. Journalists were calling me for quotes and clarifications. In the cab I dashed off a stern mail to Hamid Mir expressing my anger and disappointment at his distortion of events. On television I talked again and again about what had been said and what had not.

By now I knew that with the issue having erupted in the domestic political arena the prime minister's team would not be able to treat it with the levity that had been their first response. Sure enough, ahead of the dialogue, the Pakistan foreign secretary was tasked by Sharif to explain things to the national security adviser. And when Nawaz Sharif and Manmohan Singh finally met, the Pakistan prime minister's opening gambit was a defensive expression of hope that Singh was not 'disturbed' by what the Indian foreign minister Salman

8824688888888888888888888888888888888888888888888888888888888888888888888888888888888 stop.

Khurshid later called 'something silly like this, really a non-issue'.

With the benefit of emotional distance from the surreal aspect of my own unwitting role in that controversy, it was clear that Narendra Modi's calculated intervention was illustrative of what a smart politician he was. Manmohan Singh was taunted, mocked and jeered at by the BJP almost every day for the government's weak-willed Pakistan policy. With ten people dead in terror strikes, this was an opportunity for Modi to strengthen that argument ahead of the India–Pakistan meet. At that point, Manmohan Singh's stock was at a particularly low ebb. His party vice president Rahul Gandhi had just ripped up an ordinance the PM had given his assent to, thereby humiliating him. By presenting Manmohan Singh as a man whose authority was respected neither at home nor abroad and yet taking his side against the Pakistani premier who had dared to 'insult' him, Modi managed to make Manmohan Singh look frail and ineffectual and himself seem firm, yet fair and patriotic when it came to matters of national pride.

The motivation for drawing me into the debate remains less clear. Was it because I was one of the journalists he didn't like or was it illustrative of his often uneasy relationship with the media; or was it a chance to create a simplistic but instantly effective debate around who had passed the patriotism test? I am still not sure what the correct answer is. Of course that was Modi in the Opposition. As prime minister, his Pakistan policy soon reflected the essential contradiction he was trapped by. He wanted, like every prime minister before him, to be the man who would deliver lasting peace to South Asia, but at the same time, for his core constituency, he could not veer too far from the machismo of the man who boasted of a '56-inch chest'. In other words he was attempting to think out of the box but also felt compelled to appear tougher with Pakistan than his predecessors. The result was confusion. After Sharif and Modi's first meeting in Delhi they agreed to resume the stalled dialogue between the foreign secretaries of both countries. Then, the Pakistan high commissioner met with Kashmiri separatists ahead of those talks, as they had been doing for years, including in Vajpayee's time. The Modi government protested and scrapped the talks. His hardline supporters hailed the decision as evidence that Modi was not going to be 'soft' like Vajpayee. Around the same time guns erupted at the LoC, testing the sustainability of a decade-old ceasefire agreement. BJP spokespersons were quick to go on TV and talk about how under the Modi government the army had a free hand to respond with the might it considered appropriate. 'Our forces will make the cost of [Pakistan's] adventurism unaffordable,' warned Arun Jaitley.

But unknown to the media and certainly the public at large—and in yet more proof that basically there was nothing doctrinaire about Modi's ideological formulations—both he and Sharif had found someone to keep them connected even when things got difficult. When the two leaders first met one on one in Delhi they discussed whether they wanted to repeat the back-channel model the previous governments had followed of deploying veteran diplomats in the role of special envoys. The model had permitted the conducting of discreet dialogue, usually in a neutral territory like Dubai, free from the pressure of political and public opinion. But those in the know say both Modi and Sharif decided to keep the reins of the relationship in their own hands instead, leaving them to decide when to pull back and when to let go. However, they agreed that it could be useful to talk informally through a mutual acquaintance they both felt comfortable with.

The unexpected conduit was the steel magnate with movie-star looks—Sajjan Jindal—brother of former Congress legislator Naveen Jindal. When Sharif was in Delhi, Jindal hosted a tea party for the Pakistani premier right after his meeting with Modi. It attracted little attention in the Indian media but in Pakistan, Sharif drew flak for finding time for Jindal and not for Kashmiri separatists (Sharif was the first Pakistani leader to visit India and not meet with the Hurriyat Conference or mention Kashmir in his public statements).

It was no secret that Indian steelmakers, both state and private players, were looking to foster friendly relations with Pakistan; they needed this to happen so they could ferry iron ore from Afghanistan by road across Pakistan from where it would be shipped to ports in western and southern India. When Sharif was in Delhi for Modi's swearing-in he invited me to Delhi's Taj Mansingh Hotel to have a cup of tea with him. In the lobby, I bumped into Jindal escorting Sharif's son Hussain for lunch. I was struck by how friendly they seemed but assumed it was something to do with Jindal's business interests. However, Jindal's relationship with Sharif appeared to have gone beyond that of a businessman seeking to build a relationship with a head of state to further his business interests; they appeared to have become confidants.

Jindal kept the confidence of both prime ministers, never revealing the occasional unofficial role he had been entrusted with. Unlike special envoys in the past, his role was obviously not one that involved negotiating tricky matters of geopolitics. He was more like a covert bridge that connected them if either wanted to reach out to the other side sans protocol or publicity. Because Jindal's part in the Indo-Pak drama was strictly off the record, it came with plausible deniability. When I was first told about the arrangement by a principal protagonist in the know, I considered reporting it for the news but decided against it, as I knew not one of the key players would go on record except to repudiate it.

But enough people in diplomatic and business circles in both countries knew about Jindal's mediatory role. Except the media— which had been badly thrown off the scent by the seemingly frosty dynamics between Modi and Sharif when they met in Kathmandu in November 2014 for the annual conference of South Asian nations. Television anchors were airing the usual speculations about whether the Indian and Pakistani prime ministers would meet. Everyone was looking out for 'the handshake'. There were precedents to this sort of conjecturing, especially where SAARC summits were concerned. In January 2002, Pervez Musharraf took India by surprise by striding across the room and clasping Atal Bihari Vajpayee's hand in a firm grip. Taken aback for a second, Vajpayee then rose from his seat to reciprocate the gesture amid loud cheers from fellow delegates. This was just a few weeks after the attack on India's Parliament. Then there was the 'Thimphu Thaw' where Manmohan Singh and his counterpart Yousaf Gilani came together and posed for cameras their hands interlinked in a show of warmth. This time around, there didn't seem to be much chance of such amity.

The television channels were broadcasting footage on a loop that appeared to have caught a grim looking Modi studiously examining a newspaper whilst an equally impassive Sharif walked past him to make his address. There was no eye contact between the two men; they seemed to be ignoring each other altogether. It was evidence, journalists proclaimed, of the frostiness in ties between the two countries. The more 'patriotic' channels termed it a grand snub. At the close of the two-day conference, when Sharif and Modi finally shook hands and smiled for the cameras, flanked by other heads of state, the media was excitable and ready to draw conclusions. 'Finally!' said one headline, 'Summit salvaged by handshake' said another, once again suggesting that the two countries had just about come back from the brink of a total collapse in communication.

But as the op-eds were being written and the limitations of 'the handshake' were being debated to death on prime time television, a 'secret' meeting between Modi and Sharif had gone entirely undetected. Bombastic commentators, including those of the BJP, were decreeing the Nepal trip to be yet more proof of a tough new Pakistan policy. Even at the leaders-only retreat at the resort in Dhulikhel, an opportunity to talk more casually, the interaction between the two had been described as strictly an 'exchange of pleasantries'. The public image of enforced politeness and actual friction between the two was authentic only to the extent that a structured encounter was never part of the plan. However, on reaching Kathmandu, the prime minister had called Sajjan Jindal and asked him to hop on to the earliest flight to Nepal. Jindal was asked to discreetly reach out to his 'friend' across the border. Subsequently, the two prime ministers were able to meet quietly in the privacy of Jindal's hotel room in Nepal, where they are said to have spent an hour together. Elections in the sensitive state of Jammu and Kashmir were just a month away and Modi explained that while he was keen to find ways to reopen some formal channels, circumstances did not permit him to do so immediately. Sharif, in turn, told him about the constrictions imposed on him by the security establishment in Pakistan—his negotiating power with the army had been gradually whittled away. Both agreed they needed some more time and greater political space to move forward publicly. This under-the-radar encounter paved the way for Modi to openly reach out to Nawaz Sharif two months later through a phone call that was positioned as an innocuous good-luck call for the World Cup, but could be traced back to that moment in Nepal when both sides set the ball rolling.

I was told this story of Jindal's role as an intermediary at a dinner where many big names from the business community were present. I was asked, more than once, how the media had missed it altogether. The telling part of the story to me was the contrast with the memory of that night in New York when Modi's fierce outburst at an election rally in Delhi had drawn me into its vortex and made its impact felt on the first and last meeting Manmohan Singh ever had with Nawaz Sharif. A pragmatist had clearly replaced the polemicist.

There were other noticeable shifts in Modi's foreign policy that were a clear departure from his years in the Opposition. The land boundary agreement with Bangladesh's Sheikh Hasina, for instance, which involved a swap of enclaves between Assam, West Bengal, Meghalaya and Tripura with Bangladesh. The agreement had been signed between Manmohan Singh and Hasina in 2011 but needed a constitutional amendment to make it operational. Right up to 2013, the BJP had bitterly opposed the move and argued that the territory of India could not be altered by an amendment to its constitution. Once in power, Modi argued that it would be one way of stopping illegal immigration and would bolster ties with the Awami League government. Steering the passage of the legislation he then walked across the aisle to personally thank Sonia Gandhi and other Opposition leaders for their support.

One could be clichéd and label these modifications, some subtle, some dramatic, as 'U-turns' that are typical of Indian politics. But, because in so many ways Modi himself had been the main issue of the election that catapulted him into power, and because never before had there been so many assumptions about and expectations of a prime ministerial candidate, his shifts were more significant than the prosaic flip-flops that we were used to. He was certainly going to leave us all guessing.

■

To conclude this section on Narendra Modi, I'd like to describe his relationship with the media. He was instinctively suspicious of journalists; especially those he believed had been critical of him after the 2002 Gujarat riots. While he was chief minister, successive political victories had made him impervious to the comments of the media. The scale of his win in 2014 made him think that his office in Delhi would not need engagement with the press either. He dispensed with the post of media adviser and stopped journalists from accompanying him on his aircraft when he travelled abroad. Most media people still hot-footed it on their own, shadowing his every move across the globe, but typically neither he—nor any senior official in his government—would even meet informally with the press corps on these trips. Unlike Manmohan Singh—who never gave interviews and faced the media officially at a press conference only three times in ten years—Modi did give interviews when he became prime minister. However, these were only to journalists he did not dislike.

At first, when Modi was still CM, I would follow him on the campaign trail just as I would any other politician. As his 'rath' criss-crossed its way across the state, reporters would hop on for small stretches of the ride where he would give them short interviews. As a professional it was my job to try to get an interview as well, and so I did. Until I discovered that while Modi would talk to even local stringers in the interior villages of Gujarat, he would not talk to me.

Over the years I came to believe that while Modi may have disliked some of us, more than any personal antipathy he rather enjoyed the idea of doing battle with whichever media person he had designated as an antagonist or enemy; just as he battled his 'foes' in politics, so did he fight his 'enemies' in the media. He seemed to relish a good scrap—and even better, a victory. The 'othering' of the media—or at least sections of it—was part of this. Modi, who felt the English language media had vilified him during the riots, did not forget who had said what. And now he believed the tables had turned.

I only had one brief conversation with Narendra Modi before he became prime minister and that was at the Chennai wedding of the son of my friend Shobhana Bhartia, the well-liked owner of the *Hindustan Times*. Bhartia's son was getting married to the daughter of Mukesh and Anil Ambani's sister Nina and there were several politicians, film stars and businessmen in attendance.

I moved aside as I saw Modi arriving, not wanting any awkwardness at the table I was sitting at. In the course of the evening, I saw well-known lawyer Raian Karanjawala and adman Suhel Seth at the same table as the man who would be prime minister. They waved to me to join them. Modi was polite and we made some small talk; I even managed a half-joke about how I thought he would not wish to talk to me. He (half) joked back saying he had no intention of giving me an interview; talking was just fine.

Later, after he became prime minister, Modi began to meet groups of journalists at dinners organized at Arun Jaitley's residence. The only two people I knew who were not invited to meet him were my former NDTV colleague Rajdeep Sardesai—who had fronted the coverage of the Gujarat riots—and myself.

Yet, for all the antipathy he displayed towards some journalists, Modi was the most media-savvy politician India had ever seen. He was also the one whose deeply felt dislike for the media would express itself in phrases like 'news traders', which he coined while in the Opposition, and 'bazaaru' (bought) which he used while canvassing for the Delhi state elections. His relationship with the media aside, there was no question that Modi was a brilliant communicator (which was what made his silences—whenever his partymen made inflammatory statements or when there were incidents that deserved stiff and unequivocal condemnation—worthy of comment and speculation). He was also a successful practitioner of a new kind of politics that the rest of the political class was still trying to catch up to.

You could call it the 'Modi'fication of Indian politics or perhaps more accurately the Americanization of our democracy. Raymond Vickery, a former member of the Clinton administration, once told me that Narendra Modi was 'simultaneously the easiest and hardest

kind of partner for the United States to deal with—easiest because
in some important ways he is so American in his outlook and the
hardest for the very same reason'. The show of strength for Modi at
New York's Madison Square Garden, with repeat performances in
Australia and Canada, was seen as an American-style statement of
clout that several commentators compared to the atmosphere of a
presidential nomination.

The cult of personality, the emphasis on charisma and
communication, the assertion of fierce and complete political
supremacy—Modi had effectively pushed politics from a
parliamentary model to a presidential one where the fortunes of
parties now depended on the personas of their leaders. More Indira
Gandhi than any other comparable figure, his capture of power inside
his own party was complete. The geriatric rebels of the party had
literally been put out to pasture. During the election campaign
one of them, who was likely contesting the last election of his life,
whispered to me before the cameras came on that the 'BJP was now
a dictatorship'. But beyond the carping, faced with his own electoral
irrelevance, there was not much he could do. Even ministers like
Sushma Swaraj—widely considered one of Modi's most charismatic
colleagues—seemed diminished compared to her years as a fiery and
voluble Leader of the Opposition. When Modi was initially putting
together his Cabinet, Swaraj had insisted that she be treated like an
equal. She told the prime minister she would only become part of his
Cabinet if he treated her as a peer—like two people sitting together
on a sofa, she said, and having a conversation and not a situation
where one person is expected to sit at the other's feet. But once in
government it was the prime minister who overshadowed her foreign
affairs ministry, relegating the talented Swaraj to the sidelines. When
the Lalit Modi cricket scandal hit her (and in Rajasthan, the chief
minister, Vasundhara Raje), and when an admissions controversy
engulfed the Madhya Pradesh chief minister, Shivraj Singh Chouhan,
the word in the party was that Modi had demolished all three leaders
who could challenge him or who had taken Advani's side against him
in the past. When Advani and Joshi were appointed to the party's
'margdarshak mandal' (advisory board), Nitish Kumar, ally of the

BJP for seventeen years and now Modi's bête noire joked to me, 'Rajnath will be the next leader to be banished to the margdarshak club.' This, about a minister holding a portfolio once regarded as the second most powerful in government. Modi's hold over the party was complete and nothing but electoral defeat in the states was going to dent that. By becoming more important than his party Modi marked a new phase of politics where the model of political domination he constructed began to be replicated in other newer parties as well, including the Aam Aadmi Party.

Modi had understood that India's new politics was a marketplace of ideas in which the leader is a branded product and the voter a perennial consumer of political content. He heralded a new communications age wherein fiercely individualistic leaders seek a strong connection with the masses to reinforce the imprint of their own personality on the larger political ecosystem. It's what Bernard Manin, professor of Politics at New York University has called 'audience democracy', in describing a new kind of representative government where politics is mediated by the mass media and 'the electorate responds to the terms that have been presented on the political stage'. In his book, *The Principles of Representative Government*, Manin outlines three kinds of democracy—parliamentary democracy, party democracy and audience democracy—arguing that the most recent variation of image-driven politics is as legitimate a form of representative government as any other. So, if political dialogue previously took place inside Parliament, now it unfolds in the public domain, in television studios, on social media, or even in gossip around the digital version of an old-style water cooler.

Modi's made-for-media politics in which strategic communication was a key component was constantly on display. A perfect example was the visit of President Barack Obama to India as chief guest at the country's Republic Day celebrations in 2015. The manly hug between the two leaders, the hard to miss symbolism of Modi, once a tea vendor, pouring tea from a silver teapot for arguably the world's most powerful man, the intimate setting of the joint-radio broadcast, the huddling under umbrellas on a rain-soaked Rajpath—this was strategic communication at its best.

Several parallels have already been drawn between Modi and Obama, their rise from modest backgrounds (the grandson of a cook and a tea-seller's son as the US president described it), their self-proclaimed status of being outsiders to Delhi and Washington respectively, and their embrace of social media and technology to run intensely personality-driven election campaigns. But they were also similar in their flair for showmanship. In an age of hyper-information and shrinking, overloaded attention spans both understood the value of telling a good story. Even the fact that Modi did not hesitate to cry in front of the camera was not typical of the conventional Indian politician. To be personal in public was the American way.

Obama's parting shot on the need to uphold religious tolerance in India—'India will succeed so long as it's not splintered along the lines of religious faith'—may have pointed to the limitations of packaging, oratory and theatrics. But it did not detract from the dramatic transformation that has taken place in Indian politics where, as technology-enabled outreach increases, the actual relevance of journalists is declining. Once upon a time, when private television began in India, 'camera-friendly' referred to politicians who would play the role of jesters for television. Think Lalu Yadav in the years he would never be photographed without his cows or Farooq Abdullah diving into Dal Lake. Their antics and affected buffoonery were designed to draw laughs and some affection, but never did it give them control of the political narrative. Today, as politicians learn the art of creating news events to stay in the headlines, they have understood that the media will never look away from a moment of drama. As long as they can keep generating drama they can actually avoid institutionalized engagement with the media. They can be the news without talking to the press.

III

If Rahul Gandhi's communication strategy was ineffectual and Modi's was masterful but hostile to large sections of the media, one man's embrace of the media space was complete—at least in the initial years when he was still an anti-corruption activist and not yet a full time politician.

I first met Arvind Kejriwal when he was a Right to Information (RTI) activist and a winner of the Ramon Magsaysay award who sought the support of our television network to campaign for transparency in governance.

Even in his pre-politics years there was a brooding intensity and a single-minded focus to him. Unlike Rahul, who would effortlessly alternate between Polo-tees, open-collared shirts, bomber jackets and kurta-pyjamas, and Modi whose trademark half-sleeve kurtas even compelled Obama to call the prime minister a fashion icon, Kejriwal, who used to rotate just two sweaters through the entire Delhi winter, had no interest in clothes or appearances. His shirts were unstarched, his feet were usually shod in chappals and all he wanted to do was get on with the task at hand. Kejriwal was a man in a hurry. His impatience betrayed a simmering restlessness that he was able to channel into the birth of a new political party.

India's anti-corruption movement took root in 2011 against the backdrop of a slew of corruption scandals that had embroiled the Manmohan Singh government. Telecom, coal, the Commonwealth Games—it appeared as if in almost every corner of the economic life of the nation you could find examples of the unsavoury links between big business and the state. Ashutosh Varshney and Jayant Sinha—who is now a minister in the Modi government—had dubbed the season of ceaseless scams as 'India's Gilded Age'. The reference was to a term coined by Mark Twain and Charles Dudley Warner in 1873 to describe a phase of huge economic growth in American history that was accompanied by wide-ranging corruption. As activists of what was known as the 'Progressive Movement' trashed their country's super-wealthy business families as 'robber barons' and accused them of manipulating the system for private profit, they vowed to clean up politics. Kejriwal was the Indian version of the Progressives, fashioning an entire party from the middle-class disillusionment with corruption and their craving for a third alternative to the BJP and the Congress.

Kejriwal swiftly occupied a place in the national imagination that the so-called third front—the non-BJP, non-Congress regional parties—should have but couldn't pull off. Though individually,

state satraps remained firmly entrenched in their fiefdoms—Naveen
Patnaik in Orissa, Mamata Banerjee in Bengal, Jayalalithaa in Tamil
Nadu, Mulayam Singh Yadav in Uttar Pradesh—and were treated
with deference even by the Modi government which needed their
legislative support in the Rajya Sabha where it was short of a
majority—none of them were seen as a 'third pole' in the country's
dominant bipolar model built around the BJP and Congress.

Now, a space had been made in the collective imagination of
voters for a third personality—someone other than Narendra Modi
or Rahul Gandhi. Initially both a maverick and a sort of political
guerrilla, Kejriwal was like an insurgent in permanent revolutionary
mode. From the inception of Kejriwal's India Against Corruption
movement, to his shoot and scoot press conferences—where he
attacked some of India's most powerful people—he understood
that Indian politics is increasingly mediated by the mass media.
On social networking forums the troopers belonged (and still do,
for most part) to only one of two armies: either that of the BJP or
AAP. The effectiveness of this approach was reflected in how much
air time Kejriwal managed to get in the 2014 elections, even though
he was only the leader of a regional party whose sphere of influence
did not extend beyond Delhi. He was also good at learning from
his mistakes. His decision to apologize to the voters of Delhi after
impetuously walking out of government the first time they elected
his party, was a first for Indian politics. The voters forgave him and
voted him back to power with an overwhelming majority.

His nascent political journey has not been devoid of accidents
and serious missteps. His party has already had severe public
meltdowns with some of its most prominent members, psephologist
Yogendra Yadav and senior lawyer Prashant Bhushan, being ousted.
Yadav once told me that his enforced exit was akin to a 'Stalinist
purge'; Bhushan called Kejriwal a dictator. His initial patronage of
unsavoury characters like Somnath Bharti, accused by his wife of
domestic violence, remained another blot. While controversy never
left his side, nor did the media attention.

Kejriwal 2.0 was a much mellowed politician who even smiled
every now and then and seemed to have ironed out many of his

rougher edges. He had also finally abandoned all delusions of grandeur and hunkered down to focus on Delhi instead of chasing a premature national ambition. What made him interesting to a political observer was that he combined some of the traits of both the Congress and the BJP. Unlike many leaders of the Congress, he was culturally rooted in a more traditional Indian ethos—'Bharat Mata Ki Jai' and 'Inquilab Zindabad' were slogans you heard at AAP rallies and not those of the Congress. But unlike the BJP, which claimed the same rootedness, he did not carry the baggage of Hindutva politics.

Either way, like Narendra Modi and Rahul Gandhi, he represented the shift that had taken place in Indian politics, where the personality of the leader—and how voters responded to the individual—had become more important than either the party or even an ideology. The Americanization of Indian politics was complete.

Seven

A SOCIETY IN FLUX

I

ON 26 DECEMBER 2004, the sea literally rose to swallow the coastal town of Nagapattinam; a tsunami had hit the southeastern coast of India following a massive earthquake in the Indian Ocean.

It was the season when the rich and famous typically moved to Goa or Koh Samui to bring in the New Year. For many of these people, the tsunami was of interest only to the extent that their tropical holiday destinations to escape north India's winter suddenly didn't seem so safe anymore. What a bore, they thought, and once the worst was over they simply packed their Louis Vuitton bags and went on holiday to some other place.

When I began my journey to the scene of the catastrophe I was sure that I would find that the devastation was enormous but I was not prepared for what I would discover. The unceasing rain on the morning after the tsunami struck was nature's final act of cruelty; the strong currents of water were sucking in the few material belongings—a wall clock, a slipper, even money—of the helpless survivors who were looking on. Many of the people I spoke to in the ravaged fishing town said they were determined to leave, even though they had nowhere to go.

One man motioned to us to follow him towards the fishing boats that lay in a heap, blocking the entrance to the nearby village of Akaraipatti. There was only a narrow channel to crawl through under the boats. One by one, we went down on all fours, and squeezed our way through the tiny passage to the other side. No district official had bothered to go past the boats.

I felt a wave of nausea when I stood up and shook the water out of my nose and eyes. We were looking at a beach that had become a mass grave of children overnight; so many that we couldn't bear to look or count. The women and children of the village had been sleeping out in the open when the raging waves rose to devour the shore. When the water rushed back into the ocean, it had taken many of the tiniest and most vulnerable with it; those it left behind had been battered to death. Now the mothers who had been spared, stood silent and forlorn in the rain as the fishermen placed milk and powder on the lips of their dead children in a final farewell ritual.

When they counted the bodies across the coastal districts of the southern states, especially Tamil Nadu, they discovered that more than 2,000 children had died. Hundreds of others had been orphaned. At the local children's shelter, older siblings worried about how they would look after their brothers and sisters, a five-year-old boy held on to a teenager he didn't know for comfort; both had lost their parents. There was a little girl who had been born blind; her parents had saved Rs 12,000 over several years for an eye operation that doctors believed could partially restore her vision. That money, too, had been swept away by the water.

When I filed my stories on the 'Children of the Tsunami' I had thought there was no special eloquence needed to convey such visceral sadness and loss. Children dead in their thousands in one of the worst natural disasters the country had experienced—this was a story that told itself. But that night, after the telecast, I got a call from a friend who said, 'Do we really have to watch this depressing stuff on television right now?'—as if life's grim reality was an optional item on a movie menu in a hotel room and you could pick out only the cheery stuff to view. In several of my reports I actually began editorializing more than ever before, appealing directly to those vacationing in happier, sunnier spots to pause and at least think about these children. The callousness of the well-heeled was eye-opening. To be reminded that for a section of Indian society the deaths of the children of poor fisherfolk mattered not at all was both disconcerting and disturbing.

Had fifty children from middle class or rich families died in metropolitan India, people would have spoken of nothing else for weeks. Sadly, all that the death of these children seemed to evoke in the hearts and minds of the wealthy was a desire to switch to another TV channel or change their beach destination. But my disappointment with the reactions of people I knew wasn't the only thing that struck me. Beyond the calamitous scenes I witnessed, what leapt out at me was that even amid the death and devastation, there was the pernicious presence of one of India's oldest fault lines—that of caste discrimination.

For the past forty-eight hours a group of about a hundred men had been working tirelessly, wading barefoot through the water on the beach, removing rocks, stones, planks and other debris obstructing their passage, trying to drag out the bodies, many of which had already started decomposing. An overwhelmed local administration was terrified that the putrefying corpses would pollute the water and cause an epidemic on a scale that would multiply the rising number of fatalities. It was already too late. And yet, no one among the local rescue teams had been prepared to do this job.

Sanitary workers had to be brought in from Madurai to clear the dead bodies that no one else was willing to touch. These were workers belonging to the 'untouchable' Arunthathiyar community of Tamil Nadu, considered the lowest of the low because of their traditional occupation—working in cremation grounds and government mortuaries, and clearing villages of dead animals. Although they were not directly tied, geographically or emotionally, to the tragedy of the tsunami, it was left to them to scrub the stains of death from the beach. They worked with their bare hands and torn gloves, pulling out body after body—I counted thirty in just one hour—and heaving them on to a truck to be taken to makeshift funeral pyres on the beach. The inescapable irony was that most of the dead were fisherfolk belonging to the 'higher castes'. In life, they would have recoiled from any social contact with the same men who were now pulling them out from under the wreckage to ensure they at least got a dignified, final farewell. But kindness to the dead was no guarantee of appreciation for the living.

Even as the sanitary workers braved quicksand and medical maladies, news was coming in of discrimination in the relief and rehabilitation camps that lay further inland—Dalits were being told they would get food only after it was first distributed among the fishermen's families. In school buildings that were doubling up as night shelters, there were families who refused to share physical space with Dalits who were then shunted to accommodation in plastic tents. Many Dalit families were left with no option but to live out in the open. Fishermen had borne the brunt of the tragedy because they were the immediate victims of the rising waves. But Dalits had also suffered, losing their livelihood, cattle and, crucially, access to drinking water. Yet they were being forced to the back of food and water lines and in some cases were not even being allowed to use the temporary toilets that had been built by international agencies. Unable to cope with the scale of devastation and the work that needed to be done, some aid workers found it simpler to provide separate relief facilities for the Dalit community than to fight, at that moment, the engrained biases of caste. It was sobering to think that the enormous power of the earthquake and the tsunami it had generated had managed to kill 230,000 people in fourteen countries but had still been unable to break down the wall that separated India's Dalits from their countrymen.

As I followed the sanitary workers around, a hospital mask tied loosely over my face, I was struck by how diligent and uncomplaining they were about their work. Most of them worked without special protective gear or tools and, in some cases, without shoes. It was backbreaking work. They would clear away the larger pieces of debris, then extract the body from the rubble and lift it onto a mat on the beach from where it would be transported to the pyres. Locals stood around, watching from a safe distance as the corpses of their friends and neighbours were retrieved, their faces wrapped in swatches of cloth in an effort to block the smell of rotting human flesh. As the flames enveloped body after body, I began to feel nauseous; the antiseptic lime powder, the sea breeze, none of it could mitigate the overpowering odour of death. Within a few hours, I was unable to stand there any longer. I ran to where the other onlookers were standing and threw up. But the sanitary workers carried on, impassive, committed and focused on delivering the last rites for people who would not have allowed them to pray in the same temple as them, had they been alive. They did all this for the paltry sum of Rs 75 a day.

Two days later I fell sick and had to leave Nagapattinam for Chennai where I was admitted to the Apollo Hospital for a medical examination. It turned out that I had picked up a severe bacterial infection from my brief exposure to the disintegrating human bodies. I thought of the men on beach and the abysmal daily wages they were paid—if they fell ill where would they go? But there was no one in Chennai I could have that conversation with. Just 300 kilometres away, the city seemed entirely untouched by the violent crash of water on the state's shores. After the initial shock had passed, Chennai went on with its annual Carnatic music festival. The *New Indian Express* interviewed a young student hanging out at a mall who explained his apparent disconnect to the lives lost by arguing, without embarrassment, that 'it's good if India's population is reduced'.

The self-absorbed upper classes, the forgotten poor, the oppressed Dalits, the resigned scavengers—the vignettes I carried back from the tsunami painted a portrait of a deeply unequal country.

All this was meant to change after 1991. Forced into liberalizing the economy, India's financial managers, across parties, made a dramatic ideological shift in opening up once protected markets to global forces. They now believed that growth and the trickle-down effect of capital would run a bulldozer over other social inequities. Capitalism would subsume caste; free enterprises would give birth to dreams liberated from a socialist past.

At Nagapattinam, I discovered that in the collision of caste and class, the country that was booming outwardly was in fact in grave danger of imploding.

II

In the summer of 1901, a ten-year-old-boy and his brother (and their sister's son) were looking forward to a train ride from the tranquil hill town of Satara in the Western Ghats of Maharashtra to Koregaon, another town in the district, where their father, a retired army officer, had taken a part-time job. New clothes had been stitched for the journey—caps embossed with coloured stones, dhotis with silk borders and new shirts. The children had never been on a train before and they were excited. They each had two annas to spend and as they got on board with their lemonades, they couldn't have been happier.

But when the boys got off at the Masur railway station they discovered that their father had not sent anyone to meet them. Later, it would emerge that their father's domestic help had forgotten to pass on the message of their arrival. Whatever the reason for the absence of an escort, the children now had to figure out how to reach their destination. Noticing their plight, the station master began making enquiries. The ten-year-old blurted out that they were Mahars, a community considered 'untouchable' because of the 'lowly' jobs traditionally assigned to them, including cleaning village streets and skinning and clearing animal carcasses. By recruiting them as soldiers the British Army had offered some freedom to the Mahars from, what was in effect, bonded labour—but the army background of the boys' father did nothing to change what happened next. On discovering their caste, the station master shrank back in revulsion and withdrew into his office.

Thirty minutes later the boys were still stranded on the platform. The sun was beginning to set. The worried children decided to hire a bullock cart to ferry them to their father. They even offered to pay double the fare. But the station master had spread the word that the boys were 'untouchables' and no one was willing to have any contact with them. Finally, a solution was negotiated. The boys would have to steer the bullock cart themselves and, in return for the payment, the cartman would walk alongside at a 'safe' distance.

That ten-year-old boy was Bhimrao Ramji Ambedkar. He would grow up to be a scholar, a lawyer, a Dalit icon and the architect of free India's Constitution. He would describe this incident in his life as the first time he had ever questioned why he had to accept abuse in the name of caste. Until then he, like millions of others, had quietly endured the social code which could neither be resisted nor challenged. At school, he was not allowed to touch the tap and help himself to water. 'Unless [the tap] was opened by a touchable person, it was not possible for me to quench my thirst,' he wrote. In class he had to sit on a separate gunny bag, one that the school's cleaner refused to wash. So he would bring it to school and take it back home with him every day. His elder sister was the one who would cut their hair—no barber was willing to provide his services to 'untouchables'. All this he accepted as a 'matter of course'. But on that day—when their joyous train ride to meet their father culminated in humiliation—he felt a rage rise within him like never before.

Exactly thirty-five years later he would write his seminal speech calling for the 'annihilation of caste', an address that would remain undelivered because it was too radical for the organizers.

In 1936, the Jat-Pat-Todak Mandal (Caste Destruction Society) that emerged as an offshoot of the Arya Samaj reformist movement, convened a meeting in Lahore and invited B. R. Ambedkar to address the forum. He sent them an advance copy of his speech. Ambedkar argued that the tyranny of caste and the Chaturvarnya—the four basic classes or varnas in Hindu society: Brahmins (priests), Kshatriyas (warriors), Vaishyas (merchants or farmers) and Shudras (labourers)—had been sanctioned by the Dharmashastras, ancient texts that outline the codes relating to Hindu social and civil law; and hence, the only way to escape caste was to leave the Hindu fold. The organizers asked for some of the remarks to be expunged, in particular the reference to the Vedas. Ambedkar shot back, 'I will not alter a comma.'

Ambedkar's revolt against the tyranny of caste would bring him into confrontation with another of the country's founding fathers—Mahatma Gandhi. Even though both were true revolutionaries who had taken on the upholders of orthodox and divisive traditions, they approached the challenge of caste in different ways. Gandhi opposed any form of caste discrimination but did not see the resolution outside the framework of Hinduism. In fact, he believed, at least initially, that the varna-defined hereditary occupations helped integrate Hinduism as long as there was perfect social equality between all groups. Later, he called for a single varna to enable the 'root and branch destruction of the idea of superiority and inferiority'.

Ambedkar, who once described himself as 'repugnant to the Hindus', called for an end to the absolute sanctity of Hindu scriptures:

'[T]he enemy you must grapple with is not the people who observe caste but the Shastras which teach them this religion of caste.'

Gandhi and Ambedkar had their biggest confrontation over the demand for separate electorates for 'untouchables'—Gandhi thought this demand by Ambedkar was 'absolutely suicidal'. The Mahatma went on a fast unto death demanding the British withdraw their assent to Ambedkar's demand. Finally, in what came to be known as the Poona Pact of 1932, Ambedkar compromised. Voters would not be segregated by caste, but there would be a fixed number of seats reserved for candidates from the 'depressed' castes. By 1935 the Simon Commission had given the nomenclature 'Scheduled Castes' to all the 'untouchable' castes identified by the census; the act was modified to include Scheduled Tribes by an independent India in 1950. Caste—far from being annihilated—came to occupy a permanent seat in the gladiatorial ring of Indian politics.

III

He was getting his head shaved. Thousands were watching as the razor blade travelled down the back of his head with the precision of a cartographer's pen. After all, with this single act, he was mapping a new identity. The crowd cheered him on, Buddhist chants filled the air and monks in red robes looked quizzically at the cameras. At the end of the ceremony the man on stage had a new name—Udit Raj. The old one—Ram—had been abandoned, as had the religion (Hinduism) that he was born into. He was among thousands of Dalits who had just embraced Buddhism in a conversion ceremony performed amid raging controversy and tight security.

A former revenue service office in the government, Udit Raj was positioning himself as the newest Dalit messiah. His own journey was rather less dramatic than he made it out to be—this was not a battle of the scale and intensity waged by Ambedkar in the previous century—but it was nevertheless an important skirmish in a war that seemed to have no end in sight. And it gave me an opportunity to examine whether all the promises made towards the social upliftment of Dalits by politicians of every hue were anything more than an eyewash.

I met Udit Raj in south Delhi's Laxmi Bai Colony where the once freshly painted white walls of flats allotted to mid-ranking bureaucrats had begun to turn yellow, and satellite dishes shared space on small terraces with drying clothes and crisscrossing electricity wires. There was nothing to distinguish the apartment from any other middle-class home except the wall clock, which had stickers of Ambedkar and the Buddha stuck on the inside of its plastic surface. On another wall, somewhat incongruously, was a poster of a WWF wrestling star, all long-haired and beefed up. On the street outside his house, a small group of neo-Buddhist supporters dressed in ritual robes—recent converts to the faith—were getting their shoes polished by a cobbler. It was hard to miss the symbolism of that moment.

The cobbler's name was Mange Lal, but to most of the world he was a 'chamar', a pejorative used for those who work with leather. His customers today were also born into castes that had been shunned and persecuted the way Mange Lal still was. But as they thrust their shoes forward for just a bit more shine they obviously believed they had swapped their birth castes for a new identity—one that gave them more dignity than Mange Lal, to begin with.

I stopped to talk to Mange Lal when he was done with his customers. The slogan scrawled across Udit Raj's car caught his attention. Might there be something in it for him? 'Hamara to beet gaya lekin ho sakta hai bachchon ke liye kuch ho sakta (It's too late for me, but maybe my children can be saved from their plight),' he said. Behind me a loud argument had broken out between the monks and a passer-by. I turned to find an old man, out for a morning walk, engaged in an unpleasant debate with them. 'They should not convert. Why are they converting?' he began shouting when I asked him what he was objecting to.

'But they have to face discrimination in their own faith,' I argued as gently as I could, initially respectful of his age.

'Who says? These people converted because they didn't do their duty. They converted because they thought preference milega. Yeh log pehle kya thhe? Dalit thhe. Unka kya kaam hota hai? They should have just done their jobs,' he said aggressively.

'This is the twenty-first century, sir, why should only Dalits do some jobs?' I said, repulsed by his twisted logic.

'Even a Brahmin today does the work of other castes,' the man was carrying on, undeterred, getting more and more cantankerous and shrill in his responses.

I finally ventured to ask him his caste.

'I am a Brahmin,' he said, proudly.

'And what do you do?'

'I retired as an under secretary in the Ministry of Personnel,' he said, before giving the monks one final glare and stomping off.

'Dekh liya aapne (Now you see),' said one of the monks to me.

The blatant prejudice the government official displayed had shocked me even though it was an ever-present reality in the lives of millions of my fellow Indians. For most of my life, until my work led me to explore social fault lines, I had absolutely no idea what my caste was. I would aggressively dismiss queries about it by declaring that I did not believe in it as an identity marker. But of course that disbelief came from a position of privilege, from never knowing what it meant to be ridiculed and abused for an accident of birth. I used to think it was my education and upbringing that allowed me to disregard caste entirely. But the vitriol displayed by the 'educated' official I had just met made me realize how simplistic my thinking was. His outburst had captured two realities—the continued stranglehold of caste, even in urban, educated India, and the simmering resentment of many towards those who tried to escape it by converting to another faith.

The blistering row over conversions captures how caste intolerance continues to fracture Hindu society and, even more dangerously, has the potential to blow up into larger religious conflict. Sociologist Kancha Ilaiah, the author of Why I am Not a Hindu, told me, 'The Dalits have no alternative but to seek a spiritual system for themselves. These people are now demanding the Right to Religion.'

But critics of mass conversions, the RSS prominent among them, have often called for the 'ghar wapsi' (homecoming) of all those who have left the fold of Hinduism. In December 2014, within months of Narendra Modi taking charge as prime minister, RSS chief Mohan Bhagwat hijacked the BJP's development headlines by declaring that those who had 'lost their way' must be brought back 'home'. 'Woh log apne aap nahin gaye, unko loot kar, laalach de kar le gaye (Those people didn't go of their own volition, they were "looted" and bribed into converting),' Bhagwat said while addressing a Virat Hindu Sammelan in Kolkata, playing on the familiar trope that proselytizing faiths like Christianity and Islam were 'stealing' Hindus with inducements and threats. 'Abhi chor pakda gaya hai. Mera maal chor ke paas hai. Aur yeh duniya jaanti hai. Main apna maal wapas loonga, yeh kaunsi badi baat hai (If a thief is caught and I find my belongings with him, will I not retrieve my belongings? What's the issue in that)?' he went on to say.

What was less clear is what caste a reconvert to Hinduism would become, though affiliate groups of the RSS like the VHP promised that anyone 'coming back' could choose their caste, reinforcing the links between conversions and upward mobility.

In January 1927, the Mahatma had this to say about conversions: 'I am against conversion, whether it is known as shuddhi by Hindus, tabligh by Mussalmans, or proselytizing by Christians'. Ambedkar, his intellectual antagonist, who had already declared that he would 'not die a Hindu', converted to Buddhism in 1956, just two months before his death.

By May 2014, Udit Raj, the man who had vowed to uplift millions of India's downtrodden by encouraging them to change their religion, joined the BJP. It was no ordinary political irony; the BJP was the most trenchant critic of mass conversions. For India's Dalits, Udit Raj was one among many politicians who had used the collective oppression of the community to climb up the ladder of ambition. In fact, it was increasingly becoming evident that traditional Dalit politics had failed to bring about transformative change. Even the Bahujan Samaj Party—founded by Kanshi Ram and built by Mayawati on the provocative slogan of 'Tilak, Tarazu or Talwar, inko maaro joote chaar (Thrash the Brahmin, the Bania and the Rajput with shoes)'—eventually had to move to a more inclusive caste formula that brought Dalits and Brahmins together. Even so, the party drew a blank in the 2014 Lok Sabha elections. Many leaders in the Dalit community believed that their future could no longer bank on the power of politics—or even affirmative action alone.

IV

'Capitalism is our only weapon to eliminate caste,' the excitable Dalit scholar Chandra Bhan Prasad would tell me, sometimes leaping out of his chair to underline his argument. He would often come on my television shows armed with a hand-drawn doodle of the 'only goddess' he said his atheist self could ever worship. Needless to say, she didn't belong to the Hindu pantheon. He called her 'The Goddess of English' and he built a modern mythology around her borrowing heavily from the symbol of America's Statue of Liberty. He even began to build a temple to her in a village of Uttar Pradesh where more than half the population was Dalit. The goddess wore a hat and gown; like Ambedkar, she held a copy of the Indian Constitution, but to root her in a more contemporary idiom, she also had a keyboard and a pen, and stood atop a computer screen. Chandra Bhan called her a symbol of 'Dalit renaissance'.

It was in the potential mobility of class, even with its capacity to create new social disparities, that many Dalit groups saw their exit from the claustrophobic confines of caste. That lion of the Dalits, Ambedkar, was always presented in a blue three-piece suit—one hand holding the Constitution, the other upraised as if acknowledging the cheers of followers. His dress and manner were in stark contrast to the more traditional dress code and imagery used by the average Indian politician. It suggested that the Dalits aspired to join India's English-speaking elite. The statue presented him as a man of enlightenment, a middle-class intellectual who had successfully shrugged off the victimhood of caste by being unapologetically westernized when needed. At a time in Indian politics when 'suit-boot' had come to be a political paraphrase for elitism and cronyism, Ambedkar's suit and boot was worn like a badge of honour. For many of my Dalit friends, it was a symbol of elite acceptance. An alternative iconography for the traditionally oppressed was not strictly a new idea. Even in the face of scathing criticism, caste-leaders like Mayawati had built sprawling Dalit memorial parks in cities like Lucknow and Noida. But these had also included statues of her, suggesting not merely narcissism but also copycat feudalism, an imbibing of the very characteristics that 'outcasts' had been stigmatized by.

A former Naxalite who had once been an ultra-left revolutionary, Chandra Bhan had travelled across the ideological spectrum to become a passionate advocate of the power of markets over Marx. He did not believe that converting to another faith would make any difference to the social or economic status of his community. 'Out of every hundred Dalits, forty-nine are landless labourers. It is immaterial for them if they declare that they are Buddhists today or Christians tomorrow. The conversions have no impact on their economic conditions. In fact, it's just the opposite. The energy of the Dalit movement is getting wasted,' he argued.

But would their betterment come from capitalism alone as Chandra Bhan believed? Almost twenty-five years after the advent of economic reforms, data released by the government was anything but encouraging. The latest socio-economic caste census conducted between 2011 and 2013 confirmed how fundamental structural inequities of caste and class continued to be the big unreported India story. Seven out of ten households in India remain rural and most lived on less than Rs 200. More than half of all rural families were landless, and 70 per cent of all Scheduled Castes fell in this category.

In other words, the oppression of caste compounded by the hierarchies of class ensured that India's most oppressed social community, the Dalits, remained at the bottom of the social totem pole.

∎

It was clear that in the twenty-first century, India would not be stepping back from its somewhat confused and tentative, yet warm and welcoming embrace of capitalism. From time to time, governments would fall back on populism or protectionism, and various parties might resort to welfare schemes, but there was one word in the Preamble (introduced through an amendment in 1976 in the aftermath of Indira Gandhi's Emergency) that people would not miss, and that was the self-description of the country as 'socialist'. Even B. R. Ambedkar had opposed its inclusion, arguing during the Constituent Assembly debates that 'how society should be organized in its social and economic side are matters which must be decided by the people themselves depending on time and circumstance'.

No one wanted to go back to the years of queuing up for a phone connection or paying bribes in exchange for an out-of-turn allotment of a gas cylinder; from telecom to aviation, services by private players were lapped up. Had political parties united to alter the amendment that first tagged India as socialist, I don't think it would have evoked any significant popular backlash.

Activists like Chandra Bhan did not dispute that the original ascent of caste-based parties in India, in particular Dalit-driven groups like the Bahujan Samaj Party, were emblematic of a new political assertiveness by those who had been marginalized for centuries. But its impact had stagnated, there was no second wave of social reform—the Dalit vote had empowered the politicians more than the community. Now many of them looked towards a combination of wealth creation and anglicization to provide the upward mobility that affirmative action or political slogans had failed to for decades. In an aping of the business culture of India's power elite, they began to form Dalit Chambers of Commerce. Like the saccharine profiles of the rich and the famous in *Fortune* and *Forbes*, they too wanted the Dalit millionaires in their community to be feted and fussed over. Milind Kamble, the understated chief of the Dalit Chambers of Commerce and the owner of a construction business, once told me proudly, 'Main Sharad Pawar ko paani pilata hoon (I give Sharad Pawar water to drink)'. His company had built the pipeline that supplied water to the pocket borough of one of the most powerful politicians in India. That it was water made its own statement—from separate village wells to separate kitchen tumblers, the controlled access to water had been one of the most wretched and visible aspects of social bigotry. Kamble excitedly shared how he had been featured in an upscale glossy. 'They said that before me Ambani and Tata had sat in this very chair for a photo-shoot.'

Chandra Bhan introduced me to Kalpana Saroj, the glamorous Dalit CEO of a business enterprise valued at over $100 million. Kalpana was the daughter of a police constable who had been unable to resist community pressure and had married her off at the age of twelve. At her husband's home she was expected to mop the floors, wash clothes and cook food for a household of ten. She would be kicked around and beaten at the slightest pretext. Eventually, not able to bear her suffering and humiliation, her father brought her home. 'They taunted me in the neighbourhood and accused me of bringing shame to my family,' Kalpana told me. 'I had tried everything—the military, nursing school, a police recruitment camp, but I was either too young or too uneducated. In desperation, I drank a bottle of poison. I didn't want to live.'

When I met her she was trying to decide whether her company should invest in a private chopper. The turnaround of her life had been dramatic and inspirational and all the more so because her success was entirely self-made. When she survived her suicide attempt she started stitching blouses for an income of a few rupees a piece. When her father lost his job it fell upon her to support her siblings and parents on her tiny tailoring business. It was when her younger sister fell fatally ill that her ambitions altered. 'Her words haunt me even today, she begged us to save her. But we did not have the funds to provide her medical help. It's then that I decided that life without money is useless and I was going to make lots of it.'

Starting with seed capital from a government scheme, she started making cheap knock-offs of high-end furniture. Gradually, she ventured into real estate before reviving the ailing metal and engineering Kamani Tubes Company. She would go on to become its chairwoman.

I asked her if she no longer faced discrimination. Had her caste ceased to be a factor now that she was a wealthy entrepreneur? 'No, not entirely,' she admitted, but proudly introduced me to her son-in-law, a Brahmin by birth. Was this love conquering caste or wealth flattening out prejudice, I asked Kalpana. The question seemed to confuse her. Love was her preferred answer but she was proud of what she had created for her family and the new stature and access it afforded her. This was some of the change post-liberalization India was going through. New money was creating new barriers and bringing old ones down. Yet, it could not be said that India was today a more equal society than at the time of its birth as a republic. For every exception like Kalpana Saroj there was a daily atrocity committed in the name of caste or class, sometimes both.

I met Pawan Malviya, a young man from Madhya Pradesh who was surprised to find that anyone outside of his village was interested in him. When he got married he wanted to sit on a horse, just as upper-caste grooms did and take his wedding procession to his bride's house. Outraged by this cultural assertion of equality, the other villagers threatened to stone him if he persisted with his audacious plans. The local administration's proposed solution spoke to the truth of an India we are too embarrassed to confront. To try and make peace between the warring factions the district officials suggested that the 'offended' parties shut their windows and doors when the procession passed by so they didn't have to witness the abomination of a lower-caste Hindu appropriating their custom. The groom's wishes prevailed, except he wore a helmet and rode his horse through a cascade of stones and bricks, while the police looked on helplessly.

In fact, as more and more Dalits and others who had been victimized by the hatred of the relatively privileged were asserting their rights, the social backlash against them was mounting. In Uttar Pradesh, two Dalit brothers, who were sons of a daily-wage labourer, made headlines after securing admission to the coveted IIT in Kanpur. But right after that announcement and the public commitment by politicians that their tuition fees would be taken care of, the rest of the village gathered to throw stones at their home.

We like to believe that in the melting pots of the country's sprawling new cities these historic discriminations have been eliminated by the imperatives of economics and the realities of modern urban living. So how do we explain the impotency of industrialization when two infants, a two-year-old and his nine-month-old sister, are burnt alive by feuding 'upper-caste' neighbours—right on the edge of Delhi—in Faridabad, a township that was among the first to become a commercial hub for factories and manufacturing? We imagine that capitalism has conquered caste, but its insidious imprint is everywhere, often unacknowledged, even unnoticed. Most kitchens still keep a separate tumbler for the woman who comes every morning to mop and clean, reinforcing the age-old Brahminical association of

Dalits with so-called 'impure' occupations. There was, until recently, the infamous 350-metre-long 'Uthapuram' (untouchable) fence in a village in Tamil Nadu built across the length of the panchayat area to segregate Dalits from the rest of the residents for three decades till it was forcibly brought down. But that isn't the only atrocity some of our countrymen have to deal with.

In satellite towns connected to the national capital by multi-lane expressways, where swanky showrooms for Volvo and Mercedes have replaced wayside dhabas, you can still be killed for marrying 'below' your caste. And despite the committees and commissions, bills and bans, the railway lines that run through the major cities of India are still cleaned by manual 'scavengers', all Dalits and mostly all women, who carry human shit off the tracks, and are ostracized for doing this 'dirty' job. The 'Bhangis', as people belonging to the sweeper caste are known, are treated as outcasts; they are the lowest of the low—'a people apart, even among people apart' as political scientist and journalist Harold Isaacs once described them. In India's elite drawing rooms however, the word is sometimes used as a pejorative for an absence of social sophistication. Among the comfort of friends who naturally believe they are too evolved to ever display caste-bias, there are still sniggers about Dalit politicians who 'look like Chamars', a reference to the tanning community that derives its name from the Sanskrit word for leather workers—Charmakar. Once again, however innocuous these jokes—that these words are used as synonyms for unattractive or ugly makes a mockery of the claim that urbanization and the growth of cities would flatten out the caste divide.

At one level, it would seem as if the semiology of the broom (and thus the status of the sweeper) had dramatically changed. The 'jhadu' is the party symbol of the activist turned chief minister, Arvind Kejriwal. It is also the centrepiece of the prime minister's Swachh Bharat Abhiyan (Clean India Campaign). Now fashionistas, industrialists and movie stars wanted to be photographed, broom in hand, sweeping the streets in a moment of glamorous and trendy egalitarianism. The Modi government deserves credit for mainstreaming the subject of sanitation and toilets. But as recently as 2014, India's Supreme Court had accepted that the 'practice of manual scavenging continues unabated'.

India passed a law in 1993 mandating the demolition of all dry
toilets. Two decades later, the official census still placed the number
of manual scavengers at 750,000. Activists argue that the statistic is
at least 1.3 million because those who pick human waste from the
thousands of kilometres of rail tracks crisscrossing India have not
been factored in.

Caste having consigned them to this life, most women who are
manual scavengers believe they will never be entitled to alternative
sources of employment. No state is willing to admit to the continuing
practice of scavenging but you don't have to go very far down the
multi-lane expressways to meet Indians whose survival remains
tethered to a variation of modern-day slavery.

Maya Gautam was one such person. She came to meet me
from Meerut, a bustling industrial hub no further than seventy-
odd kilometres from Delhi. Resplendent in a purple sari, her eyes
lined with thick black kajal, her nose ring as shiny as her wide-set
smile, Maya's personal resilience had helped her stay alive though
she had contemplated suicide more than once. 'I stayed alive for my
children,' she said, detailing the fifteen years she had spent cleaning
shit from homes in her immediate neighbourhood. 'Even beggars
shun us, people who have no money to eat don't consider our caste
clean enough to ask for alms,' she said. It wasn't just the stomach-
churning stench of her daily livelihood or the exposure to infection
and disease that made her life hell, it was the denial of personal
dignity. She was considered 'dirtier' than the bathrooms she cleaned.
When she entered the loo, she was forced to leave her slippers at
the door. When her employers paid her, they flung the money on
the floor to avoid contact with her hand and watched her get down
on her knees to pick it up. Until, one day, she fired back: 'How do
you know I won't buy vegetables with this cash? How do you know
the money won't recirculate in the market and come back to you
through some shopkeeper?'

V

Maya Gautam's retort to those who humiliated her would not

have been possible without the bold step taken by one man whom many feel has not got his due. When Manmohan Singh got up in Parliament to implement the vision of his then boss P. V. Narasimha Rao, prefacing the budget that transformed the lives of millions with a Victor Hugo quote, 'no power on earth can stop an idea whose time has come', it was one of the greatest turning points the country has ever experienced. As we have seen throughout the book, that moment wrought change everywhere in Indian society. Without it, there would have been no India Shining, the rise and rise of Narendra Modi would probably not have occurred, nor would we have witnessed developments like India's ambition to become the world's newest nuclear superpower and its current status as the world's fastest growing major economy.

■

Before 1991, most of us who identified ourselves as 'middle class' were the children of salaried professionals—bureaucrats, journalists, military officers and company executives—with a somewhat childish and irrational air of cultural superiority, especially to those who were from 'business' families. I went to school in the eighties when our exposure to foreign brands was mostly through advertisements that we saw on videotaped reruns of the great Pakistani romantic drama *Dhoop Kinare*. College began in the nineties, right on the cusp of India's first wave of economic reforms. Until then, to be a middle-class Indian meant you displayed a slight scorn for and embarrassment at any obvious display of money. Middle-class values were all about a premium on education and reading books and bringing your children up to be progressive, pluralistic and even somewhat rebellious.

At Delhi's Modern School, as prefect, I made myself vastly unpopular by confiscating the Nike and Reebok socks that the wealthier children insisted on wearing instead of the dull, blue uniform gear mandated by the school. Looking back, my self-righteousness must have been unbearable. But at the time it was a natural extension of the middle-class values I had been shaped by. We rode the school bus, scorned the carpool and when we stayed back after school to play basketball or write for the magazine we travelled back home in overflowing public transport, pushed and shoved against sweaty palms and groping hands.

Later, in college, at Delhi's St Stephen's, we even had a whole different way of classifying those who were richer, more glamorous, drove or were driven to university and spent their afternoons smoking cigarettes bought from over-generous weekly allowances. They were called the 'Dhaba type' because their college haunt was the legendary samosas and nimbu-pani shack run by old man Rohtas, who came to be more famous than the institute's big-name alumni. But the categorization was cultural not locational. It captured a sub-culture of fashionable, unapologetic opulence that was distinct from the 'leftie types' who dressed down in shabby chic, walked the corridors in floppy rubber slippers, had animated debates on the conservatism of stifling social mores and economic inequities and considered themselves to be the more grounded sliver of India's middle-class with authentic claims to ordinariness.

I belonged to the latter tribe. Wealth creation among our lot was never an aspiration but educational pedigree was. Yet, we thought of ourselves as deeply egalitarian and overlooked our innate snobbery about intellectual labels. My college sweetheart was the son of a naval officer whose mother spoke of a time when money was so short that she used giant steel trunks dressed up with colourful throws as substitutes for sofas. When we spent an evening out it was often on the back of his decrepit 'Vijay Super' Lambretta—a twenty-year-old scooter which was a hand-me-down from the clerk in his grandfather's office. Both he and my best friend worked hard to get themselves a world-class education. I managed to land myself a scholarship to Columbia University's journalism school without which I would have had to turn down the admission offer because even if my father sold all his investments and assets we would never have managed the Rs 14 lakh annual tuition. I mention all this simply to show how important education was to our lives and how we scorned conspicuous consumption.

None of us had much money and we (immaturely) scrambled to hide anything that could be even remotely considered flashy. When my father brought home a second-hand Mercedes after a seven-year residency posting in New York my sister and I wondered how we would explain it to our friends at school. Our family car till then had been a grey Padmini Fiat whose roof-carrier doubled up as a bed under the skies for us girls on balmy summer nights of load-shedding in Delhi.

Now, how were we going to explain the Merc? Remember, this was the eighties and 'foreign' cars were still a rarity. My sister christened the car 'Benzy' and we secretly loved the magic of its sunroof that opened up to the elements. But we remained sheepish about the existence of this fancy creature in our driveway, in an odd and telling juxtaposition with our shabby makeshift swing—an old car tire strung from a tall tree. For years we continued to fib and tell our friends, when the subject came up, that our car was a Fiat.

Even the movies were different in the years before globalization both glamorized and standardized storytelling on screen. Today's Hindi cinema characters, with their perfectly toned bodies and coiffed hairdos, rarely tell the story of the Everyman or woman. As shooting locations moved out from Kashmir and Ooty and Shimla to the Swiss Alps, Spain and New York, the target viewer became the 'global desi'.

This was the upwardly mobile Indian—a product of the new middle class—who loved both her samosa and sushi, her KFC and Karva Chauth. She was at home in the world, but preferred her own society to be ordered in a reasonably conformist way—that was a reflection of herself. She did not go to the movies to see the angst and struggle of the underclass or the rage of the honest cop against a corrupt system. For her, the film itself was another element of an evening out in a swanky multiplex where 'American corn' and 'nachos with salsa' supplemented the humble popcorn. And if you were willing to pay a little more, waiters would bring your food to your plush seats. You couldn't get this sort of luxury in London or New York unless you had access to a private theatre.

In many ways, the single-hall cinemas of pre-liberalization India and modern multi-screen cinemas showed the ways in which the country was changing. While it could be argued that the old-style cinema emphasized differences in class because the 'balcony' seats of yore used to separate the rich from the poor who sat below in the 'chavanni class', back then people from a lower economic strata were part of the same movie-watching experience as relatively richer Indians. In today's India, the halls do not have segregated seats but the entire experience of watching a movie is much more exclusionary. You rarely meet a poor person inside a theatre, in fact, you rarely see a poor person on screen. If you do see a poorer, small town character on screen the film is usually classified as arthouse cinema.

Chronicling the changes in Hindi films post-liberalization, writer Rachel Dwyer comments on how cinema has changed to reflect these economic ambitions. 'Big-budget Bollywood films have become part of the metropolitan imagination, open to those who are or who aspire to be metropolitan but far removed from the mofussil towns.' And Dalits? Dwyer says that Dalits are only characters in 'political films like those of Prakash Jha', underlining how heroes still have north-Indian, upper-caste surnames like 'Malhotra' and 'Khanna'.

The movies we watched as children growing up in the seventies and eighties were very different. My mother allowed my sister and I one movie a week and most of them were about the extraordinary virtues of the ordinary. The protagonists were angry, honest men and women, who wore rumpled kurtas or ungainly, non-branded bell-bottomed trousers or simple cotton saris that billowed clumsily in the wind, but always fought the good fight. Before 'item numbers' were specially written into movie scripts to serve as flamboyant, rhythmic, over-sexed showstoppers, moments of romance would feature the likes of Deepti Naval and Farooq Sheikh who embodied a million middle-class fantasies when they rode pillion on a rusty two-wheeler to buy a 'softy' cone served to them by liveried waiters in elaborate headgear at restaurant tables with pink paper napkins neatly arranged in a slightly stained tall glasses. And when they drove home from their 'date' their 'barsati' flat was done up—not in Italian marble or laminated wood—but in sparse, unfussy bamboo 'chitais' matched with soft white muslin curtains draping windows that allowed far too much sunshine in. By the time I was an adult and a working journalist, the India I grew up in had been transformed radically. So had its cultural moorings. In an environment exploding with mobiles and McDonald's, economic and social ascent became the key drivers of dreams, creating a country within a country; one in which citizenship was no profound, or even, argumentative pact with nation-building but almost a corporate membership in a rewards programme designed to give maximum returns. Liberalization and rapid growth had also played midwife to the birth of a neo middle-class consumed by its own daily battles for survival and self-fulfilment.

In fact, now it was this class that had become the biggest proponent of economic liberalization. The ascent of India's new middle-class (very different from the old) could be graphed against the fluctuating lines of what political scientist Leela Fernandes has called its experience of 'alienation and resurgence'. Economic liberalization was embraced by the middle class because it coincided with a phase in Indian politics when they were threatened by the sudden assertion of subaltern and lower caste groups. These were turbulent years. In many ways, Rajiv Gandhi—the youthful Indian Airlines pilot turned politician who spoke of modern things like computers and telephones—had the potential to become the perfect urban hope as prime minister, but his career nosedived a few years after takeoff. His successor V. P Singh's contentious decision to have quotas for 'Other Backward Classes' (as recommended by the panel called the Mandal Commission, which I've referred to in an earlier chapter) in government colleges and jobs further spooked the middle class and distanced it from mainstream politics. Politics had begun to let down its barriers to include regional backward leaders like Lalu Prasad Yadav and Mulayam Singh Yadav. They were extraordinarily powerful in their own right but their rustic style was antithetical to the self-image of the English-educated middle class. Then there was the BJP, dipping its toe in these shifting currents to see if the ripples could become a Hindutva wave.

When liberalization announced its arrival with the grand promise of unlocking a closed economy, nobody welcomed it more than the middle class because, as we have seen, it believed that the imminent arrival of more caste quotas would undermine merit and take away their economic opportunities. It's what academics Stuart

Corbridge and John Harriss have called the 'protest of the privileged'.
They went one step further to argue that middle-class anger had
intersected with the emergence of reforms, writing that it was possible
to 'describe both economic liberalization and Hindu nationalism with
their sometimes contradictory but often surprisingly complementary
agendas for the reinvention of India as "elite revolts". Both reflect
and are vehicles for the interests and aspirations especially of the
middle class and highest caste Indians'.

The anti-Mandal agitation of 1992 was India's first middle-class
protest. I was part of it. I often look back at those years to try and
understand what made me march down the streets in opposition to
something I barely understood. Every morning, at college, we would
listen to the fiery speeches on the murder of merit made by young
men who were aspirants for the Indian Administrative Service (and
thus, especially worried about the quotas reducing the number of
seats open to competition). Many of us were either ignorant of caste
or indifferent to it. So what made us do it? Maybe we were just a
generation in search of a cause—we wanted something to get angry
about. The day we got sprayed with water cannons and dragged into
the Parliament Street police station we felt a heady adrenalin rush
and thought we had become revolutionaries. But mostly the cause
had our support because the narrative that hard work and talent was
going to be swept away in a tornado of political opportunism was
too compelling to disagree with. I may have a much more informed
opinion on caste reservations today than I did as an eighteen year
old, but back then I represented the average middle-class Indian who
found politics too cynical to engage with and was ready to take to
the streets to agitate.

If the first wave of protests against the Mandal Commission
driven quotas were elitist and not entirely thought-through, the
brazen politicization of reservations over the years had the danger
of reducing affirmative action to a farce. Despite a Supreme Court
mandated cap of 50 per cent on all quotas—a number that was
meant to include both scheduled castes and OBCs—competitive caste
politics led several states to openly flout the legal limit. Tamil Nadu
and Rajasthan were among states where more than 60 per cent of

seats in government institutes fell in the 'reserved' category.

It was the forces unleashed by liberalization—and the social aspirations they created—that would prove to be the biggest challenge to all the old calculations about which community was 'backward'. As more and more people aspired to white-collar jobs and a life in the city it was no longer enough to be born into a caste that had traditionally wielded influence.

For Narendra Modi, who had positioned himself as the market reformer who understood the dreams of the emerging middle class of modern India, as opposed to the Congress that was stuck in an archaic politics that romanticized poverty with a culture of doles, the collision between liberalization and old caste politics came back to bite in the form of a man called Hardik Patel. A virtually unknown young twenty-something, Patel was able to galvanize lakhs of people in the powerful Patel community, traditionally BJP voters, to rise against the government's quota policy. Though overtly his demand was that the Patels too be made beneficiaries of affirmative action, his stir was in effect an anti-quota stir. Either caste quotas should be scrapped, he argued, or they should be recast to include an economic criterion. That the agitation had erupted in the prime minister's home state carried its own message, both about the limitations of old-style caste politics and the difficulties of managing competing aspirations in a changing society.

Others argued that it was precisely the emergence of this neo-middle class that was a challenge to old social bigotries. Either way, the middle class, once alienated, now resurgent, channelled its new political identity through what Leela Fernandes has called 'class and consumption'. The ever-growing numbers of those who came to fall within its ambit—conservatively, it has been estimated it will number over 500 million by 2025—created a potential new powerhouse of consumerism. With an eye on them being the next big spenders this was a constituency favoured by both the markets and the media. But the middle class had come to be remarkably insular, inward-looking and disengaged with the realities that lay just outside the boundaries of their own nation-state. They wanted to read, hear, watch and discuss mostly their own issues. So, in an irony of the information age, as private media proliferated with more than 400 television channels, the stories of India's poor fell off the airwaves.

In the competitive hysteria of the media battlefield 'poverty' stories were not attractive enough to score TRP victories over your rivals; they apparently won you international awards, but not eyeballs. Perhaps Indians rising up the economic ladder felt far too uncomfortable in being confronted with stark destitution or perhaps they were inured to it. Either way, while post nineties India sought to dissolve the differences of caste, language, region and religion in the all-encompassing embrace of globalization, inequities of class had only been exacerbated to virtually create islands of affluence in an ocean of poverty. People were getting richer but the gap between the rich and the poor was widening. Wealth concentration, a key characteristic of this widening imbalance continued to raise questions over whether economic growth alone could solve the problems of our staggeringly unequal society. Soon enough, it was clear that the opportunities thrown up by liberalization were available to just a sliver of the population. Inequality in earnings had doubled in the past two decades according to the Organisation for Economic Co-operation and Development. It pointed out that India was 'the worst performer on this count of all emerging economies'. The top 10 per cent of India's wage earners now made twelve times more than the bottom 10 per cent, up from a ratio of six in the early 1990s. 'Wealth managers' in banks commissioned entire reports to study patterns of spending. One such report helpfully informed us that 'exclusivity' now drove choices among the super-rich. According to the authors of this report one such big spender had imported nine crates of Japanese whiskey priced at $750 per bottle for a wedding party, partly because the drink was difficult to source in India. India now had annual 'luxury summits' tapping into this new culture of competitive (and conspicuous) consumption. So what if 190 million people went hungry every day. All that was somewhere else, it was too remote to feel real, comfortably far away from the gilded borders that now demarcated the rest of India from this private middle-class Xanadu. Now, there was greater media attention on the 'boom' in the luxury market than there was on dying children. The International

Monetary Fund held a mirror up to India when its managing director, Christine Lagarde, did the not-so-tough math to reveal that the net worth of the billionaire community in the country had increased twelve-fold in fifteen years and was enough to eliminate absolute poverty in India twice over.

VI

Many of the dramatic changes in post liberalization India are healthy and democratic and represent the power of hope. Millions of Indians now have the opportunity to leave the circumstances of their birth behind. Young women in small towns learn English and train to be airline stewardesses or beauticians in spas or salons. Men from the hinterland come to the cities to work as drivers for private households but also for twenty-first-century taxi services like Meru and Uber. Middle-class and upper middle-class families find it much more difficult to get full-time domestic help because the women who once used to migrate from the villages of Jharkhand and Bihar to urban India to find employment as nannies and ayahs now want jobs in malls as saleswomen at Burger King or Zara.

But the churning currents of a society in flux also claim victims—men and women who are pulled under because of thwarted ambition, unsustainable dreams, entrenched prejudice and remorseless competition. Cases from the lower end of the socio-economic spectrum are legion but headline-hogging stories about people from the highest levels of society who come undone are also becoming fairly frequent.

In recent years, two women came to represent the social fault lines that are being drawn and redrawn at the top—Sunanda Pushkar and Indrani Mukerjea. Although there were some similarities between their profiles, there was one very importance difference—Sunanda committed no crime while Indrani was accused of perpetrating a ghastly murder. But rather than go into the specifics of how the promise of each of their lives was cut short, I would like to comment on how they were regarded by society and the media while they were at the height of their powers, as also at the time when they fell. They were both photogenic, glamorous, self-made women from small towns. And this caused a lot of heartburn in urban Indian society especially among the Establishment types who saw them as interlopers and celebrated their downfall. Their ambition was held against them, more particularly because they were women.

The daughter of an army man, Lt Col P. N. Dass, Sunanda Pushkar graduated from a Srinagar college and worked for some time in the city before moving to Dubai. There, she joined an ad agency and soon became part of the city's social circuit. She eventually founded her own event management company. Sunanda came to the Indian media's attention as a result of her relationship with Shashi Tharoor, who was then a minister in the UPA government. Shashi is indisputably one of the brightest and most articulate of India's politicians. His unlikely presence in politics—after a long stint as a diplomat—is also indicative of social change. Perhaps his not being from the old-school wink-wink, nudge-nudge brand of politics is one of the reasons why he so often finds himself in the middle of controversy. This time around however the charge was serious. Sunanda and he made the headlines when it was revealed that she had been given a stake in one of the cricket team franchises of the Indian Premier League (IPL).

The IPL grew out of post-liberalization India and displayed its best and worst characteristics—its energy and its dynamism, as well as the corruption and shallowness. The confluence of politics, film stars and big business within the organization went a long way towards creating one of the most successful and addictive brands the country had ever seen. Its success notwithstanding, the way it was financed, and the complex ownership patterns of its overt and proxy owners, made it the subject of a Supreme Court investigation.

Much like many of the stars of the new India, the IPL came to believe it was a country unto itself. This became evident to me when its founder—the brash and controversial Lalit Modi—and I had a row in 2009. In an interview, P. Chidambaram, the then home minister, told me that the IPL would need to rearrange its schedule that year because the security forces available were required for the imminent general elections. Modi refused, choosing instead to move the IPL out to South Africa. Modi believed me to be friendly with two men he deeply disliked in Indian politics—Chidambaram and Arun Jaitley. As a result, when he saw my report on the clash between the election dates and the cricket league schedule, he said I was prejudiced against him. A few years later it was he who would be confronted with a non-bailable warrant in the course of a money laundering investigation. But by then he had already made his home in London; his Instagram feed taunted his detractors with all the famous people he knew (including the former head of Interpol). His political friendships across party lines—Sushma Swaraj's husband was his lawyer for many years, Sharad Pawar would meet him for lunch when in London, and Vasundhara Raje Scindia even signed a testimony in support of his application for asylum in the UK—would bring Parliament to a halt and exposed the incestuous web of networks and connections that held the IPL together. But back then, Modi was still the League's big boss and his target was Tharoor. Modi was the first to accuse Shashi of holding sweat equity worth Rs 70 crore in the Kochi IPL team through Sunanda. Shashi and Sunanda dismissed the charges but the media would not let go of the controversy. Narendra Modi, then chief minister of Gujarat, exacerbated the situation by quipping during an election rally in 2012 that Sunanda was Shashi's '50 crore girlfriend'. Shashi retorted cuttingly that she was 'priceless'. The BJP, which was then in the Opposition, began clamouring for Shashi's resignation from government.

I reached out to Shashi for an interview to be able to present his point of view. After some cajoling and persuasion he did a live interview with me where he defended himself against the charges. He also ruled out resigning—this did not go down well with the party high command (read the Gandhis). Soon enough, Shashi was forced to step down as minister. As a result of this interview, and its consequences, my relationship with Sunanda and Shashi grew strained.

As time went by, we would sometimes meet at the occasional Delhi party and I got to know Sunanda socially. Our conversations were confined to polite nothings till she called me one day and told me that she wanted to go on television to speak on the debate over Article 370 in Jammu and Kashmir. As a Kashmiri Pandit she wanted the special status of the state to be scrapped; by taking this position she was echoing the Opposition's ideology and contradicting her husband's stated position. I was impressed with her willingness to take an independent stand so publicly. I was also pleased that Sunanda, so long the object of unkind, sexist whispers, appeared to be coming into her own.

Less than a month after that television appearance on my show Sunanda phoned me in tears to talk about a domestic quarrel that she and her husband were having. She said that he was having an extramarital affair; she had moved out of her home into a Delhi hotel and was planning to file for divorce. It later transpired that I was one of the four-odd journalists she had reached out to that evening. Among other things she said she was going to go public with some unsavoury truths about the IPL scam. Reminding me of the interview on the IPL controversy that I had done with Shashi four years earlier, she alleged that in fact it was she who had been exploited and used as a front. She told me, 'I know nothing about sports... I was made to take the flak for him.'

Sunanda was planning a press conference as a well as a meeting with the Congress president to reveal this. She had called to offer me the first interview. As a journalist I listened intently; the IPL scam was undoubtedly a legitimate story. But I was also uncomfortable. I worried that her judgement was being blurred by her emotional state. I was keen to separate what was a private matter of their marriage from what was genuinely newsworthy.

I tried to calm her down and told her that the interview could wait a day or two. I advised her to call a friend and not be alone. The next morning she and Shashi issued a brief statement claiming that all was well between them.

A day later Sunanda was dead. Although it was initially suspected that she died from an accidental overdose or suicide, her death became the subject of a murder investigation. The case got widespread media attention, some of it extraordinarily irresponsible. The coverage of this story—and so many others—was further illustration of all that was different about India now. Television studios had become trial courts pronouncing guilt and innocence and apportioning punishment to those they deemed guilty to the cheers of a bloodthirsty and impatient urban Indian audience that sought confirmation of its own prejudices on the nightly news. I gave a detailed written account of my conversation with Sunanda to the Delhi Police. I still have no idea how Sunanda died. All I'd like to say is that I thought that her untimely death was a sad end to someone who was trying to make something of her life.

The undoing of Sunanda was followed by that of another woman from society's highest stratum, Indrani Mukerjea. Unlike Sunanda, I did not know Indrani at all. Born Pori Bora to a middle-class family in Guwahati, she first made the headlines when she married media tycoon Peter Mukerjea. Indrani's success was cut short by extreme notoriety. She was jailed for the murder of her daughter Sheena— one of two children she had virtually disowned in her quest for a different life—only to reintroduce her many years later to the world as her younger sister. Before her fall—as dramatic and abrupt as her rise—she had been listed by the *Wall Street Journal* as one of '50 Women to Watch out For'—the power list, once again, being the ultimate aspiration of a society seeking to create a New Establishment. The crime Indrani was accused of was chilling. As more and more details emerged in the course of the investigation, in Indrani's case that desire to find a place in high society appeared to have snuffed out all compassion. But what I would like to reiterate here is that the general comments that were made about her (in addition to those that pertained directly to the murder she was charged with) revealed the sexism and elitism in our society, just as they did when similar opinions were aired about Sunanda. Some things about the country have just not changed no matter how strong the churning within.

Two women. Two tragedies. Two cautionary tales. The bright lights of the new India sometimes cast the darkest shadows you could imagine.

VII

Between the controversies of Lalit Modi, Sunanda Pushkar and Indrani Mukerjea, there was little else on prime time news for months together, least of all the stories of India's poor. India is home to more poor people than anywhere else in the world. One-third of the world's poorest 1.2 billion people live in India where 1.4 million children die before their fifth birthday—making this the highest percentage in the world. Despite a reduction in the official poverty figures and an improvement in various human development indices, one in four children is still malnourished and 3,000 children die every day from poverty. This is the India that we would prefer not to see, the India that inconveniently comes in the way of slogans and news headlines of India Shining, India galloping forward, India being welcomed to exclusive clubs of the world's rich and powerful nations.

In the summer of 2001, under the sun's unrelenting heat, I travelled to the desert state of Rajasthan. I was headed to its southernmost corner, a wretchedly poor tribal area that almost never made it to the news. Travelling with me was a group of activists from an NGO who had petitioned India's Supreme Court for the Right to Food. They wanted the country's enormous food stocks to be used to protect people from hunger and starvation. The strange paradox of plenty meant that millions of tonnes of grains would rot every year in railway yards and government warehouses. Yet millions would go to sleep hungry. India produced more than enough food to feed all her people but poor procurement, inefficient distribution, infrastructure constraints in supply chains and the lack of purchasing power in families that lived below the poverty line had resulted in a man-made catastrophe of mass malnourishment.

How to define 'hunger' and where to draw the poverty line had become the subject of ferocious political and academic debates. No state was ready to admit the inconvenient truth of 'starvation deaths' taking place on their watch. Mortalities were routinely blamed on diseases like diarrhoea, tuberculosis and pneumonia or a host of pandemics, conveniently sidestepping the truth of what more nutrients on the table may have done to save the lives of those grappling with innocuous viral infections.

Here in Rajasthan, in the village of Mewar ka Matt, 'luxury' was a word from an alien language. We were here because every day for the past few days one child had died from an undiagnosed fever—eleven children had already died. The NGO had forced a reluctant team of government doctors to come and help a people in distress. As the rickety jeep in which the doctors were travelling crunched to a halt at the last motorable point and the dry dust swirled up in clouds of muddy grey, two women peered curiously at us from behind their ghunghats. They weren't used to visitors; no one from the city ever came here.

Otherwise for miles around us we saw nobody. Two empty earthen pots sat on the rocky barren land with flies and insects swarming above, a portent of the desolation and disease we were about to witness. Word was now coming in that almost a hundred children in the village were unwell, several of them critically ill. The population of the village was scattered across an expanse of steep hills. There was no way to make an assessment of the facts without trekking up the heights. The area was so remote that no doctor or government official had ever bothered to make the journey. When the villagers needed medical help they had to first walk downhill for several miles and then look for hired transport to get to even a primary health centre. It was a shocking abdication of responsibility by the Indian state. Yet, it wasn't a situation that was going to change for the better anytime soon as the absence of healthcare for millions was not an issue on which elections were won or lost.

We were told the nearest home was five kilometres away. Up these slopes, it meant an easy two to three hours of walking. We walked slowly, our progress encumbered by the unforgiving heat of an overhead sun and a narrow trail obstructed by brambles and thorns. The mood was grim, no one felt like talking much. Then the stillness was broken by the distant sound of women crying. The sound came from a solitary thatched hut on the crest of a small hill. As we made our way towards it, from behind the tall blades of grass a man appeared, his arms wrapped around a small child draped in a white sheet. It was his five-year-old son. Jana Ram had already walked twenty kilometres that afternoon when we met him. In the morning he had carried his fever-ridden son Kesar down the hill to the nearest hospital. The journey proved to be too arduous and testing, and Kesar died on the way. Jana Ram was walking back up these hard, dry hills to bury his dead son when he encountered us.

I stood there feeling an overwhelming sense of guilt about the relative comforts of my own life, the protective cushion of class that had cosseted me and kept me ignorant and unaware of what this moment felt like to a father. Jana Ram walked quietly towards us, taking small steps, his hand trembling just a bit. He didn't say anything when he saw us, unexpected strangers standing on the hillside. Wordlessly, he took off the sheet that had been used as a shroud for Kesar, he wanted us all to see what his son's face looked like. The boy's mouth was open as if his final moment had been a gasp for air. I remember noticing his curling eyelashes. Another villager walked quietly behind Jana Ram. Together, the two men placed the child on a patch of grass and gently washed his face with a few drops of water. Then, turn by turn, they began digging up the stones and mud to create a small burial place. Kesar was too young to be cremated.

This bereavement, I thought, was because of the criminal negligence of the state—the failure of India to provide for her people, the horrifying inequalities of our society, the tyranny of poverty and the absence of anyone who really gave a damn. It seemed less like a medical accident and more like culpable homicide. But because Jana Ram and his family expected no different from a life they had internalized as their destiny, there was stoicism even in this moment of staggering sorrow. And there was hardly any visible anger.

At Jana Ram's home, Kesar's mother and the other women of the village sat on the rough ground, there was no cement or concrete floor, their heads in their arms, sobbing softly. In the centre, a few stones were placed together over small pieces of charcoal, usually used to heat water for cooking. Today, there were no vessels on the fire because there was no food at home. Most households here did not have enough money to feed their children, making even an ordinary viral fever life-threatening.

What did you feed Kesar for nourishment, I asked Jana Ram. He pointed to a corner where a woman sat hunched over an old 'atta chakki'—a hand mill used for grinding wheat into flour. On a good day, Jana Ram said, a meal was what the tribals here called 'rabri'—ground maize thinned with water so that it would last longer and feed more mouths. Hardly the best food for a sick child, he added quietly. 'I wanted to give him more healthy food, but I have no money for it. I couldn't even give him milk or dahi. This is the most we had. What could I do?' And on bad days, said Lakharam, the villager who had helped Jana Ram dig the grave for his son, we fall back on these, he said, pointing to the leaves of bushes growing in the wild outside the hut. The villagers told me it was not uncommon for people to eat the leaves.

In the official records, Kesar's death, like that of the other children in the village, was going to be blamed on fever and disease, as if to suggest that it was beyond the administration's control. But when one 'roti' is split between six children, when watery maize is considered a good day's meal, when wild leaves are still used as a substitute for food in twenty-first-century India, and there is no access to doctors or medicines—then the truth is that Kesar starved to death in an uncaring, unequal society.

EPILOGUE

MOHAMMAD AKHLAQ, A village blacksmith, had a dream. He wanted his son Mohammad Sartaj to join the Indian Air Force and serve his country. Initially Sartaj thought he should run a small business—it would make his family more economically secure. Memories of poverty and his father's constant struggle to put food on the table haunted him.

He remembered how, as a child, he would spend day after day fanning the burning coal on which his father would heat strips of metal and hammer and shape them into scythes and sickles for the residents of Bisada, their village in the Dadri tehsil of western Uttar Pradesh, where they had lived their entire lives. Yet, no matter how hard they worked, it never seemed to be enough. Sartaj would sometimes cry when he thought about the despair and bleakness of their lives.

Their plight was thrown into stark relief when you considered that their village was just fifty kilometres away from Delhi, the national capital with its myriad possibilities of a better life. And so, Sartaj, the blacksmith's son, would dream of how he could make things better for his family and for himself. Whenever he discussed the future with his father, Akhlaq, a patriot, would insist that he join the Indian armed forces. After finishing school from the Rana Sangram Singh Inter College, Sartaj became a technician in the air force.

This story would have been just another unremarkable tale of a poor Indian family which believed it could get ahead through education and hard work, except for one savage encounter with the chilling reality of twenty-first-century India that would catapult both father and son into the national and international headlines.

On 28 September 2015, even as Prime Minister Narendra Modi was wrapping up a high-profile visit to Silicon Valley, back in Dadri, a murderous mob stormed into Akhlaq's house, dragged him and his younger son Danish out of bed and assaulted them with bricks and hockey sticks. A sewing machine, which Akhlaq had bought his wife and daughters so they could earn an income from some tailoring work, was picked up and hurled at Danish's head, cracking his skull. He would undergo prolonged brain surgery before he returned to full consciousness. By the time the police got there, Akhlaq, the fifty-two-year-old head of the household, was dead.

In the United States, the prime minister was unveiling the promise of a 'Digital India' to a crowd of prosperous émigrés and Americans. Led by Facebook founder Mark Zuckerberg, millions of Indians changed their profile pictures to the vibrant colours of the Indian flag to express their support. 'The twenty-first century will belong to India,' Modi announced. Yet, at home, his words were belied, as a sectarian murder, rooted in regressive religious phobias, took an innocent life.

Ironically, even as Modi was expanding on how technology could be used to develop his nation, India was confronting the darker, more sinister side of technology—social media channels like Twitter, Facebook, Google and WhatsApp were often becoming the medium of choice to spread murderous rumours and messages of hate.

But in Dadri, what would become an exhortation to murder came the old-fashioned way: an announcement was made from the village temple that a cow had been killed and its meat had been stored in Akhlaq's house. The family pleaded with the frenzied mob. They said they had not slaughtered a cow, the meat in their fridge was mutton. But their protestations were dismissed and the murderers lynched Akhlaq. Turning the victims into the accused, the first response of the local administration was to send the meat to a forensics laboratory for testing—as if it mattered whether the meat was mutton, chicken or beef, as if we lived in an India where manslaughter was less important than cow slaughter.

Just a few days after the barbaric murder of his father, Sartaj spoke to me in an extensive interview that should have humbled and shamed every Indian who watched it. At the time his brother was still in the intensive care unit, yet when Sartaj emerged from inside the hospital to talk to me—wearing a simple checked green-and-white cotton shirt and a white skullcap—he betrayed neither anger nor bitterness. Speaking with much more dignity than any politician I had heard on the tragedy, Sartaj told me, 'I never thought something like this could happen to us. Because I am with the air force, I am serving my country, I thought I could complete my posting in Chennai in the belief that my family is safe, that the villagers would look after them. My family and I never had a conflict—not even an argument with anyone in the village—all these years. On Eid, we used to call all our Hindu neighbours home or send them boxes packed with food... Yeh mere liye bahut sadme ki baat hai ki main desh ki seva karta hoon or mere parivar ke saath aisa hota hai (It has caused me deep anguish that even though I serve my nation they would do this to my family).'

All I could say to Sartaj was, 'Every Indian, each one of us, should feel deep shame right now. We have all failed you in some way.'

His father's last, desperate call for help had in fact been to his Hindu best friend, Manoj Sisodia. 'It was around 10.30 that night when I got a call from my bhai (brother) Akhlaq. He said, "Some people have reached my house to kill me, please call the police, please somehow save my life,"' Sisodia told me. 'I had not recharged the card on my mobile phone, so I ran to my neighbour's, called the cops and then ran to my friend's house. I was there within ten minutes. But I was too late. His battered and bloodied body was abandoned on the road, there was blood gushing from his head. I was broken to see him like this. It was pitch-dark, but by now a crowd of a thousand people had gathered outside his house. I just sat by myself in one corner.' Forget riots or violence, he had never known a Hindu–Muslim divide in his village in forty years, Manoj told me. 'Not just Akhlaq, I have many Muslim friends here. We are so close that if I am ill or unable to go out, their children go and buy me vegetables and rations. I can only say that come what may, whatever anyone says, I will stand in support of Akhlaq's family in this hour of crisis.'

Those of us who denounce Akhlaq's murder cling to the story of that last phone call as proof that all is not lost in our country, that the barbarians have not yet swept all before them. We see it

as a sign that humanity and decency can still triumph over forces
of division and communal hatred, that the rumour of a dead cow
cannot destroy relationships that were decades old.

But perhaps we held on to this hope only to make ourselves feel
better. In the next days there was not much to feel optimistic about.
The families of the young men who were arrested for the murder
of Akhlaq used the women of the village to front their battle. The
media—seen by them as biased—was the prime target. Cameras had
already been attacked and stones were hurled at press cars. Holding
sticks, the women ensured that the media was kept at a distance
of three kilometres from the village. When my producer Noman
Siddiqui tried to make his way in without a camera he was stopped
at the human barricades and body searched. He heard the women
chant, 'Lathi mar de, lathi mar de (Hit him with the stick, hit him
with the stick)', and complain about the 'injustice' of Akhlaq's family
'walking away with 45 lakh in financial assistance'.

In his moment of loss, instead of rage, which is probably what
you and I would have felt, Sartaj showed remarkable grace and the
big heart to call for calm. He told me a handful of troublemakers
should not be allowed to wrest the story of India from its people—
who, he still believed, after all that had happened to him—were
generally good. But it was his words to India's politicians that were
the most powerful. 'Yeh mudda siyasat ka nahin, hamdardi ka hai,'
he told me. (This is not a moment for playing politics, it's a moment
to show empathy). They can come and meet us if they wish, but
can they please leave their political agendas behind?'

■

The Dadri lynching has exposed the all too familiar fault lines,
raised all the same questions about identity politics, the layers of
Hindutva, the failure of secular parties and the place of minorities
in today's India—revealing how tenuous the notion of a 'modern'
India remains. One of the accused, Vishal Rana, is the son of a
local BJP leader Sanjay Rana. BJP legislator Sangeet Som—already
facing charges for his role in the riots in Uttar Pradesh in 2013—
addressed a village sabha vowing help for the accused and warning

the Samajwadi Party government against protecting 'cow-killers'. BJP parliamentarian Yogi Adityanath sent his 'Hindu Yuva Vahini' to Dadri where they promised all help, including guns (tan-man-dhan-gun) to protect Hindus if they were harassed. Mahesh Sharma, the central government's culture minister and Member of Parliament from the area described the murder as an accident, as some sort of village misunderstanding, as distinct from a conspiracy to kill. His evidence included the fact that the mob had not laid a finger on Sartaj's seventeen-year-old sister, as if that somehow proved they retained an innate decency and were not bloodthirsty louts.

Once again the ruling Samajwadi Party was exposed for its failure to maintain law and order and keep minorities safe, just as it had failed during the Muzaffarnagar riots in 2013. During the riots, the party's rabble rouser, cabinet minister Azam Khan, had suspended four police officers for arresting seven Muslim men in connection with a murder. It was the sort of polarizing decision that only served to create the impression that the BJP and the SP— supposedly staunch enemies—were guilty of the same thing. One sought to consolidate the Hindu vote; the other was trying to cement the Muslim vote. Now Azam Khan, who was rapidly becoming the Muslim equivalent of Sangeet Som, threatened to take the lynching in Dadri to the United Nations. He was sharply criticized for his antics, but just like with the BJP, the question that needed to be asked was: why wasn't the SP reining him in?

Not to be left behind, the Congress jumped in, promising a day-long fast to protest the Dadri lynching even as its leaders tried to take credit for the cow slaughter ban in twenty-four Indian states. Its party leaders added that they were even ready to consider national legislation against cow slaughter.

■

Dadri was a clear indication that beneath the surface glow of liberalization and progress, the deep-seated troubles of India persist. Among the worst of these is the so-called 'beef politics.' In his book, *Hindu Mahasabha in Colonial North India,* Prabhu Bapu chronicles how the cow became part of the narrative of nationalism in the

1920s. What started off as an anti-colonial protest against the beef being supplied to British troops soon became central to the debate around Hindu identity. 'The evocation of the nation as "mother" was symbolized by the cow, turning cow killing into "matricide"', he writes. In his lifetime Mahatma Gandhi deplored the politics that surrounded the cow and cow slaughter. He wrote and spoke on the issue many times. During a prayer discourse he delivered on 25 July 1947, the Mahatma said, 'In India no law can be made to ban cow-slaughter. I do not doubt that Hindus are forbidden the slaughter of cows. I have long pledged to serve the cow but how can my religion also be the religion of the rest of the Indians? It will mean coercion against those Indians who are not Hindu.' But Gandhi's efforts did not put an end to the politicization of the issue.

In 1966 thousands of sadhus wielding trishuls and spears marched on Parliament against cow slaughter. The police opened fire and the agitators retreated, but not before torching a large number of vehicles. In the mid-1970s spiritual leader Acharya Vinoba Bhave threatened to go on a fast unto death if the centre did not introduce a national ban on cow slaughter.

There have been spirited and robust challenges to the political shibboleth that Muslims introduced beef-eating to India, most prominently by historian D. N. Jha who in his treatise, *The Myth of the Holy Cow*, writes that cows were sacrificed and beef commonly consumed by Vedic Aryans. Jha, a Maithili Brahmin, received multiple threats for arguing that the eating of beef was common in ancient India. Dalit scholars like Kancha Iliah said demands for banning cow slaughter were 'brahminic' and exclusionary towards Hindus from lower castes. In his book, *Buffalo Nationalism*, Iliah wrote: 'no one asks why the cow alone should remain a constitutionally protected animal under the directive principles of state policy'. He pointed out the hypocrisy of the Hindu elite that thought nothing of wearing leather shoes but could kill a Dalit for skinning a dead cow.

∎

Historically, the holy cow has long been an excuse for unholy, profane politics. But the expectation was that the mantra of an aspirational

India—the economic dreams of a new generation—would have finally made cow politics irrelevant.

Instead, the Dadri murder—which should have caused only disquiet and shame—seems to have unleashed a torrent of hatred and intolerance. In the twenty days after the killing of Akhlaq, two more men were murdered over rumours that they were ferrying cows for slaughter. Noman in Himachal Pradesh and Zahid Ahmed Bhat, barely twenty years old, from Kashmir, joined the list of innocent men murdered by hate-spewing cow vigilantes. 'Beef politics' is no longer confined to the 'cow-belt'; it seems to have spread like a forest fire through parts of India, from Kashmir to Kerala, areas that were not even remotely vulnerable in the past.

The lynching of Akhlaq and soon after Noman and Zahid confronted the Narendra Modi government with persistent, tough questions, whether from writers returning literary honours or even from some of Modi's own supporters. It is true that the Samajwadi Party government in Uttar Pradesh bore the primary responsibility for law and order where Akhlaq's lynching was concerned. But it was just as true that the country needed both unequivocal condemnation and a healing touch from its leader.

Not just because of those within the BJP who repeatedly qualified their criticism with ifs and buts—making an apology sound like an assault—but also because some moments in a country's history become an emblematic test of a larger truth. It happened during the anti-corruption crusade led by Anna Hazare and Arvind Kejriwal; it happened after the Delhi gang rape and it has happened after Dadri.

I asked Sanjeev Balyan, a minister in the Modi government from western Uttar Pradesh, who was also implicated in the Muzaffarnagar riots, why the prime minister did not just pick up the phone and have a private conversation with Sartaj if he did not want to make a comment in public. 'If the PM starts calling every such family that is a victim of a crime, he will be on the phone 24/7 and not be able to function as prime minister.' Balyan had missed the writing on the wall; Dadri had become much more than an isolated, single incident. It posed a fundamental dare to the government; could Narendra Modi truly move beyond the limitations of his own election

campaign? Opposition leaders were citing the many times Modi had
brought up the 'pink revolution' in the election speeches of 2014—a
reference to the rising export of buffalo meat. Could he leave that
sort of rhetoric firmly in the past? Could he—would he—become
a statesman, a leader ready to provide emotional succour?

For several days after the Dadri tragedy there was no comment
from Modi. When the prime minister finally did speak—at an
election rally in Bihar—he called for Hindus and Muslims to fight
poverty instead of each other. A perfectly decent formulation in
itself, except for the fact that he did not mention Dadri or the
lynching or Mohammad Akhlaq by name. He called upon Indians
to follow President Pranab Mukherjee's message, who had that same
week reminded Indians that our core values are of pluralism and
diversity. But Modi's message was general and not particular. And,
in the same speech before he delivered his homily, he used the beef
motif to taunt Lalu Yadav. Modi accused him of insulting his own
community of Yadavs or Yaduvanshis—traditionally a community
of cowherds. (Lalu had said some Hindus eat gau maas, but hastily
retracted the comment.)

A few days later, Modi gave another brief comment to a
journalist. The lynching, he said, finally addressing it directly, was
'very sad and unacceptable', but 'what does it have to do with the
centre?' he demanded to know. It was only after a spate of television
assaults on visiting Pakistanis by its ally, the Shiv Sena, that Arun
Jaitley came forward to say the prime minister disapproved and
disagreed with this 'disturbing trend' and believed that India should
'engage in debate, not vandalism'.

So far, the BJP had argued that the killings had taken place
in states where it was not in power. But in Jammu and Kashmir,
where Zahid (and his friend Showkat, both truck drivers) had been
assaulted with petrol bombs in the Udhampur region, the BJP was
one half of the ruling coalition.

Zahid, whose truck was set on fire by the mob, died in a hospital
in Delhi, succumbing to grave burn injuries. Within hours of his
death, the Valley erupted in street clashes between police and
protesters. In the assembly an independent MLA, Engineer Rashid,

was beaten up by a BJP lawmaker for hosting an inflammatory beef party. When he came to Delhi with the relatives of Zahid and Showkat to demand justice for them, his face was smeared with oil and ink by a self-styled Hindu Sena. The ink attack took place at the capital's press club; there could no greater irony than watching the mob violence unfold at an institution meant to stand for freedom of expression. Zahid's murder brought home how high the costs are for India. We hoped desperately—those of us who love Kashmir and worry for it—that the Valley would not erupt in violent rage.

The murder of the young truck driver will test the sustainability of the PDP–BJP alliance. It has reopened fears in an already alienated and increasingly radicalized Kashmiri Muslim community that there are clear attempts to 'Hindu-ize' them. Beef is not organic to Kashmiri cuisine—I've never seen it cooked at the home of any Muslim friend in the Valley—but the suspicion today stems from concerns about religious and political identity. For many, it has brought back memories of the Jagmohan years. As governor, Jagmohan had attempted a temporary ban on meat during Janmashtami, provoking an unknown cleric, Qazi Nisar, to slaughter sheep at Srinagar's Lal Chowk. The worry is that similar tensions will return to haunt the state.

All at once, India seems not just noisier, but also so much more bigoted. The shutting down of a concert by Pakistani ghazal singer Ghulam Ali, the smearing of journalist Sudheendra Kulkarni's face with ink because he invited a Pakistani to a book launch, the disruption of an India–Pakistan cricket meeting by the Shiv Sena in Mumbai—every day seems to start with a new headline of dissonance. Yet, far too many people with influence and clout remain silent. Will India Inc. speak up against freedom being blotted by the stains of ink attacks? Will more of Mumbai's film stars, who have the popular appeal to lead the way, take a stand to stem the tide of hatred? Is it so difficult for us as people to speak up and protect the first principles of democracy?

■

We could all learn from the dignified but strong way in which Sartaj

EPILOGUE 303

summed up his feelings about Dadri. His words contained within them both the tragedy and the promise of our country's future.

'I just want to say a small thing and make a plea. We have all read the song, we all know the words,' he told me. 'Saare jahan se accha, Hindustan hamara, mazhab nahin sikhata, aapas mein bair rakhna... If we could just follow the sentiments expressed in this song, we will be fine as a country.' The words were heartbreaking for the sheer generosity of spirit they displayed. They showed perhaps the only way in which the fault lines of this unquiet land can be mended.

NOTES AND REFERENCES

Unless they are in the public domain, all the incidents, conversations and interviews in the book have been witnessed or recorded by the author. In some cases, to protect her sources, the identities of interviewees or witnesses have not been disclosed or have been disguised. The page numbers and lines that the note refers to are in bold.

INTRODUCTION

x Kalpnath Rai, who had been accused of harbouring terrorists: Kalpnath Rai vs State (through CBI) on 6 November 1997

x Writing about the incident in 1997: Vijay Jung Thapa, 'Soundbite soldiers', *India Today,* 15 May 1997

xii petition in the annals of case law: *Prabha Dutt vs Union Of India and Others,* 7 November 1981

xii India's first woman war correspondent: Pamposh Raina, 'Why Female Journalists in India Still Can't Have It All', India Ink, *New York Times,* 2 September 2013

xiv record this conversation in his Kargil memoirs: Gen. V. P. Malik (retd), *Kargil: From Surprise to Victory,* New Delhi: HarperCollins Publishers, 2006

ONE

THE PLACE OF WOMEN

2 Dr John Hala: for more on the 'domestic issue' see Simran Bhargava, 'Dirty Linen', *India Today,* 28 February 1985

4 100 million women were 'missing': Amartya Sen, 'More Than 100 Million Women Are Missing', *New York Review of Books,* 20 December 1990

4 In 2006, the UN published another staggering statistic: and for Renuka Chowdhury's remarks, see Palash Kumar, 'India Has Killed 10 Million Girls in 20 Years', National Confederation of Human Rights Organizations, 14 December 2006

8 Vishaka guidelines: *Vishaka & Others vs State of Rajasthan & Others,* 13 August 1997. These guidelines that lay down procedure to be followed in cases of sexual harassment in the workplace were promulgated by the Supreme Court in 1997 and superseded by the Sexual Harassment of Women at Workplace (Prevention, Prohibition and Redressal) Act, 2013

12 woman is raped every twenty-two minutes: Akshaya Mishra, 'A rape every

22 mins: What makes us so complacent?', Firspost.com, 12 October 2012

14 her use of the word 'adventurous': 'Sheila Dikshit's comments draw flak', New Delhi: *The Hindu*, 3 October 2008

15 'Par kati mahila': Yadav made this remark during a discussion on the women's reservation bill. 'Women's Bill: Not fair for the fair sex', *Outlook*, 5 May 2008

15 Interview with Hillary Clinton: May 2012

17 woman raped at gunpoint in Kolkata's Park Street: 'Mamata terms rape claim of Anglo-Indian as cooked up', Kolkata: *India Today* (IANS), February 2012

18 260 candidates facing varied charges of crimes against women: 'Analysis of candidates, MPs and MLAs who have declared crimes against women including rape', Association for Democratic Reforms, 2012

19 Interview with Sheelu Nishad (and Sunitha Krishnan): We the People: Rape our National Shame, NDTV air date 23 December 2012

21 fastest growing enterprise of the twenty-first century: Judy Lin, 'Human trafficking escalates as world economy plunges', UCLA newsroom, 3 June 2009

23 marital rape as a criminal offence: 167th Report of the Department-related Parliamentary Standing on Home Affairs on the Criminal Law Amendment Bill, 2012.

23 Turkey and Malaysia: 'Marital Rape not a crime as marriage is sacred in India', Erewise.com, 1 May 2015

23 husband cannot be guilty: Sir Matthew Hale, *History of the Pleas of the Crown*, 1736

24 Interview with Anjum and Archana: We the People: A Reason to Hope, NDTV air date 27 January 2013

26 the first ever government survey: Dr Loveleen Kacker et al, 'Study on Child Abuse: India 2007', Ministry of Women and Child Development, Government of India

29 90 per cent of Indian women: Nita Bhalla, 'Almost 90 percent of India's rapes committed by people known to victim', Reuters, 21 August 2015, http://in.reuters.com/article/2015/08/21/india-women-crime-rape-idINKCN0QQ0QS20150821

29 sexually abusing her children: We the People: Everywoman's Battle, NDTV air date 6 January 2013

30 92 per cent of its villagers: 'Baseline Survey of Minority Concentration District', Indian Council of Social Science Research, 2008, http://www.icssr.org/Sitamarhi.pdf

32 Why Kali Won't Rage: Read the entire critique here: http://www.genderforum.org/issues/passages-to-india/why-kali-wont-rage/

33 proportion of working women: Report No. 554, Employment and Unemployment Situation in India, National Sample Survey Office, January 2014

34 female participation in the workforce: Steven Kapsos, Andrea Silberman and Evangelia Bourmpoula, 'Why is female labour participation declining sharply in India?', Geneva: International Labour Office, August 2014

34 'much lower and with a labour force pattern not very dissimilar from that prevailing in most Islamic countries': Surjit S. Bhalla and Ravinder Kaur, 'Patterns in Labour Force', *Labour Force Participation of Women in India: Some facts, some queries*, Asia Research Centre, London: London School of Economics and Political Science, 2011

34 self-reliance for India's women: Vinoj Abraham, 'Missing Labour Force or "De-Feminization" of Labour Force in India?', Thiruvananthapuram: Centre for Development Studies, May 2014

34 'sanskritization': M. N. Srinivas, *Religion and Society Among the Coorgs in Southern India*, Oxford: Clarendon Press, 1952

35 One of the world's most powerful women: Caroline Howard, 'The World's 100 Most Powerful Women', *Forbes*, 26 May 2015

36 'can't have it all': 'Why PepsiCo CEO Indra K. Nooyi Can't Have It All', *The Atlantic*, 1 July 2014

36 Kirron Kher and Firuza Parikh: We the People: Women, Work and Home Truths, NDTV air date 6 July 2014

38 Shabana Azmi and Priyanka Chopra: We the People: Everywoman's Battle, 13 January 2013

39 Tina Brown's Women in the World Summit: watch the video at https://www.youtube.com/watch?v=eLbw1gieFqc

40 woman in rural India walked an average of 173 kilometres: 'Key Indicators of Drinking Water, Sanitation, Hygiene and Housing Condition in India', National Sample Survey Office, December 2013

41 Her reminiscences about her childhood: Ismat Chughtai's semi-autobiographical work, *Terhi Lakeer*, translated as *The Crooked Line*, New Delhi: Kali for Women, 2000

42 'All societies on the verge': Germaine Greer, *The Madwoman's Underclothes*, New York: Atlantic Monthly Press, 1994

TWO

THE COST OF WAR

45 During the Tiger Hill operation alone, 9,000 shells were used: 'How artillery changed the tide of the Kargil war', *Economic Times*, 25 July 2015

45 'Such high rates of fire...in every 24-hour cycle': Maj Gen Jagjit Singh, 'Battle-Winning Role of the Gunners in Kargil War', *Artillery: The Battle Winning Arm*, New Delhi: Lancer, 2014

48 It lasted till January 1949: A lot had been written about the Kashmir conflict. For a brief overview see: 'A brief history of the Kashmir conflict', *The*

Telegraph, 24 September 2001

48 **4,000 soldiers and officers**: Sudhi Ranjan Sen, 'For the first time, soldiers who died in 1962 Indo-China war to be honoured', NDTV.com, 20 October 2012

49 **Indira Gandhi now bestrode**: Percival Spear, *The Oxford History of Modern India: 1740-1975*, Delhi: Oxford University Press, 1978

50 **It is one of the greatest frauds**: Maulana Abul Kalam Azad, *India Wins Freedom*, New Delhi: Orient Blackswan, 2009

50 **a major operation inside Kargil**: Read more here: 'Kargil: Pakistan's dastardly misadventure', *Business Standard*, ANI, 23 July 2015

52 **Interview with Captain Vikram Batra**: Kargil: The Remembrance, NDTV air date 26 July 2009. Captain Vikram Batra was posthumously awarded the Param Vir Chakra, India's highest gallantry award

54 **'About 10 to 15 hours'**: Gen V. P. Malik (retd), 'The Capture of Tiger Hill: A First-hand Account', Tribune News Service, 26 July 2002

56 **Writing many years later in *Force* magazine**: Air Chief Marshal A. Y. Tipnis (retd), Operation Safed Sagar, October 2006. http://www.forceindia.net/ACM%20Tipnis.pdf

57 **The thinking behind his Kargil folly…was now caught on tape**: Excerpts of the conversation between Gen Musharraf and Lt Gen Aziz, Rediff.com, 11 June 1999

59 **'that guy's from Missouri big time'**: Strobe Talbott, *Engaging India: Diplomacy, Democracy, and the Bomb*, Washington, DC: Brookings Institution Press, 2004

60 **'One way or the other, we will get them out'**: Vir Sanghvi, 'Vajpayee turns quietly assertive', Rediff news, 17 August 1999

60 **'My mandate is Kargil, not Kashmir'**: George Perkovich, *India's Nuclear Bomb: The Impact on Global Proliferation*, University of California Press, 2001

61 **On 2 July, Nawaz Sharif**: Strobe Talbott, *Engaging India: Diplomacy, Democracy and the Bomb*, Washington, DC: The Brookings Institution, 2004

62 **Clinton wanted to know**: Ibid

69 **'by denying essential equipment'**: Gen V. P. Malik, *Kargil: From Surprise to Victory*, New Delhi: HarperCollins, 2006

69 **minimum acceptable risk level requirements**: 'Indian Army faces severe ammunition shortage, won't sustain war for more than 20 days: CAG', *Deccan Chronicle*, 9 May 2015

70 **The estimation of how many lives Pakistan lost**: For Musharraf's estimates, see his memoir, *In The Line Of Fire*; for Sharif's, see his book *Ghadaar Kaun? Nawaz Sharif Ki Kahani, Unki Zubani*

70 **453 soldiers killed in 'Batalik Kargil' sector**: 'Pak Army quietly names 453 soldiers killed in Kargil War', *India Today*, 18 November 2010

THREE

TERROR IN OUR TIME

73 'heavily reliant on Pakistani sources': Condoleezza Rice, *No Higher Honor: A Memoir of My Years in Washington*, Massachusetts: Crown, 1 January 2011

73 Operation Parakram: Rahul Singh, 'Recalling the highs and lows of Operation Parakram', *Times of India*, 15 January 2004

75 'If we have to go war, jolly good': Celia W. Dugger, 'A Blunt-Speaking General Says India Is Ready for War', *New York Times*, 11 January 2002

75 The next day, Pervez Musharraf: 'The general under pressure', *The Economist*, 31 May 2002

76 In 2003, Defence Minister George Fernandes told Parliament: 'Op Parakram claimed 798 soldiers', *Times of India*, 31 July 2003

78 'The incongruous mixture of growth': H. V. Savitch, *Cities in a Time of Terror: Space, Territory, and Local Resilience*, New York: M. E. Sharpe, 2008

79 Interview with Syed Raheem: We the People: Terror déjà vu, NDTV air date 24 February 2013

81 use militant groups: 'Pakistan using militants against India: US', NDTV. com, 4 February 2010

82 'third round of jihad': Amit Baruah, 'Militant chiefs warn Musharraf', *The Hindu*, 6 February 2000

82 'wounds given by...': For the first manifesto of the IM, see: Praveen Swami, 'Was the Indian Mujahideen made by the 2002 Gujarat riots?', *Firstpost*, 23 July 2013; for its attack on the courts, see: Praveen Swami, 'Indian Mujahideen manifestos attacked judiciary', *The Hindu*, 16 September, 2011

82 'an internal security issue.': Stephen Tankel, 'Jihadist Violence: The Indian Threat', Woodrow Wilson International Center for Scholars, Washington, DC: Wilson Center, 2014

88 Interview with J. K. Dutt: We the People, NDTV, air date 26 November 2009

89 Local support: 'Mumbai police admit local support for Mumbai attack', *Economic Times*, 12 February 2009; 'Pak Plays 30 Questions with India', *Mumbai Mirror*, 13 February 2009

89 Interview with Rahul Bhatt: 'Knew nothing about Headley's Pak links: Rahul Bhatt', NDTV.com, published on 4 February 2010

97 'not allow elements that wanted to sabotage the peace process': 'India train blasts kill 66', *The Guardian*, 19 February 2007

98 'In the daytime...': Kartikeya, 'Col Purohit badmouthed Sena: ATS chargesheet', *Times of India*, 24 April 2009

98 'As a young revolutionary...': Christophe Jaffrelot, 'A running thread of deep saffron', *Indian Express*, 29 January 2009

99 the very phrase 'Hindu terror': Mala Das (ed.), 'Congress Hits Back at Rajnath Singh on "Hindu Terror" Remark', NDTV.com, 1 August 2015

99 'training camps': Mohammad Iqbal, 'Shinde blasts BJP, RSS for "inciting Hindu terror"', *The Hindu*, 21 January 2013; Sandeep Joshi, 'Shinde apologises for 'Hindu terror' remark ahead of budget session', *The Hindu*, 21 February 2013

104 biggest internal security threat: 'Naxalism biggest threat to internal security: Manmohan', *The Hindu* (PTI), 24 May 2010

105 he confessed to a 'limited mandate': Prannoy Roy and Barkha Dutt, 'Time to change tactics against Naxals, Chidambaram tells NDTV', NDTV, 18 May 2010

106 'history from below': Sumit Sarkar, 'Social and Political Movements 1885–1905', *Modern India 1886–1947*, New Delhi: Macmillan, 1983

106 'revolted more often and far more violently': K. Suresh Singh, *Tribal Situation in India*, Orient Book Distributors, 1986

107 guns and bullets would turn to water: Sumit Sarkar, *Modern India 1886–1947*, New Delhi: Macmillan, 1983

108 'Is this Salwa Judum Part 2?': Pavan Dahat, 'Salwa Judum-2 is born in Bastar', *The Hindu*, 5 May 2015

109 Lot of politics in the insurgency: Barkha Dutt, 'Stop the Squabbling', *Hindustan Times*, 7 March 2011

FOUR

IN THE NAME OF GOD

113 Yeh jo sara rona: 'Women MPs condemn Fernandes remarks', *The Hindu*, 3 May 2002

115 3,000 people were killed: 'Indira Gandhi's death remembered', BBC, 1 November 2009

115 like a 'Jew must have in Nazi Germany': Khushwant Singh, 'Oh, That Other Hindu Riot Of Passage', *Outlook*, 15 November 2004

116 fudged records: 'Betwa Sharma, Lawyer to Contest Congress Leader Sajjan Kumar's Acquittal in 1984 Riots Case', India Ink, *New York Times*, 1 May 2013

116 I have no hesitation: Hasan Suroor, 'Manmohan Singh's apology for anti-Sikh riots a "Gandhian moment of moral clarity", says 2005 cable', *The Hindu*, 22 April 2011

117-118 'action' against the burning of the train: Ashish Khetan, Probe reveals Gujarat riots were not spontaneous and sudden, IndiaToday.com, 15 April 2015; also see for police commissioner P.C. Pande's remarks

123 It may be clarified here that: 'Ehsaan Jafri killed for provoking mob, says Special Investigation Team report', NDTV.com, 11 May 2012

124 Hang me if I am guilty: 'Narendra Modi to Urdu newspaper: Hang me if I am guilty', NDTV.com, 26 July 2012

130 '...but not your or my religion': M. K. Gandhi, 'Talk with a Christian Missionary', *Harijan*, 22 September 1946, *Collected Works of Mahatma Gandhi*, Volume 92

132 **Veteran journalist Kuldip Nayar:** Kuldip Nayar, *Beyond the Lines: An Autobiography*, New Delhi: Roli Books, 2012

133 **Supreme Court judgement in the Shah Bano case:** 'The Shah Bano Legacy', *The Hindu*, 10 August 2003

135 **Interview with Girish and Tahir:** We the People: Twin Tragedies of Mumbai, NDTV air date 2 August 2015

137 **described the Shahnawaz shooting as 'cold blooded murder':** Meena Menon, 'A father's long struggle for justice', *The Hindu*, 29 March 2012

138 **A. R. Rahman response to fatwa:** Ben Child, 'AR Rahman responds to Muhammad: The Messenger of God fatwa', *The Guardian*, 16 September 2015

137, 139, 140 **Interview with Javed Akhtar, Uday Prakash and Hamid Dabholkar:** We the People: No Country for Rationalists, NDTV air date 13 September 2015

FIVE

A CHRONICLE OF KASHMIR

150 **'We were Kashmiris':** Jawaharlal Nehru, *An Autobiography: Toward Freedom*, London: John Lane, 1936

151 **'Armed Revolt In Kashmir':** Akbar Khan, *Raiders in Kashmir*, Karachi: Pak Publishers, 1970

152 **Sardar Patel and Nehru conversation:** Claude Arpi, 'The blunder of the Pandit', Rediff.com, 16 June 2004

153 **'For God's sake we are not asking for Jihad...':** Reality Bites, Interview with Farooq Abdullah, NDTV air date July 2002

154 **From a position:** Victoria Schofield, *Kashmir in Conflict: India, Pakistan and the Unending War*, London: I.B. Tauris & Co Ltd, 2000

165 **an estimated 1,500 women had no reason but the irrationality:** 'The other half: For many Kashmir "half-widows", remarriage rule means little', *Indian Express*, 2 March 2014

187 **Interview with Mehbooba Mufti:** Exclusive, NDTV.com uploaded 2 March 2015

168 **unidentified bodies in various unmarked graves:** 'J&K Human Rights Commission's SIT confirms 2,156 unidentified bodies in "mass graves"', *The Hindu*, 22 August 2011

183 **Sajjad Gani Lone called upon:** Sajjad Gani Lone, 'Beggars on the Prowl', *News International*, 11 January 2002

187 **Interview with Imtiaz Parrey:** From 'Haider' to Hope: a True Kashmir

Election Story, NDTV.com, uploaded 26 November 2014

190 **less than 3,000 Pandits left in the entire valley:** Azad Essa, 'Kashmiri Pandits: Why we never fled Kashmir', Aljazeera.com, 2 Aug 2011

190 **'There was an acute sense…':** Dr S. N. Dhar, *Eighty-three Days: The Story of a Frozen River*, Infuse Inc, 2000

196 **The sight of thirty-six bodies, all Sikh men:** 'Kashmir killings overshadow Clinton visit', BBC, 21 March 2000

205 **those numbers shot up to 38,696:** Afsaana Rashid, 'Violence Touches "each family living in Kashmir"', Thewip.com, 29 August 2008

208 **40 per cent of the children:** Margoob MA, 'The pattern of child psychiatric disorders in Kashmir', *JK Practitioner*, 3, 4, 1996

SIX

OF POLITICAL DYNASTS, JUGGERNAUTS AND MAVERICKS

210 **interview with her in Amethi:** 'Priyanka: My life, my politics', NDTV, 24 April 2009

211 **whether Rajiv would have been surprised to see her leading the party:** 'Indian of the Year', NDTV, 30 December 2005

212 **unexpectedly taken full control:** Krista Mahr, 'Priyanka Gandhi Takes Center Stage in Latest Congress-BJP Spat', *Time*, 28 April 2014

213 **the day I feel:** 'There's always a push for me to join politics', NDTV, 6 February 2012

213 **Are you serious:** 'Robert Vadra Pushes Mic Away, Asks "Are You Serious?"', NDTV.com, 2 November 2014

214 **No one in my family:** Barkha Dutt, 'Rahul thinks I should run for Lok Sabha, decision not to is mine', NDTV.com, 14 April 2014

222 **The Congress 'System':** Rajni Kothari, 'The Congress "System" in India', *Asian Survey*, Vol 4, No 12, December 1964

222 **In his classic study:** W. H. Morris Jones, *Parliament in India*, London: Longman, Green & Co, 1957

222 **Writing after Nehru's death in 1964:** 'The Meaning of Jawaharlal Nehru', *Economic Weekly*, July 1964

227 **You can insult Modi:** 'Indian media: Narendra Modi's "caste politics"', BBC.com, 7 May 2014

232 **two seats in parliament in 1985 to eighty-five seats in 1989:** *RSS and the BJP: A Division of Labour*, Signpost: issues that matter, New Delhi: Manohar Publishers and Distributors, 2001

233 **supporting the decriminalizing of homosexuality:** 'I am for decriminalizing gay sex: Arun Jaitley', Political Roots, NDTV, 27 February 2014

228 **Never make it as PM:** 'Modi will never be PM, but he can sell tea: Mani Shankar Aiyar', Firstpost.com, 18 January 2014

229 **incestuous organization of political power and social influence:** C. Wright Mills, *The Power Elite*, New York: Oxford University Press, 1956

230 **a pyramid of control:** George Orwell, *1984*, London: Secker & Warburg, 1949

230 **three kinds of people in the world:** Ibid

230 **30 percent of India was already urbanized:** Shirish Shanke et al, *India's Urban Awakening: Building Inclusive Cities, Sustaining Economic Growth*, McKinsey Global Institute (McKinsey & Company), April 2010

237 **Patriots:** *Life and Work of Sardar Vallabhbhai Patel*, Dr Ravindra Kumar (ed), Atlantic Publishers and Distributors, 1991

238 **'virulent disease':** 'Hindutva Hotheads Defiling Hinduism: Professor Jagdish Bhagwati on Modinomics vs Hindutva', NDTV, 15 January 2015

240 **Interview with Nawaz Sharif:** September 2013

243 **America feeding Pakistan millions of dollars in military aid:** 'No cut in $700 million civilian aid to Pakistan: US', NDTV (PTI), 15 December 2011

244 **'dehati aurat':** 'Nawaz called Manmohan a "dehati aurat", says Pak scribe', Firstpost.com, 29 September 2013 and 'Major row over Nawaz Sharif purportedly calling Manmohan Singh "village woman"', DNA, 29 September 2013

247 **'Our forces will make the cost of…':** Mala Das, 'Our Forces Will Make Cost of Your "Adventurism" Unaffordable: Defence Minister to Pakistan', NDTV, 9 October 2014

247 **relationship between Jindal and Sharif:** Satish John, 'Sajjan Jindal's tea party: Sharif draws flak in Pakistan', *Economic Times*, 3 June 2014

250 **land boundary agreement:** 'Why Narendra Modi made a U turn on Land Boundary Agreement?', New Delhi: *DNA*, 2 December 2014

252 **'bazaaru':** Pragya Kaushika, 'Modi's final appeal: Don't let bazaaru people mislead you with poll surveys', New Delhi: *Indian Express* (PTI), 5 February 2015

253 **he is so American in his outlook:** Barkha Dutt, Obama's India visit: Telling it like a good story', *Hindustan Times*, 31 January 2015

254 **'audience democracy':** Bernard Manin, *The Principles of Representative Government: Themes in the Social Sciences*, Cambridge University Press, 1997

254 **'the electorate responds to the terms that have been presented on the political stage':** Ibid

255 **India will succeed:** 'India will succeed so long as it's not splintered along the lines of religious faith', *The Hindu*, 27 January 2015

256 **'India's Gilded Age':** Jayant Sinha and Ashutosh Varshney, It is time for India to rein in its robber barons, *Financial Times*, 6 January 2011

SEVEN

A SOCIETY IN FLUX

260 more than 2,000 children had died: Kausalya Santhanam, 'Children of the tsunami', *The Hindu*, 23 December 2012

263 In the summer of 1901, a ten-year-old boy: Paraphrased excerpt from: Dr B. R. Ambedkar, 'Waiting for a Visa' in *Dr Babasaheb Ambedkar: Writings and Speeches*, Vol. 12 edited by Vasant Moon, Bombay: Education Department, Government of Maharashtra, 1993

265 'annihilation of caste': *Annihilation of Caste*, Dr B. R. Ambedkar, undelivered speech, 1936

265 root and branch destruction: M. K. Gandhi, *Collected Works of Mahatma Gandhi*, Volume 57

266 'absolutely suicidal': Dhananjay Keer, *Dr. Ambedkar: Life and Mission*, Bombay: Popular Prakashan, 1971

268 have often called for the 'ghar wapsi': Madhuparna Das, 'RSS leader Mohan Bhagwat justifies 'ghar wapsi', says will bring back our brothers who have lost their way', *Indian Express*, 21 December 2014

269 'I am against conversion...': M. K. Gandhi, *Young India*, 6 January 1927; *Gandhi on Christianity*, Robert Ellsberg (ed.), New York: Orbis Books, 1991

269 not die a Hindu: B. R. Ambedkar, speech at Yeola Conversion Conference, 13 October 1935

270 'The Goddess of English': 'Temple for "Goddess English" focuses on Dalits', NDTV.com (PTI), 27 October 2010

271 Seven out of ten households in India remain rural: '7 in 10 homes rural, most live on less than Rs 200 a day, reveals new socio-economic census', *Indian Express*, 4 July 2015

271 'how society should be organized...': Constituent Assembly Debates, Vol. 8, 15 November 1948

274 In Uttar Pradesh, two Dalit brothers: Indrani Basu, 'Dalit Brothers Who Cracked IIT Face Stone-Pelting Back In Their Village', *Huffington Post*, 22 June 2015

275 the infamous 350-metre long 'Uthapuram': S. Vishwanathan, 'The fall of a wall', *Frontline*, 24 May–6 June, 2008

275 'a people apart, even among people apart': Harold Isaacs, *India's Ex-Untouchables*, New York: John Day Company, 1964

275-276 'practice of manual scavenging...': "Cleaning Human Waste: "Manual Scavenging", Caste, and Discrimination in India', *Human Rights Watch*, 25 August 2014

276 India passed a law in 1993: The Employment of Manual Scavengers and Construction of Dry Latrines (Prohibition) Act, 1993; and 'Manual scavenging: Hardly an election issue', *Business Standard* (IANS), 23 April 2014

280 'Big-budget Bollywood films...': Rachel Dwyer, *Picture Abhi Baaki Hai: Bollywood as a Guide to Modern India*, New Delhi: Hachette, 2014

281 'alienation and resurgence': Leela Fernandes, *India's New Middle Class: Democratic Politics in an Era of Economic Reform*, University of Minnesota Press, 2006

282 'protest of the privileged': Stuart Corbridge and John Harriss, *Reinventing India: Liberalization, Hindu Nationalism and Popular Democracy*, Cambridge: Polity Press, 2000

283 'class and consumption': Leela Fernandes, *Transnational Feminism in the United States: Knowledge, Ethics, and Power*, New York University Press, 2013

284 'the worst performer on this count...': Praful Bidwai, 'How rising inequality threatens our democracy', *DNA*, 6 February 2014

290 One-third of the world's poorest 1.2 billion people: The Millennium Development Goals Report 2014, United Nations; and Nilanjana Bhowmik, 'India is Home to More Poor People Than Anywhere Else on Earth, *Time*, 17 July 2014

290 3,000 children die every day: 'India's hunger "shame": 3,000 children die every day, despite economic growth', NBC News, 16 February 2012

EPILOGUE

297-298 Vishal Rana, Sangeet Som, Mahesh Sharma: 'Dadri killing: Mob incited by local BJP leader's son, claims report', *DNA*, 3 October 2015; 'Dadri killing: Cases filed against Mahesh Sharma, Sangeet Som over inflammatory remarks', *DNA*, 6 October 2015

299 'The evocation of the nation as "mother"...': Prabhu Bapu, *Hindu Mahasabha in Colonial North India, 1915-1930: Constructing Nation and History*, Routledge, 2013

299 'In India, no law can be made to ban cow-slaughter...': M. K. Gandhi, *Collected Works of Mahatma Gandhi*, Volume 88, accessed online at www.gandhiheritageportal.com

299 cows were sacrificed: D. N. Jha, *The Myth of the Holy Cow*, Verso, 2002

299 'brahminic' and exclusionary: Kancha Ilaiah, *Buffalo Nationalism: A Critique of Spiritual Fascism*, Popular Prakashan, 2004

301 when the prime minister finally did speak: Amarnath Tewary and Nistula Hebbar, 'Modi breaks silence on Dadri lynching', *The Hindu*, 9 October 2015

ACKNOWLEDGEMENTS

I devour books but for the longest time I never considered writing one. For convincing me that my experiences as a journalist needed to be chronicled, for persuading me to record the biggest news events over the past two decades, and what those taught me about my country and myself as a person—I owe a huge thank you to David Davidar. This book would have never been conceived or written without his persistence and interest. He kept the faith even when my day job, as a journalist obsessed with the news, often filled all the hours of the day. Many thanks also to the team at Aleph—Simar Puneet, Aienla Ozukum and Pujitha Krishnan. As waves of panic would rise in me ever so often, they were always islands of calm— ready to help with everything from decoding Google.docs to hunting for the right research sources.

I owe thanks also to the India Initiative at Brown University's Watson Institute and to Professor Ashutosh Varshney for inviting me to be an in-residence scholar as the first Vikram and Meera Gandhi Fellow. The distance it offered me from the frenetic pace of daily news was invaluable in being able to get started with the book.

This book—and all that I have reported and witnessed for twenty years—would not have been possible without New Delhi Television (NDTV) and the many opportunities for adventure and learning it provided me. Thanks especially to Radhika and Prannoy Roy for always being encouraging and affectionate and for supporting the nomad in me during travels to war zones in India and abroad, remote interiors, and flood- and quake-ravaged parts of the country. I am very grateful to them for being fantastic enablers and for always being there for me.

None of what I do would be possible without the fantastic, super-talented team of producers, editors, camera crew, engineers and designers I work with on 'The Buck Stops Here' and 'We The People'. They have patiently absorbed my eccentricities and my over-demanding personality, and are really extended family more than colleagues. This book would not have been possible but for the fact that they always keep me standing, through good and bad. So to all of them—Juhi Tyagi, Ruby Dhingra, Noman Siddiqui, Shailander Chauhan, Mohammed Asim, Shorbani Bhattacharya, Yamini Joshi, Rohit Wellington Rajan, Manoj Thakur, Manu Nair, P. Varadarajan, G. Manjunath, Ajmal Jami, Kaushik Mani, Prafulla Mishra, Neha Kukreja, Apta Ramesh, Almas Malik, Ashish Kumar, Sudarshan, Angela Albert, Debojyoti Paul, Uma Shankar Mishra, Sonal Josh, Aneesha Baig and Tarun Shingari—you are, quite literally, the wind beneath my wings.

My interest in politics began with the stories told to me by my 'Tayaji'—my second father really—who even at ninety-one still wears only khadi in tribute to the freedom movement he witnessed as a young man. He has been my best teacher.

Finally, I owe my biggest thank you to all the people who have trusted me enough to share their stories with me—opening up to me even in moments of war, death, calamity and violence. For your willingness to let me into your lives in some of the toughest moments you have faced, I am eternally grateful. I was humbled by each one of you, I learnt from every one of you. Thank you.

INDEX

Abdullah, Farooq, 147-148, 153–158, 197, 198, 200, 236, 255
Abdullah, Ghulam Mohammed, 191
Abdullah, Omar, 157–158, 160, 170, 173, 178-179, 204
Abhinav Bharat, 98-100
abortion and women's reproductive rights, 5
Abraham, Vinoj, 34
Adityanath, Yogi, 239, 298
Advani, L. K., 55, 125, 128, 131, 133, 147, 197, 215, 226, 232, 237, 253
Ahangar, Parveena, 167
Aiyar, Mani Shankar, 228
Akhlaq, Mohammad, 140, 239, 294-297, 300-301
Akhtar, Javed, 137-138
Ambedkar, B. R., 139, 264–267, 269-271, 270-271
Ananthamurthy, U. R., 139
Annan, Kofi, 57
anti-Mandal agitation of 1992, 281–282
anti-Sikh riots of 1984, 113–116
Antony, A. K., 105
Armitage, Richard, 75
Arunthathiyar community, 261
Aseemanand, Swami, 98
Association for Democratic Reforms, 18
Association of Parents of Disappeared Persons, 167

Ayodhya campaign, 133
Azad, Maulana Abdul Kalam, 50
Azhar, Maulana Masood, 147–148
Aziz, Mohammad, 57
Aziz, Sartaj, 242
Azmi, Shabana, 38

Baalu, T. R., xv
Babri Masjid incident, 82, 130–132
Bandukwala, J. S., 144-145
Banerjee, Mamata, 15–17
Banerji, Rita, 32
Baru, Sanjaya, xvi
Batra, Vikram, 52, 70
Bedi, Kiran, 235
Beg, Mirza Aslam, 50
Berger, Sandy, 60
Bhagalpur riots of 1989, 134
Bhagat, H. K. L., 115
Bhalla, Surjit, 34
Bhangis, 275–276
Bhanwari Devi, 6–9, 12–13, 19, 21
Bharatiya Janata Party (BJP), 23, 98–100, 107, 117, 123, 125, 128, 131–135, 137, 140, 152–153, 155, 160–161, 181, 183–184, 192, 209, 212–215, 217, 224–226, 231–237, 239–240, 244, 246–247, 249–250, 253–254, 256–258, 268–269, 281, 283, 287, 297–298, 300–302
    vs Gandhi family, 214–215
Bharatiya Muslim Mahila Andolan, 31

319